I0788426

graduation
and
GIFTS

Graduation and Gifts
Untouchable #8
Copyright © 2021 by Heather Long
Cover by Crimson Phoenix Designs
Editing by Kira of Leavens Editing
Proofing by Bookish Dreams Editing
Interior Formatting: Sloane Murphy

Graduation and Gifts/Heather Long – 1st ed.
ISBN-13 -978-1-956264-11-1

For my heathens.
You are the absolute best.

Foreword

Dear Reader,

Thank you for picking up *Graduation and Gifts*. If you haven't read the first seven in the Untouchable series, I caution you to go and grab those right now and read them first.

When I first started this series—I wrote the first chapter of the first book in September of 2019—I envisioned a trilogy. That, of course, quickly changed as I got to know Frankie, Jake, Coop, Ian, and Archie. I fell in love with each guy for different reasons. There were things I saw on my side of things that the reader didn't get to see yet.

Since that first chapter, I've written eight books, expanded the series from a trilogy to ten books then ten books to twelve. We've begun releasing the series on audio and I can't even begin to tell you how fantastic it sounds with Marnye Young and Grayson Owens doing the narration. They truly bring these guys to life.

We've covered 181 days of their school year, not counting their vacations (hello Colorado, Padre Island, and Massachusetts), celebrated birthdays, watched each relationship she has with the guys flourish and grow. More, we've seen the guys grow their own brotherhood (brother boyfriends isn't going anywhere) and extend their family.

They've faced the rumors, the trials, and the neglect. Finally, they've faced truths about themselves and their families and through it all, they've managed to not only stick together, they've kept it together and become so much more than who they were at the beginning of the year.

Frankie, herself, has grown and I couldn't be more proud of her if I tried.

On the home front, we've gone through a pandemic, been crowded together at home, worked on the idea of planning for "after" it was over and, of course, rooting for vaccinations and more. The last thing I expected was to have a herniated disc in my spine hit in February just as so many other challenges hit at once including a winter storm that crippled the whole state and it took me two extra weeks to even see a doctor, having a dear friend face a health crisis while I was too far away to do anything about it, while another faced the rising flood waters around her home.

The pandemic may have isolated us, but I have never felt so far away than I did in those weeks. Writing *Graduation and Gifts* through all of this turmoil was both a relief and a challenge. I shared their joy and their triumphs while I was worried about so much more.

I talked about letting this story breathe and even when I couldn't catch my own breath, Frankie and the guys were doing it for me. Their investment in each other reminds me constantly that we build the families and the communities we need. From found families to girl gangs, I am surrounded by a community of amazing individuals and I treasure each and every single one of them.

This series wouldn't be the same without them, or my family or the readers themselves. Thank you to everyone who gives this series a shot. To those who left reviews. To those who recommend it to their friends. To the narrators who love the characters as much as we do. To the fans who make those amazing TikToks. To my friends who cheer Frankie and the guys on, who tell me it's okay to take a break, who listen to me complain, who celebrate the highs and catch on the lows.

Thank you will never seem like enough, but right now, I can't tell you how much I appreciate all of you.

And now, as always, the housekeeping notes:

For those of you who have never read a reverse harem before, first let me thank you for picking this up and giving it a shot. Second, a reverse harem means the heroine will not make a choice in this book or any other between the guys in her life. It may take her a while to reach that conclusion, but it's the journey that drives it. There are many ways to frame this kind of relationship, currently reverse harem fits it very well.

Also, this is the eighth book in a series. If you haven't read the first seven, I encourage you to pause here and go grab them. While there may be no specific happy endings at the end of each of these books, there will be one to the whole series, that I promise you. Some of these books will have cliffhangers, largely due to the size of the story, but the happy ending has to be earned as part of the journey.

Again, thank you for reading and being on this journey with Frankie and the boys. You haven't seen anything yet.

xoxo

Heather

Chapter One
GUESS WHO'S COMING TO…WHAT?

FRANKIE

"**I** was looking for Frankie Curtis," the man at the door said. "I'm Henry Jackson."

Jake's shoulders went stiff, Ian sat forward, and Archie emerged from the kitchen, but Coop and I were on the sofa and closer than the others. The man's voice sounded warm, if a bit wary. I glanced down at the near see-through pale blue tank-top and sleep shorts I had on and jerked to my feet. Ian stripped off his sweatshirt and tugged it over my head. It hit me about mid-thigh and I still had to roll up the sleeves.

For his part, Jake hadn't moved.

"I did get the right apartment?" Hesitance entered the man's voice. "Sorry, if I'm coming by late. I drove here straight from the airport and I got lost once."

My heart fisted at his words.

"No," Jake said slowly. "You're at the right place." He spared a glance back at me but didn't move from the door. I couldn't see past him and Henry Jackson couldn't see in. Brows raised, he looked at me for an answer and I hesitated.

"Breathe," Coop said as he tugged my hair free from the sweatshirt and smoothed it down. "We'll put on the coffee and clean this up." He was already reaching for the popcorn. Ian was emerging from the other bedroom with a new shirt on and I hadn't even noticed him leaving.

"Breathe," he said, repeating Coop's earlier suggestion and I blew out another breath. It came out far shakier and I folded my arms as a shiver assaulted me.

"I got the coffee," Archie said quietly, but Jake still hadn't moved to open the door fully.

Toes curling in my socks, I tried to quiet the shakes before walking over toward the door. Jake nodded once then backed up a step, even as he held a hand out loose for me to take if I wanted.

Oh, I definitely did. Unhooking my arms, I reached for him. He locked his fingers around mine and I shifted my gaze from Jake's to the door and the man standing there illuminated by the yellow outdoor lamps attached to the walls at various intervals.

He was a bit shorter than Jake, but still taller than me. Dark hair and… green eyes. The green eyes stopped me because I always thought I had Maddy's eyes, but the color wasn't exact. Mr. Jackson's...

"I'm Frankie," I told him despite how dry my mouth had gone. This was ridiculous. I wanted to roll my eyes and laugh at myself, but I settled for a half-smile and started to extend my hand. "I mean, yes, I'm Frankie. Would you like to come in Mister—or is it Professor..."

Crap, what was I supposed to call him?

He took my offered hand and his grip was a little sweaty, kind of like mine. When I dug my nails into Jake's hand, he just tightened his hold.

"Hank," the man said slowly, more than a bit of wonder in his voice. "Call me Hank." He stared at me for a moment, then said, "And I can come in or we can go somewhere. I don't want you to feel cornered or ambushed, just… You called and you mentioned graduation and I thought if you were reaching out that maybe you wanted to meet me and I've wanted to meet you."

The words came out of him in a rush and I had to bite my lower lip to keep from laughing a little. He sounded almost as nervous as I felt.

"I did want to—Yeah, it's fine, come in." I gestured him in and he let go of my hand as I started to back up.

"You have company," he said as he stepped in and the lights from the living room revealed a youthful face despite the hint of stubble on his cheeks. He glanced from me to Jake, then behind me. "I'm interrupting."

"It's fine, these are my boyfriends, you'd have to meet them anyway."

Hank paused a beat and raised his eyebrows, but he wasn't alone, Jake wore nearly the same expression as he stared at me over Hank's shoulder while closing the door. "Boyfriends?"

Well, love me, love my guys and all that so… I nodded. "Yeah, that's Jake and…"

"Ian Rhys, sir," Ian offered as he extended his hand. Hank shook it easily and then Coop's when he offered his.

"Coop Brennen," he said, grinning. "Boy next door and resident best friend as well as boyfriend."

I laughed. "Smart ass."

"Benton," Jake said as he took his turn for a handshake.

"And I'm Archie," Archie said as he came to stand next to me, he looped an arm around my waist before he offered his hand. "Standish."

Hank paused, then accepted the handshake. "Eddie Standish's kid."

It wasn't a question.

"Unfortunately," Archie told him with a half-smile. "Hopefully you won't hold that against me."

"Not at all," Hank said with an ease that had me letting out a breath as

I leaned into Arch. That hadn't even occurred to me there might be a problem, considering the history. Then again, I didn't expect him to just show up when the guys and I had settled in for the night. "Just surprised," he admitted and then glanced at me where he paused with a small smile. "I'm going to make this weird and keep staring, just ignore me for a bit. I promise I'll get over it."

"It's okay," I said with a laugh. "It is weird. I mean… Are you looking to see how I'm like you or how I'm like her?" Cause, I really had no idea how they left things.

He gritted his teeth and wrinkled his nose like he was bracing for something. "More me than her, I mean, you've got her coloring. But those are my mom's eyes and that little—crinkle right there at the corner of your right eye? That's us too. Jackson family trait. We all do it."

A family trait, it was the stupidest thing to grin about, but I was still pleased. And we were all still standing.

"Yeah, see," Hank said glancing around at the guys like he was apologizing to them too. "I'm making it weird. Kelly told me I do that because I talk, talking is my thing and I get chatty and then—well, everything kind of comes out jumbled. Great when you're lecturing, can keep the room engaged, not so great when you're meeting your adult daughter for the first time and she has no idea who you are."

His self-deprecating smile and hand gestures made me laugh. That, and he actually looked genuinely worried.

"He is so Frankie's dad," Coop murmured and I elbowed him, but he laughed and pressed a kiss to my temple. "If it's all right to call you, Hank, sir, why don't we all sit and I'll grab some coffee. We could order in food if you're hungry. We pretty much decimated the leftovers already."

"Hank is fine, boys," he said. "Boyfriends," he muttered, then shook his head. "That'll take a little getting used to. Chloe's all of seven and she's not allowed to date until she's thirty." Another flash of a smile, then he focused on me again as we all sorted ourselves out, Archie sat next to me on the sofa while

Ian settled on a chair and Jake came to sit on my other side. That left the love seat open and a second chair, but Hank chose the love seat, it was closer to me.

It gave me a minute to kind of assess him as he rubbed his hands on his jeans. He was dressed comfortably, like someone who'd just arrived on a flight. He didn't have on dress shoes, but rather a pair of running shoes that looked well worn. His shirt was *Star Wars* and he wore a jacket over it. I leaned forward.

"Chloe is your daughter?"

I'd kind of latched onto that. Wittaker had told me he had a family.

"See, there I go... yes." He pulled out his phone and flipped it around to show me a photo. There was Hank with a dark-haired woman, both smiling into the camera with two boys standing between them and a girl peeking out from behind him. They all had dark hair like the woman, but the older boy looked a lot more like Hank. "This is Kelly, she's my wife—she's also looking forward to meeting you. I thought about bringing everyone, but Kelly insisted that it should just be us at first, then when you're ready you can come meet your siblings."

My stomach bottomed out and Hank flashed me a quick smile.

"If you want. No pressure. I mean, yes, this is pressure me showing up, but really no—I... I wanted to meet you." He admitted and lowered the phone. "I'm very sorry I didn't know about you. She never told me. Not until she asked for a DNA sample because you were sick."

Wait...

"I know you're not," he continued as Archie slid his hand over my knee and gripped mine when I held on. "Mr. Wittaker explained. Of course..." He cleared his throat. "I'm sorry about that either way. And I'm very glad you're not sick."

Just when I thought Maddy couldn't get worse, she surprised me. "No," I told him. "I'm not. And I'm sorry she made you think I was."

"Yeah well, that was then and this is now and when your attorney called, I was... I was surprised but I told him I'd already done a sample and I didn't mind doing it again. Apparently, once I agreed to it, the lab released the results. I told him, I wanted to speak to you and that I would welcome any contact."

"He told me," I admitted. "I wasn't... Okay confession time, I wasn't sure about meeting you." I met his gaze as directly as I could. He'd been really honest with me. "I had no idea...and Maddy and I aren't... Well we're not close. She didn't tell me anything about you either." Maybe we'd skip the part where she named Archie's dad as mine. He'd been used enough in this particular scenario. "And maybe I was a little afraid."

Jake stood and went to help Coop who was carrying out mugs of coffee.

"That's fair," Hank told me as he twisted to take the mug from Coop. "Thanks."

"I didn't put any sugar or cream in it," Coop told him. "But we've got some."

"Black is fine." Hank nodded then took a big gulp as if he were knocking back a whiskey, and my heart kind of clenched for him.

"You were scared too," I said quietly and he gave me a half-shrug as Jake brought me a cup and then handed another to Archie. It wasn't long before Ian had one and then the guys were all there with us.

"We could give you some time," Ian offered. "If you want."

"I'm fine with you boys being here, you know until I knocked, it didn't even occur to me she might be here by herself and that would have been more uncomfortable. We've just met, but I want to earn the trust and that takes time." Then he set the coffee down and returned to the phone. "Anyway, yes, these are your brothers, Alec, he's ten, very serious kid. Don't know where he gets that from. Always has to try and be the best at everything he does. Studies twice as hard before he plays. It's a little intimidating."

I laughed at the face he made. There was so much genuine affection and pride in his voice and it left me hungry for that same kind reaction.

"This is Craig, he and Alec couldn't be more opposite if they tried." Hank frowned. "Actually, I really do think they try. They're three years apart, but Craig and Chloe are twins. So they are always thick as thieves. He's the most gregarious of them, he'll make friends with anyone. He's never met a stranger."

The older boy did look serious, but he had a nice smile and the younger had a much wider grin. His right eye had that same little crinkle mine did and it struck me. They were related to me. Hank was my father, these were my siblings. For the last decade, they'd been around, and I could have known them but...

Some days I really hated Maddy.

"This is Chloe, she's a darling, but Kelly says I'm biased. She's a daddy's girl though." He paused then looked at me. "But she's got a good sense of humor. I think she's going to like having an older sister. I'm afraid the cat is out of the bag on that one too."

"You told them about me?"

Hank made another face as he leaned back. "Well, not precisely, at least we didn't intend to, but Chloe's become a bit of an eavesdropper and she heard Kelly and I talking. She has no filter, she immediately told her brothers. Mostly because Alec wouldn't be the oldest anymore, so he couldn't be the boss of her."

The exasperation and fondness were equal in his voice.

"I'm sorry?" I offered but he chuckled and shook his head.

"Not at all. You aren't going to be a secret. I mean—if you want time to get to know me before you meet them and if you want to keep a distance, I'll respect that. But we're a loud bunch and...I'd really like to get to know you Frankie. I feel like I missed a lot and knowing my kids now, I *know* what I missed. I don't want to miss any more. But I also don't want to push anything on you that you're not ready for..."

He was perfect.

"Though maybe, I'm the one still reconciling the idea that my daughter has four boyfriends, would you be terribly opposed to not telling Chloe about that immediately?"

Jake snorted then Coop laughed and even Ian's shoulders were shaking. Archie's reaction was a great deal more guarded, but I wanted to like Hank.

More, I thought I did like him.

"Well, I don't really think it's the first thing I tell everyone but... these guys are my family. They've saved my life and they've been my best friends forever. If you're going to be my dad, then I need you to know they're important to me."

He smiled encouragingly. "I'd like that chance. I even..." he shifted a little in his seat and then stood to dig into his pockets and finally he pulled out a coin. "I brought you this." It was a penny and he placed it in my palm.

It was old. I frowned down at it. Old with a Native American head inscribed on it and... "1899?"

"Yeah, that was when my great-great grandfather came over from Poland. He came through Ellis Island, stayed with a family he knew in Brooklyn. This penny was the first one he made. He kept it. Never spent it. Gave it to his son when he finished school and then that son gave it to his oldest daughter and so on...my mom gave it to me when I graduated high school. Said that penny brings us luck because it shows a commitment to the hard work it takes to make a life for yourself."

Tears burned in my eyes and the penny wavered.

"I haven't gotten a chance to do much for you, but you come from a long line of hard workers. And you should know about them and me... when you're ready."

I blew out a breath and closed my hand over it. "What about Alec?"

"He'll be good, he doesn't know about the penny for one, and for another, it goes to the oldest child. That would be you. Don't worry, we can do other things for him when he's ready. That penny will be for your oldest child... You know when you have one. In ten or fifteen years."

There was a beat and one of the tears slipped out as I started to laugh and even Archie cracked a smile.

"We were going to finish watching the *Fast and Furious* movies, we've been having a marathon and we could order pizza," I offered. "If you'd like to stay."

"I'd love to stay," he said. "But only if you let me buy the pizzas."

"Um..." I started.

"How about you throw in for it," Jake suggested. "Frankie's a little too polite to tell you that the four of us tend to eat everything in sight."

Hank grinned. "Fair deal then."

"And I'd offer you a beer," Coop said. "But we're a little young to have it in our fridge."

"Or wine," I said drily.

"You know, I won't tell if you won't," Hank said. "But right now, I'd kill for a beer. If you point me toward the store, I can go pick us up some."

I put a hand over my mouth as he stood to follow Jake into the kitchen. They were both laughing. The penny weighed a thousand pounds in my palm, but emotion clogged at my throat. I glanced at Archie and he gave me a long look.

"He seems okay."

That was high praise.

"Yep," Coop said as he followed after them. "You want wine, Frankie?"

"Oh God, yes," I admitted, and Ian slid over to take the spot Jake had left.

Voice low, he said, "You really okay?"

"I don't know. It feels like Christmas and a birthday and.... The best surprise ever, and I'm terrified to look at it too closely."

It was his turn to press a kiss to my head as Archie squeezed my hand. "I like him," Ian said quietly. "But take your time. You don't have to decide anything tonight."

No, I didn't. I swiped at the tears from the corners of my eyes then looked down at the penny before glancing in the kitchen as Hank and Jake both laughed. They looked... relaxed with each other. Even Coop seemed to have eased up some. Only Archie was still guarded and when he squeezed my hand, I understood it.

Until we were certain, he would be.

And I was okay with that too.

Hank caught me staring and he grinned. "Everything on your pizza? Back me up here."

"Pineapple," my guys announced in chorus and Hank gripped his chest.

I just grinned.

As first steps went, this was a doozy and I was all right with it.

Chapter Two
MAD WORLD

FRANKIE

"You go," Jake's soft whisper penetrated my sleepy brain.

"No," Coop countered. "You."

"Shut up," Archie said from somewhere on the floor. "You're going to wake her up."

"Just go," Ian groaned with just a hint of impatience.

"No," Jake grunted. "I'll wait. Coop can go first."

Oh fuck me, they were not going to shut up. I slit my eyes open and it was still dark. I growled but it came out more like a whimper as I buried my face back under the covers. Jake and Coop had piled in on either side of me the night before, while Archie and Ian sacked out on the floor. Someone had dragged blankets and pillows in and they'd made their pallets. I'd totally meant to help, but I'd been dead on my feet.

Coop wrapped me up in a hug, and I pretty much passed out.

"See, now you did it," Archie scolded and I groaned again.

"Why are you arguing?" It came out muffled but mostly because I had my face pressed into the pillow. We didn't have to be at school until ten. Ten-thirty at the latest, because we would be bussed over together. Archie had grumbled about that, but it was our last "bus" ride for school, ever.

"Jake needs to pee," Coop said, and I frowned.

What?

Lifting my head, I peered at Coop then at Jake. "Then go pee." Why was this even an issue when I could be sleeping?

"I can wait," Jake said. "Go back to sleep, Baby Girl."

Collapsing back against the pillows, I blinked slowly. Most of my brain was still planted in dreamland. "Wait...why would you wait? Did one of you guys break the bathroom?"

It wouldn't be the first time and the more that thought settled in, the more I frowned.

"No," Archie assured me. "He just doesn't know if Hank's awake."

Hank.

My eyes widened as awareness swept through me. Hank. My dad. He'd slept on the sofa the night before. The guys had offered him the other room, but he said the sofa was fine. Very comfortable. On the one hand, considering what the guys and I had done in the other bedroom, I was down with him not sleeping in there.

Not that the sofa was free of such memories, but I wasn't thinking about those right now. Nope. Just better for everyone if I didn't focus on it. I still couldn't believe he'd come all this way just because I left him a message.

More than that, he'd been so *nice* and funny and warm. "I thought you guys liked him."

"We do," Coop promised then nuzzled a kiss to my forehead.

"Yep," Jake agreed. "But this is a new dynamic and you pretty much told him we were all the boyfriends."

"And we all slept in here," Coop tacked on.

"So?" What was my sleep-fogged brain not getting? "And if you make me wake up to sort this out, I may have to hurt all of you."

"Go back to sleep, Angel," Ian murmured. "They can suffer and wait it out."

Why the hell did they have to wait? "Jake if you have to pee, go pee."

"Yeah, we kind of took your dad on as a group last night, Baby Girl. Be better to not start anything this morning if he's up, and we don't want to wake him up on accident. We can wait until you're up."

Were they for fucking real right now?

"What are you going to start if he's up?" I dragged myself upright and shoved the hair out of my face. It was dark and Tiddles let out a disgruntled meow before leaping off the bed, which set Tory off. It didn't matter what time it was, they wanted to eat.

Kill me.

"Just the one on one, Baby Girl, don't worry about it." Jake tried to soothe me, but it wasn't really working. Fuck. Tiddles let out another plaintive note and I tilted my head back before I climbed over Coop.

"I hate you all."

Coop balanced me with his hands on my hips and there was no missing his morning wood. "You don't have to go out there," he said almost suggestively.

I snorted. There was a strangled laugh from the floor that had to be Archie, and Ian let out a sigh, but Jake punched Coop in the arm. Right, they didn't want to go out there and accidentally trip over Hank. No way were we having sex with him out there.

Just, no.

"I don't get it," I muttered as I climbed off Coop. "You have no problems dealing with psychotic Maddy, but Hank, who is *nice*, worries you."

"Maddy we know and hate. We also don't give a fuck what she thinks," Archie explained.

"Hank's different." Coop squeezed my hand. "You like him and you're just getting to know him."

"We're not rocking the boat," Jake finished, and I sighed.

Okay.

That was sweet. Really sweet. But I could still be asleep if they just went to the bathroom and came straight back to bed.

"It's a good thing I love all of you."

I let myself out of the bedroom along with the cats who threaded around my legs. It was pretty dark in the whole apartment. A single light from the kitchen burned, not that I couldn't make the whole walk in the dark. The bathroom door closed behind me and then the second bathroom door shut as I padded into the kitchen.

Boys.

The cats were still meowing as they raced ahead, and I faltered two steps into the kitchen as both the smell of coffee and the sight of Hank standing there hit me simultaneously and chased the remnants of sleep from my brain.

Well, look at that. I saved the boys after all.

"Crap," Hank said as he finished filling a mug with coffee. "Did I wake you up?"

"No," I said slowly. "The guys needed to pee."

Hank frowned before holding out the mug of coffee toward me. Okay, I really liked him. "And that meant you had to get up?" The side-eye he gave me was almost laughable.

"It was a whole thing," I told him. "No biggie."

"They didn't want to run into me on their own yet?" The flash of a real grin warmed his whole face, and I wanted to laugh. Still, I just gave a little shrug. Not waiting for my answer, he asked, "Where's the cat food?" My little heathens were all bouncing back and forth, rubbing against his legs as well as mine.

"Second cupboard," I said with a nod. "I can do it."

"I got it. You drink the coffee." He shot me a grin.

"If you were looking for a way to make nice with me," I told him as I took a sip of the coffee and he fed the cats. It was weirdly domestic. "You nailed it."

His laughter made me grin. "So coffee lover, check." Some of his humor sobered. "What about breakfast? Do you like bacon? Eggs? Or are you more cereal?" He had a mug of his own coffee and glanced around the kitchen.

"Um, I like all of it," I admitted. "I pretty much love food."

The corners of his mouth curved a little higher, but he hid the smile by taking another sip of coffee. "So, not a picky eater?" Curiosity inhabited the question. "I mean outside of the whole pineapple on your pizza thing."

"There's nothing wrong with pineapple on pizza," I countered, and he snorted. It was an inelegant sound, half-dismissive and half-scoffing, but it was also familiar.

"There's everything wrong with pineapple on pizza, but you're young and haven't been educated in proper pizza consumption, so I'm willing to cut you some slack."

It was my turn to roll my eyes. "Let me guess, people in Boston do it differently?"

He gave a little shrug. "Pineapple is a fruit. It shouldn't be on pizza."

"Tomatoes are a fruit," I pointed out. "But I bet you still want red sauce on your pizza."

"Touché." Saluting me with his coffee cup, he smiled a little wider before that expression faded. "I'm not making it weird, am I?"

"No," I said. "You're curious about me and I have a dozen questions about you, but I don't want to be rude."

"Please, God, be rude," he said almost begging as he set the coffee cup down. "Ask me whatever you want and I will..." He trailed off after he opened the fridge. "When was the last time you kids shopped?"

There was just the barest hesitance on that question and while I wasn't going to admit that Jeremy had been doing the shopping lately, I could admit, "We were going to go later today or tomorrow. It's just been a lot of events and family things—"

He closed the fridge and glanced at me. "It's okay to have family things with people that aren't me. We're still working on that part. Not that I plan on it being okay for long because… I want to be your dad, but I can settle for friend right now." Shifting gears, he took another swallow of coffee before he reached for his phone on the counter. "Tell you what, I'll go get breakfast for you kids. What time do we have to be ready by?"

"I still can't believe you came all this way for my graduation just because I called."

"That's why I came," he told me as he met my stare. "Because you should know parents will do anything for their kids." He hadn't asked me about Maddy and I hadn't said much, then again… "And I'm not going to ask about her. If you ever want to talk to me, I'll listen. Right now, I'm focusing on you. So, what would you like for breakfast or should I just go hit a grocery store and get the works?"

Standing, I chuckled. "Why don't I go with you or at least drive, since I know where stuff is, and we can go grab donuts."

"Donuts?" He frowned. "That's not really healthy."

"But they are tasty," I pointed out. "The little place around the corner makes the best apple fritters."

He continued to look at me skeptically, and I bit my lip. Okay, maybe it wasn't about the food.

"I'll grab some pants and we can go to the grocery store if you really want to cook. The guys…"

"They eat a lot, I figured," he told me and slid his phone into his pocket. "I'd like to make you breakfast. But we don't have to."

It pretty much killed all my reservations. "Five minutes."

I downed the coffee and headed back to the bedroom. All four of the guys had gone back to bed, mostly. Ian glanced up from his phone and raised his brows. "You good?"

"Hank wants to make breakfast." I didn't know what to do with that entirely, but at the same time I really wanted to know what it would be like. "And we need to go to the grocery store."

Sitting up and forward, he said, "Breathe. Do you want me to come with?"

"Yes," I admitted, but... "But he's really nice and I don't think it's totally fair to put a buffer between us. I mean he just fed the cats and he made coffee and he's really sweet. He said he came for graduation because I called. He came because I didn't believe he'd come just for *me*."

I had a dad.

I had a dad I kind of wanted too.

It was so weird.

Rising, Ian cupped my face and then kissed me. He tasted like toothpaste, something I needed to do but at least the coffee would help kill the morning breath. Hopefully. "If you want support because you're still finding your footing and he's still a bit of a stranger, then that's perfectly fine. I'll get dressed and we can go together."

Licking my lips, I leaned into him. "You'll protect me and I'll protect you?" I couldn't help tweaking him, just a little. All of them really, it was kind of cute.

"Something like that." Ian gave my ass a gentle squeeze. "Your call, Angel. What do you want?"

Head tilted back, I thought about it even as I listened to the soft snores from the bed. Jake and Coop really liked Hank or they'd never have gone right back to sleep. Still... "Archie? Do you want to come with us?"

"Thought you'd never ask," he answered and rolled out of his bundle of blankets. "Five minutes."

It took us ten, which was fifteen minutes after I asked Hank for five, but he wasn't complaining. I put a Post-it note on Coop's forehead in case they woke up while we were gone. We took my car, and the guys insisted Hank ride up front with me. We also swung by and got lattes and mochas before hitting the grocery store.

Somewhere between the eggs and the Pop-Tarts it hit me that I was out shopping for breakfast food with my dad *and* my boyfriends on the same day we were scheduled to graduate from high school. Holy crap.

Mad world.

Insanely mad, awesome world.

"You're kidding?" Rachel spun away from the mirror and stared at me. The bathroom door started to open, and I slammed my butt back against it. "Out," she ordered whoever it was. Granted, we probably shouldn't be hogging an entire bathroom to ourselves, but at the moment fuck the rest of them. I needed to talk to Rachel.

"Why would I make that up?" I demanded, staring at her. "Look at me! I'm dressed up and I'm wearing *heels*."

"I had noticed that," Rachel said, a sly smile on her face. Like me, she was also dressed up but then Rachel always looked nice. I swore she'd been born poised. The deep purple dress she wore would blend in perfectly with our robes. Mine were still hanging open to show off the red dress I'd put on. My jewelry and makeup were both simple.

We'd lingered over breakfast for so long and laughed so much, I hadn't really had time to do anything with my hair so I'd flat ironed it and pulled it into a sleek ponytail. I almost looked like I knew what I was doing.

Hank insisted on taking photos and then Carly insisted he ride with her and Trina to the graduation, since we were going to the high school to ride over as a class. After, we'd get a ride back to the school to grab the car and probably dinner or lunch or something.

After.

After we were officially graduates.

Oh, my stomach did a little flip flop. "This is so stupid," I whined.

"Don't cry," Rachel ordered before crossing the bathroom to grab my hand. She dragged me over to the mirrors. "Deep breaths. No panting. I don't want you to hyperventilate and pass out either." Instead of facing the mirror, she studied me and then flipped open her bag of cosmetics.

"I did my makeup," I complained.

"I know you did, but I'm just going to do a little touch up here and there. So, what did he say when he saw your tattoo?"

I groaned. "He made this little choking sound and I swore he was trying not to say anything at all, but I don't know that he liked it that much."

"Uh huh," she said, using a soft brush to flick blush on my cheeks. I didn't argue, Rachel was gonna Rachel. "But this is *after* you told him you had four boyfriends and even introduced him five minutes after meeting him."

"Well... true."

"And he not only hung out with you for the evening and spent the night, but then insisted on making breakfast this morning." She switched from the blush to something a little glittery for my eyes.

"And he made coffee first thing and he said he came because I didn't believe he would. I mean, come on, Maddy wouldn't do that crap."

"We'll put a pin in Maddy," Rachel commented. "In fact, I say we put a whole axe in her, but right now, I want to talk about Big Daddy Hank."

I grimaced. "Please do not call him that."

A laugh escaped her. "Fine, Hank."

"Better."

"He flew here all the way from Boston because you called and left him a message. He came all this way because he wanted to meet you face to face and be here for your graduation. He didn't flip his shit at your *four* boyfriends or the fact you guys are practically living together. He's funny, sweet, and he can cook. Do I have all this straight?"

"More or less," I admitted. "He's worried about making it weird, like he couldn't stop staring at me at first and I couldn't really stop staring at him. I was trying to figure out where we were alike, and you should see him talk about his kids. Rach, he's so proud of them and he just… beams."

"Good. He should beam about you today too." After dusting my eyes, she gave me a look and I closed them so she could touch up the eyelids. "I'm glad he did. You deserve the best. What do the boys think of him?"

The guarded note had me opening my eyes. At her glare, I made a face and closed them again. "They like him. Coop and Jake really like him, and Ian thinks he's nice."

"And Archie?"

"He's going to take a while to like anyone new." The fact he had his reservations wasn't lost on me and I had zero intentions of pushing him on it. Everything about Hank had been great. That would make it hurt that much worse if it all turned out to be another lie.

My heart twisted painfully.

"He's suspicious of everything. It's one of the things I do like about him." The comment made me smile.

"Are you admitting you like Archie?"

Her scoff of disgust had me laughing. "Fine," she admitted. "At the risk of regretting the admission, there are things about each of them that I like. Okay, what do you think of that?"

I glanced at myself in the mirror. I couldn't really tell what she'd done, but I looked...more. My green eyes were brighter, my smile seemed a little warmer and my face flushed. I'd gotten something of a tan going running with the guys a couple of times a week and spending a few hours in the pools after school. This was different though, everything just seemed brighter.

"I love it and I am never going to understand how you do this." I leaned forward to inspect my eyelids. There was a hint of green eye shadow on my lids, but it made my lashes duskier somehow. What kind of sorcery did Rachel know?

"When I have a beautiful canvas," she said with a shrug, "it's not hard."

"Thank you," I told her as I glanced at her. "I am so nervous."

"About what?"

"Graduating. I almost hate to admit it. I've told the guys forever that this is just a stupid ceremony." Even my robes had been bought by Jake, and Coop had made sure to pick up all my honor cords. "We're done, right? We passed. We graduate whether we walk across the stage or not."

"Sure," Rachel said as she zipped up my robe and reached for the honor cords to start arranging them. There was also a stole and other extras. Rachel and I were in the top twenty students and Rachel ranked even higher than me. "This is all pomp and circumstance."

With care, she straightened the gold stole and arranged the purple cord over it. I had two—one for honors and the other for special nomination.

"Yes, we're not getting actual diplomas today and the whole point of the ritual is to parade us in front of our parents and the community to show them look, we're all adults now. We survived our twelve-year educational sentences. Some of us are going onward," she said the last with a grin. "Some aren't. But here's the thing...ceremonies aren't just for the people around us."

Smoothing the stole, she began laying the honor cords around my neck one at a time.

"They're for us to take the time to reflect on how far we've come. To look at what we've accomplished. When else do we see that we're the ultra nerds who not only killed it with our sense of style, but also our academic achievements?"

That made me laugh. "Your sense of style cannot be argued with."

"Thank you, I love you too. Now, the other part of a ceremony?" She gripped my shoulders gently. "It's a chance for us to say goodbye to one part of our life as we prepare for the next. This was a crazy year for you."

"It was a great year in so many ways." I refused to think about the rest. "I had this fantastic secret admirer who left me the most amazing roses and wrote me sweet notes. Then when I needed them most, she told me who she was and she's the best best friend I could have had."

"Even better than Coop?" she dared me and I grinned.

"Best girlfriend," I conceded.

"I'll take it." Pressing her forehead to mine gently, she said, "You're the best friend I could have too. Thank you for letting me be a part of your year and for wanting to keep hanging out with me even if I still hit on you occasionally."

"And keep secrets," I teased her, and she grinned.

"Fine," she huffed out a breath. "His name was Garrett, we are not seeing each other anymore. He was a freshman at UNT and we fooled around."

"How did you meet a freshman at UNT?"

"I went to a party with Audra."

"Audra?"

She let out a sigh. "Audra was the girl I started dating for a bit, also a freshman at UNT. We went to a party together and turned out she's pretty bi...or very open when she's been drinking. She hooked up and that left me on my own, Garett's girlfriend dumped him at the party and we ended up hanging out. There was a lot of heavy petting and some oral... how you suck four cocks I will never know. One was more than enough for me."

The most delicate of shudders racked her.

"But, it didn't work out. He wanted more than I was willing to give, and Audra decided to hook up with him too, after I wouldn't and well..." she gave a shrug and the sadness in her eyes pissed me off.

"That bitch," were the first words that came out of my mouth. "And *fuck* him. Garrett? At UNT? I'm totally telling Jake after graduation."

Rachel's smile was still a little sad, but her eyes brightened. "You don't have to kick his ass. Trust me, he's not worth it. It was fun to explore though and maybe I'll do it again sometime or maybe I'll just indulge my fantasies about you and focus on school."

I laughed. "We're gonna be freshmen in a few months."

"This is true," Rachel said.

"And there will be parties."

"Oh, this is also true..."

"We will have your back."

She flashed me a real smile. "That I do know."

"Rach?"

"Hmm?"

"I like all of their cocks and if he was worth it, I think you might have liked his too."

Her laugh was real. We got her cords sorted out then our caps and once we were both ready, she said, "He was total shit at head. Though, he really was good at my breasts so... what are you going to do?"

"Find someone who is the whole package and understands what a fucking wonderful woman you are."

"See," Rachel told me as she threaded her arm through mine and we headed for the door. "This is why I love you."

"I love you too."

Chapter Three
POMP AND CIRCUMSTANCE

ARCHIE

"I like him," Bubba commented as he leaned against the wall opposite the bathroom. We weren't trying to crowd the area. Still we were a little gun shy about leaving her even if she was with Rachel. Not when we were all perfectly capable of waiting right here to escort them both.

"So do I," Coop admitted. "He reminds me a lot of her." The consensus among them all was positive where Hank was concerned. Henry "Hank" Jackson seemed like a good guy. Honest. Earnest. Kind. Warm. He was a lot like Frankie, right down to some of her awkward charms.

He'd also arrived at a very convenient time, as she was coming into some serious inheritance.

"Arch doesn't like him," Jake commented.

"Archie hasn't formed a full opinion of him yet," I corrected. "We spent a few hours with him and he impressed Frankie and made her smile. That's definitely a positive in his favor." That didn't mean I hadn't ordered a background check. I'd done that the minute Wittaker had a name.

"But?" Bubba asked, studying me with a measuring look. He wasn't the only one studying me.

"But nothing. He impressed Frankie. He made her smile. He appears to be asking for nothing." I shrugged. "We have graduation to focus on. And a ride on a shock-challenged bus because the school thinks we all need to arrive together. I could have arranged better transport."

Coop hid a laugh as he ducked his head to glance at his phone. Jake didn't even bother to try. "It's humbling for you," Jake said with a faint smirk. "You didn't have the privilege of bussing as a kid. Time to enjoy a little of how the other half lives before you take over the world."

I spared him a look that just had Coop doubling over in real laughter and Jake shoving him playfully.

"Is there a problem?" Bubba asked quietly while Coop and Jake got into a playful shoving match. We were all dressed, comfortably for Coop and Jake, in half-suits for me and Bubba. Though Jake had gone with slacks, Coop defied all of us and said he was going with jeans. Unless they did an actual inspection of our clothes, his black jeans should be close enough to slacks. Not really, but some days I really wanted to enjoy the color of the sky in his world. His jeans were not dress pants. They really weren't, but seriously, fuck it.

"No," I told Bubba. "Not at the moment." I didn't. The guy really did *seem* genuine, but if you'd asked me a couple of years earlier was Frankie's mother a raving psychotic fucking loon, I'd have actually doubted it, even if I thought she was a bitch.

Frankie had enough issues in her life and she was also very, very wealthy at the moment whether it had fully dawned on her or not.

Wealth came with its own issues.

"But you're already planning if there is one." That wasn't a question. Bubba and I had our differences. We'd clashed on a few things over the years, mostly involving Frankie. I didn't like how he'd been reticent and wanted to move slower and he didn't like how fast I could move when I wanted something.

"Better to have a plan in place," I said. "I'm *tired* of things and people hurting her. If he's as genuine as he appears, great. But until that's proven, I believe appearances can be deceiving and I'll react accordingly."

"Good," Bubba said, tilting his head back against the wall as he tracked Coop and Jake. "How much you wanna bet one of them is going to tear their robes?"

I chuckled. "No takers."

"We have until the end of the month in the apartment, right?" Bubba asked and I nodded.

"I'm going to have movers box it all up and we'll store it until we're ready to take it north, though we'll have keys to the new place by the first of July."

Bubba chuckled. "I can't believe you got a place for us on the Upper East Side."

"Only the best for our girl."

"She's going to kill you, you know," he commented. Frankie knew I'd been looking, but I still wanted to surprise her.

"I can handle it." Besides, getting out of trouble was half the fun of getting into it.

"Mom and Dad said they wanted to take us all out to eat after. But I'm figuring with the number of all of us there, it might get crowded."

Crowded was an understatement.

"Grandpa will want to one up that, probably take over a whole restaurant." I couldn't help grinning. Grandpa had made a point of being in town for graduation. Jeremy would make sure to get him there, and he'd promised me he wouldn't miss it. Having them there was a point of pride.

Also, thank fuck neither would see me arriving on the damn school bus. I cut a look out the window to where the big yellow buses had pulled in to await us loading up.

Kill me.

"You'll survive," Jake said, slinging an arm around my shoulders. "Everyone should ride on the bus where the wheels go round and round..."

"...round and round," Coop continued for him in a sing-song voice and I shoved Jake away, but we were all laughing.

"Round and round," Bubba picked up and spread his arms as he sang the lyrics louder.

Assholes.

They really were the best.

COOP

"Get off," Archie said with a laugh as he shoved Jake away for a second time. The grin on his face softened the words. He and Bubba were laid back and relaxed about the day. Jake was getting antsy. Maybe it was his fault the anxiety was starting to crawl through my system. Frankie had been vibrating with it this morning, though she kept trying to punch it down.

That and the excitement of Hank being there. I couldn't help but grin at the look on her face every time she glanced at him, something she'd done repeatedly to make sure he was still present. The guy hadn't proven to be a douche. So far.

Thank. Fuck.

He was also Frankie in male form. While that thought was fucking weird, it was also cool. It explained so much too. That old nurture versus nature argument replayed in my head. Despite the lack of nurturing she'd gotten from her bitch of a mother, she'd managed to turn out a lot like the father she'd never met.

Please let him continue to be cool.

Bubba had his cell phone at his ear as he paced away and I cut a look to Archie and Jake. "What did I miss?" I hadn't even heard it ring.

"No idea," Jake said. "Archie thinks it's the lawyer, which is good, cause maybe that means the producer got back to them."

"Would they call on a Saturday?" What I didn't know about the music business could fill volumes. Frankie had been emailing Kaitlyn from Torched on a semi-regular, if infrequent basis. That made sense. The girls were still finishing their tour.

I crossed mental fingers.

"You good?" Jake asked as Archie paced away from us in the other direction. He had his own phone up. I swore I could see Arch in ten or twenty years, probably dressed in a nicer suit, but still juggling a dozen different things and his phone permanently attached to his hand.

"We're done," I said slowly. "Is it me or does it feel surreal?"

He shrugged. "Yes and no? It kind of felt done when we took that last test and like we've had one foot out the door since spring break."

True. Except...

"Tomorrow, we wake up and everything high school is in our pasts." I wasn't sure I could quite put it into words. Pretty sure if I decided to have an existential crisis right now... "How are the girls taking the move?" Jake hadn't mentioned anything regarding them. To be honest, I'd also been pretty focused on Trina.

Thankfully, she was coping better.

"Becca is going to get my room, she and Blake flipped for it." Jake grinned. "She already texted this morning about how soon I could move my shit."

I laughed and the door to the bathroom opened to let Frankie and Rachel out.

Damn, my heart squeezed. Frankie seemed to glow as she came to a stop and spread her arms. "How do I look?"

With a twirl, she made me smile even wider. The happiness shimmering off her the night before practically seemed to be infused into her skin.

"Stunning," I affirmed as I crossed toward her and leaned down to press a kiss to her smiling lips.

"Do not smear the lipstick." Rachel chortled, but I slid an arm around Frankie and flipped her off as I gave Frankie a real kiss. Fortunately, she didn't complain, and Rachel just laughed harder.

The rest of our lives began as soon they dismissed us from commencement. That was the whole idea. This was that last ritual before we walked out the doors of high school forever. We were leaving it all behind, except the very best parts.

Frankie tilted her head back to stare up at me and she grinned. "What are you thinking about?"

I opened my mouth to answer her and the principal announced over the PA system that we should be gathering to line up for our respective buses. Archie was already heading in our direction, as was Bubba. Jake stole Frankie away with an arm around her and pressed his lips to her temple.

"He's being philosophical," he warned, and Frankie laughed as she rubbed Jake's hand before looking at me again.

"Because this is the end?"

"In a way," I admitted. "It struck me, this really was the end of an era for us. Yes, we're still going to be together, but... no more coffee in the cafeteria or heading off campus for lunch or waiting by your car for you in the morning."

"Oh, fuck me," Archie groaned. "Who let him get started?"

Bubba chuckled. "Leave him alone. We all have to process in our own ways."

I flipped both of them off, but Frankie let out a whimsical little breath. "But the important part is we will be together. I mean, it hasn't been 'whose house do we hang out at' in months, and it won't be everyone crashing at my apartment, we're gonna find our own place. You know, if we can pull that off."

It was Bubba's turn to tug her away from Jake and he nuzzled a kiss to the corner of her mouth. "You're encouraging him."

Laughter swelled up, she didn't have to encourage me. We were doing this. Rachel made a gagging sound as they called us to the buses again and I snaked out an arm to grab her and tucked her close.

"All together means you're with us too, Queen Cactus."

She grunted, but didn't yank away, then Frankie glanced over her shoulder at Jake. "Road trip later, we need to go beat up a Freshman at UNT."

"Done," Jake said bringing up the rear. "Just tell me how much damage you want him to feel."

"A lot," Frankie said decisively. "He's a real dick."

"I'll take care of him, Baby Girl."

When Frankie flashed a triumphant smile at Rachel, she huffed out a laugh. I glanced at the brunette who gave me an impudent look. "I'll help," I decided aloud and Frankie beamed at me. Whoever this fuck was it had to do with Rachel. I had zero trouble beating the shit out of some asshole who hurt her, and Frankie wouldn't be asking if Rachel wasn't hurt.

"We all will," Archie agreed as Bubba shot a look back at me and Rachel.

"Yep." Then Jake fell in next to Rachel while Archie and Bubba kept Frankie between them.

"The musk of testosterone in the air is choking me," Rachel commented.

"Deal with it," I told her. "You're one of us."

IAN

The line for the buses took us out into the heat. Thankfully, all six of us were on the same bus because we were in the top one hundred, which meant instead of sitting alphabetically, we'd be sitting by class rank. I'd rather have just sat together, but even alphabetically, that wouldn't happen, so this was the next best thing.

Archie grunted when I slid into the seat next to Frankie and he snagged the one behind us with Jake while Coop and Rachel took the one ahead. The air outside was already sticky, but they had the air conditioning running full blast. Maybe that was why Frankie gave a little shiver, or it could have been my fingers on her nape.

Maybe both.

She flashed a look up at me, those green eyes of hers sparkling. I loved seeing her happy like this. I wanted her to always be happy. "Attorney called," I said in a low breath, and she raised her eyebrows. So far, the only questions she'd had in the negotiations had been did I like it and did I trust it. If either answer had been no, then she'd voted no.

Was it any wonder I adored her?

"Still not happy with what the producers are pushing for and they want a full rights grab." I shook my head. After a couple of long discussions with Archie *and* the attorney, I had to agree with them. The more rights we retained the better for our future. If the producers had their way, we'd make ten to twenty percent at best off our work and our creations while they could then sell and resell it anywhere they wanted.

Granted, maybe it was arrogance on my part. Just because we got a recording contract didn't mean we'd make it anywhere. The contract didn't even mean they'd release it. Honestly, I just wanted to make music with her. I wanted to write with her, sing with her, and just share it with her.

If all we ever did was record for ourselves, then fine.

She bumped my shoulder. "Then we keep negotiating or we tell them to take a leap. If one producer wanted us, then another will too. Remember what KC said."

Yeah, KC, Kaitlyn, had been fantastic. She'd critiqued our demo and it had been mostly positive, but she'd also made a few suggestions, particularly where we could both feature our voices individually as well as in combo. I hadn't even realized that I'd done more about featuring Frankie's voice than mine.

Frankie had given me a scolding. It had earned her a lovely spanking, but I wasn't really sure who got chastised more in that situation. Color bloomed in her cheeks as if she, like me, was thinking about that particular conversation. Studio time had become one of my favorite parts of the week. The soundproof walls and privacy gave us a lot of freedom.

We also had a rope class in a couple of days, I was a little more nervous about that, but she was looking forward to it. Truthfully, so was I.

Linking our fingers, I gave her hand a squeeze. Seniors packed onto the buses... well I guess we weren't seniors anymore. We were graduates. Fuck. There were a lot of familiar faces that we never had to see again.

The girls. Some of the football players. Fuck, for every face we liked there were at least four or five I didn't care if we ever saw again. It didn't take long before we were rolling out. The principal was on our bus and began waxing poetic about the future ahead of us, but my future was sitting around me and right next to me.

There really was no rush for the rest of it. Archie had told us to clear a few weeks right at the beginning of summer for a surprise trip. No details on where we were going, yet. He promised to give me a heads up a couple of days before the blast off. Frankie had to know we were planning something. At least that Archie was, but she didn't ask.

My phone buzzed in my pocket and I eased it out. We'd been told to keep them turned off for the duration. Yeah, that wasn't happening.

Mom and Dad sent me a selfie with the sign they planned to hold up. Kill me.

"They're adorable," Frankie said as she leaned her head against my shoulder. The purple was really working for her.

"They're not bad," I admitted. Still, there was no mistaking the wistfulness in her voice.

"They're the best," Frankie teased me, then gave me a gentle jab. "Who else would have come up with brother boyfriends?"

Thankfully, she kept her voice pitched low, so it didn't set off Jake or Archie again. I was never living that down, and Coop's laughter? I thought the guy was gonna pull a muscle.

"Fine," I conceded. "Though if she puts that on a sign, I'm disowning them."

The drive proved uneventful and while Coop and Frankie had been the anxious ones, they were both calming. I wasn't anxious so much as ready. Ready to be done with high school, the drama, the politics, hell, even the bad decisions. I was ready to make a clean start in a new place.

New York was going to be so fucking different from here and I couldn't wait.

We pulled into the event center and Jake made this soothing noise behind us.

"Hang in there, Arch. You're almost done, and you can add 'survive the public school bus system' to your resumé."

The sound of Archie punching his arm carried, and I grinned.

Better, Frankie laughed.

JAKE

Hell yes, I whooped as we descended the steps into the parking lot. The heat smacked at us and there were four other buses dropping off their graduates. A sea of purple. For the first time since the shit the team pulled at Halloween, I was proud of our school colors. A breeze stirred the warm air and Frankie adjusted her cap. Rachel was helping her pin it into place.

The robes looked fantastic on her. Best extra sixty bucks I ever spent. Mom had tried to reimburse me when she figured it out, but like I told her then, I did it for Frankie, I didn't want to be reimbursed.

Even better, she'd been on cloud nine since her father showed up at the front door. Hank seemed like a cool dude. He even rolled with it when Frankie said we were all her boyfriends. She flat fucking amazed me every time.

Hank's reaction had been surprise, but he'd taken the news and just gone with it. The guy reminded me of her so much that I didn't doubt for a second he was her father. There'd been this one little moment in the kitchen when we'd talked about pizza that he'd looked around the apartment and asked if this was where Frankie had grown up.

The surprise on his face had also been touched by sadness. There were little touches all over the place that were hers. Fuck Maddy Curtis. Frankie should have gotten to know this guy while she was growing up.

Then again...

If he'd been in her life, maybe we wouldn't have been, and every cell in my body rejected that idea.

Fuck that.

"Jake." The hint of impatience in Frankie's voice tugged me back to the present, and I grinned at her.

"Someone else you want me to beat up for you, Baby Girl?" Couldn't wait to find the walking dead man whose ass my girl wanted kicked.

She snorted, but curled her finger. "No, they want us to line up by rank."

Right. We were ahead of all the losers. I gave them a smirk as I caught her hand, but Rachel was a step ahead and moving with us.

"Yeah, yeah," Archie grunted. "Fuck off."

I snickered.

Honestly, none of us cared where we placed in the ranks beyond being in the top percentage to get the scholarships and admission. We were in at NYU, and that path was decided. Everything else we'd figure out as we went.

Together.

I was a couple of spots ahead of Frankie and Rachel was three ahead of me. She was in the top five, her wink and adjustment of her cap with her middle finger made me laugh again.

It wasn't long before we were heading inside, I kept one eye on Frankie, though I needn't have worried. She handled those heels on the uneven pavement like she'd been walking in them forever.

The march inside had the cool air conditioning hitting us as we followed in single file toward the stadium. The music had begun to play, the school song followed by Pomp and Circumstance for us to head to our seats. As soon as I cleared the first doorway, I glanced toward the arena seating we'd secured for our families. We'd traded tickets around until we'd gotten a block for all of them together.

I half-stumbled when I saw Dad there in his uniform, a broad grin on his face, and the girls squealing and cheering next to him. Even Mom looked happy. Klara was sitting with them and she winked when she caught me looking.

Fuck. Me.

He came.

They both did.

Bubba's dad stood right behind mine and he wore the broadest smile. Somehow, Joe had a hand in this. He and my dad had been friends for too long. There was Coop's mom and dad. We had friends there too. Marsha from the diner had come. I thought that might be Lyssa from the club sitting with them, but would Bubba and Frankie have invited her?

Archie's grandfather stood clapping with Jeremy and, ugh, Archie's mother was there as well as his father. Poor guy. I mean, I guess it was good they showed up, but still.

As promised, Frankie's dad was right there with them. He wore the strangest expression though, his smile proud but strained and when my gaze skipped past him, I realized why.

My dad wasn't the only surprise guest. There was an older couple also seated there and from the photos, I recognized Frankie's grandparents.

But they weren't who made my blood boil.

Maddy "fucking" Curtis was there too.

Goddammit.

Chapter Four
DON'T LET ME BE MISUNDERSTOOD

FRANKIE

All through the speeches, the accolades and the calling out of special achievements—even when they called my name—I remained intensely aware of the fact Maddy had shown up.

She'd shown up *here*.

At my graduation.

Where the guys were.

Where their families were.

Where Hank was.

That was the part that infuriated me the most. Hank had come all this way on the *chance* he could see me graduate. A child he'd never known about, while Maddy, the woman who had raised me—that whole phrase was fucking laughable— couldn't even be bothered to tell him about me or vice versa. A woman who only wanted what she wanted when she wanted it and fuck everyone else.

Hating her probably wasn't healthy, but Erin told me I needed to be honest about my feelings. Right now, I really fucking hated her. The only saving grace was all of the guys' families were between Hank and Maddy.

That was something. I hadn't noticed whether she was sitting with Eddie or not. Fuck, poor Archie. The last people he wanted to see here were his parents. My stomach roiled, and I focused on keeping my head up. The speeches droned on, but I couldn't focus on them. None of the guys were sitting close enough to touch and even Rachel was one row ahead not far from Jake.

When they started calling out the names, I exhaled a huge sigh of relief. I wanted so badly for this whole thing to be over. It was like all the giddiness from earlier had deflated from my day. The first row rose and lined up so they could cross the stage. We'd rehearsed it, and when they got to the halfway mark, I rose with my whole row and we trundled into place.

Thankfully, I didn't trip over my heels and I didn't turn my head or look back. I had my eyes on the stage when they called Rachel's name. Her family let out a huge burst of sound in the center. They were noisy as hell and she made a face at them before she tugged her tassel over to the opposite side and accepted the folder from the superintendent. When it was Jake's turn, there was another burst of sound, and I put two fingers to my lips and let out a shrieking whistle for him.

Fuck the rules.

Okay, maybe I should calm down, but my heart hammered and Jake's almost feral grin when he glanced at me as he left the stage pulled a real smile to my lips. I winked at him and his mouth pulled a little wider, and then I was climbing the steps.

"Francesca Curtis." Fuck me, I hated my name.

But the cheers came from not only guys, four sets of whistles along with Rachel's "Yes bitch!" carried and some of my fury gave way to warmth. They were here for me. Just like I was here for them, and as I accepted the empty folder, I looked out over the crowd. Coop, Ian and Archie were all in the line behind mine, but Jake held up both thumbs toward me. Then beyond him, I glanced at the stands.

My grandparents were here, and they were both clapping. Maddy wasn't sitting with them. She wasn't sitting with any of them, really. Not even Eddie. Instead, she sat at the end of the row with a few seats between her and all of them. But Hank was where I forced myself to focus. I didn't want her here.

I didn't want her to be part of this.

The moment my gaze snagged on his, he put a hand over his heart and mouthed "Congratulations," or maybe it was "I'm proud of you," or something. I was too far away to really make it out. What I could see, however, was the pride reflected on his face.

The pride he'd worn when he talked about his kids back home.

I dropped my gaze for a moment and blinked back the tears as sound rushed in and I shook the superintendent's hand before I moved my tassel and headed off the stage. I was almost numb by the time I made it back to my seat.

The girl next to me let out a shuddering breath. For the life of me, I couldn't remember her name. Maybe it was Dawn? "We did it," I murmured to her.

And she let out a ragged little laugh before she bumped my shoulder and grinned. Then Archie strode across the stage like he owned it and I whistled for him just like I had for Jake. There was a wild burst of applause from our families. The same for Coop and Ian when they had their turns. I locked gazes with each of them as they exited the stage.

This was it. We'd done it.

Graduated.

No more high school.

No more mornings in the cafeteria. No more pop quizzes. No more library make out sessions.

No more bullshit notes on my locker or worrying about vandalism to my car.

Weirdly, no more donuts or coffee runs.

I mean, we'd have all of that, but it would be different.

No more watching the guys with other girls. Or worrying about girls trying to make friends with me to get their attention.

That alleviated some of my melancholy, but we still had another five hundred students to pass through and that took time. There was a moment where the band played. More remarks from some of our teachers, and even Diane was up there giving us a few last encouraging words before the principal congratulated our graduating class and dismissed us for the last time.

Despite being scolded to not throw our caps, we all hurled them skyward. Some of the kids had decorated theirs and spontaneous hugs were offered. I even got one from Maria, before she grinned and slid away. Ian got to me first and scooped me up for a hug. Coop wrapped his arms around me from behind. Then Jake and Archie were there. They dragged Rachel into our group hug and I let out a noisy breath.

"Let's make a break for it," Archie said as we pulled apart. "I'll call for a car to come and get us."

"We can't," I told him. "And more...I don't want to. I want to see Grandpa Ted and Jeremy. I want to see Marsha and the rest of our families." More, I wanted to see Hank.

"Whatever you want, Angel," Ian promised me. "They would understand."

I cast a glance over my shoulder. Like the kids, the families were heading outside. One of the announcements indicated we'd be exiting through a different set of doors and meeting them on the other side of the event center.

Fingers linked together, Jake tugged me toward him. "Then let's go get this over with."

"Your dad is here," I murmured to him. I hadn't missed the uniform. Even in all the emotional noise generated by the arrival of Maddy, I'd seen Jake's dad and Klara with his mom. She had to have known they were coming and she made it a surprise for Jake, which was awesome.

He deserved all of that and more.

"I know," he said. "Yours too. Apparently, all the dads showed up today." He cut a glance over my head as Coop handed me a cap. I had no idea if it was mine or not. We collected six of them and then Rachel hooked her free arm through mine.

"You good with this?" she asked as we walked toward the exit. We'd be among some of the last out and to be honest, I didn't care. I wanted the time to cool down before I laid eyes on Maddy.

"We graduated," I told her, grinning. "I'm gonna be fantastic. Besides, I want you to meet Hank. And I saw your aunts were here."

Rachel laughed. "They're all here. Even my mom. She's dying to see you again. Says she likes me having a normal friend."

I snorted. Normal was not a word I would usually apply to myself, but fine. Archie and Ian took point with Coop strolling behind us. It wasn't lost on me that the guys were constantly forming up like a barricade. Some distant part of me resisted the notion that I needed bodyguards, but the rest of me adored them for it.

Ian wasn't the only one who wanted to take care of me. But right now, I had Jake while Ian had Archie. Coop would probably move between us as needed. Eddie and Muriel being here was not ideal. Jake's dad, though? That was a huge surprise. The emotional distance between them was this huge divide and while he'd been attempting to bridge it the last few months, it didn't mean it was all that easy.

I liked what I'd managed to learn about him while we'd video-chatted the couple of times I'd joined him. When I squeezed his hand, he smiled down at me. "I'm good, Baby Girl."

Like Jake's dad, my grandparents being there was also a huge surprise. They'd sent me a card the week before and addressed it to Miss Frankie Curtis— at least it wasn't to Francesca. They'd done that the first couple of times, but Patience really did seem to be trying. The card had included a check with a ridiculous number of zeroes on it.

She'd wanted to buy me a car for graduation, but they'd seen the photos I'd sent them of the car the guys had surprised me with on my birthday. So the card had told me to make one dream come true. The whimsy of that had made me smile. I hadn't decided what to do with the money yet.

The heat slapped at my face as we stepped outside. There was a coolish breeze that made the shade tolerable, but I accepted my sunglasses from Coop. I didn't even know when he'd snagged them. He also had my diploma holder along with Jake's and Rachel's, apparently. He winked at me when I threw him a grin over my shoulder. Rachel had hidden a purse under her robe cause she was clever, but Jake had my wallet and I hadn't bothered with keys since I was with the guys.

They all had keys to the apartment.

I tucked my glasses on, then steeled myself with a breath. We'd all planned to do photos after, talk to our families, and maybe head out for lunch together. There was plenty of stuff we could do. I wanted to introduce Hank to everyone. He and Carly seemed to hit it off all right when she'd insisted he ride with her and Trina. I also wanted to rescue him if he was at all uncomfortable.

However, there was one thing I needed to do before anything else.

We circled the building and even with Archie and Ian ahead of me, I caught sight of the group that made up our families. Well, I spotted Jake's sisters first who were staring at those crowded together with worried expressions.

Jake's hand flexed around mine and he pulled ahead. He had to have spotted them too. When I eased my arm from Rachel's, all she said was, "Do you have this?"

I locked gazes with Maddy. Her eyes were so chilly, even at this distance they cooled off the heat of the day.

"Oh, I have this. Talk to you soon?"

"You know it."

Another hand squeeze and she cut away from us. Her family had gathered away from ours. Probably the smart ones. Coop narrowed the distance between us. Archie cut me a look, but I shook my head. He could deal with his parents. I would deal with mine.

A year ago, the idea of confronting Maddy terrified me. Even when I couldn't admit it to myself. I understood that any showdown with her would include tears, usually hers, and pain, usually mine, as she twisted every conversation around to how I'd done something to her.

Questioning her, or pushing her for answers, was tantamount to declaring war. It was always so much easier to just let it go. Smoothing things over and letting it go had been my modus operandi for years. All that had ever earned me was more pain and neglect. I didn't know why Maddy was the way she was, but her behavior and responses were not my fault. She'd put me—hell, she'd put *us* in this position.

Her choices had cost her. Who she slept with wasn't my responsibility and whatever happened between her and Edward? Well, they'd made their respective beds. They didn't get to demand the rest of us deal with changing their dirty laundry.

As we closed in on the group, I caught sight of Grandpa Ted standing with my grandparents. He looked almost protective, with his stance putting him firmly between them and Archie's parents. Muriel and Maddy glared pure daggers at each other. Ian's parents stood with Jake's, while Coop's parents seemed mildly bemused by the drama unfolding.

I didn't spot Hank right away and my heart kind of bottomed out. The last thing I wanted was for Maddy to have chased him off. So, I headed straight for her. No pussyfooting around this particular issue. I didn't know what she hoped to accomplish here, but I wasn't interested in her games.

Not anymore.

You know what? Not ever again.

The breeze pulled at my robes as I marched straight toward Maddy. I could almost feel the anxiety rolling off my grandparents, but I didn't let that distract me. They'd walked away from me because Maddy threatened to kill me. Just what every girl wanted to hear, you know?

Even more, they enabled Maddy's destructive patterns of behavior. Could they have fixed it when she was younger? I had no idea. It might be naïve to even consider that had been an option. All I knew was I didn't have to suffer her anymore.

Someone was right behind me, but then I knew my guys. They weren't letting me wade into any fight alone. It also didn't surprise me when I caught dark hair from the corner of my eye. Archie and I had each other's backs when it came to our parents. He'd had to fight those first battles for me.

Fuck, that stupid country club dinner.

"Maddy," I said, not bothering to disguise the hostility in my voice even if I kept it cool. "I don't recall inviting you to crash this event."

The woman had the temerity to sniff once. "Frankie, I understand that you're angry with me. But could you really expect me to miss my only daughter's graduation?"

I snorted. Legit snorted, and didn't even attempt to disguise my disgust. "Your only daughter. That's convenient. I've been more of a doll. One you take down off the shelf to parade around when you want people to applaud the poor put upon professional raising her child alone. Then dismissed to take care of myself when you didn't have the time or wherewithal to put up with me." The words just flowed out. "I may be your 'daughter' and I use that term loosely, but you've never been a 'mom.'"

Her expression transformed.

"Maddy," Eddie said suddenly appearing next to her. "Maybe we make an appointment with the kids another time."

"Don't you dare," she snapped, yanking her arm out of his hand. "You already let her poison our relationship because she wasn't yours. Don't pretend that we're anything at the moment. If we were you wouldn't have had your dick down another of your secretary's throats."

He let out a pained sigh and next to me, I swore Archie chuckled. It was a quick, blink and you'll miss it sound, but I had to bite the inside of my lip.

"She's not my daughter," Eddie said drily. "Despite your attempts to make it otherwise." He met my gaze briefly. "But she's a clever, intelligent girl and she made more than a few solid points about my parenting. I wouldn't want me for a father either."

Yeah, okay. Whatever. I cut a look back at Maddy. "Well, sounds like you and Eddie are on round one hundred and whatever of this crazy fucking merry-go-round you like to ride. Do us all a favor, take it somewhere else. Today is about us, not you."

Muriel laughed. I swore to God, she laughed. It began like brittle glass breaking, but it turned into something a lot warmer and filled with far more humor.

"You're absolutely right—" Eddie began, but he couldn't finish before Mad Maddy erupted.

"You ungrateful little bitch," she spit out, rage heating her eyes. There she was. This was who I'd been waiting for...

"Watch your mouth," Hank said abruptly, his back filling my vision as he cut between me and Maddy. "I was going to take the high road about your choices and behavior. I wasn't going to call out your lies about her health or how you decided to involve a child in your delusions, but you're not talking to or about *my daughter* that way now or ever again. I don't know what can of crazy you popped open to drink this morning, but that shit stops right now."

I stared at Hank's back, rooted to the spot. Even Eddie looked mute at the words Hank delivered in a steely, almost cutting tone. My heart fisted in my chest, not only at his swift defense, but the immediate sense of safety I felt rolling off him.

I wasn't afraid of Maddy. Not anymore. I refused to let her terrorize me. Not when I had a chance at a much better life. But having him step into the gap and shield me...

There weren't words for it.

"How dare you talk to me like that?" Maddy floundered, but the fury in her voice was unmistakable. "You were a nobody. I slept with you out of pity."

Voices murmured behind me. People shifting. Hopefully moving the kids away from this ugly scene.

"Really? Interesting. I slept with you because I was drunk. I never could figure out how you maneuvered yourself into my apartment or my bed." Hank gave a shrug. "But it was a one-night stand and you said nothing, and it was better to leave it alone."

"Then why the hell do you care now?"

"Because the moment you became pregnant, that one-night stand became *my daughter*, and you stole her from me. You stole her, and you robbed her of me."

"Oh, like she needs you..." Maddy scoffed. "This is ridiculous. Eddie..."

"No," he said firmly, taking a step back and putting his hands in his pockets. "The professor isn't wrong—you made these choices and every single one hurt her. Hurt me. Hurt him. Hurt our families. I'm hardly innocent, but I know when it's finally enough. This is it."

Then, as if the whole world hadn't shifted and pigs sprouted wings as it snowed in hell, Eddie looked at Hank.

"I'm sorry," he murmured. "She's an amazing kid." Then his gaze went past me. "Just like mine. At least I know you won't fuck it up like we did."

The hand on my lower back kept me steady. I hadn't even realized I'd swayed. Those were words Archie deserved to hear, but it seemed so strange they were coming right now. This was not the moment.

Maddy seemed too stunned to speak. Her eyes actually filled with tears. "Eddie..."

"Stop it," he said. "You should go. You're making a scene, and this is their day." With that, he glanced at us again. "If you have a moment, I'd like to speak to both of you when you've finished visiting with your families."

Then he stepped away.

The look on Maddy's face was equal parts stunned and furious. She glanced at Hank, but he hadn't moved. "You heard the man," he said coolly. "Keep walking. Frankie doesn't want you here and I'm pretty sure I speak for every other parent here, you aren't invited to stick around."

"On that," Carly said, suddenly stepping up next to me and just behind Hank's shoulder. "I couldn't agree more. Go away, Maddy."

"Agreed," Sara said, stepping up on my other as Archie wrapped an arm around my middle and flattened his front to my back. "This is extremely inappropriate. You should go and take some time for yourself."

"Maybe go and seek out some help," Alicia suggested, but they were forming a barrier between me and Maddy. Hell, they were forming a barrier for Hank too. Ian's dad was there, Jake's, and even Coop's. The guys were fanning out next to us. Thankfully the sisters were away from the tempestuous storm breaking.

The hum of vehicles and dozens of other conversations filtered through the abrupt quiet.

"Or you could just go straight to Hell," Muriel suggested into the silence. "If you really need advice."

"Muriel," Eddie sighed, but she just scoffed at him.

"Madeleine," Patience said. "Please."

"Why are you even here?" Maddy demanded as she snarled at her mother.

"Leave her alone," I said, pushing forward. Not that I got far with Archie and Hank both acting to shield me from both sides. "I invited her and my grandfather. I'm surprised they made it, but *they* are welcome."

Shock traveled over her face and for a few seconds, she ripped her gaze from them to me and I read every ounce of the hatred shimmering in those eyes. Yeah, that expression would have had me tucking tail before and keeping my head low, but I refused to do that.

Not now.

Not ever again.

"Hank," I said, deliberately turning away from her. "Would you like to meet my grandparents? And Grandpa Ted? Maybe even Jeremy?"

Oh. I hoped he was still here.

Hank glanced down at me and then up again toward Maddy and he twisted. Archie loosened his grip on me. Jake had his gaze pinned on Maddy behind me, so did Archie. Ian swept a look over me before he started watching her too. Coop winked and made a face like, *holy crap, could I believe this craziness?*

Why yes, yes I could.

My life had definitely gotten crazy this last year. I glanced from Coop to Hank's face then to my grandparents. Patience looked pale, but my grandfather glared at Maddy. He hadn't said a word to her. Ted had also maintained his defensive posture.

Crazy, yes.

But I wouldn't trade my family for anything, not when Hank offered me his arm and I tucked mine through his and let him guide me through the guys as they closed ranks behind us. Maddy said my name, but I didn't respond.

"You know what I'd really like?" Hank asked as we continued toward my grandparents.

"A pony?" I suggested before crossing my eyes and making a face. Because if we were going to be in the theatre of the absurd, we might as well really go for it, right?

He laughed. "Maybe later. No, I wanted to get a photo with you if that would be all right?"

Oh hell, I was about to cry all over again. I took the time during introducing Hank to Ted, then to Maddy's parents to try and compose myself. Like Hank, they wanted a photo with me too. Grandpa Ted pulled an envelope out of his jacket pocket, as did my grandfather. They both offered them to me after photos. They did the same with Archie.

Then to my enormous surprise and delight, they gave envelopes to all the guys. There were photos. Lots and lots of pictures. The guys and their families. All of us. Me and my dad, man that was so weird to say. Archie and I even managed to get Jeremy to pose with us. Marsha and Lyssa hadn't lingered after all the family drama, but they did give us hugs and wish us well.

After pictures with my grandparents, and when the heat seemed to get to them, Jeremy went to fetch the car. Archie and I promised them we'd come for breakfast the next day. They were staying at the club rather than Archie's.

Somewhere during all the craziness, Maddy left. But Eddie lingered, as did Muriel. Jake pulled me over to talk to his dad and Klara. He said he was gonna go grab dinner with his family and when I offered to go with them, he gave me a kiss and murmured, "Next time, Baby Girl. Go spend time with *your* dad, yeah?"

My dad.

Wow.

Yeah.

"See you in a few hours?"

"Definitely," he promised. I got hugs from all the girls and then we had to assure his dad and Klara that we would join them for dinner another night. Alicia gave me a fierce hug, and when I asked her if she was okay with all of this, she smiled at me.

"I'm just fine, sweetheart. Go enjoy time with your dad. I like him," she said with a nod.

"Me too," I admitted. I liked him a lot.

Even more, he seemed to like me.

Not just how I made him look.

As Jake left with his parents and siblings, I glanced over to the shady area where the guys waited, with the rest of our—wow it really was kind of our—rapidly expanding family.

We'd graduated. We'd survived senior year. Holy hell, we'd done it.

Ian held out a hand to me, and I hurried back over to join them. Today was an awesome day and I didn't give Maddy another thought.

She'd taken up enough of my time.

Chapter Five
A QUESTION ABOUT PRIORITIES

ARCHIE

We took the time for photos. Despite the lingering sense of tension left behind after Maddy's not so gracious exit, the early afternoon turned out to be relatively pleasant. We hadn't even left the event center grounds yet, though Jake and his family had left to go get a meal together. I half expected Frankie to go with, but she stuck it out with her dad instead.

Made sense.

Currently, she and Hank were chatting with Bubba and his parents. Grandpa had taken the Graysons back to the club with him. Jeremy had given me a nod and then cast a look at my parents. Yeah, I still needed to talk to them. Shockingly enough, they'd remained throughout the chaos of photos being taken. Neither had stepped up to be in any photos save one that Grandpa requested, and I'd acquiesced. It was one of the three of us—me, Grandpa, and Edward. Muriel had not been invited, and she hadn't tried to intrude.

Most of us had shed our robes, and Coop loped over from where he'd walked his mom and sister to their car. "Hey, you think we're going to try and head out to grab food together somewhere?"

"Maybe." I shrugged. "But I think Frankie and Hank are going to be attached at the hip for a while. So, if your parents and sister want to grab lunch with you, go. I've got our girl."

He chuckled, and then glanced over at her. "A part of me would rather stay here."

"Then stay," I gave him permission. "But you're not the guy who runs from his issues and you and your father are at least talking again." At his surprised look, I smirked. "What? You think you're the only one who listens when you wax on about the psychology you're always reading about?"

"So, if you're listening, does that mean you're taking your own advice?"

As much as I wanted to resent the question, I couldn't. Our fathers had one thing in common that I would prefer to have never known about. They'd both had affairs with Maddy Curtis. Maybe Coop's dad was a passing fancy and mine...? I glanced over at Edward. He and Muriel were actually speaking together in quiet tones where they sat together on a bench in the shade.

Mine had been on the hook, quite literally, for years.

Didn't make it any better.

Then again, he told her off today. But how long would that last before she crooked her finger and he went running back?

How much did I actually care?

Except...

"Arch," Coop said. "Talk to them. You have nothing to lose. You've already written them off. They owe you a lot. So, if they plan to make a payment, no matter how paltry the installment, listening is free."

"Can you forgive him?" The question came out of nowhere, for me at least, but if it threw Coop, he didn't show it. "After everything that happened? He's trying to make amends. Can you forgive him?"

"Forgiveness isn't for them," Coop said. "It's for you. I'll forgive him eventually when I'm not living on the anger. And I'm not—not as much as I was. I hate that he hurt Mom. I don't think that part will ever go away, but I also…I kind of feel sorry for him."

"Because he got used." I didn't have to wonder at that.

"Yeah, and not only did he get used, he lost a lot too. I don't think he realized how much he lost at first either."

I glanced at Edward. "He never really valued his relationship with Muriel." Or me, but I didn't want to say that aloud. I wasn't that kid anymore, trying to find something, anything that would make his father happy. "If I ever have a kid…"

"Same," Coop told me and gripped my shoulder. He had no idea what I was about to say, but there wasn't an ounce of hesitation or doubt in his voice. "I'm gonna tell Frankie I'm going to eat with them. I'll catch you guys back at the apartment. Text me if plans change?"

"Done." Before he'd gone two steps, I said, "Coop?"

"Yeah?" He squinted as he glanced back at me.

"If you figure out how to not live on the anger at him, show me?"

"Man, if I could, I would. But then…you can fix anything. Think about how you'd fix this for Frankie." With that, he winked and strode away. I shook my head. If Hank did to her what Maddy had done, I might fix it with a shovel. I wanted to know how the hell Maddy had even gotten a ticket to sit in that section.

As it was, I still hadn't figured out exactly what we were going to do with her. I wasn't the only one worried about how much more dangerous she might get. Maybe we'd move our plans up to head on our summer vacation sooner, then just make the move to New York. The guys didn't need Frankie here to come back and see their families.

The more distance I put between Maddy and Frankie, the better.

Frankie caught my gaze as she gave Coop a hug. A tiny frown tightened her brow, but I shook my head at the question in her eyes. I didn't need her to come rescue me. As it was, I glanced over to Edward and Muriel again. Time to take care of this.

Hands still in my pockets, I crossed to where they continued to speak. At my approach, Edward rose and Muriel even attempted a smile. I didn't reciprocate. Neither said anything as we all stared at each other in silence. After a few more seconds of that, I raised my brows.

"You were the one who wanted to talk," I reminded him.

Muriel let out a sigh, then to my surprise she put a hand on my arm and brushed a kiss to the air next to my cheek. "I'll leave you both to it. I don't suppose you will take me up on the offer, but you are welcome to stay at my place when you're in New York."

"You're right—I won't take you up on it." I was never living with either of them again. Besides, I'd already made arrangements. "Are you flying back today?"

"Tomorrow. Your grandfather invited me to dinner," she said, then glanced at Edward. "Unless either of you want to make me a counter offer?"

"Pass," I stated. Unsurprisingly, Edward snorted.

"Muriel, he's eating with the Graysons."

"Of course he is," she said with a purely satisfied smile. "They will likely be discussing just how horrid their bitch of a daughter is. I will enjoy that."

I didn't roll my eyes and Edward didn't rise to the bait.

Look at that, maybe we were growing emotionally.

Or maybe we were just that bored with the same old games. I didn't doubt Grandpa invited her to dinner. He'd very specifically invited Frankie and I to breakfast, so he'd make sure the field was clear for us.

With a little bit of a huff, she paced away from us with a click of her heels. A dark car pulled up to the curb and just before the driver jumped out to open the back door, Edward said, "A hundred says her latest conquest is waiting for her inside."

Ugh.

I caught sight of a pant leg as the door opened and turned away to face Edward instead. "Pass."

He gave me a faint smile and nodded. "Good plan." Even his sunglasses couldn't disguise the way he glanced to where Frankie and the others still gathered. Sara and Joe were speaking animatedly with Hank, and Frankie leaned into Bubba. She looked happy, content. But I caught her glancing at me and I shook my head when she raised her brows again.

The wrinkle of her nose promised me a scolding later. I looked forward to getting out of trouble. After one last glance, I turned to face Edward again. "What did you need?"

"Walk with me?"

"Sure," I agreed and fell into step with him. Why not? Anything to get him farther away from Frankie. He'd mentioned speaking to both of us, but frankly, I'd rather vet anything he wanted to say to her through me first. We followed the sidewalk along the side of the event center. The place was bordered by a park and a greenbelt with shade trees. The heat rose off the pavement in waves.

"I honestly don't know where to begin," Edward admitted after we'd walked in absolute silence for several yards.

"If it's about the company, my answer hasn't changed. My shares will vote with Grandpa for now."

"I expected that," Edward said. "Where you vote, Frankie will."

I shrugged. Honestly, Frankie and I hadn't discussed what her shares meant. We were due for a meeting with the accountants in the next week or so, because I wanted her to understand the state of her finances. Particularly in light of the decisions the Graysons had made with regard to her trust and how much money was actually in it.

That said, I wouldn't *tell* Frankie how to vote. She was more than capable of reading the reports just like I was, and after her brief internship and the light in her eyes when business came up? I had a feeling she was going to be telling me how to vote and I was okay with that too. I liked the idea of having someone who could share the passion of the business.

Such as it was.

Edward sighed. "About Maddy..."

I paused and faced him. "What about her?" The last thing I wanted to discuss was Maddy *fucking* Curtis unless it involved a restraining order or a psychiatric commitment. For now, putting several states between Frankie and that bitch would have to do.

"You were right to bring up your concerns about her," Edward admitted. "I know she's troubled."

"Is that a polite way of saying psychotic?"

He exhaled a long sigh and tilted his head back. "Archie, you have every right to be pissed at me and to be dismissive. I deserve it. That said, if Frankie was the one who was troubled, would you want to call her psychotic or get her help?"

"Then why aren't you getting her help?" Also, fuck that noise. "Frankie was in trouble. She was isolated and alone. A manipulative bitch was using her to achieve her own ends and you fell for it hook, line, and sinker."

"I did. And I hurt you in the process." He actually looked upset by the prospect.

The snort escaped me before I could stop it. Not that I would have bothered. Not really. "Edward, you haven't given a solid damn about me ever. To be honest, the last time you hurt me, I was nine. I've long since gotten over it. You're you. I just lowered my expectations."

Brows gathering together, Edward ducked his head. "Fair."

"It is what it is." Except... "You know she threatened to kill Frankie once?"

The reticence and unease fled Edward's expression as he focused on me. "She couldn't have meant that. She loves her."

"Does she?" I challenged. "Or does she love how Frankie makes her look? For more than a year, she's neglected her. Vanished for days at a time on 'business' trips. Worse, when Frankie was hurt and in the hospital, no one could get ahold of her or you. Not really feeling the love there, Edward, what about you?"

Because the fact it took me hours to even track down *where* they were had been irksome enough. That they hadn't responded to messages and chose to appear *days* later? Yeah. Fuck that.

Edward sighed heavily, and he seemed much older. A part of me felt for him. A distant, uncynical part of me that wondered why I'd had to compete with the ghost of a woman he'd loved for attention. At the same time, I wasn't willing to ask him for that explanation or anything really.

Not anymore.

"I will do what I can to keep her calm," Edward admitted. "Though today made it clear the fractures in our relationship may be irreparable."

"Well, maybe next time don't bang your secretary. Fidelity seems to be a sticking point for her." That he'd continued getting his rocks off at the office hadn't been lost on me during my last visit. The fact he had the woman of his dreams back and still couldn't keep it in his pants? "You know, there's counseling for that."

Edward laughed.

It wasn't harsh or brittle or even empty. It was a genuine laugh that seemed to work its way up from his chest. He raked a hand through his hair and for a moment, the unruffled, undisturbed poise of Edward Archibald Standish Jr disappeared.

Maybe for the first time, I saw "Eddie."

"Counseling. That's never been my strong suit. Problems are not something we share with the world."

"Weaknesses can be exploited," I said, repeating the advice both Edward and Grandpa had often repeated over the years. "Having a weakness isn't the problem. Revealing the weakness is."

"When you say it like that, I sound like an asshole."

It was my turn to chuckle. "You are an asshole. Doesn't make the advice any less useful, but it shouldn't be applied in all things. Flaws. Weaknesses. Imperfections. We all have them. It's the people who stick with you despite all of them, who have your back when others would have walked away or already had, they are worth keeping. More than worth it. In fact, you fight to keep them. I'm not afraid of my flaws."

Edward studied me for a moment. "If I asked, would you tell me if you're in counseling?"

"Yes," I admitted. "For the record, not regularly." Though I planned to attend the group sessions with Frankie as she'd asked. I'd been as skeptical as the next person about therapy to be frank, but in the weeks that followed Homecoming, as we'd all had to watch her struggle, my opinion changed.

Therapy had helped her. It showed in her attitude. How she would confront issues directly. And how the nightmares faded. The smile on her face and the light in her eyes was no longer clouded under some dark shadow. Would it do me any good? Who the fuck knew? But I didn't discount it anymore.

"And let's be blunt here, Edward, what do you have to lose? Your marriage is over. Your position in the company is nothing more than a glorified figurehead now, you have no negotiating power. You could spend your weeks golfing, and no one would notice your absence."

He winced. "Ouch."

"I'm calling it like I see it. The only major flaw in your life right now is your choice of companions."

"After today, I sincerely doubt Maddy will want to see me. It could even be months before she deigns to acknowledge me again...and that is a good thing. The woman..." He looked to the distance and it hit me, there were lines of age around his eyes, a hint of gray in his hair and deeper grooves round his mouth.

Edward was getting older.

"Maddy has always been one of mercurial moods. But she never responds well to attacks."

I said nothing as he spoke.

"It might be a good time to take Frankie on a trip." He focused on where she continued to chat with Hank and Bubba's family. "Maybe take all of you on a trip. If you need some..."

"I've got it," I said. "You said you could handle her." That was before the much clearer breakup. We'd discussed this very fact a few days prior.

"I didn't expect her to drop by the office yesterday and got..."

I rolled my eyes. "Yeah, you keep telling yourself that. If you wanted out of the relationship, why don't you man up and just end it. The drama play, the backstabbing, the cheating? All it does is make you both miserable. It made Muriel miserable. It definitely didn't do me any favors."

"Because...she's a singular woman," Edward admitted. "While I know a lot of people think you're too young, I see the same look in your eye when you look at Frankie that I felt when I looked at Maddy."

"Then or now?"

"They run together, if I'm honest. She's still the girl who takes my breath away. The woman who pushes me and challenges me. She's the one I want to win, that I would pursue..." He grimaced then ran a hand over his face. "So maybe you're right, maybe I should just be direct with her and end things like adults. But when I'm with her, I'm not a rational man."

She was toxic for him. That was what Grandpa had said. Defeat seemed to weigh down his shoulders.

"I can't tell you what to do. I can tell you that I think she's unhinged and dangerous. I think she's already committed crimes." What Hank had said earlier, about waking up to find her in his bed and he'd been drunk and didn't remember it, that was definitely taking advantage of someone. The neglect she subjected Frankie to. Blatantly threatening her life if Maddy's parents tried to intervene... Those were just the things we knew about. "If she really thinks she's lost you," I said slowly, "there's a chance she could turn that anger on you."

"Worried about me, Archie?" The pained smile Edward wore, he'd earned.

"I don't wish you dead," I said flatly. "I don't have a high opinion of you…"

"Clearly, a fact you detailed when you wanted to protect Frankie from the monster that is me."

I shrugged. "She is my priority."

"She's a remarkable young lady, and maybe this is too little, too late, but what she said to me will not go away. I missed out on a lot with you, I'd like to miss out on less. I know you're not fond of golf but…"

"Possibly," I said, raising a hand. "It's not my favorite game, but Frankie loves mini-golf and if she wants to come along to learn…we could test the waters. But Edward…" I leveled a stare at him. "Maddy shows up, and all bets are off. I don't want her anywhere near Frankie. And it may need to wait because we're heading out of town in a few days."

"Have you decided on where?"

"Yes. Jeremy will know how to reach me." Frankie's apartment would be packed and cleared out before we returned, but I wasn't going to provide him with that information. Edward was reeling on several fronts, give him time to get his bearings and his feet back under him and that might very well change.

It wouldn't be the first time.

Holding out a hand, he said, "You might not believe this, but I am proud of you."

"I'm an epic son," I confirmed and clasped his hand for a brief handshake. "You'd be hard-pressed to deny that, regardless of what you'd heard or seen."

He laughed again. Man, the first laugh had been strange. The second was downright bizarre. "Your wit is enjoyable when it's less pointed and aimed at slicing me."

Sliding my hand back into my pockets, I shrugged. "Not going to give you an apology."

"Not asking for one. But I am asking for a second chance. Maybe not to be your father, I have a feeling that I have missed far too much to get there, but I'd like it if we could at least attempt to be friends. To get to know each other."

Frankie's father flew thousands of miles and drove to her apartment on the slim chance he'd get to lay eyes on a daughter he'd never met. Edward wasn't really going that far out on a limb here, but...

"Consider therapy. Look at getting some help and get your life sorted and we'll talk." It was the best I could do, and honestly, I didn't think he could do any of it. But my family came first and if he wanted to be around them, then I had to be able to trust him.

Right now, I didn't.

Did I want to?

Eh… The jury was out on that one.

He only nodded, then said, "Archie? Congratulations on graduating and on NYU. I know Senior would have preferred that you go to Harvard. Legacy is fine, but making your own path is something to be respected."

Then he slipped his sunglasses back into place and walked away.

I could say that was honestly the weirdest conversation I'd had with Edward in my entire life.

It might also be the longest.

Soft arms crept around me and gentle hands flattened against my chest as Frankie brushed her lips to my ear. "You good?"

Twisting, I hooked an arm around her and pulled her close. "Always," I promised. "We ready to grab the other brother boyfriend and your dad and get some food?"

Her eyes lit up. "Oh, no one's said that in front of Hank yet."

Glee filled me. "You love me, right?"

Her soft groan and laugh were all the permission I needed. But I did walk us back over to them. It was the least I could do and, so far, Hank had been taking all the challenges like a pro.

I was looking forward to his expression on this one.

What?

Can't a guy have a little fun when testing out the worthiness of his girl's sperm donor?

That's what I thought.

Chapter Six
FRIENDSHIP BEFORE LOVE

FRANKIE

Joe and Hank walked ahead of us. We'd ended up going to the lake and eating at one of the little cottage restaurants overlooking the water. It was laid back and relaxed. The seafood had been a great choice. Ian and Archie followed behind, while I walked with Sara. I'd kind of hoped Rachel and her family would join us, but the huge noisy crowd had made plans of their own.

Rachel and I were getting together later in the week for a girls' day before she jetted off to Europe for her summer vacay. I refused to be envious, while at the same time, I was wild with jealousy. She planned to hit several art centers in Europe, backpacking for parts of it, but basically photographing her way across the continent.

"Come with," she'd invited. "I'm pretty sure we can work it out for you to come along. I'm staying in a lot of hostels and stuff, so it's not like we even have to worry about reservations."

Beyond tempted, I still said no. I'd promised the summer to the guys. I'd taken last summer away, so we hadn't had our last high school summer blowout together. Though, they'd certainly done their best to make it a summer to remember. This year was about us and Ian's birthday and really living it up between high school and college.

In all likelihood, Archie had planned something. He loved planning, and the guys were his more than willing accomplices.

"Fine," Rachel huffed. "But next summer, we do a couple of weeks somewhere. Just us girls where we go and explore the history and the art."

That, I agreed with. I just had to find a way to break it to the guys that Rachel and I were going to run away together for two weeks of fun.

Sara bumped my shoulder. The sun had dropped in the west, and though we were walking slowly along the boardwalk toward the cars, the breeze off the lake had turned the day beautiful and cool. "How are you feeling, sweetheart? I really haven't had a chance to talk to you alone."

While we weren't totally alone right now, we did have some privacy. "Better than I could have imagined," I admitted. "I like Hank. I like him a lot. I'm still stunned he came all this way. I loved that Lyssa and Marsha came to graduation, and all of you. Thanks for the cheering, by the way."

She chuckled. "Of course, we told you, you will always have a mom when you need one."

My heart squeezed. She, Alicia, and Carly had all made that clear. They would be there for me whenever I needed a mom. The fact I had earned such a crappy one, but somehow found three fantastic ones, left me a little teary.

"And I like Hank too, and I think Joe does. He's stopped interrogating him, and now they are just arguing sports." She rolled her eyes playfully and squeezed my arm. "You've grown up to be such an amazing young lady. I'm glad he has gone out of his way to meet you, so he can get to know you too."

Hank had rolled with all of it. The moms. The dads. The questions. Even Maddy. He'd handled her like a champ. Once we were back at the cars, I got a hug from both Joe and Sara. Ian was coming back with us, but he promised to see his parents later. We had family dinner coming up.

The drive back to the apartment was almost silent. Ian drove, and Archie offered Hank the passenger seat. He'd given Archie an amused look before he accepted. When Archie wrapped an arm around me, I tucked my head against his shoulder. It had been a long day, but it had also been a good one.

I had so many photos on my phone now. Photos of all of us. Of Hank—my dad.

My dad.

My. Dad.

At the apartment, he didn't intend to come up. "Actually boys, if you'll excuse us, I'd like to talk to Frankie alone for a few."

Archie studied him for a long moment, then glanced at me. I appreciate the trust and the quiet request in his eyes. I nodded. I got it, he continued to be wary, and I loved him for it. Hank—Hank seemed genuine, and as much as I liked him and hoped I wasn't wrong about him, trust had to start somewhere.

With a gentle kiss to my temple, Ian murmured, "We'll go look after the cats. You want us to order anything?"

I considered that because I was kind of hungry… "Maybe pizza and those cinnamon bread sticks?"

He grinned. "You got it."

Hank and Archie shared a brief handshake before he headed up the stairs, with Ian following him.

"You're leaving," were the first two words out of my mouth. I eased my feet out of the heels. I'd managed to wear them all day, and currently, my feet were kind of numb. The warm pavement under them felt great.

Instead of denying it, he just leaned against the hood of his rental car. "If I could, I'd stay the rest of the week. I want to, but I still have a job and I have summer term coming up that I have to prep for."

"We've barely even gotten to talk about that," I admitted. He was a professor at *Harvard*. "We were actually up at Harvard a few months ago, on spring break. We kind of gave ourselves a tour and then had a snowball fight."

Inane as that sounded, he grinned.

"I wish I'd known…" he said, and I lifted my shoulders.

"But we didn't," I said. "I mean, I know that we might have had the test results then, but I wasn't ready."

"There's no problem with you waiting until you were ready, Frankie," he told me. "You're an amazing young woman, I am so damn honored to have met you and gotten to spend this time with you. Even more, I'm hoping you'll do more visits? Maybe come up and see Kelly and the kids? I'd love for you to meet them and for them to meet you."

My stomach bottomed out, both from excitement and a little bit of fear. "They may not want a big sister appearing out of nowhere."

He snorted. "No, I think whatever minor resentments they could possibly nurse will be utterly outweighed by the cool factor."

"The cool factor?" What cool factor? However, he just grinned at me.

"Trust me, you're way cooler than their professor dad and real estate mom."

Folding my arms, I lifted my shoulders. "If you say so. I think you're pretty cool. I mean, you're teaching at my dream school." How weird would it have been if I'd actually gotten into Harvard, then ended up in his class or something?

"That's the other part of what I wanted to talk to you about," Hank said. He glanced toward the apartment, then back to me. "You guys are all going to NYU…"

"That's the plan. I was wait-listed at Harvard, and it took me a little time to get over it, but I'm good now. The five of us—well six now if you count Rachel—we like the idea of going to the same place. Even before we were dating, the plan was to go to the same school, be roommates, and you know, build a life."

Even before we were dating. I might as well have said back when I was oblivious to the fact they wanted me, but there were some things that he really didn't need to know. The fact I had been dense definitely seemed to fall into that category.

"Sounds good, and forgive me if I pull on my dad hat for a moment, but I want you to think about your life as stages and that this is the next stage, not the rest of your life…"

"Hank, we're not getting married, but they are my life. I get what you're saying, and none of us are interested, you know, in changing that anytime soon…" Okay, maybe I shouldn't just assume. "It's not a topic we've discussed. We are focused on building our best lives. Ian and I want to record. Archie and Jake want to build and design. Eventually, Archie will be involved with Standish. I might help with that, I kind of like studying business and focusing on getting a project through from concept to creation to launch. Coop's gonna be a psychologist. But we've kind of known that for years. None of that is going to happen overnight."

He raked a hand through his hair. "That's fair and a really good attitude. College is a challenging time. You're becoming adults, away from home and… Well, I suppose you've been away from parental supervision a lot longer than you probably should have been."

"Probably, but it means I can handle the day-to-day stuff. Though wrangling Archie and chores is fun and balancing a grocery budget seems like an impossibility. But it's half the fun too. He loves to do things grander, and the other guys are learning to cook or already do cook."

"So Archie doesn't cook?" He cocked his head.

"No," I mouthed with probably more force than necessary. "He's brilliant with machines though." And the worst cook ever.

Hank chuckled softly, then sobered and stared at me with such serious eyes. "Fair, fair. What I wanted to tell you was that if Harvard is still the dream, I can make it happen."

"I don't want money to open any doors…"

"It's not money, kiddo. It's me. I'm a professor and a tenured one at that.

I earned it pretty early, and while Humanities isn't the full-on sciences, I do have a pretty heavy class load. As my daughter, your admission would be easily handled and your tuition wouldn't be an issue."

It was probably the sweetest thing in the world to offer me.

"And selfishly, I'd like it if you were closer. Now that I know you exist, I don't want you so far away."

"We're moving to New York, that's a lot closer to Boston," I promised. "And a few months ago, I might have leapt at the offer." Maybe. I'd had a couple of offers to grease the wheels and get me in, but I still wanted it on my own merit. The nepotism of being a professor's biological issue didn't seem any more fair than using money to open the doors. "Thank you so much for thinking of me. But it would still be a no because Coop and Ian didn't get in there. We want to be together, even if our classes are different and the stuff we chase is different. We want to be in the same place."

"You really love them." It wasn't a question.

"More than I can describe. They really saved my life. They've had my back, and even when I didn't totally understand what they meant to me, they knew what they wanted. It just took us some time to figure it all out."

"Then I will do my best to support it, but I'm on your side. First and foremost," he told me, and my heart did this little weird stretch. "Can I… I know we're working on the friendship thing, but can I give you a hug?"

I didn't hesitate. Maybe I should be more guarded. But I adored everything about Hank. If I'd dreamed up a dad, he would have been like him. The fierceness in his embrace made tears spark in my eyes.

"Thank you," he said. "Thank you for letting me get to know you and them. Thank you for letting me come to your graduation and including me in this day."

I returned the hug with the same ferocity. "Thank you for wanting to know me. Thank you for standing up to Maddy for me."

He leaned away and met my gaze. "Every day. That's what a dad does.

He's got your back, and he doesn't let anyone treat his little girl like crap. So we may still be on the friendship portion, but my goal is to get you to call me Dad and for you to know and trust that the relationship is there for you. Those boys all seem great and I love how they look after you, but one step out of line, and pop…they are going to deal with me."

I couldn't help it, I laughed. "They'll probably have to deal with Rachel too."

"Oh, good. She's a lot scarier than I am." His expression softened into a goofy smile. "You're an amazing kid, Frankie Curtis. And if you ever want my name, it's all yours."

That added to the waterworks, and I let out a shuddery breath. "I have your number, and you have mine. Call me when you're home? Let me know you got there safely?"

"Deal. Your boys were talking about a trip…"

I pressed a finger to my lips, and he quieted. "It's a surprise. Though I'm kind of on to them this time, but I'll call and let you know we're okay. Then once we're settled in New York, we can make plans for that visit."

"Anytime," he said. "I mean that. The kids are going to want to meet you sooner rather than later, but we'll take it one day at a time. Deal?"

I grinned and then gave him a hug that he returned with a sigh. "Deal."

My eyes were still a little damp when he finally climbed into his car— almost an hour later. He kept finding one more thing to mention or share. It seemed so strange that my heart could be so full and aching so much at the same time. I missed him before he was even out of the parking lot.

Only after the red tail lights were gone and a mosquito had bit me did I finally head up to the apartment. The pizza had arrived while we'd been talking, and I grinned when I found Coop sprawled on the floor, while Ian and Archie vied against each other in some game.

"Hey," he greeted me. "All good with Hank?"

"Yep. He's got an early flight in the morning, so he's going to a hotel at the airport so he's close." I would have preferred he stay, but it might be easier to say bye now than get up at three or four in the morning and do it.

"You good?" Ian asked as they paused the game, and I smiled.

"I'm great. I'm going to get changed and then come back and eat."

Coop trailed me into the bedroom and tugged down the zipper for me, but he just fell back on the bed while I slipped out of the dress.

"You sure you're good?"

Glancing over at him, I reached up to loosen my hair. Oh, my scalp ached as the hair fell free. Well, free was relative since it seemed semi-frozen into the shape of the pony tail. Raking my fingers through it, I loosened it up and wanted to groan at the same time. I forgot how much a tight hairstyle hurt after a few hours. My scalp, like my feet, had gone numb.

"I think I'm great, actually." I laid the dress over the back of a chair. It would need to go to the cleaners. It was too nice for the washer and dryer. The shoes, I set in the closet, and if they didn't look so pretty, I might burn them for being the torture devices they were. I unsnapped the bra and slid it off before shimmying out of my panties.

Coop groaned. "Are you torturing me on purpose?"

Laughter bubbled up as I discarded both items into the dirty clothes bin and padded over to the dresser. "No, I just need to change. I've been in all of that *all* day and I need to find a brush for my hair and maybe some Tylenol for the rest of me." I pulled out his old boxers and dangled them at him before I stepped into them and snagged one of Archie's shirts. The guys preferred me in their clothes at night. Or out of them. They weren't that fussy.

"I'll brush your hair," he volunteered, and I smiled 'cause I wouldn't say no to that. "But I wanted to make sure that after Maddy…"

I held up my hand, and he hushed.

"She was a speed bump in an otherwise perfect day. I'd rather talk about how cool it was that Hank stood up for me or that your mom is a badass or that Jake's *dad* showed up."

With a smile, he shoved off the bed and looped his arms around me. "Have I mentioned how awesome you are today?"

I made a big show of thinking about it. "No, I don't think so…pretty sure I'd remember that."

With gentle hands, he traced up my arms to my neck, then into my scalp. At the first stroke of his fingertips to my abused scalp, I wanted to melt. I did groan.

"You're amazing, Frankie Curtis. The best bestie a guy could have and the best girlfriend to boot." He brushed a kiss to my lips. "Today was awesome because we were all together."

I opened my eyes and smiled up at him. "I couldn't have said it better myself."

When he increased the pressure of his scalp massage, I really did moan, and he let out a soft chuckle. "Could I convince you to make really profound moaning noises while they're stuck out there?"

"Like they haven't heard us having sex before?" I pinched him gently.

"True, that's a great idea. Let's do that." Then he flipped me onto the bed, and I landed with a bounce and burst out laughing. Instead of following me down, he caught one of my feet and began to massage it.

Holy crap.

I groaned, loud and long.

"That's my beautiful girl," Coop said with a wicked grin. "Let them hear how good this feels." Fuck, when he hit that spot in my arch, I didn't even have to pretend. My moan came out more a little shriek because it hurt so good. The sound of thuds from the other room just barely registered as Coop worked my foot flat and then curved again.

He gave the best foot massages. "Just keep doing that," I said with a sigh. "More."

"Fuck me," Jake said from the doorway with a laugh. "I was all set to player three your ass, and you're massaging her fucking foot."

I slit my eyes open and lifted my other foot. "I have two, feel free to join the game, player three, you might even earn enough XP to escalate to the next level."

"I'm in."

"Hey," Archie protested as Jake joined us on the bed, but the moment he took possession of my other foot, I stopped paying attention. This was *amazing*. "I thought you wanted pizza."

"I can want more than one thing," I murmured. "I'm complicated like that."

He chuckled. "Fair enough. Bring this party out to the living room. We can all take turns making her purr."

Oh, that sounded amazing.

"And it's not even my birthday…"

The swat Jake delivered to my ass made me laugh, but so did the fact that he let me climb on his back and he piggybacked me out to the living room. True to his word, Coop brought out the brush and ran it through my hair. The guys took turns giving me foot rubs in between games, and I got pizza.

"We're done," I murmured a little later while we debated a movie. Currently I was curled up in Ian's lap and had zero intention of going anywhere. I was a boneless wonder, and he was warm and cuddly.

"Yep," Ian answered. "But only with high school, we leveled up. Achievement unlocked."

I let out a contented sigh. The guys were still arguing about a movie. They were going to put in the action film.

It was always action.

Honestly, I had no idea which one they ended up choosing. I was asleep before the opening logo played.

SUBJECT: CONGRATS!! FREEDOM!

Seriously, that's sooo cool! Thanks for the pictures. Don't get weirded out, but I like how normal all that seems. We've been homeschooling or doing online school on the road for so long, I'm probably going to bomb the minute I walk into Blue Ivy, but you know what? IDGAF. Taking time off is about letting us work on us.

Also, girl. The daddy drama. We need like a weekend, some alcohol, and maybe some weed. It might take all of that for me to confess all of mine, but I'm glad yours seems to be cool.

So what are your summer plans? Have you and Ian worked on your new sound yet? I want to hear a remix where you get his voice some more airtime. If he gives you any trouble, remind him you hold the key to the va-jay-jay. If he wants penis tunnel time, he's going to have to cooperate. Besides, no lie—his voice is panty melting hot.

And on that note, hit me up with new lyric sheets. We have three more weeks on this freaking tour, and then I swear I'm going to sleep for a month. Send me music.

KC

Chapter Seven
LEARNING THE ROPES

IAN

We'd taken the bike tonight. If there were a chance Frankie would need aftercare before we left, I'd have suggested her car. However, our *class* this evening was for me to learn and her to observe. The feel of her arms wrapped around my waist and breasts pushing against my back were both sensations I never wanted to end. Since we had time, I took us for a ride around the lake. The days were getting sultrier, but a flash storm earlier had cooled the humidity and left it gorgeous.

We hadn't discussed our next steps, but Memorial Day weekend was coming and Archie wanted to spring the surprise then. I was good with that. It gave us time to get a couple of classes in with Lyssa and Richard. Yeah, I couldn't call him Master anything unless we were in a scene, and here was hoping they didn't require that tonight.

Frankie calling me Sir Ian was heady as fuck, but I didn't need it or want it from anyone else, no matter how much I teased Coop.

Longer days meant the sun was still out when we pulled into the industrial park where the club was located. Frankie's eyes were bright as she danced off the back of the bike and pulled the helmet free. "I could ride for hours," she admitted, and I grinned.

"Maybe we'll do that. Take a drive over to Louisiana and find the Blue Dog Café for gumbo or something."

Laughter bubbled out of her. "Sold."

"You'd have agreed without the food stop."

"Oh, absolutely," she said as she shook out the waves of golden blonde hair. "But you've put gumbo on the table, Sir, and I'm afraid I'll have to hold you to it."

Amusement unfurled within me as I slid off the bike and set my helmet on it before taking hers and adding it. Then I cupped her face in my hands and kissed her. Frankie didn't ask any questions as she pushed up on her toes, her lips parting for me beautifully. The gentle glide of her tongue was intoxicating, but it was the soft moan she exhaled that sent all my blood southward.

Still nibbling, I tested my own restraint as she leaned into the caress, but no other part of her body touched me. Just her face, where I cradled it in my hands, and her lips, which opened to me in eager surrender and potential demand.

Breaking the kiss slowly and more than a little reluctantly, I found her eyes half-closed and her body swaying a little in my direction. The lack of tension in her expression satisfied me on a level so primitive, I didn't want to examine it too closely. I *needed* to keep her safe and make things easier for her. The bliss on her face was my objective.

"You ready?" We'd discussed this with Lyssa and Richard the week before over dinner. Funnily enough, the first lesson hadn't been a lesson so much as a getting acquainted to help remove some of the awkwardness. I appreciated the effort. I also appreciated the fact they had the names and numbers of a couple of similarly-run clubs in New York—one in Manhattan and the other in Brooklyn.

"Is it weird that I'm excited to watch?"

"Nope," I assured her, then traced my thumb over her cheekbone. Sometimes it was easy to think of her as fragile, but she wasn't. "I didn't know voyeur was your kink, but there's nothing wrong with it."

Her laughter wrapped around me like a hug. "Not sure I get off on it like Coop does, but I'm excited to see what you're going to get to do with the ropes. I mean when it's me, I can't see what you do."

That made sense. "I'll make sure I take pictures if you ever want to see the designs." Because there would be designs. Nearly every single thing I'd devoured on *shibari* and the art of rope was that it was an art. Frankie would be the canvas.

"That both scares and excites me… The pictures part, I mean."

"Well, one step at a time then, yeah?" With that, I slid an arm around her shoulders and we headed inside. One perk of membership was we just had to show our dog tags with the club ID stamped on them, and then we were through the doors to the kitchen and lounging area.

Lyssa was brewing a pot of coffee, and she grinned at us. "Hey, how are you both?"

"We're good," Frankie answered as she stripped off her jacket. Neither of us really needed them for the weather, but we definitely needed them for the bike. The reinforced biking jackets had just *appeared* in the closet one day. They matched perfectly, and I didn't have to look far for the culprit. Archie just smiled. Considering he just wanted her safe, I let it go, but I did look up how much they cost and paid him back.

Much to his chagrin.

Gifts, I had no problem accepting, but these weren't gifts so much as his attempt to control what he could. I appreciated that. But we had to have some kind of balance.

"Thanks for coming to graduation," Frankie was saying, and Lyssa flashed her a quick smile.

"Oh, honey, my pleasure. Sorry I didn't stick around for the drama though. Just not my scene." She motioned to the coffee. "You want some? Ian and I can't have any, but you're welcome to it."

"Why can't you have it?"

"Because," I answered for Lyssa, "we don't want any of the senses inhibited, particularly while I'm learning."

Frankie twisted to stare at me. "Ian Rhys, you didn't say anything about no caffeine. This might be a deal breaker."

I cocked my head to the side and stared at her. Her green eyes glittered, and her nose wrinkled up. Yeah, I didn't believe her either. "Really?"

"No," she said, making a face. "But I love my coffee."

"I promise to make it worth the sacrifice."

"You two are *adorable*," Lyssa said with a grin and poured Frankie a cup of coffee. "Also, saw your dad Frankie. He's a hottie."

Lyssa absolutely knew what she was doing, but Frankie's face made me laugh anyway. "He's a nice guy," I cut in, because I got it. Let's not talk about our parents here. "But Frankie's right—we really do appreciate you coming to graduation. It was thoughtful."

She smiled. "Again, it was my pleasure. Thank you both for inviting me. My only regret is that graduation means you're both moving soon, but you'll be back for holidays, yes?"

"Some, yes," I told her as Frankie smiled at me. "My parents are still here, and we have a few other ties."

But Frankie didn't. Well, she had the ties to our families, because our families rallied around her and were all making it a point to support her. Mom, Dad, Jake's and Coop's moms. I counted Jeremy in that number, but I had a feeling he'd picked her over all of us except for Archie a long time ago.

"Well, good. Then we keep your memberships so that you can come and visit with us too, and I know Richard gave you some numbers for New York. I know a few people too. A couple of good subby groups." She winked at Frankie.

"Sometimes, it can be lonely when you're starting out and you don't know who to ask questions of. Ian will do everything he can, but he's not a subby."

No, no I was not.

"I appreciate that. There's gonna be so much to do when we get to New York. It'll be nice to have others I can talk to who won't think it's weird when I ask about my desire to be a brat."

Lyssa chuckled and I snorted, but Frankie's wide grin delighted me. "You don't need a reason," Lyssa answered before I could.

"She would know," Richard declared as he strolled in wearing a suit and tie. He also had a duffel bag over his shoulder. I had no idea what he did in his day job life. He didn't offer, and I didn't ask. "I am running late, my apologies if I kept you waiting. If you don't mind giving me ten minutes, I'll go change and we can get started." He gave Frankie a quiet nod, but held out his hand to me. I shook it once.

"No problem. We've been catching up with Lyssa."

"Excellent. No coffee," he said to Lyssa, and she stuck her tongue out at him.

"It's for Frankie."

His expression was indulgent. "Of course it is, but a reminder never hurt anyone, unlike bratty behavior."

The connection between them amused me. I couldn't tell if they were just dating or together. One of the things they'd both stressed in the beginning was BDSM could be a component of a relationship or it could be the whole relationship. But just because they did scenes together didn't necessarily mean they shared a sexual relationship as well. The power exchange was one aspect, the sexual relationship was another.

Part of why I understood that I wouldn't really look for someone else to share the power dynamic with. I wanted it all with Frankie. Even coming here in the beginning to learn and try to explore my interests, I hadn't wanted to just find someone to work a scene with, even after observing. There had been more joy in the play Frankie and I had done, unstructured or constrained, than anything I'd seen here.

Not that I was judging, either. I wanted to learn. I wanted to know everything. Richard and Lyssa were both open, direct people. Richard might be more reserved than Lyssa, but I got that impression from a few of the more dominant partners I'd met here. They were more guarded, especially around their sub. Since I did the same thing for Frankie, I definitely got it. I also appreciated their candor more than I could describe. Making it safe and joyful for Frankie would always be my primary goal.

Frankie had the large cup of coffee in a refillable tumbler ready to go. At her raised eyebrows, I just smiled. I loved that she always wanted to make sure I was okay with something too. Honestly, I'd have probably been more nervous if I were doing this to Frankie right now *with* an audience. I was less uncertain about having her there to watch and learn with me.

"All right, you two," Lyssa said with a grin. "Enough with the googly eyes. You're killing my teeth here. C'mon, let's take you back. We're in the quiet room tonight. I thought it would be easier for you and that you may not want an audience for your first tying session."

"Thank you," I told Lyssa as I held my hand out for Frankie. "Do I need to change?"

"Are you comfortable in what you're wearing?"

I was in jeans and a T-shirt. Our jackets were hanging up. Like me, Frankie was in jeans and she had on one of her Torched T-shirts that she'd fallen in love with. Neither of us had on motorcycle boots, but I'd added those to the list of items we needed to add to our wardrobes, particularly for longer rides.

"Pretty much."

"Well, then unless Master Dick," she said the last bit with a wink and a conspiratorial smile at Frankie, "says otherwise, you're fine." As we followed her, Frankie slipped her hand right into mine. "As you get the feel for it, you'll know more about what you're comfortable in."

Richard—yeah not calling him Master Dick unless absolutely required, bratty subs and all that notwithstanding—seemed fairly relaxed when he offered advice. But his commands were absolute, and it was interesting to see how he spoke to and handled Lyssa in a scene versus outside of it.

The quiet room was just that—the walls were a little thicker and padded to help insulate against sounds from outside. The room was set up so they could arrange what they needed in it. There were hooks and eyelets in the wall for running ropes and an armbar that extended out for suspension work.

We were definitely not there yet.

Richard was already in the room when we stepped inside, and he had an assortment of materials from rope to silk ties and more. He nodded to Frankie, then to a pair of armchairs set up in the corner.

"Be good," she teased me with a whisper. "I expect good grades."

Yeah, I swatted her on the ass as she skipped away from me, and her laughter eddied back. Brat.

Lyssa grinned as she slipped off her shoes. Like us, she was dressed in street clothes and casual. Though her pants were more leggings and she pulled off the T-shirt to reveal the body hugging top underneath.

"Better for you to see form," was all Richard said. "Clothing is something you're also going to practice with and without eventually. You just have to remember that when you're binding, clothing can also bind."

Okay, that made sense.

Instead of sticking with us, Lyssa padded over to the corner and settled into the other armchair.

"We're not quite ready for her yet," Richard continued as he set out the different types of restraints. There were leather ties. Handcuffs. Different kinds of rope. Silk ties. Even regular pieces of torn cloth. "Let's go over the merits of each, then remind me what you know about coiling your ropes and knots."

The next hour was a bit grueling. Richard was a very precise man, which I appreciated. One of the very first demonstrations I attended had been in ropework, and he'd gone over the different ways of coiling the rope. Once you began tying, you wanted the rope to stay smooth and the motion to be even, as it was better for the rope bunny and easier for the knotmaster.

I had three knots I was comfortable with, two that were quick release. For suspension work, the third knot would be better for when we were securing to something higher.

That made sense.

Periodically, I glanced over to find Frankie leaned forward and watching. She had no phone or notepad or pen. But I swear, you could see her mentally taking notes on everything

Only after I'd coiled and recoiled the ropes twice and selected the type I was most comfortable with, and the least likely to cause friction burns, did Lyssa join us. Her smile was open and affable.

"Don't be nervous," she teased. "I'll be gentle."

"That's one," Richard warned, and Lyssa winked at me. I probably shouldn't have laughed, but her teasing coupled with his sternness did make this a bit easier. I did not want to screw this up. "As for you, breathe. If you're tense, you convey that tension to your sub. They're trusting you to take care of them, so you have to be in the right headspace to do that."

He had a point, and it was why he was a good teacher. I concentrated on evening out my breathing then focusing on the rope I had coiled. Richard directed Lyssa to kneel, and then he began looping the rope around her wrists and then binding them together. It was simple but elegant, the knots were more decorative, but still offering a semblance of binding.

Then it was my turn. Richard loosened his ties and removed it, and I worked the rope around her wrists, wrapping slowly. Then setting the knot. I'd actually practiced this one, so it was pretty straightforward.

"You don't want to go too loose," Richard said. "If she relaxes, which they will over time because the ropes offer that soothing effect, this might slip off. So if you adjust the knot, you can tighten and loosen as needed."

Three more times, we repeated this set. He would do her wrists and tie them off, then remove it and then I would. The goal wasn't to do the exact same set of knots, but to get a feel for the tension and setting it. Soon, we were binding up to her elbows, and Lyssa just knelt there, her eyes a little glassy and her breathing slowing.

When Richard lifted her so she wasn't kneeling anymore but allowed her to sit, I waited while he rubbed her feet. Gradually, awareness bled back into her face as she winced.

"In the beginning, you have to check frequently, you'll learn their cues. Lyssa, for example, can go so still, she forgets that her limbs will start to go to sleep, and since part of taking care of them is making sure they don't hurt themselves, this is where you have to make the call. So now, we can continue with some more light work or we can end it. What do you think?"

He was giving me the choice?

I frowned and then glanced at Lyssa, studying her. Her breathing was far more normal, her pupils not so glassy or blown, and there was the barest hint of a smile on her face. "I'd be game to continue if you think she's up for it," I offered.

"Tell me what you see," Richard instructed, and I sighed.

"You can do it." Frankie's voice was so soft that I barely heard it. I hadn't forgotten she was there, but the encouragement skirted the reluctance. She was right—I could do this, and I needed to do this.

So I described Lyssa's physical responses. "If she were Frankie, I'd know what this meant. I feel like I'm guessing because I don't know her as well."

"Fair," Richard told me. "But that's part of what you're learning, so think back to what her responses were when we began." Good point.

"Lyssa, are you comfortable with a little more practice?" I'd say her physiological responses all pointed toward yes, so that just left consent.

The nod and quiet smile from Richard told me I'd chosen correctly, and Lyssa gave me an even wider grin. "I'm definitely game for more."

Every part of this was a test, but that was the point of the lessons, right?

We spent the next couple of hours going over more knots and ties and different ways to start. By the time we finished, I'd bound her wrists, her ankles, her wrists to her ankles, and her hands in front as well as in back. We'd bound them up, then down.

We alternated the ropes with silk ties, sometimes with leather straps, and once with the handcuffs. While we were learning ropes, he wanted me to understand the different reasons to use different bindings. Sensation was chief among them, but also purpose. For suspension, for example, the metal cuffs were always a no. In fact, the metal should only be used for stimulation play and then traded for something gentler on the skin.

Each time, Richard pointed out different things to watch for, and when Lyssa seemed almost drowsy, he called it. I loosened all the ties and coiled the ropes as he picked her up to cuddle. Aftercare was something I was already familiar with. "Go ahead and set that all down, and I'll take care of it after I take care of her."

"Thank you, Lyssa," I murmured to her, and she gave me a sleepy smile. Over her head, I caught Frankie watching me in absolute fascination. She'd sat there for hours during this, and outside of the occasional encouragement, she'd been so quiet. I put up the ropes and nodded to Richard. "Thank you both."

"We'll talk soon," he said, carrying Lyssa over to the chairs to sit with her a while, and I held out a hand to Frankie. She was quiet as we made our way out. We passed a few other scenes in the outer room, but neither of us were in the mood to watch.

Jackets in hand, we headed outside, and instead of just pulling hers on, she wrapped her arms around me at the bike and hugged me tight. That I could do, so I tucked her in close and closed my eyes. It had gotten late while we'd been inside, and the sun had gone down. The sound of traffic in the distance accompanied the sound of the cicadas and the hum of an air conditioner.

A sigh escaped me, and I tightened my arms around her. I hadn't actually realized how much I needed this hug. "Someone is looking after me," I said after a long moment of soaking it up.

"Mmm-hmm, deal with it," she teased and rubbed her hand against my back. "You did wonderful in there. But now you look wiped."

I kind of was, a little. "Not tired so much as…" I looked for the words. "I don't know her as well as I do you," I admitted. "I think it would be easier to make sure I wasn't pushing her more than she can take, and yes, that was why Richard was there too, but…"

"You worried," she murmured, and I pressed my lips to her hair. Yes, I had, and she got it. "I thought you were wonderful. Thank you for letting me watch."

I laughed and pulled back some. "You sure you weren't bored? It was a lot of tying and untying then retying…"

"You get this crinkle right here…" She ran her finger between my brows. "When you're very focused. You do it when you're working on music too. Every time you worked on a new knot, you did it, and I could almost see you trying to figure out what order to do it in next, how it would play when you worked it into the bigger piece."

"You liked that?" Curiosity filled me as I studied her. Under the street lamps, she had a warm glow to her skin, but it left her eyes a pair of shadowy pools.

"I loved it. Because I know you're going to put it all together in this wonderful piece that I get to enjoy. Now, if you're up for it, would you mind if we hurried to get home? I'd very much like to strip your clothes off and ride your dick if you'll let me."

Let her…

Real laughter burst out of me before I kissed her soundly. She'd managed to comfort, encourage, and tease me all in the same set of sentences. "Let you?" I said against her lips. "Just for that, I might make you lay there and get yourself off for me while I watch."

She shivered.

"But you were being sweet, and you were exceptionally good tonight."

"So were you," she insisted, and I sighed as she bit my lower lip gently. "I love you, Ian, I love all the care you take. I'd also love it if you'd let me take care of you."

"Jacket on," I murmured, then kissed her once more before taking her jacket and holding it so she could slip it on. Then she snagged mine off the bike where I'd set it and held it up for me. "You're going to brat it up some, aren't you?"

"I think I've earned it," she remarked, and I turned and let her help me into the jacket.

Fair enough.

"I think you have too."

"Yay," she said, letting out the little cheer, and I chuckled. I straddled the bike and held out her helmet to her, but she had her phone in her hand. "One sec. I'm making sure the bedroom is clear."

I snorted. "You give Coop enough warning, and he'll accidentally wander in."

"Not tonight, I want you all myself."

"You always have me, Angel."

Chapter Eight
ALL WE ARE

FRANKIE

The whole ride home, I clung to his back. Funnily enough, just like the ride in, he took us back around the lake. The darkness was soothing and the air cooler. Honeysuckle bloomed in a thick patch, and I swore it fisted around my heart. The longer we wound around the lake, the more I realized Ian needed the soothing as well, so it didn't surprise me when he pulled off to a rest area. We didn't talk, just drank in the sight of the moon, the water, and the swaying trees. There were lights visible across the lake. Life going on. When he touched my hands, I tightened my grip, and he got the bike started again.

At the apartment, he pulled into the slot next to my new car. I still couldn't believe they'd gotten me a Tesla. The other car was now stored at Archie's until Trina needed it. Even after we moved, the house would remain here. Closed up for the time being, but here, and there would be groundskeepers looking after it.

When we came down to visit the guys' families, Archie and I would probably stay there. Apparently, his mom had signed the house over to him, so it wasn't his parents anymore. So much to do before we moved—

Moved.

I blew out a breath as I slid off the bike, aware of Ian's gaze before I'd even tugged the helmet off. He studied me for a long moment. "It's hitting you, isn't it?"

"After the conversation about Manhattan and Brooklyn? And the ride around the lake and the fact that we're ordering boxes to start packing up the apartment?" Somewhere in all of that, I thought it had already sunk in, but tonight? Yeah, tonight it hit me. "It's hitting you too."

The corner of his mouth kicked up as he turned off the bike and dismounted. "Yeah, I was thinking about the lake. About the first time I kissed you out there…"

"And our helmets clacked together?" I grinned.

He chuckled, tucking me under his arm to walk together up the short set of steps into the apartment. Only the light in the kitchen was on. Ian helped me out of my jacket and then hung both of them on the hooks they'd put up behind the door. Too many jackets and coats made it easier to keep track of them there.

A note on the fridge said Jake was crashed in the other room, Archie would probably be late, but he was out with his grandfather for dinner and business. Coop had gone home, but promised he was just around the corner if we wanted company.

Ian snorted at the note. "Told you."

"Except," I pointed out, "he removed himself from temptation." It was the only reason he would have gone back to his mom's apartment. He really did respect the boundaries Ian had, we all did. And I liked my time with each of them individually as much as I did together. I had the best of both worlds, and I planned to savor every second of it.

"True." Ian brushed a kiss to the curve of my ear, and a shiver went through me. "Get some water? You hungry?"

"Not right now," I murmured. "But I could probably go for ice cream later…" I glanced at him over my shoulder. There really was only one thing I wanted at the moment, and I was looking at him.

His eyes darkened, and another shiver went through me. I might have been asking him to let me spoil him tonight, but that expression promised so much more. "Get a couple bottles of water then, Angel. Then back to the bedroom."

"Yes, sir," I whispered, and he gave me a knowing look before he turned away and headed out of the kitchen. A little shiver went through me in his absence. I half expected the cats to greet me, but they'd probably all crawled in with Jake, which meant Ian and I had my room to ourselves. I paused in the bathroom long enough to use it and brush my teeth before I headed into the bedroom.

Ian turned around when I walked in, and I forgot how to breathe for a moment. He'd stripped all the way down to a pair of boxers only, and he wore the most amused smile.

"What?" I asked as I leaned against the door and closed it. I didn't want to take my eyes off him. Sometimes, I had to remind myself that these guys were mine. They were all beautiful. Ian had broad shoulders, cut muscles, and he was leaner than Jake in some ways, but it didn't detract in the slightest. I loved the way he moved and looked.

He already had the first signs of his summer tan coming in. We needed to spend more time in the pool. Not that I was opposed to that idea at all. Summers in the pool had always been a part of our friendship.

Except for last summer.

Last summer, I'd been here and they'd been off…

"Hey." Ian's voice yanked me right back to the present. His soft smile had vanished as he narrowed the distance. The warmth rolling off him chased away the odd chill. "What happened?"

"I'm being…weird." I made a face and would have looked away, but he caught my chin and tugged my gaze up to his.

"About what?"

"We were talking about leaving and it's hitting me, and I was thinking how beautiful you are." My face flamed. You'd think I wouldn't be remotely embarrassed about that kind of honesty, but getting to tell them I loved their bodies was still kind of new for me. He stroked the line of my jaw with his thumb, waiting. "I was thinking I loved how golden your tan is and that we needed to swim more because summers and swimming go hand in hand. Or it always had except for last year."

"And you got sad," he whispered. "Because you started thinking about what we missed."

I let out a little sigh, and his whole demeanor gentled. "I hate that we lost those few months and it was partially my fault."

"And ours," he reminded me. "We were all to blame, but we're all together now and there won't be another missed summer like that. Not this one. Not the one after it. Or the one after that."

"I like your enthusiasm."

"It's called commitment, Angel," he said, the words feathering over my lips as he leaned in close. "I'm committed to you. To us. To all of us."

Each word sent shivers racing up my spine, and my thighs clenched a split second before his mouth claimed mine. I leaned into the kiss, opening to the sweep of his tongue as he dragged me forward. It went from just the connection of his fingers and our mouths, to his arms around me. The water bottles hit the floor, forgotten as I wrapped my arms around his neck.

The heat from his skin seared me through my shirt. The ache the memory of the past summer opened up in me eased with every nip of his teeth and stroke of his tongue. When he lifted me off my feet, I just clung to him. Even expecting it, I wasn't ready to let go when he set me by the bed. Then he pulled back long enough to tug my shirt up and off. The bra went right with it.

The air conditioning kicked on, and the first brush of the cool air against my nipples tightened them even further. He traced his fingers down my sides to my jeans. He kissed each breast as I settled my hands in his hair, and then he was peeling my jeans down. The kiss to my navel had me shifting my feet, but he slapped my hip lightly and I locked my feet, lifting them only when the jeans reached my ankles. The shoes and socks came off with a tug to each so he could peel the jeans the rest of the way off.

My panties followed. I only half remembered I still had them on.

"I was supposed to be taking care of you," I protested when he traced his thumbs along my calves. The warmth of his hands as he switched to his palms along my skin had another series of shudders racing through me.

"You take care of me by letting me take care of you," he informed me. "And you were there for me, Angel. Never doubt how much that meant to me, knowing you were there to support me and not once did you get jealous or upset or even protest that you couldn't play yet."

A real smile pulled at my mouth, and what shadows lingered from that past summer vanished in the warmth burning in his eyes as he looked up at me. Fuck, when he knelt on the floor in front of me like that and gazed at me with those deep blue eyes, my whole world faded to just him.

All I felt was adored.

"I love you," I whispered. Every single time I got to say it was a thrill. Even more, I loved how he would light up at the admission. How they all did in their own ways.

The slow massage of his fingers up and down my legs had me alternately relaxing and tensing as I wanted his fingers to stroke just a bit higher, but he always skated away from touching my ass or my pussy. I sucked my lower lip between my teeth as he edged higher. He knew what he was doing, and I could protest.

I could shift my leg and demand the contact.

Or I could be patient.

Let him give me the touches he wanted to. The awareness of his observation flooded through me, and I swore my thighs tightened as I rubbed them together. I expected the sting of the slap a split second before it landed.

"Feeling impatient, Angel?" he teased, but maybe we both needed this. The sadness was still there, but so was the elation. I'd let it discolor our evening, and he wanted to chase it all away. Or at least ease it until the roughness of those memories was gone.

"I need you," I whispered. Not a lie. I did. More every single day.

"You have me," he promised in a soft voice. "What else do you need?"

"Whatever you give me."

He chuckled.

"Sir," I said, tacking that on, and he laughed a little harder but there was real joy in his eyes.

"I love when you call me that."

"I know," I admitted. It gave me a thrill too.

"Bend over the bed, Angel," Ian told me. "On your knees here…" He tossed a pillow down at the foot of the bed and then guided me to it. I knelt onto the pillow and then leaned over the bed until it was my ass that was up and my legs that were down. "Close your eyes."

A part of me wondered why, but the rest of me relaxed into the feeling of the comforter. It smelled like the guys. Even freshly laundered, some elements of them clung to the material. The woodsy scent of the soap Jake and Coop preferred, along with the hints of the spicy aftershave Archie liked to use, but above all of that was the sweet scent of Ian. I loved the way he always made me think of sunshine…

A crack of his hand against my ass brought me right back to the present.

"No drifting, Angel," he murmured as he rubbed the heat into that spot, and I melted a little more. Coop asked me about the spanking once, a faint glimmer of concern in his eyes. If anyone had asked me a year ago would I enjoy being spanked, I'd have probably laughed.

Still, there was a simple, almost elegant truth I found whenever Ian spanked me. Jake liked to slap my ass, and he got playful when he got rough.

Those moments were always a thrill and made me clench harder. Yet when Ian spanked me, it was about being in the moment with him. The pain was so fleeting but also freeing, and it only left pleasure behind.

Another slap—this time to my other cheek—jolted me, and a laugh slipped out on a gasp.

"You're dropping fast tonight," he murmured against my ear. The whole weight of him stretched against me, thigh to thigh, his cock resting against my ass and his chest against my back. "You sure you're up for this?"

Was I? "I think I enjoyed your lesson more than I realized," I whispered. He rubbed his dick up and down along the seam of my ass as he nuzzled a kiss to my throat. When he turned my head, he stroked his hand through my hair. "I just want to lose myself in you."

"Look at me," he commanded, and I opened my eyes and met his gaze evenly. I never asked him what he looked for when he studied me, but he always seemed to weigh my reactions against something he found in my eyes. "We can just make love," he murmured. "I can sink my dick in you right now and we can chase our pleasure until you're sated."

My nipples peaked at the thought, and no lie, I swore I grew even slicker at the suggestion. "Or?" I asked, licking my lips.

"Or I'll finish what I was about to do, and then I'll let you ride me until you come."

I almost laughed. "You make that sound like a hard decision."

"But you still have to choose, Angel."

"I just want you, Sir Ian," I told him simply, not once looking away from his steady gaze. "I trust you." And I did.

No question.

No doubt.

His expression melted, and it damn near undid me. Sometimes, it was easy to forget they had their own insecurities and… The thought faded as he fisted my hair and helped me up until our mouths collided and my thoughts vanished in a singe of ash and burning desire. The twist to my body kept me pinned against the bed as he plundered my mouth, but he angled himself away.

The first slap sent a whimper through my throat, and then the next landed on the other cheek. He took his time, never quite finding a rhythm I could anticipate. Sometimes, the sting was sharp and pulled tears to my eyes, and other times, it was just loud and spread out. My ass flamed from the spanking, but the only thing that mattered was how our tongues danced. I didn't take a single breath he didn't give me, and when my ass was so hot I could feel slickness on my thighs and tears on my cheeks, he eased back and then helped me up.

I swayed on my feet but followed him willingly as he turned and lay back on the bed, pulling me astride him. When he fisted his proud cock, I smiled down at him and straddled his thighs. The burn as I sank down on him had me clenching so tightly, he gritted his teeth.

"Fuck me, Angel," he whispered, and I dropped down to brace a hand on either side of his head. My hair was like a curtain, and it isolated us.

"I am." It was my turn to promise, but I had to relax to take him, because my core muscles clenched too tight. He dug his fingers into my sore ass gently, tiny pricks of awareness flaming through my system as I eased up and then down again. Between us, we worked him into me until we were both grunting little explosive breaths.

Honestly, I devoured his expression, savoring every time his jaw tensed or his lips constricted. I flexed around him, the feel of him incredible as a counterpoint to his fingers alternating between digging into my ass and massaging it. The fire stoked from both sides, and as much as I wanted to take over the pace, I let go of that thought and followed his cues.

"Fuck, Angel," he groaned. "You are so perfect. That's it, my beautiful girl, ride me."

He thrust upward to meet my next downward stroke, and my head tilted back. I wanted to keep looking at him, but he felt so good inside of me. Every little jolt teased my nipples against his chest, and then he ran his hands up my sides and cupped each breast. With a gentle push, he urged me higher, and I began to rock against him.

My body knew his, and with very little nudging from him, I rolled my hips and twisted a little with each thrust. He massaged my breasts and teased my nipples until all that was left of me was sensation. I was so close, but it was like that orgasm was just right there, just out of reach, and I needed just a bit more…

He flipped us over until he was on top and then powered into me, and I came screaming. Even as he kissed me, I cried out against his mouth, the thrust of his hips powerful and pushing me higher on the bed. Every stroke sent sparks through my system, and he didn't relent, pushing me into a second orgasm before he let go with a groan of his own.

I swallowed his cries as he spent himself, the heat spreading inside of me a feeling I never wanted to miss anymore. I loved the intimacy of him emptying into me. The connection and the feel of being together.

With light kisses and soft brushes of his hands, he eased me down from panting shallow breaths to longer, sweeter sighs, and when he lifted his head and stared at me, I smiled.

"Better?" he asked.

No shadows in evidence. Every single one pummeled and destroyed in the warmth and light of his love and affection. Corny? Maybe. I didn't care. "So much better," I whispered. "I can't wait for you to tie me up like you were learning today. Then play with me however you see fit."

"Yeah?" he said with a slow grin. "*Any* way I see fit?"

"Hmm…yes."

"What if I want to tie you up, get you wound up and soaking wet so I can come back and play with you whenever I feel like?"

I shivered. "I'd love it."

"And if I let the guys come in one at a time, let them play with you however they liked?"

"Whatever you want, Sir."

He chuckled and nipped my lower lip, then kissed me softly. "Angel… look at me." Arms braced on either side of my head, he cupped my face, and this close, I couldn't see anything that wasn't him. Hell, he was still inside me, soft but there and connected. "Last summer without you sucked. But you never lost us. You never lost me. We might have been apart, but we were always with you. You were always with us."

"Never again." Ferocity tore through me.

"Not like that," he agreed. "No matter what life throws at us, you will always remember that I love you. That you have my heart. You have had my heart longer than I even understood what that meant. You have always been the only one for me."

Sometimes, I wished I could say that to them, but at the same time… "It's only ever been you guys."

"I know," he said smiling. "You're mine. Just like you're theirs, but that doesn't make you any less mine."

No, it didn't. It had been so hard for Ian, in some ways, because all he wanted was to protect me. Protect me from the world. From them. From myself. "We're safe together," I whispered, and this time when we kissed, it was all sweetness and gentle delight. He rolled onto his back and pulled me with him until I collapsed against his chest, cradled safely to him. He stroked my back and teased my hair back.

"How's your butt?" he asked with just a hint of teasing.

"Sore," I told him honestly. "But I like it. I can feel your hands on me still. It's warm and kind of like how my vagina feels at the moment—hot and well-spanked."

He chuckled. "I didn't break your vagina this time?"

A groan ripped through me. "Oh my god, you guys are never going to forget that."

"Nope," he said without a hint of remorse. "It's an achievement unlocked. Though I am tempted to find out if I can do it on my own without any back up."

That was the only warning I got before he thrust into me again, and my eyes rolled back into my head.

Oh hell.

It was going to be a glorious night.

We never did get to the ice cream.

SUBJECT: SUMMER PLANS

I'd kill to see you guys in concert again, but currently, I don't know what our summer plans are. Archie is being very cagey. Yes, I know he's the one making them, but considering our spring, I'm not going to say no to anything. That said, we'll be in Manhattan before August. If you really are enrolling at the school in Connecticut, we won't be that far away. Maybe we can lure you into the city to come listen to us practice.

Are all of you going? Or just you? I don't even know much about the school. I did see it when we were up there. My grandparents live pretty close by. As for lyric sheets, see attached. Ian and I have studio time this weekend, but we've been swamped with some other stuff. We're going to re-record and remix.

Weird question, are you going to miss touring? I swear, I think you girls have been on tour since I first started listening. (Also feel free to ignore the question.)

F.

Chapter Nine

BE STILL

FRANKIE

I wandered out from my shower to find Archie and Coop in the kitchen with Jake. They were razzing him, and his eyes gleamed when he caught sight of me. "Good morning, Baby Girl. Glad to see you still walking."

Pausing, I raised my brows. "I was not that loud."

"Oh, yeah you were," he said with a wide grin. "And I was here for it. But I found a happy volume on the headphones."

Laughter escaped as Archie snorted, and then warm arms wrapped around me from behind. "Be nice," Ian scolded a moment before he kissed the back of my neck. "And we were going to go out for breakfast if you guys want to join."

I leaned back into Ian as he cradled me to him. The night had been wonderful. Honestly, I don't think we'd really slept that much. Yet I was so relaxed, it didn't matter. There was no school today. No school again until we were in college. We still had to go to orientation, but we signed up for one at the beginning of August. I'd wanted the earlier one, but the guys all campaigned to avoid me launching into back to school mode before summer even began.

Like I was that bad.

My phone buzzed in my back pocket. Ian tilted my head back for a quick kiss before he let me go so I could tug the phone out. The best part of not being in school was my denim short shorts that didn't meet their stupid length requirement. Dress codes were a thing of the past…well, mostly. I'd survive.

Shaking that thought off, I blinked at Hank's face staring up at me from the phone. He'd texted since he left, but this was the first time he'd called.

I swiped across the screen as I pulled it up to my ear. "Hello?"

"Good morning," Hank greeted me. "Sorry to call, I tried to not make it too early, but then I wasn't sure what your schedule would be when you weren't in school, and while I've got the end of May-mester and office hours this afternoon, plus you probably have plans, so I took a risk. If you're busy, I can just call you later or leave a message. Probably should have just done that."

The rush of words had me grinning. "It's fine, I just got up a little while ago and I'm going to get coffee…"

"You haven't had coffee yet? Shit—I mean, well wait, you're eighteen, I can say shit." He grunted. "Hang on a sec." The phone muffled, and I found the guys looking at me in question as I poured my coffee. Bless them, they must have put on a fresh pot when I headed into the shower.

"It's Hank," I said. "I'm gonna talk to him before we go, and I'm good with pretty much anywhere for breakfast. Are you guys still good for the appointment today?"

"We're fine, babe," Archie told me with a sweet smile that made my toes curl. "Go talk to your dad."

My dad.

That was never going to get old. I lifted my coffee mug toward them and then turned to wander back into the living room. Tiddles tracked me to the sofa, and as soon as I sat down, I had a lapful of cat.

"Sorry," Hank said, huffing out a breath. "I had to settle a dispute between Alec and Chloe, but that's actually why I called."

"Because of a dispute between Alec and Chloe?" At this point, I'd seen more pictures of the kids, and his wife had sent me friend requests on social media. I hadn't answered those yet. Sorry, that was still just a *bit* weird. Not bad weird.

Rachel totally stalked her and reported back that she seemed cool, though she had some bizarre obsession with running. Like miles and miles every day. It made me laugh, because I had to admit to Rachel that I'd been running more with the guys. Not every day, 'cause um no, I liked sleep. But a few days a week.

I didn't think she'd ever looked so disappointed in me.

It had been hilarious.

She also sent me links for deprogramming sites.

Smart ass.

"No," Hank said. "Well, not exactly. Chloe wants to set up a video call to meet you since you can't make it up here yet and I'm not pressuring, but she has been campaigning all week and this morning, she presented me with a three-part argument to present the idea to you and let you decide whether you would like to speak to her or not."

I had to bite back a laugh. "A three-part argument?" Okay, not going to lie. That tickled me. "What were the three parts?"

"You sure you want to listen?" The amusement vying with pride in his voice remained goals. But this was the same man who flew across the country to see me graduate after only knowing about me for like five minutes. The same man who shut Maddy down and stood protectively between us. I could probably listen to him all day, even if I didn't know what to do with him.

"I promise, I want to listen. If she worked that hard on an argument, then it wouldn't be fair if I didn't at least listen to it, right?"

"See!" came a triumphant, younger feminine voice in the background. "I told you she'd want to hear my ideas."

Laughter burst out of me, and I nearly sprayed coffee as Tiddles gave me a disgruntled look. I couldn't help it. Particularly when Hank sighed. It was such an aggrieved sigh that I had to giggle. Coop shot me an amused look as he strolled through the living room. With a wink, he vanished around the corner, and the bathroom door closed on him.

"Chloe," Hank said in a very patient voice. "Go on back out and play. I'll talk to Frankie and…"

"But they're my arguments," the young voice protested, and I swore I melted. "I should get to make them. And it's not fair 'cause you've already gotten to meet her. She needs a reason to meet me."

No I didn't.

He sighed.

"I don't mind if she wants to present her own arguments," I said quietly. "I actually think I'd enjoy it."

"Fair," Hank said slowly. "All right, Chloe, close the door and come here. Frankie, you're on speaker… Frankie, this is Chloe. Chloe, say hello to Frankie, *and* be polite."

"Are you going to tell her to say hello to me?" The scandalized, yet imperious voice had my lips twitching. Trina had done that. So did Jake's sisters. Not as much as they used to, but it was still adorable. Maybe it was a sibling thing.

My heart wrenched. I had a sibling.

Siblings.

"Of course, I'll say hello," I answered before Hank could. "I'm really looking forward to meeting you."

"You are?" Uncertainty flickered in those two syllables.

"Yes," I assured her. "I know this is probably a lot for you, and I've never had siblings before so I wasn't sure how to do this."

"I have siblings…well, I have brothers." The sheer level of disgust there pulled another laugh from me. "It's not that hard."

"Chloe," Hank warned, and I wanted to tell him it was okay, but that precocious little beauty did it for me.

"She gets it, Dad, let me talk. You get it, right, Frankie?"

"Well, not exactly. But since I have you, I think you can help me with brothers. I've never had those either." The closest would be Coop, and even at our tightest, he'd never been a brother. He'd been my best friend. He was still my best friend, but we weren't fraternal.

A little shudder went through me at the few days of coping with the notion that Archie *might* be my brother.

Nope.

"I can tell you *all* about brothers." The world-weary and wise sigh there.

"I can't wait."

I really couldn't.

"But tell me your argument now. I have to hear it. I love a good argument."

"Awesome." She damn near glowed through the phone, and I took a sip of my coffee as she launched into her reasoning why we needed to meet via video call first. The number one reason?

We were sisters.

I loved her already.

I ended up talking to Chloe and, by extension, Hank for nearly an hour. Jake brought me fresh coffee when I finished mine, and I ended up curled up in his lap as the guys migrated out to the living room. It didn't take long for them to figure out Chloe's campaign, and they seemed to enjoy listening to her as much as I did.

Once I was off the phone though, I found all of them studying me. "Come on, Angel," Ian said before anyone else could say anything. "Let's go feed you. Then we can talk plans. We have time before the appointment with Erin."

Excitement and nervousness vied for my focus as I let him pull me to my feet and out of Jake's lap. "You guys are awesome for going."

"Yeah," Archie said without a trace of humbleness. "I know I am, not sure what their excuse is." Then he hooked an arm around my shoulder and slid me away from Ian. I was laughing as I stuffed my feet into a pair of flip-flops, and then we were out.

A part of me wanted to take the Tesla, but Jake angled for his SUV first and that was fair. Coop slid into the backseat with me and Archie, while leaving the front passenger for Ian.

"What is up with you guys?" I glanced from one to the other as Jake smirked at me over his shoulder.

"You screamed a lot last night, Baby Girl."

"And?" I refused to be embarrassed. It was hardly the first time one or more of them had made me scream. Apparently, I was noisy. Fine. I could own it.

"Some of us had to get it thirdhand," Archie griped as he slid his fingers through mine and tilted his head back. "'Cause some people are assholes."

Ian groaned. "You didn't."

"Oh," Coop said with a laugh as he rubbed my thigh. "He did."

"Jacob Benton." I growled his name, and he glanced at me so utterly unrepentant. I kind of wanted to punch him.

"Baby Girl, when you're louder than the music, it requires the rest of us manning up. Bubba now leads in most orgasms in a row, and that record cannot stand."

Oh. My. God.

Okay, now I wanted to cover my face with my hands, but the assholes in the backseat captured them and wouldn't let them go.

"It's fine," Archie soothed. "Totally fine, babe. Trust me. Balls deep in that perfect pink pussy, and I'd be damn proud of all those screams too, but it just means we have to up our game and let me just say…challenge fucking accepted."

"I hate you all."

"Nah," Coop teased and kissed me behind my ear. "You love us. And you're kind of stuck with us."

Ian snorted, but there was no mistaking the flicker of pride on his face or the pleased little smile. And really, was I going to complain? No.

"I don't know," I mused as Jake pulled out of the parking lot.

"You don't know what, babe?" Archie asked.

"I don't know if I'm stuck with you. Rachel told me if I ever went vag, I'd never go back, and the four of you seem completely taken with mine."

The silence in the car had me wiggling my fingers free of Archie's long enough to lick the tip and then mark a sizzling point in the air.

"That's just mean, Angel," Ian said over his shoulder. "I approve. They can use the notes."

Laughter exploded around me, and then they were talking over each other. It was pointless to remind them how safe they were. I really did prefer dick, but the compelling arguments they offered were worth listening to, right?

After breakfast, the guys took me shopping. More my speed than Archie's, but he didn't complain. They wanted me to look at bathing suits. Though I had a perfectly good one, I accepted the challenge and threw one back of my own.

I let *them* pick out my suits. The gleam in Archie's eyes was worth the ridiculousness as Coop and Jake stared at me like I'd sprouted a second head. Only Ian had hidden a smile as he watched the three of them wander off into the swimsuit area, and I tilted my head. "Not going hunting for one too?"

"Nope," he told me. "I love you in everything. What do you want to do?"

"That was really smooth," I admired as he took my hand. "And I don't know. Clothes shopping has never been my favorite, but I suppose we could look for something to wear for the audition photos." That was something else Kaitlin had recommended. Sound wasn't the only thing that sold. We had to have a look or a feel for our music.

I wasn't sure about that part, but she'd been in the business a long time and if she was willing to give us advice, the least we could do was listen.

A whistle stopped us as we wandered toward the dresses. Not that I was going to try on dresses. Nope.

Dresses made me think of changing rooms.

And changing room sex.

And… Yeah, let's not with all four of them here.

They were being weirdly competitive today.

Pausing, we both found Jake staring at us with a pair of bikinis in hand.

"Dude," Ian said almost drily. "You'd never let her wear those."

"I'd let her wear them," Jake argued. "Then I'd peel them right back off. Win-win." He held up the first string bikini then the other, and I rolled my eyes.

"You know I could help if I knew where we were going."

"Nice try," Archie murmured as he strolled out with three suits dangling from his fingers and a hint of a wicked smile on his lips. "Come try these on for me."

Oh, and there went that pair of panties. Dammit.

"Hang on." Coop slid out, and he had a pair of suits too. A one piece and a sorta one piece. I glanced at all their suits and sighed.

"All right." I gave Ian's hand a squeeze and then collected the various suits. "But there will be no cameras. No pictures. No following me in to help me out…" I paused at the open door to the changing room and stopped Archie with a hand on his chest.

His delightful grin melted into a pout. "But we know how helpful I am."

"We do," I promised him and rose up on my tiptoes to kiss him lightly. "And I won't ever forget it. But right now, I'll try on the suits and…" I raised a finger before they could toss out terms. "I'll show you the ones *I* like."

"Fine," Archie conceded.

"Yep," Jake said with a nod, but Coop eyed the suits in my hand and then me.

"I want to see you in mine, please."

I considered it. "Okay." I winked and closed the door.

"Hey," the others protested, and Ian's laughter made me grin even wider.

They really were all in a mood and it was glorious, if a bit nuts.

To be fair, they made some good choices. Even if I wasn't sure I could pull off Jake's deep purple string bikini, I kind of liked the way it fit me. It wasn't super revealing, though I'd want to knot some of those strings, no way there wouldn't be tugging.

Fuck, they'd have it off in one small version of tug of war.

I snapped a picture of it with my phone. The second string bikini had to be a joke. "Jake, I really love this blue one."

His absolute snort made me grin. Seriously, there were three itty bitty triangles and nothing to cover my ass.

Yeah. Nope.

The red bikini from Archie caught my eye. It was different from the ones that had been at his place. These also had no strings.

The bottoms formed a vee with three lines on each hip connecting front to back, and the top was a strapless molded bit. I appreciated the vote of confidence but there was no way I could dive or play without a nip slip.

I was almost sorry to just snap a picture and go.

The black suit that I'd thought was a bikini turned out to be more tankini, and it was freaking adorable. It also wasn't just black, it had glittery kind of paw prints amongst what looked like leaves. It was tropical but feline, and I adored it. It was also securely meshed against my body and left me plenty of skin on display without fear of it vanishing at one tug.

Yep, picture.

Okay, that left Coop's. The standard razorback suit was the most familiar, so I went for the one piece that made me think of a sexy X-Men costume in black and yellow.

I should've looked like a bumblebee or something, but I didn't, it was... Wow, it was perfect.

Oh crap.

Now I liked each of them for different reasons.

Snap.

I flicked through the images and then grouped them and fired them over the group text to the guys. The dings of their phones right outside the thin changing room walls made me grin. Then I frowned.

Wait, they were *right* there, and I couldn't hear them chatting?

I blew out a sigh. They really were plotting something. It was a good thing I loved them so much, or I'd get irritated. As it was, I sent Rachel a text before I changed back into my clothes, and the guys started debating which suit they liked best.

Rachel answered immediately. She couldn't say a word, but yes, she did know what they were up to, and she promised it was all good.

Me

Thank you.

Rachel

I got you. I promise. Also, make them work for it. They're cute, but they aren't as cute as they think they are.

Me

Do I want to know what that means?

Rachel

Nope. Love you. Have fun at therapy with the boys. I bet Erin wants to write a dissertation.

I laughed.

We still needed to road trip to UNT. Maybe I'd see if Jake would let me hit the asshole first.

No surprise, I got all three suits. When the guys gave Ian shit about it, he just grinned. "That just means I get her in her birthday suit."

And then we started all over again.

Rachel was right—Erin was going to have a blast with these nutjobs.

Chapter Ten
BREATHIN'

COOP

Erin was not what I expected. Not that I had a lot of expectations, to be honest. For over six months, she'd been Frankie's lifeline and, in some ways, her anchor. She'd been a steady hand to help her cope with everything that had happened. While I wanted to be that person in Frankie's life, I understood that sometimes, it was the person standing outside the equation who could see it the most clearly. That, and she gave off a strong maternal vibe. One that probably helped ease Frankie into talking to her.

"So this is Coop," Frankie said, introducing me, and I extended my hand to shake Erin's. "This is Ian and Jake." They followed suit. "And Archie." Of the four of us, Archie had been the last to agree to this session, and I understood his reservations. Even now, his expression remained guarded, though his eyes warmed whenever he glanced at Frankie.

"Thanks for coming, gentlemen," Erin said by way of greeting. "I appreciate the effort to support Frankie."

And that was it in a nutshell.

Of course we were going to support her.

"Normally, I conduct sessions in my office, but all of us would make that very crowded, so I've borrowed the conversation room." She guided us into what looked like a comfortably appointed living room with sofas and thick armchairs. The plush rugs and heavy wall hangings probably added to the sound insulation, and the half-wall window looked out onto a manicured garden with a fountain.

Very peaceful.

Serene.

It probably worked to minimize distractions and possible external stress. We didn't really plan ahead how to do this, but Frankie sat near Archie on one of the loveseats, while Bubba took an armchair, and I flopped on the opposite sofa with Jake. If I were Erin, I'd probably read that as Bubba was the most isolated and that Frankie was most worried about Archie.

She'd probably be on the money about the latter, but Bubba was less isolated than he was comfortable. Lucky bastard had been riding high all morning, and why shouldn't he? I bit back a grin when he gave me a bland look.

Yeah, yeah, focus on why we were here.

"Before we get started, do any of you have any questions?" Erin glanced around at us, but I wasn't alone in shaking my head. Frankie made a face as Erin focused on her. "Do you have any questions?"

"No," she said with one of those smiles that had come to her easier and easier since Christmas break. I hadn't realized how much those had faded in recent years until they came back. The ease in her smiles, the brightness in her eyes, even the quickness of her sharp tongue. While we might quip and tease, she was no slouch. "I still think it's weird you wanted me to invite everyone, but we're here."

"Well, it's not unusual to talk to partners and to close family of patients at some point during the therapy. You're standing on the cusp of a huge transition, this on the heels of a lot of other big changes."

Mouth twisting a little, Frankie gave a reluctant nod and leaned back in the seat, her shoulder butting up against Archie's. His hand closed over hers almost automatically, and I swallowed back my own smile. There was no mistaking how much he'd needed her a few months ago or the subtle, but indelible shift between them that had cemented into something they both relied on.

The fact it steadied them both, even when they faced uncertainty, just made it even sweeter.

"I know, and we did talk about that," Frankie admitted, casting a look at all of us as she responded to Erin's description. "I guess…it just seems like right now, it's not so much upheaval. I mean, it's all good stuff. I got to meet Hank—Oh, I didn't get to tell you about Hank." Then she launched into a quick description of meeting her father. The clear affection she'd already developed made me thankful as fuck that Archie said his background checks came in clear and that he came across as a genuinely nice guy when we met him.

The full forward press with her was mitigated only by distance, but the man clearly wanted to be a part of her life. I liked him. We all did.

Well, all of us except Arch, and Archie didn't *hate* him, so we'd call that a win.

"That sounds like a lot," Erin pointed out. "Also, you need to remember that positive stress, it's still stress. You've graduated high school, congratulations to all of you. You're enrolled in college. You're about to move out of your apartment, and you're planning to move across the country. You're going to test your relationships, because with growth and change comes new challenges. How prepared for that are you?"

"I have no idea," Frankie admitted, and the open honesty filled me with pride. "But I'm not scared. We're gonna have each other's backs. Even when it gets hard."

"What about you?" Erin asked, focusing on Archie. Yeah, if I were going to pick the most reticent one in the room. I'd have focused on him too.

Archie met her gaze evenly as he shrugged. "I'll handle it. Whatever it is."

Oh, hell. I tilted my head back to stare at the ceiling. Talk about waving the red flag at the psychologist.

ARCHIE

"By you'll handle it, you mean you'll fix any problems encountered by anyone?"

The psychologist stared at me like she wanted to pry into my brain. Pleasant expression aside, I recognized a bulldog when I saw one. She'd been amazing for Frankie, and I was happy to be here for Frankie.

I was not planning on letting her pick me apart.

Frankie squeezed my hand though, and I bit back the automatic sharp retort. The woman wasn't the enemy.

"I meant I'd handle it in as much as do what is needed when I can, and otherwise help or support if I can't address the issue directly." I could fix most issues. We *had* fixed most of the issues. Once we got Frankie far away from Maddy, that would help resolve one lingering issue. I wanted Frankie beyond Maddy's reach.

"Do you feel that handling those issues are your responsibility?"

"I think taking care of Frankie is my responsibility," I said, then added, "One we all share. We're getting pretty good at balancing those needs with our own and looking after her at the same time."

The stroke of her thumb along the side of my hand pulled my attention. Frankie studied me, but there was nothing but encouragement in her eyes.

"She looks after us too," I admitted. "Probably does a much better job than we do."

She only rolled her eyes a little before she crossed them, and I grinned.

"You're making light of it," Erin stated. "Do you always downplay your contributions?"

"I am well aware of my worth," I countered. "Trust me. I know what I bring to the table." That had never been one of my doubts. Being worthy of *her*? That was something else altogether. "But I take care of my family, and these guys are my family."

"At the risk of seeming like I'm picking on you, Archie," Erin continued, utterly unfazed by my cool stare. Impressive. Annoying, but impressive. "You and Frankie are the closest when it comes to family dynamics, not to mention the fact your parents were involved with each other…"

"I'm going to pause you there," I said, raising a finger on my free hand. Agreeing to this session for Frankie was one thing. "Their toxic nightmare of a relationship has nothing to do with us, by our choice, not theirs."

"Your anger at them, Frankie's anger—the anger of your friends on your behalf—that is a part of your lives."

Not for much longer. Edward offered a form of detente and seemed to have developed something of a conscience. I hadn't decided whether I was interested in pursuing his offer or not. "I wouldn't say anger, specifically," I began.

"I would," Jake stated flatly. "I'm pissed for both of you. Your parents are assholes. Well…not your dad, Frankie. I like Hank. So far so good, but the rest. Pfft."

I didn't smirk, because Coop gave Frankie a pained smile before he said, "Pretty much."

Bubba shrugged. "But I don't blame Frankie or Archie for their parents. If anything, we want to protect them."

Okay, that was a tad on the humbling side.

"How can you protect them from their parents?"

"By being better than them," Bubba said flatly.

"By sharing ours," Jake offered.

"By just being there." Of the three of them, Coop seemed the most certain.

"The difference," I interjected before Erin could ask another question, "is

I had support from other areas. I had my grandparents and I had Jeremy." Frankie had fucking Maddy.

"I've had you guys," Frankie reminded us, and if that didn't shut up any other arguments, I didn't know what would. "To be honest, I wouldn't have gotten through this year without all of you. Not sane anyway."

"Nah," Jake said. "You're incredible. There's nothing you can't do. We just like being a part of it."

And that was it in a nutshell. "Still, there are things you shouldn't have had to face. We like Hank so far, though I have my reservations. He seems good for you, and you seem to enjoy getting to know him. As long as he doesn't do anything that hurts you, I'm good."

"And if he does?" Erin asked, plunging the room into silence. I wasn't the only one who stared at her. Jake's and Bubba's expressions had become set in stone, and though he still seemed laid back, I knew that look in Coop's eyes.

"Rachel will probably get even for me, because she'd do it with a little less bloodshed."

At Frankie's utterly nonplussed response, laughter broke through the room, and Erin gave her a small smile.

"I know," Frankie said. "We've discussed this. But sometimes, you have to laugh or you'll cry. I like Hank. I like the fact I have siblings. Getting to know them is fascinating right now. Will it always be easy? No. Will moving to New York and starting college be easy? Maybe. But probably not. The five of us have figured out how to balance our relationship now. Will that change in New York? With college? With graduation? With finding our careers? Probably."

"Then we just find our balance again," Bubba said.

"Every time," Jake added.

"We're pretty good with the learning curves in this group," Coop threw on top. "I mean, we used to screw the grade curve all the time, so between the five of us, we'll figure it out."

"And we'll fix it," I confirmed. "Because that's what we do."

What we would continue to do.

Every.

Damn.

Time.

JAKE

"How are you handling the changes?"

Okay, the psychologist lady was nice, but she asked weird and somewhat irritating questions. "What kind of question is that?"

"A straightforward one. You went from being primarily a friend group dating multiple girls to a group that now dates one girl. You're living together. You've already faced several challenges. Now you have a lot of life issues facing you. How are you handling the changes? Not just as a group, but individually."

Before I could growl out an answer, Coop leaned forward elbows on his knees. "I think we're all handling it like we did before. We talk. Sometimes we argue and debate. But at the end of the day, it's an individual call on the personal issues and we do our best to support each other."

"Even if you disagree with how one or more of you is handling something?" Erin studied us in turn, and I had to wonder what she saw. One thing Frankie had been clear about was that she had discussed us with Erin, not invasively, but our relationship. There was no judgment in the woman's eyes or her tone.

The fact Frankie liked her so much was a plus in her column, but the whole process was making my skin itch.

"We try to ask questions if we don't understand something," Bubba offered. "Or we try to head off questions by being honest ourselves. You don't always know what everyone needs to know or understands if you don't share."

I didn't laugh, but he had a point. He had actually come to me and talked to me about the play he and Frankie liked to engage in, and I was glad he'd told me. As intriguing as it all was, I'd probably have hit first and asked questions later if I'd ever found him tying her up. Now? Now it intrigued the hell out of me.

Then there was Coop's voyeurism. Bubba hadn't totally gotten that, so I pointed it out and it had helped.

"Sometimes, we can talk to each other when we get something one of the others doesn't." Rather than use those examples, I said, "I've known Frankie a long time. Coop's known her longer. Sometimes, he sees stuff that even I don't. He can give us a heads-up if he notices something amiss. That said, Bubba pays pretty good attention to the shifting dynamic, though one might say he's had to get better with words."

Not missing a beat, Bubba flipped me off.

"That said…" I continued with a grin this time as I glanced over to find Frankie watching me. The warmth in her green eyes eased some of the tension right out of my shoulders. "Sometimes, we have to just confront each other and not let the other one get away with burying or dismissing what they're feeling or thinking. It's easy to say what is happening to them is more important than what is happening to me."

"Even when we're not always thrilled with the confrontation," Frankie pointed out. Then she blew out a breath. "At the beginning of the school year after I'd avoided them all summer, they found different ways of calling me on it. Jake tends to be more direct, while Coop prefers sneak attacks." She glanced at Archie and then Bubba. "Archie and Ian are a lot more subtle."

I snorted. "Archie is *not* subtle."

"Bite me," Archie retorted with a smirk. "I can be subtle."

"'Can' and 'are' are two *very* different things," I countered. "You tend to bulldoze your way into or around a situation until you can take control. You also prefer ambushes."

Archie's eyes narrowed, but it was Bubba who cut a look at me. "Sometimes, we prefer patience and letting everyone else figure out what they are doing before we decide to take the matter out of their hands."

"Until someone decides to confess something that doesn't just involve them but throws everyone else under the bus." Coop's tone was idle, but the faint whiteness around his knuckles wasn't.

"Point," Archie said. "We don't get to make arbitrary decisions for each other."

"Oh, we don't?" Bubba's tone was mild, but there was a crackle of tension in the air.

"And this is where I whistle because they are going to start arguing," Frankie said almost patiently, and I flicked a look to her. "Or I let it go, because for the most part, they can settle the disputes on their own."

"How do their disputes make you feel?"

It was like someone snapped a switch, and all of us focused on her.

"Sometimes they frustrate me," she admitted, picking at some invisible piece of lint on her shorts. She also shot Archie an apologetic smile, but he just kissed her hand and I had to bite back my own rolled eyes response. I could hate the guy, but he just did it. He charmed her. He always had. It wasn't even something he had to fucking try at.

Asshole.

"Other times, I think they're ridiculous," Frankie said with a wry smile. "Sometimes, I just want to leave them to sort it out, and sometimes, I want to throw things at them so they'll knock it off. But I always know they care about each other and that if they are fighting, it's because they have their own points of view. I just never want them to fight over me."

"That's gonna happen, Baby Girl," I said before the others could jump in, and it was my turn to lean forward and study her. "We love you. All of us. We all want what is best for you. Now, we don't always agree on what is best, but I'd like to think we've figured out a few things along the way."

"Agreed," Bubba said slowly, and Coop nodded. That just left Archie, and as I stared at him, he gave me a slow smirk.

Really?

"Yeah," he admitted with a faint chuckle. "Fine, I've learned that I can't fix everything, even when I want to. But I also know it's easier to fix things when I have backup, and there's no one else I'd rather have at my back than you idiots."

"Oh man, dial down the love," Coop said with a gasp. "You're going to make me blush."

Frankie laughed, and for a split second, I forgot we were in the middle of this group session. It was just us, hanging out, figuring things out.

That was how we would make this work.

Even when we struggled, we'd find a way to talk and to laugh.

When all else failed, yelling worked too.

IAN

The session went on that way for a while. Erin would poke us with a question and get us talking. It took a little time, but everyone—especially Frankie—relaxed. I supposed that was the best time for the psychologist to ask her next question.

"What do you think will be your biggest challenge over the next few months?" Erin looked at Frankie, and so did I. Honestly, I thought our biggest struggles would be keeping Frankie from vanishing into college academia. She loved a good challenge, and it had been a while since she really faced one. College was going to provide her with so many opportunities.

I was both hungry for her to discover them all and worried about how fast she'd burn out trying to balance all of us, the singing, the classes, business with Archie, and that was just off the top of my head.

"Finding a new place to live," Frankie said slowly. "We've talked about living together for college forever, even before we were dating." The corners of her mouth tipped up a little higher. "And before we wander back down the garden path of Frankie is dense, I know part of that was because you guys wanted to keep me safe as much as anything, but now it's like we're moving our whole household."

"We are," Archie pointed out. "We've all been living in the apartment, more or less, for months."

"Except," I pointed out, "here we can go back to our parents' places for a night or two. We can create privacy for Frankie or for Frankie and someone else." Like they had for us last night.

"That's gonna be harder in New York," Frankie mused. "Places are so expensive there. I mean, the apartment here is a tight fit for five of us, how hard does it get when all five of us are jammed into a smaller place?"

Coop chuckled. "Archie is not gonna let us get stuck in some cramped apartment, Frankie. Seriously, have you met him? He's going to find us a really swanky place, then convince you it was a fantastic idea, and you'll argue, we'll harass him, and in the end, we'll move into it because we need the space and he can afford it. Even if the rest of us are going to have to find a way to add to our portion."

"Actually," Archie said, tracing a finger against the back of Frankie's hand, "I'm not the only one who can afford it. Besides…this isn't about money."

"Yes," I agreed with him. "It isn't specifically about the money. But at the same time, we have our pride, Arch. We want to be participants. It's not just Archie takes care of Frankie and we bum along for the ride."

"I know that." Archie scowled. "I have the money to make things more comfortable. You guys bring as much to the table."

"Yeah, but when it comes down to providing—" Jake began, but it was Frankie who cut us all off.

"We're not doing this part," she said and then looked at Erin. "There are sore points. Money is one, and it has been between Archie and me before. He is one of the most generous people I know, but supporting myself is important."

"But you just came into a great deal of wealth," Erin offered.

"And I have no idea what to do with that," Frankie said, and she glanced to us. "That's something I still have to figure out. The point is, we're a team. Maybe someone has a little more money and someone else knows how to cook."

"Not Archie," Coop sneezed with a grin, and Archie flipped him off. The rest of us laughed. But well, Coop wasn't wrong.

"I think we all push each other in different ways. But I don't ever want to get tied up over the money."

"You just want to be tied up over other things," Jake teased, but I stared at him until he spread his hands. Right. Teasing her was one thing, but Frankie barely noticed it.

I did.

"I think what we're all saying here is that each of us takes point on something. Sometimes we're content to go with the flow, sometimes we want to drive. Archie fixes things, we all know it. In this case, finding a place for us to live together, and if it costs a little more, he's going to fix it. But I'm keeping a tab going. I want to be a partner in this, and if that means I pay more in later to cover today, I'm okay with that."

Archie locked gazes with me for a long moment, then he nodded. He didn't like it. He didn't have to like it. The point was to make sure we were all partners. That meant sometimes one got a little more and that was okay. It all evened out in the end.

"What I want to know," Coop said almost too idly, "is if I'm tackling more than my fair share of the cooking since some of us don't, does that help even it out too?"

"Absolutely," Archie said. "And you can do all the cooking you want. I'm down for the laundry and the cat litter boxes too if you want those. I think that's equitable."

Frankie groaned, but the comments had perforated the tension, and if my read on Erin was right, she was pleased with what she saw amongst us. We weren't perfect.

Far from it.

But we were good for each other.

Frankie was good for us.

Best of all…we made her happy.

That goal alone made working through everything else worth it.

Chapter Eleven
EVERYBODY WANTS TO RULE THE WORLD

FRANKIE

The group session went way better than I'd expected. Even with the guys being wildly competitive and making little digs at each other, Erin seemed to like them. Well, like might not be the word. We had a brief talk at the end without the guys, and she applauded me on the communication and openness we demonstrated.

"Even with all the one-upping they're doing?" Don't get me wrong, I adored them, and that behavior had always been a part of their charm. It was normal for them, but it had been absent for a while.

"They hold genuine affection for each other, and they are all very much bonded in their desire to protect and take care of you," Erin said with a smile. "I'd be more worried if they didn't have that kind of a relationship. It shows just how relaxed they are with each other. That's wonderful. But let me ask you that same question—how do you feel about the competitiveness?"

"For the most part, it's them," I admitted with a little sigh, then grinned. "Teasing and ragging each other has always been part of their charm. Usually, they reserve it for video games." I rolled my eyes and then laughed. "But it happens other times too. It's just been a while. So maybe you're right—maybe they are relaxing too."

"Remember, if you're worried or have questions, ask them. Don't assume."

"Oh no, I won't be assuming again." I knew better now. The previous summer had been a very uncomfortable lesson on that subject.

"Good. I have a couple of questions for you. You don't have to answer me now, but I want to give you time to think about it."

"All right."

"Question number one, do you feel like you want to continue therapy once you get to New York?"

I hesitated. I actually hadn't thought about that.

"Question number two, if you feel like you should continue and would like some references, I actually have three or four recommendations for you."

Erin was the best.

"Do you think I need more therapy?" Despite my initial leeriness about seeing a shrink or even admitting that I had any kind of problem, I'd found a strong ally in Erin.

"That's a question only you can answer. That's why I want you to think about it. Okay?"

I grinned at her. "Okay."

The guys were quiet after therapy, but Jake and Coop were both planning to do some deliveries. I debated it, but Archie caught my eye and raised his brows in question. He wanted to talk to me, and I'd been somewhat avoiding the financial discussions for the last few days.

I wanted to groan, but that wasn't fair to him. Ian glanced between us, then dropped a kiss on my lips before he left us alone.

"I promise," Archie said as he tugged me toward the sofa, "it's not as bad as you're thinking."

Making a face, I dropped onto the sofa next to him and sighed. "Archie, you're going to ask me what I want to do with all of it, and my answer hasn't changed. It didn't change when we had breakfast with our grandparents… Also, how weird is that to say 'our' grandparents?"

An indulgent smile creased his face. "I know, babe, and it's kind of cool to say it. Grandpa Ted adores you already. But you knew that."

Eyes rolling, I couldn't help but grin. "I like him too. Even if he makes me want to ask him dozens of questions."

Archie chuckled. "Fair. Now…" He covered my hands with his. "You have no idea what to do with the trust fund or how to assess your current financial standing, particularly in light of the Standish stock."

"First of all, the Standish stock should be yours."

"Edward gave it to you."

"Because he thought I was his daughter." Another shudder of revulsion went through me. I never wanted to live through those days again. It had been such a hellish time.

"Hey," Archie squeezed my hands. "When he gave you those stocks, he knew you weren't his daughter."

Head tilted back, I sighed. "That makes it worse somehow."

"I don't know, it makes me think he's human, which has been in doubt for a long time."

Cutting a look at him, I frowned. "I am still surprised he came to graduation." We hadn't discussed Maddy's presence there, and frankly, I was quite content to continue ignoring it.

"Honestly, I was more surprised by Muriel." Archie shrugged. "Then again, I made it clear I was done with her, and she's taking it seriously. A part of her probably doesn't want to be cut off from potential future funds, though I imagine the divorce will leave her with a tidy sum."

Disgust curled through me. I hated his parents so much. "But Edward being there didn't surprise you?"

"No, he's already made a couple of moves to try and test the waters where a relationship with me is concerned."

I narrowed my eyes.

"Down, beautiful girl," he soothed, going so far as to lift my hand to kiss it gently. "Edward has a lot to answer for, but I put my need for their approval to bed a long time ago. If he wants to make an effort now, I'm inclined to allow it. That doesn't mean I trust it, nor am I going out of my way regarding it."

"Still…"

"Still, you want to protect me, and I love you for it." Another kiss to my palm. "This is not about that. This is about sorting out your finances so you're comfortable with them. I don't know if you're aware of just how much money you came into."

A sigh rippled through me, and I fell back against the sofa. "I looked at the numbers the other day when you guys were killing each other in that new version of *Halo*."

"It wasn't *Halo*, but I get it." Archie leaned into the sofa next to me. He sat sideways so he could stare down at my face. I loved the way his brown eyes would soften and almost seem to lighten a shade when he looked at me. I loved how the tense lines at his mouth always eased and the sinful smirk relaxed into something far more affectionate.

Archie Standish might be brutal in how he handled others, but that side of him never touched me. Not that way. "I love you," I told him.

"And I love you, stop trying to distract me. Even if you presented me with your delectable breasts and begged me to suck the nipples until you were so wet, I could lick your juices from your thighs, we still need to talk about this."

Goddammit.

I shifted on the sofa and pressed my thighs together. His utterly unrepentant grin made my stomach do a flip-flop. "You know exactly what you do to me."

"Mmm-hmm," he replied, humming a pleased note. "It's only fair since you utterly devastate me. Now focus, Frankie, before we have to resort to birth names and you threaten my balls."

Laughter bubbled up through the desire he kindled, and I cupped his cheek. "You're terrible."

"And all yours, so deal with it."

Yes, he was mine.

"Focus, Frankie," he continued, and I stuck my tongue at him. He only winked. "The point here is you have access to a great deal of wealth, and I want you to be comfortable with it. You do not have to make a lot of decisions right now, but some are necessary. For example, the shares you have in Standish gives you voting rights."

I groaned.

"Hush and listen, my beautiful, brilliant lady. That mind of yours is as sharp as your heart is big. You can handle this."

The encouragement was almost as sexy as the dirty teasing. Pulling my legs up so I could sit crisscross, I turned to face him. "Okay, I can handle it. Tell me what you're thinking, because I know you. You have a plan."

"I have the elements of a plan," he conceded. "I cannot, however, dive into it without involving you. This has to be your call, even if I would be delighted to deal with every single battle for you, this one included."

"But you trust me to make those decisions for myself." I don't know which of us was more impressed. Archie or me. Still…

"I trust you to know your own mind, Frankie. I trust you to follow your instincts. Making those decisions for you might protect you in the short-term, but it doesn't help in the long-term. You want to be partners, not the princess."

"Who says I can't be both?" Not that I had any desire to be the princess, but Archie got that and his eyes warmed.

"You'll always be my princess, and I will always protect you," he told me in the most sincere tone that could have been sappy as hell, yet wasn't. "But as your partner, I want to advise you that your income has increased significantly. The amount already available to you from your trust fund will not only pay for the relocation to Manhattan, but cover all four years of your college and probably two years of a master's, as well as cost of living in the city with extras thrown in. Easily."

I wanted to throw up.

"Breathe," he told me, tracing his fingers up to my temple before beginning to massage my scalp as he brushed the hair away from my face. "That doesn't take into account the fact you have a scholarship to cover college."

Right. That kind of seemed unfair now. Someone else…

"You earned it," Archie reminded me in a tense tone, as if he could sense the direction of my thoughts, and I wrinkled my nose. "But that said, your shares in Standish will also pay dividends quarterly. At the moment, you're looking at earning somewhere between three and six million per year, depending on our financial returns."

Holy.

Shit.

"Now, you can turn around and reinvest that money or put it into a portfolio that we can then diversify. But before we make any calls like that, I want you to get a financial manager, preferably one vetted by me and Wittaker, with Wittaker taking an advisory role."

My head kind of spun for a moment. It was a lot to take in. "Wait…you don't want to do it?"

"Babe, I have a financial advisor," Archie told me, and I blinked. "But in the effort of total transparency, I don't want you to think I'm taking over your money or trying to control it. I want you to have the control. I want you to understand the decisions being made. More, I want you to make the decisions with me and to tell me what you think. I love the way your brain works, but this—this is not what you're used to."

He wasn't wrong about that. "Archie…I don't know what to do with all of it. Wittaker wanted me to talk to the financial advisor the week after my birthday when they released the trust to me, but I honestly don't know what to do with that kind of money."

"First, you stop being afraid of it," Archie told me almost sternly, and I scowled.

"I'm not afraid of it."

"You are, a little. Because you know how to live paycheck to paycheck. You know how to stretch a dollar out. You know how to use coupons and find the best deals."

Honestly, I was so proud that he listed those attributes as positives not negatives that I leaned in and gave him a kiss. He caught me close and kissed me again, this time possessing my mouth with a sweetness that had me sighing as his tongue sought mine. I would never get tired of kissing him or falling into his orbit. He pulled every part of me.

"Okay," I admitted when he released my lips. "I don't want to become someone else because of the money."

His expression gentled. "There it is. Do you think I'm so terrible?"

"Of course not, but…"

He raised his eyebrows, a hint of shock on his face. "But? Did you seriously end that sentence with a *but*?"

A giggle escaped, I couldn't help it. "Archie, you're so *you*. You're not remotely terrible, but you are a force of nature. You storm through my defenses, and you throw money around with such ease. You are comfortable with huge price tags and exorbitant fees. It doesn't seem to faze you in the slightest."

"And that's bad?" he checked.

"No, I think you're the best rich person I've ever known. You're not a snob. You are hands down one of the best people I've ever known, period. You are so focused on others and caring about them. You are generous to a fault. You are as far from terrible as you can get."

He laughed. "Well, that doesn't sound too bad. I think you'll be an even better rich person than me." The teasing light in his eyes took any sting from the words, except…

"I don't think badly of you." It was very much the last thing I wanted him to think.

"I know, babe, seriously. That said, I'm not the only wealthy person you know."

A sigh escaped me. "Your parents aren't totally wretched."

"That you can even say that with a straight face after everything that's happened just proves to me how much better than both of them you are." Before I could protest, however, he pressed a finger to my lips. "Listen, please?"

It was the please that secured my silence.

"Okay." He exhaled the pair of syllables as if he needed to steel himself in the coziness of our living room to dive into this topic with me. Guilt struck in the next second. Archie should not have to gird himself to have this—or any for that matter—conversation with me. I cupped his face, and he quieted.

"I know you want me to listen, but, Archie, nothing you tell me is going to change how I feel about you. I might get mad or I might yell, and I've even been known to throw things when I'm not being an utter delight." As I spoke, I climbed over to straddle his lap, and his eyes brightened, even as the corners of his lips tilted upwards. "Don't ever be afraid to talk to me."

"I love you," he said, hands on my hips as I wrapped my arms around his neck. Then with a little sigh, he gave me a squeeze. "Now sit that beautiful ass still so I can talk to you about this without you trying to distract me."

The playfulness was back, but he meant what he said. As tempting as teasing him was, I bit the inside of my lip and saved that for later.

He groaned. "I know that look."

"What?" I protested. "I didn't say anything."

"You didn't have to. You're going to make me pay for that statement."

I raised my eyebrows. "Didn't you want me to listen?"

"Yes." He gave my hip another squeeze, and I returned the favor by tugging his hair lightly.

"Then start talking."

He pinched my ass, and I jumped. "If you insist." At my rolled eyes, he pinched my ass again, and I laughed.

"If you think that's going to deter me…"

Nipping my lower lip, he gave it a gentle tug, and I hushed. Forehead resting against his, I waited.

"First step, financial advisor. Wittaker has put together a file with six names, I marked the three *I* liked, but I want you to review all six of them. Then if you have questions, we can discuss it. The final decision will be yours."

That didn't seem so bad.

"Wittaker will arrange for your first meetings, if the advisors are out of state, we can do it over video call or take the meeting to them."

Yeah, I wasn't going to touch that one, instead I soothed myself by playing with his hair.

"The first couple of meetings will be the worst. You need to know every asset at your disposal. Everything listed in your name, every dime and dollar coming to you as well as when it is coming to you. A trust isn't just a stagnant pool, if handled correctly, it also continues to earn interest and income that will then help the trust grow. Sometimes, the funds it earns are used to pay the administrators, lawyers, and advisors, which means your nest egg isn't touched."

My head ached at the idea of how much money would have to be present to earn the incomes of three different people—or at least the fees of three different people. Wittaker couldn't be cheap. While Archie had never told me how much his fees were, I figured somewhere in the five hundred dollars per hour range.

Rubbing a hand against my back, he grinned.

"Don't freak out."

"I'm. Not. Freaking. Out." Okay, so maybe I was a little. I closed my eyes and sucked in a deep breath. The caress of his hand running up and down my spine made me sigh. "Okay, I'm freaking out a little."

He smiled. "I know you are, that's why I wanted to talk to you about this alone. You'd probably be even more wound up if the guys were here. Money isn't a fun topic for a lot of people to talk about."

"Unless you have money," I pointed out. Money had never bothered Archie.

"That's because it's a resource. For some, it's status. For others, it's survival. For me? It's just another resource I have to make life easier for the people I love."

Warmth bloomed inside of me.

"And now, you have that resource too. Not that I won't still insist on paying for meals and spoiling you with presents." He curled a lock of my hair around his finger. "I guarantee you the guys will feel the same. Boyfriend privileges."

Yes, they had made that very clear. "Brother boyfriend privileges."

Archie threw his head back and laughed. The sound was so open and joyful, it chased away some of my nerves. Still chuckling, he gave the lock a gentle tug. "No distracting me."

"I would never." I lowered my lashes, and he snorted.

"*Anyway*… We need to lock down your financial advisor before we move out of here. Ideally, we'll have that first meeting set up so you don't have to worry about things for a few weeks…"

"Is this the part where I find out where you're planning to whisk me away for the summer?"

"No," he said without missing a beat and winked. "This is the part where we discuss the annual shareholder's meeting that takes place at the end of August every year."

I groaned. "Archie…"

"Babe," he plowed ahead. "Ten percent of Standish means—"

"Wait."

He paused.

"Ten percent of the whole company?" It was the first time that registered, I thought. Maybe. "I thought it was just ten percent of his shares, which is still too many because those should be yours…"

"What's mine is yours, so I'm fine with it," Archie told me. "And yes, ten percent of the company. Between us, you and I control about twenty percent. Grandpa actually has forty-nine percent. That leaves Edward with roughly thirty-one percent. And he'll likely lose another five percent to Muriel, now that the prenup has been fulfilled."

I frowned. I hated that whole prenup nonsense and how Archie dismissed himself in it. At the same time… "If you have shareholders, how does the family hold so many shares? I mean, that's a hundred percent, right?"

"Of the master stock in Standish Enterprises? Yes, we own the majority and controlling interest. Now, we have subsidiary companies that also have stockholders, and we are also accountable to them in some ways."

Oh, I felt a headache forming behind my eyes, but at the same time…

"There's a brief on this, right?" Because when I'd been at Standish, there had been briefs on everything.

Another smile slid across his lips. "Yes, there is. And I've had all the materials compiled for you to read."

"You could just vote my shares for me."

"I could," he agreed, sliding his hand to my nape. "But I won't unless you really discover you want nothing to do with it. I will never fault you for that. Right now, Grandpa holds my proxy, but eventually, this is going to be mine to run or to hand off day-to-day control to someone else. Though I'm not sure that's what Grandpa wants."

"What do you want?"

I smoothed my hands over his shoulders and down his chest. The shirt was soft under my fingertips.

"You."

I laughed. "Besides me."

"Oh," he grunted as I traced my fingers to the hem of his shirt and slid them under to stroke his abs. "I haven't decided on that. Grandpa wants me to think about it, but I really want to work on my degree, fuck you, design and build things with Jake, fuck you, play video games with the guys, fuck you, maybe take you skiing every winter, and you know…"

"Fuck me?" I grinned.

"Every day and in every way. I love to hear you come. I love to see you come. But there is nothing like the way you feel when you come, all hot, silky, and wet as you pulse around my cock."

I went to work on the buttons of his shorts. "Are we done discussing my finances?"

"Are we agreed on your financial advisor and reviewing the brief so you not only understand your finances, but control them?"

The zipper was loud in the silence as I slid it down. I ran my knuckles along the very stiff erection waiting for me and already peeking out of his boxers before I stood up. I pulled the shirt I was wearing up and over. "Well, let's see," I continued, leaving the dark green lace bra in place. Archie rubbed his hands against his thighs as I reached for the buttons on my shorts. I hadn't worn this set yet, and since he'd already soaked my panties, we might as well enjoy them. "Wittaker has six candidates, you like three of them, but you want me to look over all of them and maybe narrow it down to two that I meet and discuss things with."

The shorts pooled at my feet, and Archie's eyes darkened as he eyed the sheer lace green panties. I tugged his shorts, and he lifted his ass so they slid down easily and then off. I didn't remove the boxers.

I was rather fond of them. They had a game controller on them with the space for his 'joystick' around the slit. I'd picked them out myself, and his wicked grin had been worth it.

As I wrapped my hand around his length and gave it a couple of slow pumps, he blew out a breath. "Correct."

"You would also like me to make the decisions this week before we have to move out of the apartment." A bead of pre-cum glistened over the slit, and I smeared it over the head with my thumb.

"Very much so," he said on a sigh, and a muscle in his jaw seemed to be twitching like he was holding himself back.

"Then there's the briefs on the stock portfolio because that will also earn money and it comes with voting rights, even if the stock shouldn't be mine." I stroked his already hard cock and cut off his objections as he clicked his teeth together. Easing my thighs forward as I straddled him, I took advantage of the height difference to lean down and nuzzle a kiss to the corner of his mouth. "And I'm assuming after I've educated myself, I can assign my proxy to whomever, and they can handle that while I'm in school. With you. You know, hanging out, fucking, studying, fucking, playing…"

He groaned. "Fuck me, Frankie, hearing you talk like that is almost as sexy as imagining how wet that pretty pink pussy of yours is."

"That didn't answer my question," I whispered after trailing a path of kisses to his ear. I scraped my teeth over his lobe as his hands finally gripped at my waist. "After I've done all this, I can assign my proxy…"

"You can do whatever you want."

I squeezed him a little tighter. "I wasn't done."

His swift inhale made me smile, and I traced my tongue over the whorls of his ear. "After I've studied and fucked you, maybe ridden this hard cock until you explode inside of me and I can't see anything or feel anything but you, or maybe I'll suck you into my mouth and swallow every drop of your cum… Hmm, I could do both. We have the rest of the evening. After all of that…"

In a move I'd half expected but still delighted in, he pulled me to him and bit down lightly on my nipple through the lace. "Anything you want, babe, I mean it." Then he sucked and teased at the nipple until I had to tilt my head back to try and hold onto my rapidly shredding control.

Fuck it, I nudged my panties aside and just dropped down on him in one thrust. It was a bit of a stretch at this angle, but I savored the fullness of it and the way his expression went taut.

"Fuck," he groaned.

"That's the idea," I said and began to move. The roll of my hips, a bit of a twist, and I could ride him. It didn't quite hit my clit every time, but Archie slid his fingers between us, even as he raised a hand to fist my hair, and then he was stroking my clit and kissing me.

There was nothing rushed or hurried, even as we tried to devour each other. I wanted to feel him come apart, and at the same time, he swallowed my cries as he ramped me higher. I was clenching so tightly around him, it made it hard to move, and still, we enjoyed the lazy heat of it.

As hard as I tried to push him over first, he sucked my tongue, twisted one nipple, and applied so much pressure, I came on a scream. Then he dropped his hands to my hips and began to thrust up, fucking me right through that orgasm, and when he came, I swore I saw stars too.

Collapsing against him, I ignored our joint mess and the fact he still had on a shirt. I'd fix that in a minute.

"Good talk," I whispered. "Can we do all our financial discussions this way?"

He roared with laughter and then stood. I had to wrap my legs around his waist so I didn't lose him, not that he seemed to have any intentions of dropping me. We were almost to our bedroom when it occurred to me, he had been getting a little harder with each step as we ground against each other, and I clenched down on him.

"As you wish," he told me before we fell together onto the bed. "Let's discuss terms…"

Chapter Twelve
INDEPENDENT WOMEN

FRANKIE

"You are not driving up to UNT with the guys to kick his ass," Rachel informed me as she slid into the booth opposite me. We were at Mason's. Marsha had already waved at me, and the girl who'd taken my job—okay in all fairness, she earned the job, but I might still be a *little* salty about it—was our waitress. She was toothachingly sweet though, so I couldn't complain.

Much.

"Yes, we are," I told her. We were taking a day for us. Okay well, Rachel was making a day for us. She'd shown up to 'kidnap' me, and the lack of argument from the guys told me they were all up to something and I was looking forward to the day with her, so what the hell. Besides, I'd been woken up by both Jake and Coop this morning when Jake decided to skip the morning run, and I ached in all the right ways.

Honestly, I wasn't complaining.

"No, you're not and stop grinning like such a smug bitch who got laid this morning."

I snorted. "What makes you think that?" Not that I was denying it.

"The looseness in your stride, the fact you can't stop smiling, and the pair of fresh hickeys you're showing off at the top of your boobs." She delivered the last line with such utter sweetness, I scowled and then laughed before adjusting my tank top. I didn't mind the hickeys, but four boyfriends and they could get out of hand, so the guys *tried* to put them out of sight, *most* of the time.

Jake, however, liked that little stamp to be on display and those were both from him. Coop's were currently on the curve of my ass, a matching set because he didn't want me to feel unbalanced.

Grinning, I took a sip of my chocolate shake and shook my head. "Stop trying to change the subject."

"There is no need for it to be a subject. What's his name is no longer even a factor in my life."

My heart hurt for her. "I still want to beat the crap out of him."

"I love you too," she said, before tossing a rolled up straw paper at me. "Now let it go. Today is not gonna be about idiots…well, at least not about ex-idiots. We'll make an exception for current idiots."

I rolled my eyes, but held my response as our lunches arrived. We'd both gone for the big and thick burgers to go with our shakes. In a lot of ways, this was a farewell meal. Yes, we'd be back, but this place that had been so important to me for the last few years was going to be a memory.

"Stop it," Rachel ordered as I went to take bite of my burger, and I hesitated. "No, not the burger. Eat that. I meant stop being so maudlin."

I made a face. "I just feel weird," I admitted, then sank my teeth into the burger. Rachel let me eat in peace while she took a couple of bites of her own.

"I get it," she said finally. "There's been a lot of changes this year. And we're looking at even more. You more than most."

"Not all the changes have been bad." It sounded defensive, even to me. "Yet I can't shake the feeling that even when we come back, nothing will be the same and that's okay, but it's still weird. I don't even know if I can explain it."

"You're moving out of a place you've lived for most of your life," Rachel supplied. "And you're moving in with the four Peenketeers."

Thank fuck I'd swallowed that bite before she'd said that, or I would have choked. I glared at her, and she smirked before pointing a French fry at me.

"Yes, you've been living with them for months, but they've been living with *you* in *your* apartment. Now you're going to move into a place that will be all of yours and you'll be living together for real, like as more than a default but as an open choice."

The evenness of her voice coupled with the directness of the statement robbed it of any kind of patronizing tone.

"That's a lot. For anyone, that would be a lot. You're basically committing to four guys and agreeing to live with them in a joint space, and there's so much to that. Trust me, there are like eleventy hundred people that live in my house or have over the years. You think you know a person until you cohabitate, and then you discover that some eccentricities that are cute when they live elsewhere are downright fucking annoying when they are in your space *all* the time."

"You're a barrel of sunshine." But I appreciated the bluntness too.

"I know." She smirked.

"And I like living with them. Yes, it's taken some juggling, but—"

"But," Rachel interjected, "they can leave to go back to their parents' places right now. That won't be an option in New York. It will be all five of you, all the time. That would make me nervous. Hell, it makes me nervous now, so being nostalgic makes sense. Everything works here, right now, and you're asking yourself, is it going to keep working when you're there?"

"Well, I wasn't before," I argued. "God, Rachel. I was going to ask you about moving in, if we get a big enough place…"

"Nope, I'm good. I'll get a dorm room and an irritating roommate who will hopefully be hot, so the scenery is good. But I don't need to hear you guys fucking on every surface or wondering if I'm sitting somewhere you had a screaming orgasm."

My face flamed, and Rachel dug into her burger with a happy smile.

"Bitch," I grumbled, and she nudged my foot with hers.

"You love it."

"I love you, there is a difference."

"Ha," she said with a chuckle. "You say po-tay-to, and I say po-tah-to. It's all the same when it's deep fried."

Head back, I stared at the ceiling.

"Besides," she soothed. "You're not so maudlin now that you're picturing strangling me."

"Clearly," I retorted and flipped her off before taking another bite of burger.

"As for living with you, you're sweet, but no, I really don't want to move in, thank you so much. It's kind of like when you wanted me to ride in the limo to homecoming and I skipped out on that…"

"By texting Archie and the driver, instead of me."

"You didn't even notice I wasn't there."

To be fair, she wasn't wrong. We said we'd get her, and then I was just caught up in the guys all the way to the dance. "Okay, fine, I'm the worst."

Flicking a French fry at me, she scowled. "I wasn't telling you that to make you feel bad, I was just pointing out that some things are meant for the five of you and I don't want to be the outsider looking in."

All at once, my irritating vanished. "Rachel…"

"Oh my god, Frankie, go back to calling me a bitch. This is not feel sorry for Rachel day. Bless your heart, but I am *fine*. Besides, dorm living could be a blast. I'm hoping it's coed so my pool widens for easy hookups."

I groaned, but no matter what I did, Rachel wouldn't let me apologize. "You're really fucking annoying," I said when we were finally done with the meal and heading outside.

"Thank you," she declared as she slid her sunglasses into place. At least I'd managed to pay the bill before she had, much to her irritation. I'd done it when she went to pee. A fact to which she'd cried foul when she figured it out.

Too bad, so sad.

Outside, the heat of the day wasn't so bad yet. At least it wasn't the wet slap it would be by this time the following month. The breeze was still cool, and the sun was hot. It was kind of the perfect day to go swimming, but Rachel and I had other plans.

Girlfriend plans.

Nails.

Hair.

Then laser tag.

We didn't invite the guys and I might get in some serious shit for it later, but this was Rachel-time—her words, not mine—mostly because she left for Europe in three more days and the guys would likely spring their surprise on me by then, and well, it could be two months or more before Rachel and I got to see each other again.

In that vein, I let her pick out my nail polish, a *fuck me* red as she labeled it, and I let her talk me into a temporary color streak in my hair. She'd wanted me to go all Madison Kate pink—her words, not mine—but I elected for Torched blue. The single streak filled out a curl from my roots to the tips. We snapped a selfie, and I fired it off in email to KC.

I hope she enjoyed the tribute. Rachel threatened to post the same shot, but I promised retaliation if she did. I didn't want the guys to see it on social media before they saw it on me. As it was, they weren't gonna necessarily be thrilled with me coloring my hair. They'd all been rather impassioned when I suggested dying the whole thing blue.

The lady at the hair place said it would probably last about a month, but it would fade rather quickly if I didn't take care of it. I liked it. I wasn't sure I was the girl who could pull it off, but I liked it nonetheless.

At the laser tag place, we got geared up and waited for our numbers to be called. There were a lot of younger kids there. Okay, so freshmen and sophomores weren't *that* young, but they were still in the other queue. We'd drawn blue team, and Rachel rolled her eyes at me. The red team we'd be facing was a group of four, three boys and a girl. They were too busy picking on each other to pay attention to us, and some of that nostalgia might have hit me again watching them.

Rachel snorted and shoved me ahead of her into the chute. I hadn't played laser tag in forever, but thankfully, I'd also played with the ruthlessly competitive snots who were forever trying to take each other out, so I had learned some skills. Rachel, as it turned out, was pretty ruthless herself. She got all three of the boys in the time it took me to stalk and take out the girl.

We went three more times, and each time, they offered to let us add more players to our team, but Rachel and I were having too much fun on our own. As it was, we lost only one of those three games, and I was comforted by the fact that Rachel got taken out almost as fast as I did. Still, by the time we were done and turned in our stuff, we were both ready for a break.

The laser tag place included a bowling alley and the best chips and queso known to man at their food bar. The rest of the food was shit, but their queso was to die for, so we got an order along with some sodas and found a spot. When Rachel side-eyed the bowling lanes, I snorted.

"Talk to me about Europe."

She gave a little shrug. "Not much to say other than I wish you were going with," she admitted. "But it's gonna be fun. I'll send you postcards from everywhere. I guess I can mail them to Archie's place here and they can make sure they are forwarded on to you—you know, wherever you might be."

"Since you know, you're probably just gonna send them to my supersecret destination."

"Who says there's a supersecret destination?" she countered.

"Uh-huh."

"And even if there was, who says they have mail?"

I rolled my eyes. "*Anyway*… What are some of the things you're going to be doing? You are always so careful with the details. I swear you're a vault."

"'I'm going to see the sights, and not just the tourist ones, but actually spend time staying in each of the cities and kind of going about my day. I want to take pictures and walk until I find myself."

Impulsively, I reached over the table to take her hand. "Promise me that you're really all right and that you going on this grand adventure is just that—an adventure?"

"Or what? You going to buy a ticket and come with me?"

Studying her, I grinned because… "You know what, I totally can do that."

Her jaw fell, and she gaped at me. Shocking Rachel did not happen easily, and I was always delighted when I managed to get her.

Eyes narrowed, she stared at me. "You're serious."

"Yes, I am," I confirmed, and I really was. Frighteningly enough… "I can afford it. So, if you really need someone…"

"Girl, I love you," Rachel said. "But I am not dealing with those four following us everywhere, or worse, mooning over the fact you're with me instead of them. So no, as much as I adore that you would do that for me, I'll be fine. I'm really looking forward to being a stranger in a strange land with only my itinerary and myself for company. I need the break from my family, from people…from everything."

I blew out a breath. "If that changes, for any reason, you call me. I'll be on the next flight I can book. You know what, Archie owns interest in an airline. We'll charter a flight. The boys can survive without me for a few days."

"You sure about that?" But her whole demeanor softened, and her eyes warmed. "I really do adore you."

"Right back at you," I confirmed. "I hate the idea that I'm not going to see you every day this summer."

"You didn't see me every day this spring," she pointed out dryly, and I sighed.

"You really just had to go and ruin it."

"Not ruining anything, just pointing out the logic. Besides, you're going to be busy with your guys and residence hunting in Manhattan, which I'm going to guess is going to be a lot easier for you than I thought. Especially since my girl is loaded."

I tried to shrug it off, but she wasn't wrong. Wrapping my head around that much money still seemed wildly impossible, and yet in that moment of offering to fly to Rachel at a moment's notice? As crazy as it sounded, it felt good I was in that position.

She squeezed my hand. "How about your dad? Any movement on that front?"

"Actually…I talked to my little sister."

My little sister.

Yeah, that wasn't gonna get old anytime soon. Rachel listened to my story about Chloe and her three-part argument about why I should video chat them first. Her smile turned indulgent when I also told her that Hank had texted me every single day since he left, no matter what, he texted. Even if it was just a hi, how are you kind of message.

"This is gonna sound a little strange, but I think that's the part of him I like the most at the moment. I can count on the exact time he's gonna text me every single day. Maddy, she disappeared for days at a time, and I never knew when I'd hear from her. I hate that there are days that I still miss her or the idea of her. But at the same time, there's this guy who really wants to know me just for me. He wants to know what I did in my day, if I had fun, what are my plans. He sometimes just wants to say hi and that he's thinking of me."

"Good," Rachel said. "That's what a parent is supposed to be, and trust me, I have a very annoying mother who texts me all the time. Just a word of advice, if he texts and you don't answer him right away, be prepared for him to call in the National Guard after about an hour."

I laughed. "He promised to give me two hours and only after he texted the guys. He has all of their numbers now too."

She chuckled. "He is such a dad."

A grin stretched my mouth wide. He really was a dad and he was mine, and I was loving having one that it still made me want to pinch myself. "I love him, Rachel. I want him to be as real as he seems to be. It's like a Hallmark movie moment, and I don't want it to turn into some made for TV true story turned into a Lifetime special."

"I think you're in good shape, besides, Archie hasn't lost his shit, right? And if I know Rich Boy, he's done a full background check and crossed all his t's and dotted all his i's. Besides, if he turns out to be at all fake, I'll kick his ass."

I wasn't even going to argue that point. Archie was gonna Archie. We finished our queso and chips, drained our drinks, and left the bowling alley and laser tag center arm in arm. "I'm kind of jealous, though."

"About your dad?"

"No," I said, bumping her with my hip. "Of you, and by jealous, I mean envious. I love that you're going to go to Europe, that you're going with you, and that you're going to do the pictures and the touristing. You're gonna be this independent woman, and I love that so much for you."

"Then plan your own trip," Rachel told me. "You have the money and fuck knows you have the intelligence."

"I would, but…"

"You don't want to be away from your guys for that long."

"It's less not wanting to be away from them as much as wanting to share it with them. Kind of like I want to share it with you." I made a face. "I guess I'm kind of a greedy bitch."

"Yeah, but you're my greedy bitch, and I'll cut anyone else that calls you that." She pressed a smacking kiss to my cheek, and we both laughed, pulling apart when we got to the car. "Ice cream, you bottomless beauty?"

"Hell yes, and drive out to the lake?"

Head back, Rachel let out a little whoop. "Hell yes."

We'd taken Rachel's car, so she drove. I checked my phone when we got to the store. The guys had all checked in subtly via our group chat by rambling in it.

Cute.

It also let them see *when* I read their messages.

Amused, I let them know Rach and I were heading out to the lake and promised to text when we were heading back.

"You are so hopeless," Rachel teased when she caught me and read some of their messages over my shoulder. "Why do they have to put the furniture back where it goes?"

"They probably moved the sofa and the chairs to set up for optimal video game playing."

"Uh-huh. Like I said, hopeless."

I chuckled, tucking my phone away as we headed back out with our purchases. "You know what, I'm okay with being hopeless. They picked me, and I picked them. It works."

"Yes, sickeningly so," Rachel agreed. "And for that, I am beyond grateful."

We drove out to the lake and found our way to the same picnic table we'd sat at before. This was so much nicer than that night we'd driven out here after Ian and I broke up. Well, after I broke up with him. It might have been the first time I'd really leaned into the friendship with Rachel, but I was happier with where we all were now as opposed to then.

"How are you really doing?" Rachel asked, turning the question back on me that I had been asking her all day. "With everything? Your mom? Archie's dad? The arrival of Hank and his ready-made family that seems too good to be true? Graduation? College? Four boyfriends? Did I leave anything out?"

I considered it. "Relocating?"

"Right, moving." She bumped my shoulder. "And discovering that you're basically an heiress with wealthy grandparents who want to give you everything? I mean, there's gotta be a psychological malfunction related to that."

I laughed. "I'm doing amazing. Every time I get nervous or scared, the guys are there and they listen. They talk to me. Archie sat me down about finances this week. Ian has me singing. I'm running with them. I'm doing all kinds of things that I never thought possible. I mean, Jake and Coop keep giving me tips about being the oldest sibling. Course, I've been around their sisters forever."

"You're happy," Rachel said with some satisfaction.

"I am. Even when I'm scared, I'm happy."

She grinned. "Cool. That's the best, really."

"I'm gonna miss you, Rach."

"Not for long," she promised. "Come autumn, we'll be in New York together. Broadway. Central Park. The Statue of Liberty. We're gonna have a great time, and we're going to catch up on everything we did over the summer. And like your new dad, if you don't answer my texts, I'll do more than call out the National Guard. I'll come hunting you myself."

"Hmm," I said as I spooned out some more ice cream.

"Girl, you do not want me coming to find you *just because*."

"I don't know," I said. "It *might* be fun."

She laughed. "Bitch."

"Yep," I agreed, and we pretend clinked our pint cartons together.

We sat by the lake and talked for hours. It was almost midnight before we went home, and my boys were waiting up for me. There were exclamations and side-eye over the blue streak, but Archie summed it all up with a, "Huh, I kind of love it."

Jake grinned as he curled it around his finger. "Me too. It's sexy."

"Very," Ian murmured, but his eyes sparked with humor. I was in a little bit of trouble, and I was definitely here for it.

Coop just gave an exaggerated yawn before he grinned. "It's definitely hot. Like, rock star hot. I'll be your groupie any day!"

They teased, but they weren't kidding about liking it, and that satisfied me. Granted, even if they'd hated it, I wouldn't have regretted it 'cause I liked it. But the guys encouraged me to be me, and right now, a blue streak in my hair was definitely me.

I climbed onto the sofa between Ian and Jake as they battled it out on the screen and curled up happily as they trash talked each other through another couple of hours of games.

Not that they were fooling me. The apartment was superclean, and there were boxes neatly stacked in the corners. I bet if I checked our closet, there would be suitcases packed for our "trip." Unless they'd already had those picked up. The cats were still here because Tiddles settled in my lap and Tory was curled up on Coop's back where he lay on the floor. Tabby just watched us all with disdain.

Yep, my boys were up to something and Rachel was in on it, and I was fine with that. I'd find out soon enough, I had no doubt.

Chapter Thirteen
SPLAT! YOU WERE SAYING?

FRANKIE

When Archie woke me just before dawn to go running with them, I regretted my decision from the night before. Last night's Frankie was a bitch. He chuckled at my groan, and when I wrapped my arms around him for a morning kiss, the thickness of his erection suggested I might be able to persuade him otherwise.

Then Ian pushed the door open and flipped on the light. "Let's go, Angel. You said you wanted to run with us."

Have I mentioned how much I hated them sometimes?

I stared at Ian past Archie's head, and even if the light had me squinting, it was hard to stay mad at his indulgent smile. I was so fucking lucky.

"It's a good thing I love all of you," I settled on as Archie rolled off me and then tugged me out of bed. I wasn't wearing anything, but lately, going to bed in clothes meant they got stripped off me anyway, so why make more laundry?

The scent of coffee teased my nostrils as I dug out some shorts, underwear and a tank top. It wasn't likely to be hot yet, but running would definitely work up a sweat. Aware of the eyes tracking my every movement, I was so tempted to make it a show. As tempting as teasing them was, the coffee called to me. I was dressed in under five, socks and shoes on.

As I turned, I caught Archie pulling the sheets up and making the bed. He caught me watching and smirked.

"I do pay attention, and this makes you feel better."

"I know, and I adore you."

His smirk turned into a pleased grin, and he sat on the bed to pull on his own shoes. I ignored the stack of boxes in the corner. All of my artwork and posters were off the walls. The memory board with all the photos of us I treasured had been carefully put away and the photos organized. To be honest, the room had been nearly stripped, save for the huge bed that could sleep all of us if we got cozy, but still usually only ended up being two of the guys with me at any given time.

If I didn't look at the stacks of boxes, I could avoid the butterflies that would take flight in my stomach over the thought that I'd be leaving here soon. Ian blocked my path at the door and grinned.

"Pay the toll," he murmured, and I chuckled. Like that was a hardship. I twined my arms around his neck and nipped his lower lip.

"Sorry about the morning breath," I whispered a split second before he fisted my hair and claimed my mouth in a furious kiss that set my whole body on fire. If this was his way of encouraging the run, I was gonna be superfast so we could get back here and finish that off.

As it was, my fresh panties were damp and my nipples strained against my sports bra. When Archie pushed right up against my back and tugged my hair to the side to kiss my neck, I about died.

Images from my birthday flew through my mind, and I whimpered. God, I was such a mess. A hungry masculine groan answered me, and Ian's fist in my hair tightened. The tug lit up my scalp and sent another electric pulse through my body.

A whistle cut through the air, and Ian lifted his head slowly. Heart pounding, I fought to remember how to breathe. "Coffee's ready, Frankie," Jake called like a siren promising me everything, and sandwiched between Ian and Archie, the twin temptations threatened to undo me completely.

"Later," Archie promised before nipping my ear. He'd slid his hand under the edge of my shirt and spread his fingers against my abdomen. Considering the fact I was still plastered against Ian, he had to be aware of what Archie did. Goosebumps raced over my skin, and Ian chuckled.

"Later," he agreed and then released my hair before cupping my face, and I was up on my tiptoes to strain into the sweet kiss he gave me. They both steadied my swaying form as they let me go.

"Y'all are mean," I complained in a breathy tone, and Archie just laughed, but Ian gave my ass a swat that had my pussy clenching as I passed him.

"You love it," Jake taunted, his eyes practically dancing as I approached. He had a cup of coffee in hand, but he held it out of reach. "Miniboss."

"Nothing about you is mini," I teased and earned a wonderfully warm smile for it, but I slid right up against him, lips parted in invitation. Like Ian before him, he nipped at my lower lip, then teased my tongue before deepening the kiss with a sigh. He had one arm braced around me, and when I jumped, hitching my thighs to his hips so I could bring my face up level with his, that arm braced my ass and kept me in place.

"You know, you assholes dragged me out of bed for this," Coop complained, "when clearly we all want to be naked in bed. Orgy? Anyone?"

Laughter bubbled up between Jake and I, the hum of it delighting me. When I lifted my head, he grinned up at me. "Player three is getting antsy."

"Player three can always enter the game."

"Good to know," Coop chortled before he tugged me right out of Jake's arms and into his. He tilted me backwards, like he dipped me in some seductive dance, but his waggling eyebrows and faint twitch to his nostrils killed the drama. "Player three entering the game," he whispered, and then claimed my mouth for a very slow and thorough kiss that finished the decimation of my panties and sent me up in flames.

With great care, he straightened us both and then settled me on my feet. Jake passed me the coffee, and I fanned myself with one hand. "Good morning, boys."

Almost in unison, they said, "Good morning, Frankie."

I was still tingling from their kisses as I wandered into the kitchen. The cats were hanging out around the table, and no wonder. The bag of cat treats—usually kept above the fridge—was sitting on the table. Tiddles sat in a chair, tail swishing as I approached, and Tory let out a little yowl from under the table.

Poor tortured felines. No one had given them something to eat in the last five minutes. I took a deep drink of my coffee and just savored the hum of the guys razzing each other as they filtered into the kitchen. Someone had already fed the cats. Coop delved out some treats and scattered them among the cats.

"He just loves spoiling your pussies," Archie said without an ounce of irony. I snorted, and Coop slugged him in the arm.

"Like you don't."

"Oh, I definitely like spoiling her pussy," Archie confirmed with a wink.

"Huh," Jake said. "Then which of you is gonna get pierced first?"

My face flamed. "Jake…"

"What, Baby Girl? You said the idea turned you on."

Well, he wasn't wrong about that, but with his avid audience, I could wish to be somewhere else.

"Piercing?" Ian prompted with a doubtful look.

"Frankie's latest book obsession," Jake mused aloud. "It had a dude in it that got this thing called a Jacob's Ladder on his dick."

Archie snorted, arms folded as he leaned back against the fridge. The tank top he wore was that moisture wicked material, but the red looked so good on him and so did those gray sweatpants.

Everyone else was in shorts, but Archie's gray sweatpants kept his dick on prominent display for me. Yeah. I looked.

Sue me.

He caught my gaze and winked.

"Not piercing my dick, don't care if it has my name," Jake said. "But Frankie's curious, so since you two are all about pleasing her pussy, you might consider it."

Coop had his phone in hand, and he let out a grunt. "Um…"

"Right?" Jake said with a grin, and I gave him a gentle kick. Ass. He laughed at me. "Notice which one of them looked it up. My money is still on Coop."

"Hey," Archie argued. "I didn't say no yet." At the same time, he glanced at me. "Do you really want one of us to do that?"

"No," I said firmly. "I said it sounded good and it did." Yes, my face was still on fire, but I didn't shy away from any of their gazes. No, I didn't want to have this conversation in front of all of them. Yet considering the intimacies we'd shared, discussing their dicks should be pretty simple. "Particularly how the author wrote it. The guy also had a pierced tongue, and I dunno…it was sexy as fuck."

"Good to know," Archie mused, and Jake laughed wickedly.

"Don't say I never did anything for you, Baby Girl," Jake said with a chuckle, and I laughed.

"Don't be an ass," I scolded, but I couldn't stop grinning. Neither Archie nor Coop said no immediately, however… "Guys, I'm not asking anyone to do it. I can't imagine that doing it would be comfortable in the first place." And I wasn't going to ask anyone to hurt themselves.

"If I wanted you to pierce your navel," Archie said, "would you consider it?"

I stared at him a beat. "Yes."

He grinned. "Good to know."

Ian raised his brows. He'd been quiet until now, but at my glance, he gave a gentle shrug. "You've already agreed to everything I want."

A shiver went through me. "Ditto," I told him.

"All right," Coop said as he shut off his phone's screen. "We need to do this run thing before I stage a revolt and drag Frankie back to bed."

That spurred a fresh round of laughter. I finished my coffee and rinsed out the cup. We only had a handful of dishes still out. The guys had packed up everything in the kitchen, including the pots and pans, save for the ones they decided were not worth taking. Those boxes were stacked in the corner.

Yep, not looking at boxes.

"Let's do it."

Ian held out his hand to me, and I crossed to take it. It was still dark outside, that was how early we were up, but I didn't comment on it. We piled into Jake's SUV, and he took us out toward the lake. We'd been running farther each time, and I'd gotten pretty good. The guys liked to do ten miles, and I could almost do half of that without hating them. The last half sucked, but I didn't want to slow them down either and they would take breaks to walk for me.

So, win-win.

As it was, I looked forward to the running. It was more than spending time together. Not that I didn't adore the time. It was about endurance and building strength. Jake still worked on my punching. I was getting pretty good at boxing, and Rachel and I planned to take some self-defense classes together in New York.

Jake loved the idea and promised to go with us.

"So when are you guys telling me where we're going?" I asked as we reached the halfway point of our circuit of the lake. The sun was edging up on the horizon, and the breeze off the lake helped to dry the sweat soaking through my shirt.

"Who says we're going anywhere?" Archie challenged. "We have a lot to do before we move to New York."

I snorted. No takers here. We were walking. The half-mile break let me catch my breath. The burn in my legs wasn't as bad as it had been. Months of running with them was definitely increasing my endurance, even if I did miss lounging in bed and waking up slowly as Coop pressed into me.

Shaking that distracting thought off, I focused on Archie. "Well if we don't have plans, would you guys mind if I tagged along with Rachel for a couple of weeks..."

"Yes," three voices answered in unison, and I grinned. Archie just gave them a bland stare before he tapped my nose gently.

"Trust me?"

"Always."

Without any hesitation or reservation.

"Then be patient, babe. I promise it will be worth it."

Head tilted back, I let out an exaggerated sigh. "Fine, but I will let you know that the anticipation is killing me."

Because with Archie, literally anything was possible.

Four hours later, he proved my point when we arrived at Fort Splat, the paintball place with indoor and outdoor courses. We hadn't been here in two years. Well, I hadn't been here in two years. My last trip had been the summer between sophomore and junior years. If they came the previous summer, I had no idea.

"How are we picking teams?" 'Cause I wasn't sure about the rules anymore. We wouldn't be even if we split up. And I didn't want to have to pick sides. I refused.

"We're not," Ian told me as we headed toward the front doors. "We signed up as a team of five."

"Yes," Coop said with a fist pump. "Hashtag Team Frankie."

"I was thinking Team Standish, myself," Archie said with a wicked grin.

Jake snorted. "Team Jake and Coop for the win."

Ian locked his gaze with mine as I laughed. "I'm all Team Us," I said ducking under his arm as he held the door open. "You can't change my mind."

"Did you hear a challenge?" Archie straightened.

"Oh, I heard a challenge." Jake fist-bumped Coop, and I rolled my eyes.

"Let them play, Angel," Ian said as he looped an arm over my shoulders while Archie headed for the counter. The air conditioning washed over us. It was kind of a perfect day outside so far. Warm without being sweltering, sunny but low humidity, and a breeze to chase away the heat. Still, I welcomed the air conditioning.

"You're not playing?" I was more curious than anything else.

"Didn't say that, but I know you're on my team," he said with a grin, then pressed a kiss to my temple. "And I'm always team you."

Warmth bloomed in my chest and then settled in my belly. I was team them every day of the week.

"Okay," Archie said as he turned around. "There will be two other teams out there with us. It's open wargames. So, we're gonna gear up." He handed me a ticket. "You get to go to the ladies dressing room. Someone will help you, and we'll meet you on the other side."

Excitement threaded through me. Paintball could hurt, but the last few times we'd done it, I always had fun. I had to wonder if the guys were trying to rebuild some of our more fun memories.

I paused mid step and turned back. "Was paintball a date?"

Coop's whole expression softened. "A friend date, yes. A romantic date, no. Though if we'd had a brain between us, we'd have all pursued you together from the beginning."

Grinning, I pivoted and headed for the changing room. I wasn't the only girl in there, but there were only four of us. The other three were on the other two teams. We had a couple of workers running us through the use of the paintball guns and the gear.

No face shots.

No groin shots.

Anyone who violated those rules would be booted immediately. All shots needed to be in the chest region, where the armor we'd be wearing was thicker. Also, legs were fair below the groin.

I remembered most of it from our last few times doing this. Junior summer, we'd gone paintballing more than once. It was fun as fuck. Kind of like laser tag, but with more of a kick. It also amused me that the guys were impressed that I was such a good shot.

Jake and Ian were machines at this, Coop—like me—tended to hang back and just have fun with it. We'd gotten snarked at more than once for joking. But Archie? Archie was next level. I swore these games amped his competitive side to the max. By the time I left the changing room and met them outside the course, they were all there and ready. Archie had a map open on his phone, and they were studying it.

I didn't have to ask. My money was that it was a map of the outdoor course, and when I leaned against Jake's heavier armored frame, I wasn't disappointed. He flashed me a swift grin and swept his pale blue eyed gaze over me. "Hot, Baby Girl."

A snort escaped me before I could stop it. "You're looking pretty good yourself."

"Right?" Coop quipped. "He looks even better with the full face mask."

Jake elbowed him, but we all laughed. Archie scowled. "Focus, children."

"I'm older than you," Coop pointed out.

"By days," Archie said with a sniff. "And Jake isn't."

The flash of Jake's middle finger settled that particular line of thought. There was a horn sounding, and a voice came over the speaker to tell us to get ready. We'd have ten minutes to get into place in the course before the war games started.

We had two options to win the game—defend our flag and eliminate the opposition, or take their flags while not losing ours.

Fortunately, our teams were about even. Two teams of five and one team of six. Jake said we would need to trim that team first. He and Archie debated a plan as we moved to where our flag—blue—was placed.

Coop bumped my shoulder. "As much history as you and Jake watch, it always kills me that you don't want to plot strategy on these."

"You know strategy as well as I do, and you don't leap into these debates either," I pointed out, and he shrugged.

"Archie lives for this shit. Jake and Bubba work together well because of all the years of football. So why mess with a good thing?"

I grinned. "And it's fun to watch them go all alpha."

"That it is," he admitted. "They aren't even doing it to impress you. They really care how this comes out."

"You care," I told him. "You like to win."

"So do you," he began but paused when Archie glared at us.

"You're supposed to be paying attention," he reminded us.

"Oops," I intoned with wide eyes. "We're in trouble."

The playful tone was the right thing to do, because Archie grinned and shook his head. "Keep it up, babe, and I'll get into this spanking thing you like."

Yeah, my pussy might have clenched at that threat. "Not sure that's a deterrent," I teased, but out of deference to seeing him smile, I focused on their plan. I had to admit, they had worked out a good one.

And that ten-mile run earlier might not work out in my favor if I had to play bait, but that was what they wanted me to do. Lure out their players so Jake could take a higher position and knock them out. In the meantime, Coop would go with Archie to nail the red flag first. Ian would stay to defend our flag.

We did have little headsets and radio control. I wanted to laugh at how serious they were, especially when we went with call signs, but I had to admit, there was a certain amount of thrill to this whole idea.

For the next two hours, it was a blast. We weren't the only one who went after the red team first. The green team had also gone after them. They were the team with the six members, and they took enough body shots—I managed to knock out one on my own, even with Jake covering me from above—that they were out of play. Archie snagged their flag in the melee and took out a green team member at the same time.

But almost at once, our aggressive play turned defensive, because the green team came after us. Three of them moved together in a triangle pattern, and they nearly got me. I had taken four of the five hits needed to eliminate me from play.

Jake fell back with me and took two hits meant for me, then we took out one of our assailants. Buying time for Archie and Coop, we went on the run and kept their team after them.

Two on two, we were racking up the shots.

I got eliminated just as Archie claimed their flag and the buzzer sounded through the whole place.

Hot and sweaty afterward, the guys were still riding high on their victory. "My place tonight," Archie announced. "Jeremy already picked up the cats, and we're going to finish moving the last of your stuff out, babe."

It almost felt too soon, but we went back to my place long enough to shower and change. I packed up an overnight bag and my toiletries. All our cars were coming with us, which meant we were driving separately. The bed had been stripped down to the mattress, and there were new boxes.

I would scold Jeremy and Archie later, but a part of me was truly grateful. Leaving the apartment was bittersweet. I'd grown up here. I had a lot of bad memories here.

But I had good ones too. This year? This past year with them had been the best. This was where we'd become us, even if we'd had to go to Colorado to really sort it all out. This was where I'd slept with Jake and Coop the first times. Archie had told me he loved me for the first time in his Ferrari right outside. Coop and I had grown up here. It'd also been the site of an amazing birthday I was never going to forget. I met my father here for the first time.

So many memories.

The guys trickled out, and for once, they let me have a couple of minutes alone in the place. With the cats gone, the art off the walls, and everything packed, it held an element of emptiness I wasn't expecting.

As much as it had been my home, it wasn't anymore.

My home was out there waiting for me.

Blowing out a breath, I turned off the lights and headed for the door.

It was time to leave the apartment in the past and take the memories with me. Still, I hesitated at the backdoor and glanced at the kitchen one more time.

It was one more goodbye in a couple weeks of goodbyes.

I locked the door and headed to the parking lot, where my family waited next to their own vehicles.

Joy invaded the bittersweet, and I grinned.

"French toast for breakfast tomorrow?" I asked, and Archie grinned.

"Like Jeremy would make you anything else."

Chapter Fourteen
PAINTING THE ROSES RED

COOP

Breakfast at Archie's was everything you could want, right down to the fact the cats wandered through the dining room while we fell on the feast Jeremy prepared for all of us. None of them were on the table, though I'd caught Tiddles eyeing it with his tail thrashing like he just waited for the right moment to commit mischief. There was a huge platter with bacon and sausage at the center with stacks of pancakes and a special heated dish with French toast—which every single one of us knew better than to even approach until Frankie had hers.

She'd already expressed appreciation while she sat, in her pajamas, in one of the highbacked chairs, knee up and cradling a fancy coffee that Jeremy had prepared right down to the whip cream. Her blissful sigh sent a ripple of laughter around the table. While this was hardly my first meal at Archie's place, I had to admit, it was the warmest. Jake stretched over to serve himself up five pancakes, while Bubba did the same. Archie hadn't touched any of the food, a cup of coffee in one hand and his phone in the other.

While we didn't know all the details of *Frankie's Great Adventure*, which was what we'd dubbed this summer vacation plan of Arch's, we did know today was launch day. We weren't willing to let her linger a moment longer than necessary. The apartment was packed up and emptied. The movers had picked up some of my things for me while they emptied her apartment. From there, they went to Jake's and then Bubba's. All personal items were being shipped to New York ahead of us.

Well, everything except some of the more important personal pieces. "Are you sure you don't mind the cats running all over the house?" Frankie asked for like the tenth time since we arrived the night before to find that Tabby had claimed the formal living room while Tory had made herself at home in the kitchen and what I thought had to be Jeremy's rooms.

Tiddles? He pretty much swanned all over the house like he owned the place, and I'd already seen him head up the stairs via the railing. No way there wouldn't be claw marks.

"They'll get cat hair everywhere…"

"That's what a vacuum is for, and I assure you, they're fine. Mr. Archie already approved that they could go where they want. I have their toys and trees in the solarium, but for now, they seem to be enjoying themselves exploring. I promise it's not an ounce of bother. Now, drink your coffee, Miss Frankie, and then eat. You've a busy day ahead of you."

Archie flicked a look up at him, but Jeremy ignored the warning in Archie's expression. "My house is your house, and your house is the cats' house, so the cats belong here, babe. Jeremy *loves* having them here. It gives him something to fuss over, so stop raining on his parade."

Well, that was one way to get Frankie to stop arguing about the cats. She made a face, and it was Jeremy's turn to give Archie a look.

Yep, never getting in between those two laser stares. Particularly not when there was food to eat. Instead, I slid my free hand over her foot and gave it a squeeze. The swift smile curling her lips righted everything, and detente was reached in the stare off as Jeremy nodded and Archie went back to taking over the world or whatever it was he was doing on the phone.

"That producer is back with another offer," Archie said, and Frankie froze with the bacon halfway to her lips. "I still think it's a lowball, and no way are you giving up the rights to what you write. They can lease your music exclusively for a set period of time, but no direct sales. That'll cut into long-term profitability for you."

"You mind if I read the offer now?" Bubba's droll tone held not an ounce of hostility.

"No, you should, but forewarning—I think the guy's a dick."

"You haven't even met him," Bubba pointed out as he lifted his own phone, one he'd been ignoring. We'd changed our plan the week before. Now all five of us were on the exact same one, our phones cued to the same cloud so we could save images, and all of it shuttered behind a firewall Archie insisted on building. My phone had all kinds of crap I wasn't used to yet, and I didn't really care about figuring out. Except you could play pool, something Jake and I had taken to doing on nights we were both working.

"He writes like a dick," Archie continued. "You shouldn't have to do business with assholes."

"But he can do business with you," Jake pointed out, and I rolled my eyes at his shit-eating grin. He just couldn't help himself. Frankie still hadn't eaten her bacon, so before any arguments could break out, I caught her hand and leaned forward to nibble the bacon right from her fingers, all the way down until I could lick her fingers clean.

Hers wasn't the only shocked grin thrown my way.

"I'm telling him that we need time to review the offer," Bubba said after pinning me with a look. "If he gets pushy after that, you can tell him to fuck off."

"Yes," Archie said with a pleased little grin and a raised brow at me as he lifted his coffee cup.

"Save me," I whispered to Frankie before dragging her over to sit in my lap. She laughed, but I didn't miss the promises of retribution in the eyes of my best friends. It was all good. No tables were injured in the path of this potential disagreement.

Our leisurely breakfast ended with Jeremy frowning as Frankie carried her used dishes into the kitchen. Jake, Bubba, and I followed suit, because we knew better than to leave dirty dishes on the table. Archie's long-suffering sigh as he joined us followed by Jeremy's chuckle was a bit like winning the lottery.

We were not allowed to do dishes. In fact, Jeremy chased us out with a firm reminder we needed to be ready to leave in ninety minutes. Jake half tackled me on the stairs as Frankie scooted ahead of us. Bubba just laughed as he circled round, but Archie moved with purpose.

Dammit, I elbowed Jake. Now Frankie was gonna share her shower with Archie rather than me. Eh, I'd steal her away later. We'd crashed in Archie's room and the one attached to it the night before. He'd gotten a bigger bed at some point, and I didn't ask. It was just nice that there was room to share.

But we each did actually have *rooms* with en suite bathrooms, so I ducked into mine, and the sound of running water had me grinning from ear to ear. I locked the door and tugged my shirt over my head. I hadn't been in this room to do more than leave my clothes for the trip and my toiletries the night before.

Since I damn well knew which rooms the guys had gone into, there was only one person who could be in my shower. I shucked shorts and boxers. Her pajamas sat primly on the counter, next to a stack of clean clothes for both of us. The clear shower door was foggy, but there was no mistaking who waited for me.

"What did I do to get so lucky?"

Her laughter was the only invitation I needed. "Do you need to do something to get lucky?"

"Maybe." I slid into the shower next to her, and when she turned and wrapped herself around me, I counted every lucky star I'd ever made a wish on that I got to hug her, hold her, kiss her… Even before the thought finished, she fisted my hair, and then I forgot to count those reasons as I sampled her lips.

The sweet taste of maple, sugar, and cinnamon was a heady combo with the coffee she loved and the inescapable sweetness that was Frankie. "Fuck, I love you," I murmured in between strokes of her lips on mine. I didn't have to hear her response to know she loved me too.

Frankie loving me had never been a question for me. I slid my hands down to her ass and lifted her. I wanted her face level with mine as her lips parted and her tongue dueled with mine. Her soft groan echoed through me as I rubbed my cock against the damp slickness of her pussy.

This intimacy was what I'd longed for. The tease of her fingers as she reached between us had me groaning. I let go of her lips and lifted my head so I could watch her as she wrapped her fingers around my cock. In the beginning, those touches had always been tentative, a little hesitant. But they'd grown more assured and playful. Right now, she literally held my pleasure in her hands, and I could not have been happier.

Touch me. Torture me. Tease me. Just let me be here with her.

"You never have to *earn* my attention," she whispered as the water pounded down on us and the steam kept rising. "I never want you to think I don't love you as much as I love them."

Fuck. Before she could utter another protest, I pressed her up against the cold tile, aware of her hiss at the contact and the contraction of her nipples as they tightened. I was aware of everything where she was concerned. "I know you do," I assured her in between biting kisses because she gripped my cock in her slippery hand and it was taking everything I had to not start thrusting to her palm. "I know you love me. I was teasing."

Lifting my head, I met her green-eyed stare head-on. The openness in her eyes, the way they sparkled when she smiled just as they were right now with the faint curing tilt of her lips, wrapped me up in an embrace that defied everything. Long before we'd been lovers, she'd loved me. Fuck knew, I'd loved her. "Good." She accompanied that single syllable with stroking the head of my cock against her pussy, and I swallowed another moan. "I love to feel you too, you know."

"I know, I love that you can take me." Sometimes I had to go slow, other times, she wouldn't let me and would instead slam down on my dick until we both saw stars.

The huskiness of her laughter deepened my smile. "Would you…"

The hesitation in her voice had me sharpening my focus on her. Uncertainty flickered in her expression as she raked her teeth across her lower lip.

"Would I pierce my dick for you?" Yeah, I hadn't missed those conversations.

"I don't know," she said with a wince. "Maybe? I wonder if there's a way to test it. Not like I find a guy with…"

One moment, she was stroking me, and the next, I pushed into her with force that left us both gasping. Impaled on my dick and pinned to the wall, Frankie stared at me with startled eyes. I kept one hand on her hip, bracing her against me, and the other I curved against her cheek.

"The only guys you're fucking are us," I told her with way more force than necessary. Jealousy was an ugly thing, one I was well aware we had no business exercising around her. Frankie's loyalty was *not* a question. In fact, a part of my brain registered the comment was just that—a comment. She'd started it out with the word not. And I wasn't stupid, I could complete the rest of the thought.

At the same time, my lizard brain engaged and possessiveness swarmed through me as I kept her gaze on me and flexed my hips as I pulled out and then pushed into the velvet grip of her pussy. The contracting walls fluttered over my cock and stroked me better than my hand ever could.

A whimpering groan fell from her lips, and I grunted. Every stroke seemed to push her up on the wall, and then I'd drag her back down on my cock.

"No one else," I repeated. Yeah, apparently, I had some cave man in me, but Frankie just gripped my hair as she rubbed her breasts against my chest and tried to pull me closer with every thrust. "Are we clear on that?"

"There never has been anyone else," she protested.

"And never will!" I ground my hips against hers, and there was a bit of a twist on the thrust that always made her eyes roll back as she huffed out a short cry. Yes, that was the spot, and I made it my personal mission to strike it with every push until I pulled that low keening cry from her we all loved so fucking much.

Then her mouth was on mine, and we collided with a clash of teeth and tongue. It was as much a wrestling match as a deep, tongue twisting kiss. I dug my fingers into her hip and then back to the curve of her ass. She was dragging her nails down my back, and there were no words necessary as we kissed, stroked, petted, and pounded together.

I worked my hand down between us as she gasped between kisses. The thrusts were less about pulling out and more about straining and grinding to be closer to together. Every time I hit the right spot, she whimpered and dug her fingers into me harder, and I swore my dick was ready to explode, but I fought the urge.

Frankie first.

I grazed my fingers against her clit, and she jolted, yanking her mouth from mine as that sweet cry fell from her lips and every muscle in her pussy clamped down on me. Fuck, this was a feeling I would die for, this moment right here. The rest of the thought flowed into her as I came, and she held onto me or I held onto her or maybe we were just supporting each other as we shook and shuddered our way through release.

For a long few moments, the only sounds in the bathroom was the running water and our heavy breaths.

Finally, she said, "You know…"

"Yeah," I told her. "I do." She didn't need to finish the thought. She never needed it. "I didn't…"

"No," she promised me before I'd fully verbalized that I needed to know

I hadn't hurt her in my eagerness. "You felt good." When she lifted her head to rest against the tile wall and stare me, I lost myself in her eyes. "You know that…"

She was curious about the piercing but not really asking? "I do," I promised her. I brushed my knuckles against the back of her cheek. "You're…"

"Everything," she said, completing the thought, and I grinned. This, more than anything else, these moments were the ones I lived for, when we were so connected, we might as well share one brain.

"If we shared one brain, Coop," she said with a teasing grin. "We'd have died of oxygen deprivation, considering how much blood that monster cock of yours needs."

"All the better to please you with." Monster cock? Hell yes, I'd take it. She laughed, and my heart went lighter. "And if you want me to look at piercings, I will." That wasn't so hard. Not that the idea of putting something through my dick thrilled me. "If you are really interested."

"That's part of what I was trying to say earlier. I don't know if I am," she whispered and then nuzzled the corner of my mouth. This time when I turned into the kiss, it was long and sweet and soul touching. Finally, I eased her to her feet and helped her finish showering. The water had gone from hot to warm, so probably a good plan to get a move on before it went cold.

Even Archie's house might have a water limit. With her back to my chest, Frankie arched forward, and there was no accident as she rubbed her ass against my rapidly growing more interested dick. He was always interested when she was around.

"Frankie," I warned as I shaped my hands from her shoulders to her hips. The little rosette of her ass peeked at me as she bent in half, almost as though she really needed to see her ankles to do what she was doing.

"I want you," she told me, and it was as simple as that. With a heated groan, I rubbed her back as she pressed her hands against the wall, and I lost what little battle I considered waging against the need to push into her again.

She was hotter, slicker, and more swollen from the earlier orgasm. This time, we didn't tease or taunt, I just rode her with a kind of abandon that included stroking and cupping her breasts and as she rocked and twisted her hips.

Our next pair of orgasms took us until the water was almost tepid and my heart raced, but fuck, it felt good to come inside her. We finished rinsing off lazily. I didn't even care about the almost cold water. Once I'd shut it off, Frankie reached for a towel and made another fantasy come true for me as she stood there dripping wet and naked in the bathroom, running her hands all over me along with the towel and pressing kisses here and there, including to my dick that twitched with promise.

We might even squeeze in round three if we handled it correctly. The hot suction of her mouth caught me off guard, and I glanced down to find her watching me as she sucked my softened dick between her lips.

Holy shit.

It was every fantasy I'd jerked off to in the ninth grade, and she kept the suction gentle and the tongue strokes firm until I was hardening between her lips. Not once did she pull away, in fact, she increased the pressure. When my cock bumped against her throat, she made a little gagging sound but wouldn't let me retreat.

"Fuck," I whispered. "Sorry." But her eyes held no censure, and the increased pressure accompanied by her hand fisting around my base had me coming in a rush. The hot release pulled my balls up tight and had me bracing one hand on the counter and the other in her hair.

Knees weak, as soon as she pulled off, I dropped to the floor next to her and kissed her. The lingering flavor of me was not remotely a deterrent. Arms around me, Frankie returned the kiss with enthusiasm. Fuck, we had a bed like ten feet away…

"Yo," Jake called as he knocked on the bedroom door. The sound stripped away my next fantasy. "We need to get a move on. The car is here. Dress now, fuck later."

"Who says we didn't already?" Frankie called, a daring grin on her lips. "You know, two or three times. Enough that I'll be a little sore for whatever we're doing next."

"You'll be fine," I assured her. "The flight isn't that long, and we're gonna be at the airport. I guarantee Archie will have a car waiting for us on the other side."

"Lucky bastard," Jake called again, then hit the door with one thump. "Glad you're enjoying yourself, Baby Girl. But let's go. Get dressed so we can get this summer vacay off to a great start."

Frankie burst out laughing and grinned at me. "Be hard to top this."

I opened my mouth to retort, then froze. I actually had an idea of *where* we were going and *why*. "Oh, sweetheart," I said slowly. "I am so proud of you. Were you determined to screw my brains out so I'd slip and tell you the surprise?"

A saucy smile curved her lips as she stood, and a lone drop sliding down her breast to linger over her nipple before it finally fell held me transfixed. "No," she assured me. "That was just a perk."

Brat.

I pinched her ass, and she laughed. We goofed around, but we did manage to dry, Frankie blew out her hair real quick, and then we both dressed. All of the guys were waiting for us when I opened the door.

The stares I got just made me grin. Not my fault she picked me over them. Archie just laughed though and shook his head as he held out a hand to Frankie. "You ready to go for a magic carpet ride, babe?"

"Magic carpet…" Frankie said slowly, and then her eyes got huge. "We're going to Orlando."

"That wasn't a question," Jake teased as he kissed her behind one ear before thumping me. We all set off together, and Frankie practically danced in place as we made it to the stairs.

"Are we going to Disney World?"

Archie made a point of looking thoughtful. "Do you want to go?"

That earned him a stare we would normally all avoid, but not Archie. He took that look like a challenge every time and just waited her out. Finally, she rolled her eyes and said, "Yes!"

"Good," Archie told her as Jeremy opened the doors for us to reveal the limo all decked out in festive black, round ears that also sparkled under the summer sun. "Because your magical carpet ride starts right here…"

Chapter Fifteen

HAPPIEST ESCAPE ON EARTH

FRANKIE

Laughter vied with disbelief, but both failed against the utter joy of the surprise. "Really?" And yes, it came out like a damn squeal. I didn't even care as I bounced up to throw my arms around Archie. He caught me close and hugged me. Then twisted to hand me to Jake. His arms tightened around me briefly before we turned, and then Ian just picked me up, laughing, and buried his face against my neck. I caught Coop's gaze over his shoulder, and the wide grin on his face just had my heart doing somersaults.

"Did all of you know?" I demanded, and Archie hooked an arm around my middle and tugged me back to him.

With a nip at my ear, he said, "They asked me to plan it because they figured I'd do it anyway."

At Jake's and Ian's equally pointed and exasperated looks, I laughed and rubbed Archie's arm. "I've always wanted to go to Disney World."

"We know," he told me, indulgent if a little smug grin in place. "Now, get in the car, Cinderella, we have a plane to catch."

I didn't have to ask if they'd packed for me, 'cause they probably had. It also explained the various *shopping* trips I'd been invited on, both with and without the guys. Jeremy waved us off. We definitely needed to bring him a souvenir.

The guys were teasing each other about what we had to do first when we got to Florida. I settled between Coop and Archie and just grinned at their teasing.

"Maybe we should ask Frankie what she wants to do," Ian pointed out with a wink toward me.

"That's easy," Jake said with a snort and an affectionate grin.

"She wants to do everything," Coop finished before nipping my ear, and I laughed. They weren't wrong.

"I'm just glad to escape together." The words kind of dimmed the humor, just a little bit. Escape seemed like a weird word. We were moving. We'd graduated. We'd already escaped. But since graduation, I'd been waiting for the other shoe to drop with Maddy. Not that she'd made a single appearance. I'd heard from Patience regularly. My dad's—Hank's text messages arrived right on time. In fact, I got one at the airport while we were waiting for our flight to board. He told me to have a great time, and I had to laugh. Of course the guys had told him.

I caught Archie watching me, and I shifted over two seats while Coop and Jake were hunting coffee. Ian was on my right now and Archie on my left. "You told my dad." It wasn't a question.

"I'm a Standish," Archie told me. "I have a lot of ground to make up for with your father. I figure this is a little way I can prove to him we have his little girl's interests at heart."

Ian said, "It's a good idea, Angel. We don't want anything to get in the way of this relationship. As long as it's what you want."

"Exactly. Not who I am or…"

"Stop," I told Archie with a hand over his. "Who you are is someone I love, very much. Hank knows that. If he doesn't accept you…I don't care what your last name is, you come first. All of you."

Nothing would change that. Not high school bitches. Not bullies. Not where I came from or who I came from and certainly not him.

"Especially since I think Grandpa Ted is the bomb," I continued, and Archie's grin grew wider and relief flickered in his dark eyes.

"I love you, babe," he whispered in that lower register that was almost a croon. The cup of his fingers against my jaw beckoned me forward, and he feathered a kiss over my lips. The fact Ian slid his hand over my free one and interlaced our fingers as Archie kissed me slow and sweet just made my heart swell.

Even as Archie released me, a smile still in his eyes, he slid his arm through mine and then captured my other hand. I leaned to rest my head against his shoulder and then stroked my thumb along the side of Ian's hand. A woman across the way just sort of stared at me, lips tight, frown firm, and an almost prudish look of distaste in her expression.

Coop cut off my view as he appeared with coffee and a grin. His smile faded as he looked at me, and before I could say anything, he twisted around and the woman who'd been scowling found somewhere else to stare.

"Yeah, I'd look somewhere else too. Your expression is gonna get stuck like that." He was *not* quiet about it, and Jake pivoted.

"Nope," I said with some vehemence as I straightened. "Don't…"

"Eh, she's not worth it," Jake said without raising his voice. He winked at me as he handed Ian his coffee. Coop passed me my own, and Archie took his. We had to unlock from each other to take them. Or I did at least. They settled into the seats opposite us, and Coop grumbled but Jake elbowed him. "Yo, I'm the hothead. Get back in your lane."

"Former hothead," Ian reminded him. "You're trying to turn over a new leaf."

"Yeah," Jake said slowly. "Not working for me so far. Not if our Zen master is going to take the leap off the deep end."

"You don't think you can handle being Zen if you swap?" I challenged, and Coop flashed me a quick grin.

Jake snorted. "If Coop wants hothead, then I want Bubba's."

Heat swept my face.

Ian just shook his head. "You couldn't handle my job without Coop's Zen mastery."

"Ha," Coop retorted. "Besides, I'd make a better Archie. I'm *very* good at spoiling our girl."

Archie smirked. "She only needs one of me. Besides, do you want me to be the Zen master?"

"Maybe," Coop said. "If you were after Bubba's job too. Give you a little flex room. Bubba could tackle hothead."

"But what happens to Bubba's job?" Archie challenged.

They were going to kill me with this.

"If—note I said *if*—I take hothead, Archie gets Zen, and you get Archie's daddy dom…"

Had he really just said…?

"That still leaves Jake with mine, and you said he wasn't ready for it."

Coop's whole expression fell.

"And you aren't ready for daddy dom," Ian continued, and I swore my face had to be the shade of my red Converse at the moment.

"Daddy dom?" Archie said. "Really? I just thought sexy multi-billionaire genius sex god worked fine."

"Except you're not really a multi-billionaire." Ian didn't argue the other points, and I was torn between embarrassment and laughter. Maybe both. Or none of the above?

"Yet." The confidence in Archie's voice couldn't be denied.

This whole conversation. I stared at Coop.

"Don't look at me like that," Coop said. "Not my fault. Blame Jake, he told me to get back in my lane, and apparently, we have lanes…"

"Hey…" Jake protested.

"Nor did I bring up someone else's dick in the shower." He did not.

Fuck me, he did.

To say it devolved from there… Well, I focused on my phone and sending texts to Rachel. She was less than helpful.

Rachel

You could have had all this, but you went for four of them. Just saying. You gotta take the bad with the good.

I laughed.

Me

Bitch.

Rachel

Yep and you love me for it.

I ended up sitting next to Ian, and he didn't press me for an answer. But for the sake of my ass, I gave him one anyway. A faint murmur in his ear about the piercing and the fact I had admitted I had no idea what one would feel like earned me a long, studying look and him stroking his lower lip with his thumb.

A shiver went through me.

Fine, if I got spanked, at least it would be for what I said directly. Besides, we were going to Disney World, I didn't think I'd be *sitting* long enough for a sore bottom to give me issues. "It was metaphorical," I promised him.

"But you are curious," he murmured almost to himself.

"I'm curious about a lot of things," I reminded him and caught his hand so I could kiss him lightly.

He chuckled. "Fair."

Jake twisted to look over the seat at us and he grinned wide. "So that's two out of four, but I think you're gonna have to make it up to all of us."

"Oh, that's fine. I'm only going to be sleeping with three of you, so I'll have plenty of time."

Archie's soft laughter drifted up from behind me, followed by Coop's muffled oath. Ian's grin widened, and even Jake looked amused.

I wasn't going to be the only one groveling on this trip. Though, I resisted Archie's suggestion of the mile-high club and prepayment. Just barely.

As soon as we landed though, I kind of forgot all about the teasing. They did too. I was practically buzzing as we grabbed our luggage and then went out to meet the car Archie had waiting for us. I didn't even question it, nor was I surprised. Not really.

The minute we were inside, however, I squealed and then climbed over to be closest to the big windows and twisted to look out at them. "Where are we staying?"

"You'll see," Archie teased, and I groaned at him, but you know what? I didn't care. We could stay at a motel by the airport, and I'd be happy. I was with my guys and we were going to go to the best damn place ever, and I couldn't wait.

The drive out of downtown took us through sunny Orlando. I had to laugh at the road construction. There was so much of it, and the traffic thickened then thinned. We passed literally dozens of hotels. "You know, I read somewhere that the majority of jobs in this area were in the hospitality business."

"Of course you did," Coop teased. "And you wonder why we waited to tell you where we were going."

"There's nothing wrong with researching a place," I told him primly, and Jake snorted a laugh.

"Not a thing at all, Baby Girl."

When we passed the sign welcoming us onto the property itself, I swore my eyes must have grown huge. That sense of vibrating in my soul seemed to expand everywhere. We were here. We were really going. I tried to catch the names on all the exit signs to get a clue for where we were going.

The hotel was the same one that was located right on the edge of the savannah. The whole place just radiated happy energy, and the music set the mood with the rhythm and the colorful outfits. I don't think my eyes had ever been this big.

I barely heard anything as we checked in to one of the fancier suites on the club level. The view from the room itself was incredible. I had the door open and I was out on the patio as Archie put in a call for lunch and drinks. My stomach rumbled in appreciation, but nothing could dissuade me from staying out here when a giraffe wandered by. I spotted some okapi, and there was a zebra.

The birds… There were so many birds.

Jake slid his arms around me. "You happy?"

I leaned back against his chest. "Deliriously."

"Not thinking about anyone else's dicks?" The tease as he nipped my ear with teeth just sharp enough to make it hurt had me bursting out laughing all over again. One of the okapi lifted their head and stared up at me like they wanted to shush me, and I clapped a hand over my mouth.

"I promise," I stage-whispered. "I was never thinking about anyone else's anyway."

"Good," he murmured. "I'll let you make it up to me later."

I snorted, head back against his shoulder. "Only if you make up to me the fact you won't get a piercing."

This time, he bit my throat and sucked against the spot to bring the bruise up. Damn hickey monsters. "That's for being a brat," he said with an unrepentant grin.

Twisting in his arms, I hopped up, trusting in the fact he'd catch me. Jake didn't disappoint, cupping his hands under my ass and lifting me as I hitched my thighs to his hips. I nipped his lower lip with a kiss before returning his hickey with one of my own. The stubble of his beard reminded me that he hadn't shaved in a couple of days. Not that I minded it.

He looked good all rough and tumble. His chuckle as I sucked at the hickey made me smile. "Is that for me being a brat too?"

"Yep."

"Come on, lovebirds," Coop called as he tugged the door open. "Lunch is here, and then we're planning what parks we're hitting first."

"Yay!" I let out a squeal and slid down Jake with a little more contact than necessary. His eyes sparked, but I escaped around Coop before Jake could retaliate. As it was, I climbed right over Ian to use him as protection.

Lunch was all kinds of appetizers along with burgers and fries. Staples. No arguments here. Archie had out his phone and a series of brochures for the different parks. "Frankie, pick a park, any park." He fanned them out like they were cards, and I chewed my lip.

I wanted to see all of them. At once.

Four hours later, I was hoarse from screaming my way through a ride. The roller coaster in the dark, twisting and turning, was terrifying enough. The fact there were actual stars and planets to look at meant I couldn't close my eyes. Not if I wanted to see everything. Worse, there was no way to sit *next* to anyone. So I had to ride in the single seat sandwiched between Coop and Archie.

Coop took the front and Archie the back. I actually reached forward and put a hand on Coop's shoulder, and Archie had his hands on mine. It was the only thing that kept my freakout in check. Of course, I totally wanted to do it again, and this time, I rode with Ian in front and Jake behind me.

I caught almost all the stars.

We only took a break to grab some ice cream and bless them for having a Starbucks right there too. Then we were off to more adventures. We swung into every gift shop. We all had new shirts—hell, we were going to end up with new wardrobes. We each had gotten character watches, and I had to laugh when

Archie bought me a brand-new charm bracelet. My old one was getting full, and this one was already sporting new charms to mark the occasion.

I elected for matching hats rather than ears, because not all of the guys would wear the ears. Brats. But I did get some glittery ones to wear, and we stopped at every picture spot in the place and took all the photos. By the time we found a spot to watch the fireworks, I was torn between elation and exhaustion. The ground was hot, so Jake pulled me over into his lap, while Archie and Ian went to buy stuff for us to sit on.

"This is the best vacation ever," I murmured as I stared up at the brightly lit castle. My stomach ached from laughing, my cheeks hurt, and at the same time, I couldn't count how many moments had been the best because all of them were.

It was the most ridiculously awesome vacation.

"I thought Colorado was the best vacation ever," Jake murmured against my hair, and I grinned.

"It was. The best winter vacation."

"Oh, sweet save," he teased, and I laughed. The guys brought snacks and drinks back with them—it was always a time for ice cream. Even with the blanket to sit on, I stayed in Jake's lap and leaned back against his chest so I could stare up. The fireworks were a show unto themselves with music, explosions, and even flickering pictures and art from laser lights everywhere.

It was cool.

We all ended up with the most ridiculous light toys that had Archie and Jake talking about how they could improve them. If we didn't end up with lightsabers before we were done with this trip, I would have to swear I didn't know these guys. And I had no intention of swearing that.

Jake weaved one of the light necklaces, creating three different length ones that I could wear before he was done. The air cooled as the sun went down, and even though the humidity had kept all of us sweaty, I didn't care and neither did they. That was what shorts and tank tops were for, although I'd switched to a crop top after the other had gotten soaking wet.

I didn't care, but Jake got feisty at guys staring at my bra. Coop and Ian had both become roadblocks in front of me—this new possessive side of Coop was a definite turn on—while Archie laughed at all of them.

Though turnabout had proven fair play when we stood in line for one ride and there was a girl who did everything but flash her boobs at Ian to get his attention. Not that he bothered to look at her once. Didn't stop me from smiling at her, then standing on my tiptoes to give him a very solid kiss, one he returned easily and with a lot of affection. Our audience made a huffing noise, then looked at Jake.

"Taken," he informed her. "All of us are. Shoo."

That had me giggling. In fact, I giggled about it all over again when I saw that same girl as we climbed onto the ferry to head back to the parking lots. She stared at us of course. I was riding on Ian's back because my feet hurt, and as soon as we were onboard, we went up to the top deck.

"Enjoying yourself?" Archie asked, not missing where my gaze went, and I grinned at him.

"Oh yeah, and I promise to show you all just how much when we get back."

Considering how tired I was, that was an ambitious promise. That said, it was seriously the best day ever.

Until the next day, when Ian stole me out from between Jake and Coop, or later when Archie pulled me into the shower after we got back from a crazy day of play.

And the day after that.

Then the day we spent at the water parks.

On the fifth day, we headed out to the swimming pool after sleeping in. Well, after Jake woke me up with slow kisses and caresses and Coop watched us. Not that he hadn't been invited, he just waited until I was spent before rolling me over and working me all up again.

To say it was nearly lunchtime before we emerged would've been an understatement. Archie just shook his head and said that I was sleeping with him that night so I could get some actual sleep. That just had all of us scoffing.

Still, a day at the pool let me show off another of my suits. I'd worn the mostly one piece—sorta—to the water park. But I'd pulled out a bikini for lounging around the pool. The guys played and I read a book while I sunned myself, but at one point, I moved under an umbrella before I got a burn. The next day was gonna be our last, so we all voted on what would be our last stop.

We went back to the beginning, and the guys indulged me as I got pictures with every single character we could find. In fact, we divided our time between rides and photos and a little shopping.

I found some gifts for Rachel. I was pretty sure the glitter pink and fuzzy crowned mouse ears were going to be a real hit. I even found something distinguished for Jeremy, and the cats all got upgraded food bowls and a new water bowl. I might have had a little panic attack when I realized quite how much I'd been spending, but Archie talked me down with coffee and ice cream.

Then he promised me I could pay for all my purchases, but not the hotel, even if I wanted to. The hotel had been paid for, and it was a present. I wasn't allowed to pay for presents.

That logic was such bullshit, but his smile was so genuine and his eyes so earnest, I had a hard time saying no, especially when he got me a second round of chocolate chip ice cream.

"Fine, but our next vacation, I better get to split it fifty-fifty," I told him, and he just grinned.

"Babe, I love you. If you think the guys and I are ever going to let you pay a full half of—"

"Fifty-fifty, Standish. What's the point of the money if I can't spoil you guys too?"

At that, he opened his mouth, then snapped it shut as he considered me.

"Sucks to fight your own logic, doesn't it?" It was a little win, but I'd take it.

"Maybe," he mused. "I'll find a way around that."

"But until then…" We toasted with our ice cream spoons, and then I dove back into mine and Archie laughed. We were still laughing when the guys found us.

The next morning, I really didn't want to leave. "I don't want to go home," I groaned, and Archie slapped my ass.

"Who said we were going home?" He was way too damn cheerful. "Now come on, beautiful. Roll over. I want to eat you out until you scream and come all over my tongue at least twice before we shower."

Wait…what? Not that he gave me any time to process that before his sinful mouth made good on that promise.

Chapter Sixteen
NO SHOES, NO SHIRTS, NO PEOPLE

FRANKIE

We left the parks much the way we'd arrived, via limo that took us to the airport, but this time to a private airstrip rather than checking in at the commercial terminals. I slanted a look from one smug face to the next as the limo wound its way around and finally pulled up next to a private plane.

Standish owned their own airline.

Sometimes I forgot that.

The driver moved around to the rear door and opened it to let us out, even as two other crew members approached the trunk and opened it to begin removing the luggage. No, I wasn't going to admit to the moderate amount of embarrassment that not *all* our luggage was in the trunk. We'd sent some bags back to Jeremy to join our other items shipping northward, and another set had already been brought to the airport.

Archie slid out and paused long enough to hold out a hand for me. I gave him a look, and his eyes just twinkled. Behind me, Coop and Jake both chuckled. Incorrigible shits. Outside, the breeze carried elements of metal and fuel.

"Private plane?"

"Yep," Archie told me, the corners of his lips twitching as he practically vibrated with the dare.

"Hmm." I had to bite the inside of my lip to keep my expression in check. "Nice." Playing it cool was not my forte. Nor was it in my nature to hide my reactions, so I turned my back as I headed for the steps leading up into the plane itself.

I'd been on exactly zero private planes in my life. Archie's faint grunt of disbelief chased me. Beyond him, Ian's soft chuckle joined with Coop's and Jake's. I gripped the handrail and then gave into the giggle working its way free and tossed a look over my shoulder.

"Oh, you little..." Archie began, but I was already scrambling inside. Served him right. The teasing play muted some when the flight staff greeted us. Actual staff—two flight attendants, a pilot, and a co-pilot. The plane didn't seem so huge on the outside, but it was far more spacious on the inside. A table with chairs. A sofa, lounging area, an actual bathroom with a shower.

Holy crap.

There was even a bedroom onboard.

A shiver went through me.

The staff would be toward the front of the plane where there was also a galley. The pricey coffeemaker promised just how lush and ritzy the plane was.

"Good morning, we're still waiting for final clearances. Flight time to Los Angeles is expected to be just under six hours. We will handle refueling and picking up the rest of the catering for the next leg of the flight. In the meantime, can I get you anything else?" The flight attendant's nametag read 'Sandy.'

"That's great, thank you."

Once we were alone, I turned on the guys. "Explain."

"You trust me," Archie coaxed, and I rolled my eyes.

"Without question, but private plane? Los Angeles? What are we doing?"

"Friends of my grandfather loaned us the use of their island for a week, so we're heading to Fiji, where we'll take a yacht to the island."

A yacht.

A private island.

I sank back in my seat and gaped.

"To be fair," Coop offered, "the island thing threw us too."

"Not as much as the yacht," Jake murmured. "Or the plane."

"I've learned to just appreciate Archie's generosity," Ian teased. "Just like you do. But if you don't like it, Angel…"

I flicked a look at him. "How could I not possibly like it? But this is… It's almost too much." It was a kind of affluent lifestyle we watched on television or in the movies. "This is like Bruce Wayne or Tony Stark level stuff."

"Batman or Iron Man?" Archie's grin grew. "I'll take it. But seriously, babe, we wanted to take you to the beach, and we wanted you to ourselves. The parks were a blast." They had been, but we'd been surrounded by people. "On the island, we can skinny dip, you can sun topless if you want…"

Jake almost growled, and I wasn't the only one who glanced at him.

"The only people who will see her is us," Archie continued. "That's why the private island works, besides this is all about us. But if you don't…"

I reached across the table and tangled my fingers with his. "I want."

Even if I never got used to the insanity of how they spent money.

Head back, I interlocked my fingers with Archie's as I rode his dick, slow and steady. Fuck, he felt so fucking good inside of me. Every surge of his hips pushed him up to meet me. Sweat slid down between my breasts, the sensation just adding another tingle to the riot each time I took him to the hilt. Leaning upward, Archie dragged me down until my nipple was at his mouth.

The scrape of his teeth pulled at me, even as he let go of my hands and gripped my hips. Urgency had me bracing my hands on the wall above his head as he tilted my ass up. My first orgasm was right there, and I let out a cry as I chased it. He alternated between hard sucking pulls on my nipple and biting down gently. The conflicting sensations only heightened my awareness.

"There," I moaned, fisting his hair as he slammed me down on his dick. Every strike at that spot had me seeing stars, and he bit off an oath as I flexed and pulsed around him. The orgasm was both sweet and shattering. Only after he rolled me onto my back did I realize… "Archie…"

"Shh, babe. I promise, it's all going to feel really good in a minute." His cock was still long, thick, and curved. The vein along the glistening bottom of it seemed to pulse. I reached out for him, but he pinned my hands. "Trust me."

Two words that melted me every time he said them. They were both a promise and a plea.

He slid down the bed, and then his mouth was on my quaking pussy, licking, nipping, and sucking as he sent me tumbling over the edge. I was still shaking that fog when he speared two fingers into my ass and began to work me loose.

"Do you remember that first night in my bed?" he asked against my thigh just before he bit, sucking gently at the hickey he favored right there. A part of me wanted to get a little tattoo there, just for him, so he didn't have to worry about his mark ever fading away.

"Every minute." The last word rode a moan as he added a third finger. I was so used to this now, I welcomed the stretch and burn. Sometimes, the guys even talked me into wearing a plug during the day so I would be ready at any point. But this was the first time Archie had just gone for my ass alone.

He'd done it for my birthday. That and… Another shudder went through me as I thought of him and Ian filling me at once.

"Good, I'm going to keep one of those promises right now, babe," Archie whispered. He gave my pussy one last lick before he eased his fingers out and moved away. He left the bed for a second, and I pushed up on my elbows slowly. Every limb was shaking. I'd put it down to air turbulence, but there was none.

And I was floating higher than this plane if that were possible. Archie didn't leave me long, he came back with a condom on his dick, and it glistened with fresh lube. I stared at him as he knelt between my legs and teased his tip against the rosette of my ass.

"I'm going to fuck you until you come," he promised. "I'm going to fill you until the only thing you need to find pleasure is the feel of my cock bottoming out in you. Filling your pussy," he continued breaching past that tight ring of muscles with the most seductive burn. I didn't take my eyes off his the whole time. "The stroke of me in your mouth, filling your throat..."

"The taste of you," I whispered, and he thrust forward abruptly. "The salty sweetness that's all you, Archie. I love how it feels when you fill me, when you taste me, when you touch me." He bit the underside of my nipple, and I let out a sharp gasp because he'd bottomed out into my ass, then I let out a cry. Oh, so full.

This was so different from when he took my pussy, and yet I couldn't look away from him as he began a slow, punishing rhythm that demanded all my attention. The stroke of their cocks in my pussy was one thing, but my ass was something else. Too often, it was only when they shared.

"I love your pussy," Archie said, sweat dampening his brow. "I love how it feels when you flex around me, when you flutter and milk me. But this ass... Fuck me, babe, this ass of yours."

A convulsion went through me, a lazy heat that went from warm and simmering to molten and surging through my system. Archie slammed his mouth down on mine, siphoning the oxygen as he chased my tongue with his, mirroring every thrust of his dick.

Only on a handful of occasions had any of them done this, alone, and fuck me, it shredded me in all the best ways. I swore I screamed before his fingers skated over my swollen clit, but that was almost too much. Fingers dug into his shoulders, I sucked on his tongue, even as tears dampened my face and he swallowed my cries.

With one last furious and punishing thrust, he let out a shout of his own, and then we locked around each other, trembling.

I lost track of how long we lay there when Archie nuzzled a kiss behind my ear and eased himself out of me. "Thank you for my induction into the mile-high club," he whispered, and heat flushed my whole body. A first he'd saved for me.

The tears on my cheeks grew even wetter. His smile softened as he brushed them away.

"We're going to make every year better," he swore to me, and I didn't doubt him for an instant.

We landed in Los Angeles on schedule, but we didn't linger past the refuel and taking on dinner as well as breakfast. The next leg of the flight was ten hours. The guys had cards and movies. Jake tugged me back into the bedroom as soon as we'd reached cruising altitude and finished dinner. We were chasing the sunset, in a way.

Instead of getting naked, we curled up together in the middle of the bed, Jake playing with my hair and my head tucked against his chest. The steady rhythm of his heart made me smile.

"Sometimes I miss you," I murmured. He wore one of the new tank tops we'd picked up on vacation. It left his arms bare, and I could trace the muscle of his biceps with my eyes or my fingers. Tilting my head up, I found him smiling at me. He hadn't shaved in five days, and I was getting used to the itchy scruff, even when it left beard burn following his kisses.

"I'm right here, Baby Girl. Why are you missing me?"

"I don't know," I admitted. "Sometimes, you feel distant and I know it's not just you. It's me too. There's always something that seems to tug at me, pulling me away and…" I hesitated. I'd been hesitant to bring this up before, but even more so now. This vacation was exactly what we needed.

Disney World had been fantastic, don't get me wrong. But there was something insulating about the five of us on board the plane together.

"I'm right here, Baby Girl. Sometimes the other guys just need you more. I'm good with us, don't worry. If you need me or want more of me, you just say the word." He flexed his arms around me, and I rubbed my cheek against his chest. "You and Bubba are going to nail this recording deal, and then you're gonna be this big star and I'm going to be right there making sure no one bugs you."

I laughed. "I don't care about being a star. I want to be there when you and Archie invent the self-driving car that responds to voice commands or the fully automated house or…I don't know, the robot Jeremy."

His laughter rumbled in his chest. "Not sure what Jeremy would think if we replaced him with a robot."

"Me neither," I said, making a face. "But I want to support you in everything you do. I want to be right there to cheer you on. I mean, I went to some of your football games, you know."

The shake of his laughter deepened, and then he rolled me over so we were side by side, our heads on the pillows so we could stare at each other. "You support me every day. Now, is this about how much I've been talking to my dad?"

"No," I said slowly, frowning. "I'm glad you and your dad are talking again. I'm glad that you want to talk to him…even if some of those conversations haven't been the best."

They didn't always end their calls on a particularly happy note. "Dad is stuck in his beliefs," Jake said, with a shrug. "As open as he is about relationships, theirs and ours, he's still convinced that I am doing myself and the country a disservice because I don't want to enlist."

I sighed. "I would miss you so damn much."

He chuckled. "We'd manage, if it was what I wanted. See, I know you, Baby Girl." With light fingers, he traced them over my cheek. "You would cut off an arm to help any of us do whatever we wanted. I don't want to go into the military. I see the benefits and I see the drawbacks. But in the long run, that's not where I see my life in five, ten, or fifteen years."

Surprise flickered through me. "Where do you see your life?"

"Right here," he murmured, trailing his hand lower until he rested it over my breast, just above my heart. "This is where I see my future. I'm just lucky that we have the family built for this. So no more worrying about me. If I need more, I'll ask for more, and the same for you. Deal?"

The corners of his mouth curved, yet it was the warmth in his eyes holding me hostage.

"Deal," I agreed. "But…" I pressed a finger to his lips. "We have one other serious discussion to have." His eyebrows raised, and I grinned. "Someone wanted to get a tattoo this summer, and I'm not sure when you're planning on getting it with all this crazy traveling."

And had I mentioned how damn happy I was that we'd all gotten our passports done? Archie had one, but now all of us did. It made the seemingly spontaneous foreign travel arrangements easier.

Jake laughed and sat up, then stripped off his shirt before twisting to face me. Rolling on my back, I stared up at him. Rugged. Hot. Charming.

"So, I'm thinking dragons…" And a bit of a dork.

But he was my dork. And I loved every damn inch of him.

"Show me," I said as he began tracing where he wanted the first dragon to go. It would wrap around him from his back to his chest, with the wings on his back. Holy shit, that would be hot.

Our flight arrived a little after ten at night, local time. Private customs greeted us and stamped our passports, admitting us to the country. Cars met us and took us and our luggage to the yacht. Seriously, I couldn't wait to see it. I couldn't figure out why I was yawning. I'd slept. I'd actually fallen asleep with Jake and woken to Coop tucked in with us about an hour before we landed.

One perk of flying that way, I was able to shower and change before we landed. Still, I wanted to look and see. We had a late supper on the deck of the yacht. The ocean scents teased at us, and there were lots of stars visible, even with the light source from the island itself. I wanted to go and explore, but we weren't staying in Fiji proper, not this trip.

This trip.

I loved the sound of that. How many more trips would we take? I used to think I'd have to save up forever to travel. Yet now, I could literally travel whenever I wanted. Wherever I wanted. A part of me had always known Archie would take me if I asked, but there was a difference between having him take me and being able to go.

More, I liked going with them. In addition to our meal, there was wine, and I raised my brows. It was Jake who filled my glass and said, "Legal drinking age is eighteen here, so we're fine."

Laughter rippled around the table. Glasses raised, I said, "To you guys, thank you for this amazing vacation."

"It's not remotely close to done, Angel," Ian pointed out.

"Nor have we even had half the time on it we wanted yet," Coop agreed. "We are making up for last summer…"

"And beginning traditions. June is gonna be our month, all five of us," Archie said firmly. "From now on, no matter what we're doing or where we are with careers or school, June is the month we spend together, and if that means we spend it on tour with you and Bubba, or back in Texas visiting their families, or finding some new hot spot to travel to, then that's what we do. But this is our month together. For us. As a family."

I loved that so much.

We clinked our glasses together, and I grinned. After dinner, the guys traded out their wine for beer while I stuck with the wine. We lounged around on the deck chairs, staring at the sky and trading stories. The weather was just about perfect. It wasn't hot or cold. The breeze was comfortable, the air beautiful, and sometime between Archie and Jake's debate on something to do with circuitry and Coop settling me against his chest while Ian pulled out his guitar, I fell asleep.

The next time I opened my eyes, the sun was turning the horizon pink, golden, and red. It was…a postcard, it was so perfect. All around me, the guys slept. We'd all just fallen asleep up here with light blankets. Coop was still tucked next to me, but I was able to just sit up and stare out as the sun rose.

There weren't a lot of truly perfect moments. Yet here, surrounded by the guys, with the remnants of our lazy dinner from the night before as the sun rose— not only on the other side of the world from home, but in another hemisphere—I was flying higher than the little wisps of pink clouds painting against the rapidly brightening navy sky.

This time, a year ago, Maddy let me down for the hundredth time. No trip to Harvard. She'd gone off on business. I'd shut the guys out. I worked, hid out in my apartment, and left only for one long weekend to see Jennifer in San Antonio.

Fuck, I hadn't talked to her in months. A little laugh escaped me. Rachel was still on my shit list for having ripped the blinders off me, and now her absence was probably the only thing really dimming today, and even that couldn't do it. Mostly because I knew she was where she wanted to be.

"You okay over there, Angel?" Ian asked me quietly, and I grinned at him.

"I'm perfect."

He rose, raking a hand through all that gorgeous blond hair and looking sleep rumpled and beautiful. With ease, he plucked me up and cradled me to him. "Yes, you are."

I chuckled as I looped my arms around him. "I wasn't fishing for compliments."

"I know," he teased before rubbing his nose against mine. "Just remember how much I love you."

"I have no intention of forgetting."

"Good."

I should have known better. That heart stopping grin of his bewitched me though, and it barely registered that we were moving before it was too late. Ian jumped right off the end of the yacht into the near crystal perfect water.

At least I didn't scream too loud.

But we weren't in the water alone for long. The whoops from the guys as they plunged over the side and into the water with us just made me laugh. The crew was already readying for our departure by the time we climbed out of the water and then back onto the yacht. I rinsed off below deck and changed into a suit with a sarong I could tie around my waist. The water around us was so crystal perfect, it was right out of a magazine.

I'd pinch myself, but I didn't want to wake up from this dream.

Ever.

SUBJECT: COVER OPPORTUNITY READ ASAP

Hey! Answer me as soon as you get this. We're putting together a charity album and inviting some of our favorites to do covers of our songs. Since you are such big fans and cool (okay, let's be blunt, I like you two more than I like most of our peers), the girls and I thought we'd give you an opportunity to record a cover of one of our songs.

Pick your favorite. Pick one you like. But tell me which one so I can lock it up. If it all works out, we'll even let you guys use it on your first album, but only if you let me join you for some kind of trio moment. Or maybe a five way. Think your boy can handle four girls at once?

Okay, that was way dirtier than I intended.

Email me. Or better yet, call me. I have no idea what country we're in, but voicemail works.

Kisses.

KC

Chapter Seventeen
BEACH BUMS AND BABE

FRANKIE

The temptation to re-enact the *Titanic* scene was way too cheesy to resist. Bless Jake for hopping right up there with me on the prow. He locked one arm around my waist as I stretched my arms wide, and we yelled out that we were king of the world.

The guys laughed and there were pictures and I didn't care. The sun in our face, the ocean around us, and the way the yacht sliced through the water just added to the whole experience. I ducked below deck to change at one point, opting for short shorts over my bikini bottoms and a bikini top.

Jake grumbled a little when I came back up, hair pulled up into a pony tail. Hands on my hips, I stood by the door and waited him out. Coop's lips twitched, but his eyes were hidden behind his sunglasses. I couldn't see Archie or Ian from this angle, but neither of them usually minded how much skin I showed.

This bikini was hardly indecent, but there was side boob.

A muscle twitched in Jake's cheek, but it was hard to tell because the adorable scruff had been filling in. I bit my lip and raised my brows. The air out there was exceptional. We were all still tired, but it was a lazy kind of tired and I wanted to be out in the sun.

"I'm putting sunscreen on you," he conceded grumpily before stepping aside. Relief and delight combined to flood through me. Coop let out a low whistle and then tilted his head back as though he needed to sun himself. Archie and Ian both grinned at me as Jake became the shadow at my back.

Yes, the yacht had a crew. We'd met like two of them, the rest had just gone about their business and ignored us. I didn't even know whose yacht this was. Archie's? His grandfather's? Their friend's? Worse, I didn't want to ask because I was half in love with this vessel, and if it turned out to belong to someone else, I might cry.

Don't be ridiculous, it's probably a family yacht. Shuttling those thoughts away, I tucked my sunglasses on as I headed for one of the loungers. Once I was on my stomach, Jake tugged open the strap on the back of my suit, and I smiled. The coolness of the sunscreen on his fingers had me sighing as he began to rub it in. I'd done the same earlier, making sure all of them had their backs done. He paid particular attention to my tattoo.

"Do you guys want to work on that song this weekend?" Archie asked. "We have the island for five days, but I can probably make it a week."

"No," I said from where I lay with my eyes closed. "I mean, Ian and I can work on it some, but I want this week to be about all of us too. And you said something about boogie boarding."

Surfing. Snorkeling. Skinny dipping.

They were all on the list.

Archie chuckled. The push of Jake's fingers dipping below my waistband had me shifting to glance up at him. A smirk played at the corners of his mouth. Dammit, I curled my toes and then slid my legs apart as he worked his way down to my thighs. The top of the shorts wouldn't give him much access but...

"We can do both," Ian suggested as Jake smoothed sunscreen up and down the backs of my legs. He kept darting up the inside of my thighs and away again. "Don't worry, Angel. The point is to be together, and if we start boring the guys, I'm sure they'll make you play a few hours of video games."

I laughed. "That's not a threat. You guys just knock me out, then try to convince me to get naked."

"If I have my way, you won't be dressed at all for the next few days, so getting you naked won't be a problem." Archie raised his beer toward me, and I laughed as he took a drink. But the fact Ian just nodded as if the thought had occurred to him had me shivering all over again.

Private island.

No people.

Just us—

Jake slid his fingers right up between my legs, and I let out a little sigh as he shifted on the seat. The tease of his fingers along my labia sent a curl of lust through my system. The sun. The sea. The guys.

"Cold?" Jake asked in a soft voice, and I bit my lip. His gaze was so intent on me, it threatened to burn me up.

All the moisture in my mouth seemed to dry up, but I shifted my legs just a little further apart. "Do I feel cold?"

With one hand against my back, Jake leaned over me, and I had a feeling it was more to block what he was doing from the others than anything else. The thrust of his fingers into me had me swallowing a moan. The blunt tips of his nails scraped gently, just enough to sharpen my focus on the feel of him without injuring.

The two fingers together weren't as thick as any of them, and at the same time, when he scissored his fingers, I swore liquid heat spiraled outward from the contact. I moved on his hand, and it rubbed the seam of my shorts right against my clit. The spasms ignited by the contact had me contracting around his hand, and Jake's soft laugh in my ear was dizzying.

"You like that, Baby Girl?" He teased his tongue over the shell of my ear, and I let my eyes close as my nipples beaded tight. The urge to turn over and reach for him vibrated beneath my skin. The breeze on my overheated flesh suggested that might be a bad idea.

Ian's and Archie's voices faded as Jake's hot breath feathered over my ear.

"What about this?" He curved his hand, and it pushed my right thigh higher. The thrusting of his fingers added another sharp contact of pleasure that only increased when two blunt fingers became three.

Fuck.

The shorts hadn't seemed so loose before. I swore the breeze chased his fingers against my skin, and it only made the heat inside of me grow more intense.

"I can't hear you," Jake murmured a moment before he bit down on my ear and increased the push of his hand. The force ground me against the seam, even as he mimed the force of his dick taking me. While it didn't quite push me over the edge, it had me riding the precipice, breath coming in little explosions.

Somehow between gently massaging sunscreen onto my back and teasing me, he'd left me soaked and needy.

"Aren't you going to answer me, Baby Girl?" Jake drew me back to him, and I forced my eyes open to find him staring down at me. Wordless wonder flooded me as I opened my mouth, and then his lips claimed mine and thought erased as he added a fourth finger. The combined pressure threatened to split me apart. All subtlety failed me as I ground against his hand, the chair, my shorts, anything to get just that little bit more of friction.

The warmth of a hand pressing under my chest jerked my eyes open as Jake smiled against my mouth. The pinch of scorching fingers on my nipple sent a blood rush to my head, and I came apart. A cry tore free from my throat as Jake sucked on my tongue. Breath escaping in panting explosions, I dug my fingers into the chair.

Where we were trickled back in like the dampness escaping me as Jake eased his fingers free. The trembling in my legs and body kept me glued to the chair. A hand traced over my hair, then fisted it gently.

Jake's kiss turned softer and sweeter as he nibbled his way along my lips as though he only wanted to sample each breath. Even the click of our sunglasses glancing off each other didn't puncture the moment. Pulse galloping, I went boneless, trusting his grip on me to keep me from floating away.

"Mr. Standish…" At the intrusion of the accented voice, I stiffened.

"I'll join you in a moment, Captain." The words and tone brooked no argument. Jake soothed his hand over my back as I shivered. I missed when he'd pulled his fingers from me, then he broke the kiss to suck on one finger, then another, as though licking them clean. I couldn't miss the scent of me on him or the way his eyes lit up as he stayed so close.

The flash of his tongue had my toes curling.

"Better?" Jake asked.

I grinned slowly. "Perfect."

"Fuck yes, you are," Coop let out with a grunt of appreciation, and bit by bit, where we were registered again. I lifted my head just a bit higher as Jake glanced over at Coop. "What?" Coop demanded in a heated voice. "She's fucking perfect."

My gaze locked on Ian's though, I couldn't see his eyes through the sunglasses nor he mine, but I swore I could feel him all the way down to my toes. "Did you enjoy that, Angel?" Dark promise kissed each word, and I couldn't resist smiling at him or a little nod, because I wasn't sure if my voice would come out as more than a squeak.

"Fuck, I did," Archie said on a groan. "I'd have enjoyed it more if it had been my dick she was riding as she squirmed like that."

"You'll get your chance," Ian said, and a flush of heat crashed through me like a lava eruption boiling to the surface.

"Not arguing," Jake said, the teasing words anchoring me. They were all watching me, and I wanted to fucking preen under the attention. "Just cool down, player three."

A snort escaped me before I could stop it, and I clapped a hand over my mouth. There was a beat, then laughter erupted all around us and Jake grinned down at me. As much as Jake and I liked to push it when we were out in "public" spaces, I had great faith that no one could see me, so I rolled over and he trailed his gaze down at me as the bikini top fell away.

"Fuck me," Archie swore. "Let me deal with the captain." The scrape of his deck chair warned me of his exit.

"You're playing with fire, Angel," Ian warned.

I grinned and then stretched my arms above me. The combined heated stares kept any chill from even reaching my skin. "So," I asked. "Who's going to put sunscreen on my front?"

What fun was there in playing with fire if you didn't get burned?

Despite my best efforts at teasing, the rest of my morning sunbathing on the deck went uninterrupted. None of the crew came anywhere near us, and Archie confirmed I wasn't visible from the upper deck before Jake could complain. A part of me wanted to doze, but I enjoyed listening to them talk too much.

The captain warned us about an hour out from the island, and I sat up and let Jake tie the bikini back into place before lunch arrived. Lunch was mostly cold meats, breads, and fruit. It all came with cool water and even colder wine. I had one small glass of the wine, but I didn't want it to go to my head.

I wasn't hot at all, but I was warm. The sun off the water and the island coming into view as we sliced from deeper water into those more crystal clear had me moving with the guys to watch as the island grew bigger and bigger.

Tucked between Jake and Archie against the rail, I braced against them, not that I had to worry. They each kept a hand on me as the yacht slowed to give us our best look yet. Not only was the beach almost pearlescent and the trees and foliage green and lush, the house sat up on a little hill away from the water, but it was…almost majestic.

Excitement thrummed through me. The yacht couldn't go all the way in, so we transferred onto a smaller craft. Apparently, there was a dock on the far side that we could also use if the water was too rough, but as the agitation generated by the engines calmed, the water smoothed like glass. Well, at least until we were getting in the oversized rubber boat.

I would look up the terms later. Our luggage would come over after us. Apparently, that had been part of Archie's coordination with the captain earlier. Archie and Ian were already in the boat when I made my step over. I wasn't too worried about falling in, but they were all making sure I didn't even take a misstep.

Settled between Ian and Archie for this leg, I let out a laugh as the outboard motor fired up and we raced across the water toward the shore. I gripped the guys and the side of the boat as we skimmed. Thank fuck I wasn't the only one whooping.

The two crew members helping laughed at us. I wanted to jump off like they did as we rode right up the surf to the sandy beach. But Ian's hand clamped down on my thigh when I went to move, and I made a face at him. As soon as the crew dragged us up on the sand, I was up and we were all out.

What a beautiful freaking place.

It was a slice of paradise. Ian lifted my hand for a kiss before he handed it to Coop. I swore they were trying to keep me out of the way, but Ian joined Archie and Jake as they waited for the second skiff—that was the word—bringing our luggage.

"Grunt work or exploring?" Coop asked, and I twisted to look at him. He let out a laugh and then called out, "We're heading up to the house."

"It'll be open," Archie said, and I blew him a kiss. I could almost see his wink behind the sunglasses.

"I totally have to jump Archie, later," I told Coop as we hit the steps winding up the near tropical path to the house. "I mean, seriously jump him."

"I'm down," Coop told me with a grin. "You mind if I make popcorn before I watch?"

I paused a couple of steps above him and then gripped his face. His mouth opened to my kiss easily, and he banded his arms around my middle. Lifting me off my feet, he hugged me tight. I could drown in this kiss. It had begun as me wanting to share his joy and turned into him flooding me with it.

"I love you," I whispered when I lifted my head. "And I love that you love when I love them."

"You have no idea," he whispered. "Watching you as you come, knowing you'd do the same for me and have, while they make you fall apart, and I can just savor every little gasp, flush, and sweet scream? It's the fucking best, Frankie. I just have to ask…did you talk to Arch and Bubba?"

"No," I confessed. "They're letting you watch all on their own. You and Jake—I think you're helping them do it. And I think the fact they are both trusting me more helps."

His eyes narrowed. "They trusted you before. What the—"

BFF Coop who teased and played with me so easily would always be my favorite, but possessive and protective Coop opened up other sides of his personality that I adored. The ferociousness in his eyes heated me from the inside out.

"Not what I meant," I assured him and brushed my fingers over his lips. "I think we're all trusting each other more. Everything changed at Christmas. It changed again on my birthday…"

His smile turned sinful. "True."

"And we're all discovering new boundaries. So don't think I'm worried, I'm not." Funnily enough, that was so damn true. I was so fucking excited about where we were going and what we were doing. The journey—we were journey and destination. Anticipation quivered through me. "Now, we were going to explore?"

Coop still held me up, and I stroked his cheek. Over his shoulder, the beautiful blue ocean filled my view. The guys were below, offloading the luggage, and the yacht was in the distance. But it was so quiet and yet alive with the calls of birds, the rustle of leaves, and the soft hush of Coop's breathing.

Another kiss, then he set me down. As I turned, he landed a slap on my ass, and I startled before he gripped and rubbed the spot he'd slapped. The rush of dampness to my thighs should've been embarrassing, but fuck that.

"So is it just with Bubba?"

"No," I admitted. Though to be honest, I would always kneel for Ian. My Ian owned a part of me that he'd helped me find, and we were discovering more about her every day.

"Good to know," he said, his playful grin making me laugh. I let him get ahead of me and then retaliated, landing a slap against his ass that made my palm burn. He shot me a look as I massaged the spot. "Testing a theory?"

"Depends—would you let me?"

Boldness flickered through me, and Coop considered me for a moment as I gripped his ass. With two light fingers, he tilted my chin up as he stepped back down to join me. This time, there was no distance between us, his breath feathered my lips as he spoke.

"Frankie, we can explore anything you want. You want me on my knees, I'm already there."

Fuck.

Me.

This time, I nipped his lower lip when we kissed, then dragged my teeth over it before laving it with my tongue. At the rate we were going, we weren't going to make it to the house.

Hand in hand, we turned abruptly then raced toward the house. As promised, it was unlocked. There were huge doors and windows on either side of the living room. We pulled them open as we laughed, letting the breeze in. It fluttered the sheer curtains, then Coop and I dashed up the stairs. The first door he pushed open revealed this huge, bright room with a massive bed in the center and netting around it.

One tug, and my bikini top hit the floor, then I stepped out of my shoes as Coop reached around me to pull my shorts down, and he swept the bottoms with them. His shirt floated down out of the corner of my eye, and then he pushed me up against the window that let us look down at the ocean and his cock slammed home into me and we both let out a shout.

The fullness was too much and not enough. Hands on my hips, he moved me as I fought to just hold on. Everything was so sensitive, and I swore I could feel every ridge on his cock as he drilled into me.

"Look at them," Coop urged, and I flattened my hands against the cool glass as his every thrust rubbed my nipples against it. The competing sensations threatened to overwhelm me. Below, Archie had the crewmen facing him as he spoke. All the luggage was on the beach, but Jake and Ian were staring up at us, and I grinned slowly.

They could see me, and I opened my mouth to let the cries out. Coop's hands were so tight and sweet as he pulled me back onto him, and I swore every push forward took me off my feet.

"Come for me," Coop ordered. "Play with your clit and make sure Jake can see you dip your hand."

I had no idea how to make—Fuck it. I licked two fingers, and I swore Jake's whole body jerked, then I slid it down my front. A brief glance at Ian showed him marching toward the house, bags in hand. Though I couldn't quite make out his face, I would bet money Archie's hot gaze was on me, not the men he talked to and kept from looking at me.

Riveted to the spot, Jake stared up at us as my fingers skated over my clit, and I swore I detonated from those stares alone, even as Coop swore. He dragged me back from the window, one hand covering my breast and the other urging me forward until I was half bent.

His shouts as he came had me trembling and clamping down on him. I would never not love the warmth of how they jetted into me. I didn't think I could even explain how much I treasured that moment. It was like a part of them became a part of me, and if I tried to put it into words, I would sound ridiculous.

We kind of collapsed together onto the floor. He pulsed inside of me, or maybe that was my imagination, but he wrapped around me and the shorts he hadn't even fully removed rubbed against my legs.

Cradling me to him, Coop nuzzled a kiss to the side of my head. The sound of the door swinging open behind us had me glancing over to find Ian carrying some of the bags in. He gave me a slow smile.

"Having fun?"

I nodded, then licked my lips.

"You want to have more?"

Oh, yes please. I clenched around Coop, and he groaned. With care, he eased out of me, and then I was kneeling there on the thatched rug and staring up at Ian. His grin grew even more sinful as he carefully removed his sunglasses.

"Your turn to help offload," Ian told him, and I swore I could come from the way Ian reached for his belt.

Coop gave me another kiss. "Enjoy yourself," he murmured. "Take notes, and maybe I'll let you do the same to me."

Fuck.

I almost melted right there, but Ian shut the door behind Coop as he walked toward me. "You know what I packed, Angel?"

I raised my brows.

He had the belt looped into cuffs, and I offered up my hands.

"Behind your back." I obeyed, and he slid the cool leather over them. Sweat cooled on my skin as he opened the window and let the breeze in. A sharp slap hit my ass, and I jolted. I hadn't even heard Ian move back to join me. "Do you know what else I packed, Angel?"

Oh. Right. Question. I licked my lips. "No, sir," I whispered. "But I hope it's for us."

He fisted my hair and tugged it back, so I could look up at him. His pleased smile relaxed every muscle in my body. "Good girl, sweet girl. You want to find out?"

Please.

And I didn't even have to say it aloud.

"First, you have to earn it," he whispered, and I shuddered again as he dropped his shorts to reveal the thick length of his cock jutting toward me. "Will you work hard for me, Angel? I want to share the surprise with you."

Mouth open, I sat up a little higher on my knees and spread them. With my hands behind my back, I had to trust Ian to do everything, and it wasn't a question. His smile was so happy, I sighed as his cock slid across my tongue.

We'd just gotten here, but I'd already discovered paradise.

Chapter Eighteen
DAYS LIKE THESE

JAKE

Frankie strolled down to where Bubba sat on a chair near the water's edge. Archie hadn't been kidding about keeping her naked, and at the same time, it took my breath away to realize she was walking down there topless, hair up, the sun gleaming on her golden skin, and the bikini bottoms hugging her ass, the bright yellow visible through white almost sheer sarong she'd wrapped around her hips.

When he'd teased her that she didn't need the bottoms, she'd pointed at the sand and then said, "Abrasive as fuck. You want to keep eating me out and playing? We're not getting sand in the playground."

Sounded good to me.

Looked even better.

"You still can't get used to her just walking around outside naked, can you?" Coop stood next to me, munching on an apple, and I laughed.

"That obvious?"

"You're not growling. But you are glaring. Course, I don't mind. The more you do it, the more she baits you with it. It's all win-win for me."

I punched him in the arm lightly, but I was grinning. Bubba glanced up when she got there, and instead of just sitting next to him, she went down on her knees, and I swore my whole cock just went from spent to hard as a rock in a second. It wasn't the first time I'd seen her do it. For the last two blissful days, if she arrived somewhere he was already settled, she knelt before she did anything else.

Bubba ran his fingers over her cheek, then held out a hand to her. She took it and let him pull her up, and then she sat down in the chair next to him, legs stretched out and they were like two lounging gods soaking up the sun.

"Down boy," Coop teased. "We've got to finish prepping for dinner, or Archie will try to cook again."

I snorted. One of the best parts of this place besides the gorgeous views, perfect weather, and a naked Frankie was the absolute *lack* of other people, including a staff. The house had been stocked, there were instructions, a generator, and a caretaker who would be staying on the other side of the island and would only come over if we called him via radio.

If we'd wanted to fall off the edge of the world, we couldn't have chosen a better spot. The only drawback was we had to do all of the cooking. Which was also fine, at least until Archie decided he could do shish kabobs the day before when Coop and I had Frankie pinned between us.

Neither of us wanted to be interrupted by smoke like that again. "Where is he anyway?"

"On the phone with his dad again," Coop said, and I scowled. The satellite phone and the radio were our only contact points. The cells didn't work for shit out here, and I was fine with that. "Come on."

At his urging, I followed him toward the kitchen. "He's not yelling." That was something. The first full day we'd been here, he'd been shouting down the phone line before the phone itself crashed into a wall. You couldn't have told it from his mood after, but Frankie had. She'd dragged him out to the water to teach her to body surf. There was a better side of the island for actual surfing, but that was for tomorrow.

"Nope, so maybe it's going better. I want to stick my nose into it, but he hasn't asked for help. So…" Coop spread his hands, and I got the feeling really well. There was only so much butting in we could do.

Well, butting in they could do.

I'd been there in New York when he went to see his mother and then the follow up with his father. I'd been there for the court case and seen them both through that situation before and after. Archie was intent and he was angry, but he wasn't obsessed.

"We wait," I said. "Whatever this is, when he's ready, he'll tell us."

"Or he'll just handle it," Coop pointed out as he headed to the fridge, and I pulled down the list we'd been left for ready-to-heat meals versus the food we could cook ourselves.

"Possibly, but we have to trust him to know his own limits, Coop. What the hell is a charcuterie board, and why are we making it?" Who made this list? We might as well just do cold cuts and sandwiches.

Laughing, Coop glanced up from the fridge. "It's a cheese and meat board, snacks and stuff."

Right.

"How about we just stick with the basics? There's steak, right?"

Charcuterie. Who came up with this crap?

"Yep. And potatoes. Steak is defrosted right?" At my nod, he grinned. "Cool, we can fire up the grill on the deck and put the potatoes in so they can slow cook, then hit the water with Bubba and Frankie."

He didn't have to tell me twice. Except… I sent him down without me before diverting to the second floor, where Archie had shut himself behind a door with coffee to talk to his father.

One knock, and I pushed the door open. Archie stood in front of the open doors, swim trunks on and the phone to his ear. Like us, he had a view of the beach, and he stared down at Frankie.

Man, we were all kind of creepers. Good thing we had the right to look. I just raised my eyebrows at him, and Archie made a face.

"Edward, I'm putting you on hold a minute." He lowered the phone. "Everything good?"

"That was my question for you."

His solemn expression split into a grin, and he said, "Yeah, I'm just fucking with Edward over some stocks he wanted to rearrange. He's trying to suck up to Grandpa, but he won't commit to dumping Maddy. Actually, he hasn't actually said shit about her in days and that's weird."

"Weird weird or bad weird?"

Anything to do with the dumpster fire of her mother was suspect.

"Weird weird, hopefully not bad weird. I'll give him credit, he's using the business as an obvious ploy to just talk to me, but I'm making him work for it." Amusement curved his lips. "You and Coop done making sure I don't burn the house down?"

I rolled my eyes. "We're hitting the water, you coming down?"

His grin widened, and he lifted the phone. "Edward, I'm on vacation. We'll talk later. When you're ready to answer those questions, let me know." He didn't wait for any follow-up, just clicked it off and tossed it on the bed. "Thanks for trying to rescue me."

Ignoring his snort, I opened the door wider for him. "Clearly, you needed it."

"Clearly."

COOP

Surfing lessons were hilarious. Everyone but Frankie and I seemed to have some measure of a clue for what they were doing. It was skiing all over again, only with a lot fewer clothes and no instructor hitting on Frankie.

Okay, correction, no instructor not named Archie, Jake, or Bubba hitting on Frankie. The waves were strong on the western side of the isle where we'd driven on four wheelers to do our surfing. No lie, I liked the four wheelers more than the surfing itself. Probably didn't help that I could not pop up to my feet to save my life without falling off the damn board.

Frankie seemed to be having as much trouble as I was, but neither of us could stop laughing long enough. Jake just shook his head at us, but Archie and Bubba seemed determined to get us to do it at least once.

"Hey," Frankie called from where she straddled her board. We'd paddled out here and watched the others ride the last wave in, since neither of us had been in any great hurry. The fact we could see our feet in the water and the colorful fish below us added to the relaxing effect. Low tide was the best waves to ride, and they weren't particularly high here, at least not right now.

"Hey, beautiful, come here often?" I grinned, and she laughed.

"Smooth."

"Eh, I don't have to be smooth," I commented, dusting the water droplets off my shoulders. The fact her eyes dipped a little to check me out made me smile wider. It was one thing to be adored by her, but something else to know I turned her on. I could not fathom going back.

Not now.

Not ever.

"No?" The challenge in her voice dragged my attention up to the sparkle in her eyes. I'd always loved how green they were. They fit her mood, darkening when she was sad, growing flinty when she was angry, and shining—just like they were right now—when she was happy.

"Nope," I continued. "I'm your favorite. I don't have to impress you. You love me, warts and all."

"That's true," she began, then frowned. "Wait—you have warts?"

I laughed. "You'll just have to inspect me closer." The words did what I wanted, she flicked a look back down to my chest. We'd all been getting tanner, but she'd just turned more golden. I loved how sun-kissed her skin was.

"Deal."

Yep, I was the favorite. "I haven't forgotten about the piercing."

"Coop…"

"Nope," I said holding up a hand. "I haven't forgotten about it, and I'm not committing to it yet either. I only pierced my ear when you got yours done in solidarity."

Frankie laughed. That was such a magical sound. "So you want me to pierce something if you do?"

My mouth froze half open, and I stared at her for a moment. To be honest, that thought hadn't occurred to me. But the idea of her piercing something just for me? Okay…my cock might be really onboard with that idea. "Not your nipples or your clit," I told her firmly. Honestly, based on my reading, my dick was gonna need a few weeks if I pierced it, and that was bad enough. I didn't want her out of commission. At least I could watch while the guys fucked her if it was me.

A shiver skated up her spine. "That hadn't actually occurred to me, but fair would be fair."

"No," I said with some emphasis. "Nothing pierces those breasts or that sweet pussy of yours." Surprise flickered through her eyes, along with a hint of a pleased smile. Maybe this was why Bubba did it, but the command was less about her bending to me and more about protecting her. "But…" At the same time, the idea of her piercing something just for me?

Yeah, I loved the guys like brothers and they all had their needs and demands for her. I made few of them.

"Would you pierce something if I asked?"

She let out a blissful little breath and then paddled closer until our knees brushed. "Don't you know I'd do anything for you?" I knew she meant all of us. That didn't need to be said aloud, and at the same time, my cock and heart both thrummed at that declaration. "I'd do it, even if you didn't get pierced."

Curling a lock of her damp hair around my finger, I leaned toward her, and she met me halfway. The open-mouthed kiss was equal parts sexy and sweet. Just like her. "Your navel," I whispered against her mouth before I scraped my teeth over her lower lip. "Pierce your belly button for me. Something green, like your eyes."

"And something gray, like a steel bar, for yours?" The offer turned me inside out.

"Fuck, Frankie."

"Right now?" She waggled her eyebrows at me, then slid her hand along my waistband, tugging us closer. "We brought towels for the beach."

"You want the guys to see?" I had zero problem with this, and her eyes lit up.

"You like to watch, but do you like to show off?"

Right now? Fuck yes.

"Race you to shore?"

"First one there has to be on bottom."

Not like that was a hardship. I barely heard the guys as we laid down on our boards and started arm over arm swimming back toward shore.

Someone—probably Jake—yelled out for us to pop up, but neither of us listened. As we glided in toward shore, we slid off the boards, and I grabbed hers up to help her balance while catching up my own. I made it a half step ahead of her and got the towels spread out and settled. She grinned at me as she tugged me free of my shorts, pulled her bikini bottoms to the side and slid down on me.

Fuck.

This was the life.

IAN

Every night on the island, we ended up sitting around the outdoor fire, laughing and talking until the early hours of the morning. Some days, we were up with the sunrise anyway. Others, we slept late. The master bedroom in the house had a gigantic bed we could all share, though we were all just as likely to steal Frankie away to one of the other rooms or even out to the deck.

Tonight, it was my turn to steal her away. I'd told her no wine earlier. I'd skipped alcohol too. Most of the evenings we'd been too tipsy to play or to give Frankie her reward for being such an incredibly good girl. The fact she'd gone to her knees for me at every opportunity but hadn't once pouted because I hadn't rewarded her *yet*, made tonight all that sweeter.

I patted Archie on the shoulder as Frankie's fingers linked with mine. "Behave, boys. We'll be back in a little while."

"Don't do anything I wouldn't," Archie said in a dry tone.

"Me or him?" Frankie teased, and Archie laughed.

"You guess."

"That means lots of options," she stage-whispered to me, and I tucked her under my arm.

"Man, I wanna watch," Coop complained with a grin, but he didn't move a muscle from where he sprawled in one of the chairs, feet up and a beer in hand.

"Too bad," I told him and then led Frankie inside. The guys' laughter followed us as we made our way upstairs and to one of the bedrooms I'd picked for this. I'd set it up earlier while they'd been playing billiards. Frankie was a mean shot, even when the guys cheated by rubbing against her ass.

Served them right that she cleaned them out every time.

Math, as she liked to say, was all about the angles.

At the door to the room, I glanced down at her, and her serene expression knocked me in the gut. There wasn't anything I wouldn't do for this girl, and I'd practiced and worked it out a dozen times before I'd been ready to consider playing tonight.

"We're going slow and easy," I told her. "The only rules are it has to feel good. Anytime you want it to stop, you say stop, the ropes come off, and it's just us. No harm no foul."

She shuddered as she turned to wrap her arms around me. Rising, she kissed me lightly. "I trust you." Those three words meant almost as much to me as *I love you*. Maybe more. "I want this. I want you."

Cupping the back of her neck, I slid my hand up into her hair, and she went boneless, relaxing into my hand as if I'd asked for the surrender. She offered it up so easily and without hesitation.

"Strip for me?"

Not taking her gaze off me, she pushed her shorts down and then tugged the sleep shirt off over her head. We'd all showered and changed when we got back. Her skin had this golden burnished look to it from the sun, save for the fainter tan around her breasts and then the paler strip along her pubic bone where the bikini covered her.

She'd trimmed all the way down for the trip, not that anyone had asked her to. The thin strip of soft golden hair that matched her head arrowed straight toward her pussy, and I had to ground myself to keep from stroking it.

Bikini lines was all she'd said, but if Rachel took her to get waxed, she'd kept that to herself. It had better have been a woman, and if it hadn't been, I needed to not ever know.

Boxing away that thought, I didn't worry about it. Frankie was comfortable, and that was the important part. I opened the door for her, and she stepped inside slowly, her breath caught before she'd taken more than a couple of steps. I let her absorb the view while I leaned in the doorway, enjoying my own.

The doors were open on either side, letting a breeze flow in. It ruffled the sheers. There were no lights save for the tiki torches along the balcony that flickered in the wind. The scents of ocean breeze and dry rainforest around us on the island, including flora I didn't even have names for, filled the air. Pillows lined the floor, along with a couple of thicker throws to keep her legs comfortable if she had to kneel for a while.

With a sigh, she moved toward the pillows I'd stacked and turned to face me before she went down on her knees. The breeze stirred up her hair, and it slid over her skin, caressing it like I wanted to.

"Close your eyes," I told her, and she locked her gaze on me for a long heartbeat before her lashes fluttered shut. The inescapable trust flooded me with so much pride and affection. "I love you, Angel."

The corners of her mouth curved a little higher. She mouthed the words 'I love you too' without giving them voice. Not testing her limits or boundaries.

"While I adore this, I do miss my little brat too."

A giggle escaped her, and she dared one eye open to look at me, and I sighed at the pure mischief in her expression.

"But that's part of your plan—make me miss it so I'll savor it all the more when it returns."

I wasn't wrong, and she rested her hands on her thighs, legs apart so I had a perfect view of her pink pussy. It glistened in the light. There was even a hint of moisture on her thighs. She was already turned on.

Good.

When her eyes closed again, I picked up her clothes before I stepped into the room and closed the door. I could lock it, but I trusted the guys. They hadn't been invited, and they wouldn't intrude…

Then Jake's words from a few months earlier swirled up. An unlocked door was an invitation. I locked it before continuing to the bed where I'd left my surprise. I stripped out of my T-shirt and left it on the corner of the bed, folded neatly with hers. Uncovering the bamboo silk ropes I'd brought just for the occasion, I eyed the two lengths. One was red and the other blue.

A glance back at Frankie showed her sitting patiently, eyes closed, and head tilted up as though appreciating the breeze stroking over her skin. The blue was a little heavier than the red. This was more about sensation than true restraint tonight.

I wanted to practice the knotting on her, for the first time, without an audience. I'd discussed this at length with Lyssa and Richard. As long as I monitored her pulse and breathing and didn't let her sub drop too far, we would be fine.

Closing the distance to her, I knelt down in front of her. With a light hand, I shaped it over her hair as though stroking it and carefully brushed it away from her face. "How are you feeling, Angel?"

"Loved," she whispered.

Holy hell.

I set the rope aside, then cupped her face and kissed the hell out of her. Her mouth opened to me as I swept my tongue in to taste her. Frankie leaned into the kiss, taking and giving in equal measure. While I might control the kiss, she refused nothing and offered everything. I could drown in the taste of her, fuck, part of me just wanted to lay her back and make love to her for hours.

Restraint.

Who knew she would challenge me constantly on that level? Breaking the kiss, I rested my forehead against hers and enjoyed the fact her breathing came in quick little gasps, much like my own. With one hand, I reached for the rope and kept her still with my forehead pressed to hers.

"Do you know why I asked you to not drink tonight?"

Her teeth scraped over the pink of her lower lip, flushing it a deeper red for a moment before she said, "I know I was hoping we would play more, but I didn't want to ask."

"Because you're my beautiful, wonderful, and very sweet good girl." Mine.

She sighed. "Yes."

I ran the rope up and down her arm, stroking her skin and enjoying the goosebumps prickling her flesh as I got her used to it. The swift intake of air and the way her lips parted were exactly the reaction I sought.

"Sir?" There was so much need in that one syllable, it looped its very own knot around my dick and pulled it tight.

"Oh yes, Angel. You ready to let me practice on you?"

"How do you want me?"

I closed my eyes and grounded myself. I would need every ounce of my control for this. "Just like you are," I told her. "We're going to do a simple knot. I want to wrap your torso, your breasts, and your thighs, then your wrists, and if you enjoy that, it'll be my turn to reward you."

The little shudder she released filled me with an inescapable pleasure. If it were possible, she relaxed more. Exactly what I wanted.

"The chest harness," I began as I began using single columns to wrap the rope around her midsection, then up and over her breasts. At the first brush of the rope, her nipples pulled tighter, flushing with color, and I paused to swirl my tongue over one. Her fingers dug into her thighs, and I bit down gently. "Don't hurt yourself." The moment I gave the order, her hands relaxed, and then I sucked on the nipple I'd bitten lightly until she let out another of those breathy sighs and a trickle of dampness escaped from her pussy.

"My sweet girl," I whispered and then laved attention to the other nipple until both were wet and glistening. Only when I had them both fully flushed a deep red and her breath coming in deeper, harsher pants and the hint of a squirm in her posture did I move on. The harness took time to build, and by now, every touch of the rope had her reacting.

But my beautiful girl fought to stay still for me.

I wasn't comfortable with rope around her neck, so I framed it over her shoulders, weaving the knots until they formed two shoulder pieces like a tank top and didn't threaten that lovely column of throat.

Moving to her back, I traced my fingers over her tattoo. She and Jake had been talking about his new tattoo, and I'd seen that glimmer of light in her eyes each time they went over the different designs for the wings and the colors. When I followed the loop of my name, another shiver raced over her.

Delicate little tremors of reaction. Her wrists I looped gently, then bound to her waist. I didn't want to arch her uncomfortably, since she would be kneeling for a while. Once they were secure, I eased her back, she melted into me and let me position her against the nest of pillows.

The position kept her thighs apart and her feet flat on the floor. I ran the rope between her legs and then tied each thigh lightly to an ankle. Each piece hooked into the other. The red silk against her golden skin was probably the most erotic thing I'd ever seen beyond the way her eyes shifted when she came.

With care, I sat back on my heels and just admired her. She lay there, relaxed, no part of her trying to hold her pose. The ropes kept her legs apart and her hands down and comfortable. They also cradled her. Her breathing came, nice and even, and with two fingers, I checked her pulse.

It thrummed steadily, and the dampness between her thighs filled the air with its own musky invitation.

"How are you doing, Angel?"

"Wonderful," she whispered. "How are you?"

I grinned. "I'm blessed. Because you love me."

Her smile grew wider. "Can I see you?"

"Open your eyes," I whispered, and they flickered open to reveal pupils swollen to swallow almost all of the green until they were like pockets of the night. "Hello, my sweet angel."

"Sir Ian," she whispered like it was a revelation. I loved how she said my name. I had from the beginning.

"Can you take a little more? Can my good, perfect girl take more for me?"

"I'll take anything for you."

Yes. She would. My cock was stone, pressed so tight against the zipper on my shorts, it would likely be wearing the imprint. But my pleasure was right here, soaking up hers.

"Good girl," I praised her as I stroked my hands down her sides, then up to her nipples. I gave each one a hard, sharp tug that had her gasping. "That's it, hold nothing back." Pinching one like my fingers were a clamp, I dipped my head down to those thighs of hers and began to sample the sweet trickle of need soaking her labia.

Her sighs turned to moans as I plunged my tongue into her, coating my face in her before I circled her clit. The little bud was so swollen and flushed, it almost looked painful. I cast my glance up to find her body arched, her eyes on me. I released her nipple in the same moment I sucked her clit against my teeth, and she came with a shriek.

The cry elongated, and heat flooded me. I'd made her scream like that.

I was going to do it again.

I began to eat her out in earnest. She was the sweetest treat I'd ever have. The first one I wanted. The last I would ever want. Her sighs and moans rose and fell as she fought to hold on, but I was relentless in my pursuit of her pleasure, and when she was shaking all over, I rose, stripped off my shorts, and tugged the knots so they would come free.

Frankie's eyes opened wide as she gasped out little sounds that were the syllables of my name, but I swallowed them in a kiss before sinking into her. My cock ached to feel those shudders and spasms as she wrapped me up, and when her fingers dug into my shoulders, I exulted. My girl was flying, and she wrapped those legs around me as I began to pump into her, and my denied orgasm was right there but I fought it.

Not until she came.

One more time.

I might have blacked out when it hit, or maybe we both did. But I was right where I always wanted to be—with her.

SUBJECT: ARE YOU SERIOUS?

Sorry about the all caps, but are you serious about us doing a cover of one of your songs? I mean, I know all the words to every single one. No lie. The guys love that about me. Which is good, because I sing along to every album when they come out.

I'd offer to pinch myself, but I do not want to wake up. If you mean it, then hell yes, I would love to cover one of your songs. How does that work? Do I just tell you which one? How do I choose?

Also, down girl, I will happily share Ian's voice with the world, but the only panties he gets are mine.

Have I mentioned how awesome you are?

We're in paradise at the moment, on vacay, see the pictures attached, but we should be heading back to civilization soon. Actually, I'm not even sure if this email will go through until we're back, but I didn't want to forget to respond.

F.

P.S. Ian said I'd never forget. If I was going to leave them for anyone, it would be you three, but I think Rachel would disagree.

Chapter Nineteen
FAREWELL TO PARADISE

FRANKIE

Dawn of our last full day on the island, and I sat out on the deck watching the sun rise over the water. We'd all been up super late, but as the guys dropped off one at a time, I'd stayed awake. My body was sore in all the right ways. It had been an amazing week. I thought we were only going to get five days, but Archie stretched it out somehow and we ended up with an extra three.

I didn't ask him how he did it. Just thanked him. A light shawl landed around my shoulders, and I glanced up to find a shirtless Archie gazing down at me. Smiling, he dipped his head and pressed his lips to mine before he set a tall mug with an even taller cone of whipped cream on top of the table next to me.

He added a second one that he'd left just inside before moving around to tug me out of my chair and then down he sat and pulled me into his lap. I stretched my legs out on the lounger and leaned back against his chest.

The air was chillier than I'd realized, but the shawl was warm. Archie was warmer still. We didn't talk, he just passed me my foamy coffee with the crown of whip. The chocolaty goodness had been made to perfection. When I tilted my head, well aware of the whip cream mustache I had, he grinned and cleaned it off before kissing me slowly.

Peppermint. Coffee. Chocolate. Archie.

I sighed.

"What's wrong, babe?" Archie asked in a low voice as he drew his finger down my cheek. "Why so pensive?"

"Hmm…not pensive." Well, not really. I took another sip of the coffee and glanced down to where the ocean rolled in, the white caps of foam suggesting more agitation than normal. There had been a storm offshore the night before. We'd gotten to watch the lightning show for a while before we'd gone inside. "Maybe a little… I don't want to leave."

The last might have come out a little petulant. I winced.

"I mean…I love it here. I love us here. But I loved us in the lodge in Colorado. And in my apartment in Texas." Head tilted back. "And your house…"

"Our house," he corrected, then gave my hair a little tug. "The lodge will be ours too. I already told Grandpa I wanted it kept in our family."

A shiver went up my spine.

"You want an island, babe? I don't know if Grandpa's friends will sell this one, but I can make them a hell of an offer."

"How much would one even pay for an island?" The question popped out, and I twisted to look at him. He gave me a faint grin and a shrug.

"A few million, I'm sure. Probably have to clear it with the government, since I think this island falls under Fijian law, but we'd figure it out."

"A few million?" I was pretty sure I blanched.

"We can go halfsies…but I kind of like the idea of our very own fantasy island."

With a groan, I stared down at my coffee. "You'd do it too. Even if it would cost some ridiculous amount of money."

"If it made you smile? Hell yes, I'd do it. Though…as nice as this one is, maybe we get one in the Caribbean or the Mediterranean. Something a little closer to us."

Laughter fluttered through me. "Maybe later."

Was I seriously saying that?

"Yeah?" Archie teased, tugging the shawl down to bare my shoulder so he could kiss it. "How much later?"

"We'll revisit it…after college."

"So, bachelor's degrees in three and a half years? We can probably do a couple of really nice investments with high yield returns that would build that nest egg."

"Archie…"

"Come on now, babe, you're the one getting the business degree. An island retreat, particularly if we use a country with good banking laws, like the Caymans, means we can secure our investment capital offshore and then get what we want."

"Always thinking five steps ahead. Five days. Five weeks. Five months…"

"Five years," he murmured against my ear. "Fifteen. Fifty."

Fifty years. I snorted. I couldn't help it, and Archie chuckled before drawing the shawl back up and tugging me back against him.

"Five minutes after I met you, I knew you were something special. It wasn't five days later that I knew you were the girl for me. That you've always been the girl for me. I was planning a future with you before you even realized I wanted to date you."

The unadulterated love in those words warmed me.

"Maybe I don't tell you enough how much I love you and maybe I obsess about your perfect breasts, sweet gorgeous ass—which I very much liked fucking on the plane, by the way—or that way your pussy pulses around my cock as you come. How sweet you taste on my tongue when you lose control. Yes, I fucking adore your body, and I adore fucking your body. But loving you? I've done that forever, and I plan to go on doing it forever."

Tears burned in my eyes, and I let out a soppy little laugh.

"You're going to make me cry."

"As long as they're happy tears." He folded his arms around me and tucked his chin on my shoulder. "I can live with a few of those, but only a few. You want an island, we'll get an island. You want school? We'll go to school. You want a hundred cats? Well, we're gonna have to work on robo-litter cleaners…"

That made me laugh, and I shook with it. "You're such an ass."

"But I'm your ass," he said. "I always have been."

"Well, my ass isn't so bad-looking."

It was his turn to snort. "Your ass is spectacular."

I grinned. We sat there on the deck for another little while, finishing our coffees. Then we went back inside before heading downstairs. The guys were all passed out. I had to laugh at the fact that Coop was sprawled across half the bed and Jake and Ian were both sleeping at the worst angles to avoid his legs and arms.

Outside again, we followed the water's edge. The sand here was so fine, it was like powder. We'd kept an eye out for rocks and shells, but we'd been pretty fortunate.

"I wanted to talk to you about school," Archie began, and I glanced at him.

"Do you want to talk to me about school or your dad?"

He frowned. Like the guys, I'd been aware of Archie's calls with his father. Coop and I had heard part of one the other day before we ducked out of the house to let him have his privacy. "How long have you known?"

"For a while."

He sighed.

"I wanted to let you come to me with it, if and when you needed to."

"I wasn't trying to lie to you," he offered, and I squeezed his hand.

"Archie, I know that. I know you're not lying to me or trying to lie to me.

Things with your father are…complicated."

"That's a really generous word for it."

"It's not about being generous," I scolded him. "Archie—right, wrong, or indifferent—your relationship with Edward is *yours*. As long as he isn't hurting you or trying to hurt you, I will keep my distance. If he turns into a giant douche canoe again, all bets are off."

It was Archie's turn to laugh.

"I'm serious."

"I know you are, babe. Just like I know you'd kick his ass for me, no problem."

"I would too."

"I believe you." His tone wasn't placating. If anything, he sounded impressed. "And Jake would probably pummel him, while Bubba and Coop pinned him down."

"Well, you're not wrong." The breeze carrying in off the water pushed my hair across my face, and I ran my fingers through it to push it out of the way. "That's because we have each other's backs. All of us."

"You know that's something else you gave me," he said, and I shook my head before pinching him. Hard. He grunted. "Ow."

"Stop doing yourself a disservice. You're awesome. I can't make anyone like or care about someone else if they don't want to."

"Really?" he retorted. "Explain Rachel."

"I can't." I grinned. "That's all Rachel. You have to love her."

"Uh-huh. And why is that?"

"Because she's Rachel."

"You realize that's circular logic."

"You're changing the subject." I bumped him with my hip. "The guys love you for you. They're your friends too. They were before they were your brother boyfriends." I could kiss Sara for that term. Archie sent his gaze skyward.

"That phrase is never going away."

"Nope," I said. "But I promise never to tease you guys publicly about it."

"You can tease us anytime. You know that. We love that you're our girlfriend, and we'll shout it from the fucking rooftops. Trust me when I say there will never be a mistake made that you're *not* ours again."

Love cascaded through me. "And I'm your girlfriend. So, agreed. No others get their hands on any of us. But back to what we were talking about—Archie, the guys love you for you."

"Let's not go that far."

I rolled my eyes and twisted to walk backwards so I could meet his gaze. With the sun up and bathing us, the light highlighted all the shadows and planes of his face, from his adorable half-smile to his rough cheeks with their morning stubble and the disheveled hair that the wind kept tossing. He looked like a sexy god out for a stroll.

Or a Greek tycoon.

Yeah, Archie could totally rock Greek tycoon.

"They're your friends too. They'd throw down for you. Last summer, you didn't lose them, even when I wasn't there."

His expression tightened.

"That night we had sex the first time…that whole weekend, you had an advantage over all of them because even when I was furious with you for keeping our parents a secret and hurt about you making decisions for me, I never doubted for an instant how you made me feel or how you felt about me."

I stopped, and so did he. "Frankie…"

"I'm not bringing that up to rehash the fight we had. That's done. I'm pointing out that you and I, we made up before I made up with the others. We had sex again before Jake showed up, and when you could have persuaded me to stay, you encouraged me to go with him. To keep giving each of them a chance."

He blew out a breath.

"You did it with Ian too. After everything that happened, you still supported the idea of him and I working things out."

"You need him," Archie said quietly. "You need all of them. Even if I wanted to be a selfish prick and keep you all to myself, which admittedly, there are times, Frankie. There will be times now and times later when I'm going to want to run away with you and just have you to myself for a day, a weekend, a night."

"But you won't ever want me to leave them for good."

He let out a long sigh. "No…because those assholes need you too. We work. All five of us. What we have…it just works."

"So why can't you believe you deserve their love and support?"

"Because I'm the guy who fixes things." If that didn't define his self-view, I didn't know what did.

Stepping closer, I cupped his face in my hands so he wouldn't look away. "Even the mechanic needs help sometimes. Even if it's a lift to get the car up so he can see what's wrong or a second opinion on what's making that pinging sound in the engine. When you don't need that, it never hurts to have another guy hanging out, shooting the shit while you get the job done. Because you're not alone. You and me? We didn't do so hot with our parents, but this family? This family we got."

"I think your dad is pretty cool," Archie teased before wrapping his hand around my nape and stroking his thumb against the column of my neck. "I think you're exceptional."

"Right back atcha, Standish," I informed him as I rose up on my tiptoes and slid my arms around him. He caught me close, and the fierceness of his hug lifted me off my feet. I didn't know which of us needed it more. "Don't ever forget we all have your back, okay?"

"I won't," he promised. Then after a moment, he chuckled. "You'd probably beat my ass if I did."

Well, he wasn't wrong.

"But I'd kiss it and make it better after," I promised him. He squeezed me and then blew a raspberry against my neck before sucking a kiss against the skin and making me shriek with laughter.

"Like this?" And then he kissed me again, almost sloppily, and it made me laugh harder. "Or this?" Then he kissed me for real, and my laughter faded on a long sigh as he claimed my mouth.

"All of the above," I whispered between kisses, and then he tugged my shawl off and tossed it toward the sand. My top followed. I hadn't dressed for the walk, I was still in sleep shorts with no panties on underneath. "If you get sand in unmentionable places…"

"I'll be on bottom," he told me before we went down together. The kisses turned hotter and the touches more fervent, and in the same moment, we took our time. I was on my knees straddling him, and he kept his shorts on, so I guess I wasn't the only one who didn't want sand anywhere delicate.

Still, when he freed his cock and I sank down on it, we both sighed.

"Frankie," he murmured, fisting my hair as if to hold me still. "You know I love you, right?"

"Yes," I answered, meeting his gaze as our breath mingled. "I know you do. I love you too."

"Good," he said slowly, then thrust up into me and I let out a harsh breath. "Then hold still, babe, 'cause I'm going to fuck up into you until you come all over these shorts. I want to go back sticky with you all over me."

"Only if I don't lick it off you before we get there." His eyes flared at the declaration, and he shifted his grip on my hip as if to hold me still.

"Talk dirty to me some more," he whispered. "Tell me how much you want my cock drilling into you. How you like to feel me thrusting against these trembling walls. How every spasm reminds you of when I come and fill you up."

Yeah.

He still won at dirty talk.

I lost the battle at finding an appropriate response when the first orgasm crashed down on me.

An hour later, he kissed my shoulder in apology as he rinsed between my ass cheeks. "I promise to make it up to you…"

"Does anyone want to share how Frankie got sand in her ass?" Coop asked. "Inquiring minds and all that."

I flipped him off, and Jake dragged Coop out. "Just make sure you check that you got it all," Jake warned. "We'll go make breakfast."

"I'm sorry," Archie whispered, but it was Ian who was helping too. He took the sprayer and traced it over the folds of my vulva. Oh, this was embarrassing and kind of hot at the same time.

"It's fine," I grumbled and then laughed as Ian circled my clit. "Pretty sure there's no sand there."

"Good," he told me. "Just making sure." He was using his fingers to trace every single fold, and then Archie cupped me from behind and eased two fingers into me. I flattened one hand on the wall and gripped his Ian's shoulder with the other. "Carefully," he instructed.

"What do you think I'm doing?" Archie countered. "I don't want to hurt her."

"Then you shouldn't have flipped her," Ian responded. I touched Ian's cheek, and he flicked his gaze up to me as he kept running the sprayer over my vulva and down to where Archie pushed into me.

Honestly, it all felt good. There was no more bite of sand or grit. My nipples beaded under the contact, especially when Ian slid back to my clit again.

"Don't fight," I murmured. "I was just as guilty. We got carried away."

"Angel, we're not fighting." His voice dipped.

"And if you think we are…" Archie scissored his fingers inside of me, and I swore I rose up on my toes at the sensation. "Then we need to work on our method."

Wait…

"Exactly," Ian stated, and then he kissed me. The massage of his lips against mine sent the questions pinging around off each other in my brain. The firmness of his fingers against my clit combined with Archie's thrusting fingers forced me up on my toes again. Too many sensations competing for attention.

If it had been Jake and Coop, I would totally get where this was leading. Archie and Ian didn't… Ian's tongue thrust against mine, and Archie bit down on my neck. "I think she can handle this," he said softly. "You up for it, Rhys?"

The heavy weight of Ian's cock pressing against my hip promised me he very much was up for this. "But you guys…" I managed when Ian let me have a breath. "You guys don't…"

"Don't share?" Ian moved the sprayer aside and then shut off the water. It meant I lost contact with him, and then Archie tugged his fingers away and turned me around to face him.

"We make exceptions." Archie raised his brows. "We make plans."

Oh hell.

And then Ian began running a towel over me, and between them, they dried me off and then themselves before leading me out of the bathroom.

Plans.

They'd made plans.

In the bedroom, someone had turned all the covers back, and Archie tugged me over to the bed. "It's our last day here, babe," he said. "I meant it down there on the beach… Sometimes I want you all to myself. But you need all of us."

A shiver went through me as he kissed me, and then his hands were on my breasts and Ian's were moving down my back. The massage felt good, and then he landed a smack against one ass cheek and I let out a soft gasp.

"That's for taking risks," Ian chided me as he massaged the heat into my stinging skin. He landed another sharp smack to the other, and Archie bit down on my lower lip. "That's for thinking we wouldn't fix it."

One would think that was Archie talking.

The third slap landed, and I swore I was soaking Archie's dick where it lay nestled against my labia as he kissed a path down my neck. I had no idea when they discussed this or why it was all happening now or even if we were celebrating a special occasion, but trapped between both of them was a place I hadn't been in months and I was thrilled to feel them.

By the time Ian reached the fifth, my ass was on fire and Archie had one nipple so firmly locked against his teeth, I could barely hold back the long, mewling cries spilling out of my throat.

Ian's eyes locked with mine as he leaned over me. I stared up at him, hiding nothing, and his sudden, bright smile took my breath away. "More?" he asked, and I grinned.

"Please, Sir Ian. Give me more."

His eyes flashed. "Ask the other Sir in the room."

Holy shit, I quaked.

Archie looked up at me as I dropped my gaze to him. "Sir Archie?"

"Fuck," he swore and shifted us both, and then I was impaled on his dick. "You can have more, babe. Hold on…because you're going to have all of us." There was no time to brace as Ian delivered sharp slaps in rapid succession to one cheek, then the other. I was clenched so tight around Archie, his teeth ground as he held my gaze captive.

Then we were kissing, it was all teeth and tongue and hot breaths. I was barely registering anything beyond the stroke of skin and the shudders of his body pushing up into mine when warm lubed fingers pressed against my ass.

I was so used to this now, I swore my body went boneless.

It took no time at all for Ian to prep me, and in between, I kissed Archie or I kissed Ian. My skin was on fire, the heat from my ass seemed to suffuse everything, and when Ian pushed into me, pinning me to Archie, I started shaking.

I was so close. Too close.

The feeling of both of them holding me there… I could barely hold it together when he began to move. A keening noise escaped, and I dug my fingers into Archie's shoulder as I reached back with my free hand to grip Ian's neck. Everywhere they touched me, I lit up, and then a harsh exhale from across the room drew my eyes, and I locked gazes with Coop, then Jake right behind him and I came apart.

The orgasm took me like a storm, and I clenched down on Ian and Archie, pulling them with me. We collapsed together in a shuddering mass, and the tears on my cheeks were from pure overload.

"Fuck me," Jake said. "We're next."

"Oh hell yes, players four and five are definitely in the game now."

Elation warred with humor, and at my giggle, everyone cracked up.

We spent the day in bed, fucking, playing, teasing, and I came so many different ways that I lost count.

It might have been our last day in paradise, but we made the most of it. By that night, soaking in the oversized hot tub with the guys and leaning back against Jake, with his arms around me and listening to them talk, it all lulled me into a blissful haze.

The next morning, I was sore, and the boys indulged me by taking care of everything and insisting I rest. It wasn't a yacht that came to fetch us though, it was a water plane.

And we started another leg of our adventure. Ian even carried me out to climb aboard after they got the luggage loaded.

I wasn't going to melt, but I also wasn't complaining. Our last look of the island was a slow circle in the air before the pilots turned us back toward the main isle. I leaned over to Archie and whispered against his ear, "Start making those investments. I'm leaning toward yes on the post-college, four-year plan."

His grin filled me with another level of joy.

A private island.

Okay, maybe that was going a bit far, but a girl could dream, right?

SUBJECT: HELL YES WE'RE SERIOUS

Okay, first of all, private island retreat? A week at Disney World? Just make sure I'm invited to the wedding. Also, you need to come to one of our last shows. We're gonna be off tour for at least a couple of years. Is it weird that I'm both excited and terrified? Also, the girls are giving me shit that I have decided you're my bestie. Don't disabuse me of this concept.

Does that make me sound desperate? You know, don't tell me if it does. I haven't slept more than three hours in a row in weeks. I'm so tired, I think I forgot my own name. I know my parents have. Okay, pity party over.

Pick a song, we won't let anyone else until you two do, then tell those gorgeous boyfriends of yours to call me and tell me when you can be at a concert. We'll make sure you're all set up backstage with us.

KC

Chapter Twenty
IT'S NOT SPRINGTIME IN PARIS

FRANKIE

"Wait…what?" The last thing I expected when we reached the private plane and boarded was the announcement of where we were going.

"Paris," Archie repeated, his eyes positively dancing with mischief. "Rachel is wa—"

I leapt at him, and he caught my hug. The guys laughed at my squeal, and then he handed me off for hugs all around. "We're going to *Paris*?" The whole idea was insane. We'd just spent two weeks frolicking, and now we were…

"I told you," Archie said as I collapsed back into the seat between him and Ian. "June is our month."

Reaching over me, Ian clicked my seatbelt on and then linked his hand with mine. "And we all saw your face when Rachel said she was spending a few weeks in Paris between graduation and college."

"I wasn't trying to…"

"We know," Coop told me, turning his seat to face ours as the plane began taxiing. "All of us together changes a lot of things, but you thought about going to Paris with Rachel."

"I did, it would be amazing. But I wasn't about to leave you guys behind."

"Newsflash, Baby Girl, you're not leaving us behind. We're all tagging along." Jake winked at me.

"That said," Ian continued as he lifted my hand and kissed it, "you and Rachel will have girl time together to explore the city and the sights. We'd prefer it if you'd take one of us with you, but *no one…*" The last he said with some emphasis and stared at Jake for a beat before continuing, "No one is going to insist if you don't. We get that you girls need your time too, and we're perfectly capable of entertaining ourselves."

My cheeks ached from smiling, and I glanced over to find Archie studying me with a pleased little grin on his face, even as my ears popped from the rapidly ascending altitude of the plane.

I mouthed 'I love you,' and he winked.

Head back in the seat, I laughed.

We were going to Paris.

We played cards. We teased. We watched movies. Ian and I picked the song of Torched's we wanted to do, and we emailed it back to the girls. As soon as we'd gotten back to Fiji, our phones had blown up with messages and social media notifications.

I talked to Hank, checking in on him and the family. I also got to talk to Chloe. I hadn't talked to my brothers yet, but that was all right. When I told Chloe I was on my way to Paris and asked her what she wanted, she said a funny beanie. Considering I'd wanted something similar at her age, I laughed and promised I'd find us matching ones.

Hank wanted to know how I was doing, how the guys were, and how our vacation was going. He invited me—and the guys if they wanted to come as well—up to his place in Massachusetts before classes started in the fall. A weekend, he said, a chance to get to know the kids. If I wasn't comfortable staying at the house—the five of us would have to share one room and it might be a bit cramped—there were also a couple of boutique hotels nearby.

The guys didn't look opposed, so I promised him we'd work something out. We still had to finish our move to New York, and that meant finding a place. I had my suspicions that Archie already had that covered however.

Jake checked on his mom and sisters, as did Coop. Ian sent an email to Sara and Joe, but his parents weren't at home. They were taking a cruise of their own, and there were messages and pictures from them that came in.

I also had a number of notes from Rachel, each one snarkier than the last.

Look, it's the Eiffel Tower. Wish you were here.

Hey, check out me at this cute little café! Wish you were here.

French girls are hot. And bitchy. The boys are worse. Just kidding. Look who I ran into…

The picture of Mathieu made me laugh. But all of Rachel's snaps included similar themes. She wished I was there. Look what I was missing. See what we could be doing.

She was such a shit.

I couldn't wait to see her.

I checked in with my grandparents after we all spent *way* too long trying to figure out the time change. Archie finally just looked it up while laughing at us. They were fine, though my grandmother mentioned that Maddy had come to see them. All of my good humor dried up.

"Are you all right?" Because there was just something in her voice.

"Just fine," Patience informed me, then lowered her voice. "Your grandfather didn't take it well. I'm afraid it upset his heart, but he's going to be fine."

"What do you—He had a heart attack?" At my question, Archie's gaze cut sharply to me, and Coop just moved to sit on the couch next to me and my hand slid into his.

"No," Patience told me in too calm a voice. "Stress caused an anxiety attack. That was what the doctor told us. It mimicked a heart attack, but he's fine. They kept him overnight for observation."

Guilt ate at me. "What did she want?"

"Nothing for you to worry about," Patience said. "You enjoy your jet-setting with that Standish boy. At least he takes after his grandfather."

"Grandma." It came out exasperated. "Don't call him that boy." Standish or otherwise. "He has a name."

The quiet on the other end of the phone ate at me, but I stood my ground. This was one area my grandparents had to accept. It was all of us or none of us. Coop's hand flexed around mine, and I gave him a grateful smile. At this distance, there was no way he could miss what she was saying.

"You're right," she said after a long moment. "I'm sorry, Frankie. You're right. That was very rude of me. I've just been a bit…out of sorts."

Fresh guilt assailed me. I'd just chastised her, and she was clearly worried about my grandfather. "We can head there," I offered. "If Maddy is bothering you…"

"No, dear. She made her point, and she's gone again. She doesn't want anything to do with us and resents that you do. But none of this is your fault. She and your grandfather argued, he knows better than to let her agitate him. As it is, we've been in touch with Ted, and we've added to our security. We might take a few weeks in the Hamptons. Get away from here. Come see us there when you're back. You'll be getting ready to move into the city."

I chewed my lip. "Are you sure?"

"Yes, I'm sure. Now, go enjoy your vacation with Archie, Coop, Ian, and Jake."

I blinked.

"Thought I hadn't learned their names, didn't you?" Patience actually chuckled, and I swore it was the most relaxed I'd ever heard her. "I know we seem a bit cold to you, Frankie. Perhaps guarded and aloof."

"I wouldn't call it that."

"No, because you're polite if direct. We love you because…you're you, and at the same time, you look so much like Maddy and so much not."

I grimaced at the comparison, and it was Coop's turn to tighten his grip on my hand.

"That probably came out badly," Patience continued with a sigh. "We want everything for you, Frankie, but we're also wary of the past repeating itself. Everything with Maddy always seemed to be so much worse with Eddie. As much as we loved Ted… But, for your sake and for Ted's, we're going to stop holding up that mirror. If you can be patient with us a bit longer?"

"Grandma," I said slowly, the fact it had slipped out so easily earlier surprised me. I kind of liked testing the syllables on my tongue. "We'll figure it out. But is he really okay?" I didn't know my grandfather as well as my grandmother. He was every bit as aloof as she'd described. She wasn't. Of the two of them, she'd been the one to reach out time and again, to persuade him to loosen up my trust for me, not that I'd asked. Of the pair, I thought he was the one who really didn't want me to be like my mother and who feared it the most.

"He is, I promise. The stubborn old goat just has to learn to listen. But do come see us in the Hamptons. It will be good for him."

We talked for a few more moments, and I promised to come and see them. Our cars were going to be in New York with us, even if we didn't use them that much in the city itself.

"Is he all right?" Coop asked, and I nodded.

"I'll call my grandfather," Archie promised. "Make sure they have everything they need."

The corners of my mouth tilted up, but at the same time, I couldn't help but worry. Particularly since Maddy had something to do with it. I'd managed to not think about her for the last couple of weeks. Honestly, I hadn't missed her.

"Thank you."

Ian studied me for a moment. "We'll check on them after we land," he said. "And if you're really worried, we'll cut the trip short."

The last thing I wanted to do…

"Don't start, Baby Girl," Jake informed me. "Family first, and you're just getting to know them. But I have a feeling Archie's grandfather is already on it."

Probably. Grandpa Ted was like that.

"Now would probably be a good time to mention that we have videos of the cats," Coop teased. Then he held out a hand, and Jake passed him one of our laptops. Fuck, we hadn't even looked at the laptops in days and I still had…

Jake snorted. "Now she's worried about school."

"I can fix that," Ian teased. "Watch the videos, Angel."

Coop didn't give me much choice, and of course, the moment I found Tiddles trotting with Jeremy on his morning walk around Archie's—our house, that mental amendment would take a while—I started to smile.

Tabby sunned herself in the solarium atop the largest indoor cat tree house I'd ever seen, but Tory took the cake. She gleamed almost pure white like she'd been groomed and sat in another cat tree in the kitchen, eating daintily out of crystal.

The videos had little time-stamps, though someone had cut it all together to give me the last couple of weeks over the course of an hour. By the end of it, I was laughing so hard, I had tears running down my face. I thought my favorites were Jeremy reading in the garden with the cats sprawled out and playing, or when he was having his morning tea and Tiddles sat scolding him because Jeremy refused to feed them until he'd finished his first cup.

It helped.

A lot.

Coop holding my hand while I rested my head on his shoulder helped too. By the time I'd finished the video, Archie assured me his grandfather had it under control and my grandparents were being well looked after.

My guys were the best.

It was a long flight, including two stops—the first in Kuala Lumpur and the second in Dubai to refuel. I pressed up to the windows as we circled to land in both cities. They were stunning. A part of me was that girl still back in Texas, living in that two-bedroom apartment, desperate to get into Harvard just to get away. The rest of me… If I could only go back and tell her where we would be just a year later.

Not only did we get away, we did it in style. I wasn't running from anything anymore. Not if I could help it.

By the time we were landing in Paris, I was showered, rested, and thoroughly relaxed from Ian's admission to the mile-high club. Coop didn't complain because he got to watch, though he called dibs on the flight home. Jake said he'd get his ticket punched at the same time, and the imagery just made me laugh.

I had no idea what time it was. Midmorning, I thought, but the day was confusing 'cause it was like midmorning on the same day we'd left the island. Yeah. Don't ask me, I wasn't going to try and do that math again. Despite the food on the plane, I was starving. The guys promised we'd grab food as soon as we cleared customs.

One perk of flying on a private plane? Customs came out to meet you.

Or maybe it was a perk of money, but I was excited to get through and find food, but more than that, I wanted to see Rachel. Sure enough, she was waiting for us in the private lounge, phone in hand and looking all kinds of boho elegant in her black skinny jeans, white T-shirt with a black arty print on it, and a black denim jacket. Her reddish-brown hair was pulled into two long braids, and a pair of sunglasses perched on the top of her head.

"Bonjour, Rachel, espèce de salope sournoise!" I cried out, because she really was a sneaky bitch, knowing all about their plans and not cluing me in.

Jake and Coop had plucked my leather backpack purse and carry-on from me before we'd even exited the terminal to the lounge area, so my hands were free. The rest of our bags were already on their way to our hotel. All good things, because I hurried across the space separating us.

The red gloss of Rachel's lipstick positively gleamed as she grinned at me. "*Bonjour ma chérie*." She was still laughing when I reached her. She stood and had the wisdom to brace herself, because I half tackled her with my hug. "*Bienvenue à Paris!*"

"Fuck me," Coop muttered somewhere behind me. "I forgot how hot that was."

"*Vous ai-je manqué?*" she asked as she squeezed me tight before pulling back and giving me a once-over.

"Terribly," I admitted. Because I had missed her.

"Liar," she teased, tweaking me. "You look too fabulous to have missed me. And, bitch, you got laid on the flight, don't even try to deny it."

I grinned. "I would never."

Her snort just ballooned the happiness in me all over again. "Right." She flicked a gaze past me toward the guys, and for a moment, horror filtered through her expression as Coop gave her a hug.

"Just shut up and take it, Manning," he teased her.

"Don't touch me with your boner."

"I wouldn't," he promised, then dropped a kiss on her cheek. Jake burst out laughing at Rachel's scowl, and I hooked an arm through hers as Jake followed Coop's lead with an air kiss rather than a real one.

Ian and Archie stared at her a beat, and then she glanced at me and groaned.

"Fine." Dropping my arm, she gave Jake a side hug, then crossed over to welcome Archie and Ian with air kisses to each cheek before backing off. Ian winked at me with a grin, and Archie rolled his eyes but his own smile warmed. "Thank you for bringing me Frankie."

"You're not keeping her, Manning," Jake said. "Just remember that. We're sharing. 'Cause we're nice like that."

"Really nice," Ian added.

"Like gift from the gods nice," Archie tacked on, and I couldn't smother my own laughter at their snarking.

"However," Coop said as he wrapped an arm around my shoulders. "I do insist that you do all the French from here out, because Frankie's is way too much of a turn-on."

I elbowed him lightly, but he gave me such an intent look that I realized he wasn't really kidding. Oh boy.

I could have a *lot* of fun with that.

"Let's go, ladies. Frankie is starving." Archie motioned us toward the doors. "The car should be here."

"It is," Rachel said, falling into step with me and linking our arms together. "Your people swept in to pick me up last evening and moved me over to the new hotel… That was really not necessary, I was enjoying the hostel."

"You'll enjoy five-star room service too," Archie told her. "And there are enough arty types in Paris to distract the pair of you that I'd rather know you were somewhere secure at night."

"Aww, Rich Boy is worried that I'll seduce you with my bohemian ways," Rachel teased, and I rolled my eyes.

"Nah, we're pretty sure we have Frankie all locked up, but we don't want her to have to keep telling you no. Then there are all the French boys." Jake's rumble carried just a hint of seriousness that I cocked an eyebrow at him. "Not that I expect you would," he continued. "But I don't want to get arrested on your first trip to Paris."

Outside, the cooler air hit me, and I shivered just a little. After the warmth of the island, it seemed awfully chilly.

A car met us at the curb, and the driver was already out to take our overnight bags. We could have sent those with the other luggage to the hotel, but I'd wanted my laptop and stuff and so had the guys. Besides, we were heading there right after food. Rachel and I slid inside while the guys talked to the driver, who greeted Archie in English.

"He's cute," Rachel said as soon as we were tucked in. "The driver. His name is Arnold. He's doing this job to help pay for university. He's twenty-two and very sweet."

I stared at her. "You learned a lot about him."

"I'm experiencing the continent," she told me, and her grin widened. "And don't be so dirty. He knows a lot about the city and has a good eye for out of the way places. The place he sent me to for supper last night was divine. He also recommended a great café for us right near the banks of the River Seine so you can have your first truly French moment."

"I love you," I declared.

She wore a satisfied expression. "I know."

"Hey now," Jake warned as he climbed in with us. "Remember, you love us too."

"I would never forget it," I promised. I loved the fact there was real laughter and a gleam of teasing in his eyes. He'd never quite lost that growl of possessiveness, and I wasn't complaining. But I was dying to roam Paris and to catch up with Rachel on *everything*.

The café was everything Rachel said it was, and she only teased me a little about being so goggle-eyed at everything. She could afford to be cool and erudite, she'd been here for ten days already. Probably got her crazy American tourist out of her blood, but not only had I never been to Paris before, I'd never left the country.

I mean, my first trip out of Texas had been Colorado, then Florida. Technically, I'd been to Fiji, and we'd landed in Kuala Lumpur and Dubai, but we hadn't gotten off the plan in the last two. And the private island had been a heavenly paradise, but this was…

"Champagne," Rachel ordered, along with a series of appetizers.

I apologized to the waiter and glanced at the menu. They had escargot but no one, no matter how French or urbane it was, could convince me a snail was more than a snail. Nope.

Not happening.

The menu was extensive, so I added beef burgundy to my order and a couple more appetizers.

We were seated outside. Notre Dame was across the way, and I was torn on where to look. The Seine. The shops. The cathedral.

So many places.

The waiter returned with the champagne, and Jake hooked his foot against my chair as Coop tapped my foot with his from the other side of the table. Archie looked more amused than anything else, and like me, Ian studied our surroundings. There was a man with a guitar playing a few shops down, and if I strained, I could just make out the music.

Everything was just so perfect.

"So," I said, glancing at Rachel and trying to rein in my wandering attention. "Tell me everything."

"Everything?" she dared me.

"Yes," I told her as the waiter returned, this time with cheese boards. I could probably eat everything on the table, so I settled for a drink of the champagne that tickled my nose. "Everything."

"Well, the first night I was here," Rachel said, "I was exhausted from the flight. I couldn't sleep the whole way over—which reminds me, you totally need to read this new series by Lucy Smoke, it's dark as fuck, but I adore Avalon. And Dean has piercings…"

The guys groaned, and Rachel smirked. I almost snorted my champagne, but saved myself. Just barely.

"Anyway," she continued, utterly in her element. "I found a little café not that far from the hostel I was staying at, then settled myself in for the next twenty-four hours. I basically slept, read, found something to eat, then slept some more until my body clock was on the schedule here. A really cute guy named Hans was in the room across the hall, and we hit it off."

"You picked up a guy your first night here?" Coop asked, almost looking impressed.

Rachel rolled her eyes. "No, I wasn't his type. However, he did show me where a few of the best bars were for picking up girls and guys, so we spent a couple of days seeing the sites." She held out her phone for me, and by sites, she meant sights. There were some beautiful girls and guys scattered amongst the shots from around Paris.

When I found a shot of Mathieu, I glanced up. "You really did run into him."

"I did, at the Louvre of all places—see the *Mona Lisa* there in the background? He was there working on a university project with his girlfriend. That's her in the next shot."

"Oh, she's pretty."

"She is," Rachel said, popping a cracker in her mouth. "By the way, I have to tell you—Mathieu…you might have missed out, just a little."

I widened my eyes, and the conversation among the guys ceased. "Excuse me?" Jake growled.

"He and his girlfriend invited me over for the night." Rachel grinned wider. "Just saying—the boy can do more with his tongue than speak French."

"Rachel." Laughter exploded out of me, and I stared at her. She looked like the cat with the cream. Why not? She was single, free, and exploring her sexuality to her heart's content.

"You're not mad, right?" Rachel hesitated, and for the first time in a long time, I caught a little worry in those dark eyes of hers.

"Not even a little bit. I'm happy for you." I just wished…

"I'm not you, Frankie," she said with a flash of relief in her expression. "I haven't found the loves of my life hiding in plain sight."

And that made me kind of sad.

Jake grumbled, and I elbowed him, then handed him my empty champagne glass with a pointed look. He gripped my nape as he took the glass from my fingers, and his mouth closed over mine. The heated kiss demanded a response, and I licked and sucked at his tongue until he settled.

"You good, Captain Caveman?" Rachel asked as I caressed Jake's beard. He'd let it all grow in, and it was well past the prickly stage.

"I'm fine," he said, not looking away from me. "You don't feel like you missed out, do you, Baby Girl?"

Jake had not liked Mathieu. Not even a little. Neither he nor Archie had even made an attempt. But that was all water under a very far away bridge. "Not even a little," I assured him.

"Good," he grunted, then frowned. "You know…"

"Jake, no explanations are necessary."

"She knows we hated Frenchy," Archie said. "But Frenchy is also not our problem. Or a problem. Rachel can totally take him for the team."

I groaned, and she snorted. "Yes, that's totally why I rode his face—so I could take it for the *team*."

"We really don't need the salacious details," Archie began. "But if you want to compare tongue technique, tell me, did he pass your test?"

Oh, God. They were both going there.

Jake refilled my glass, then Rachel's with champagne.

"He *excelled*," Rachel said, then glanced at me. "How many times in one session have they made you come?"

"Oh hell no," I commented. "You two leave me out of this."

"I think our record is seven right now," Archie said. "Or is it eight?"

That earned a speculative look from Rachel.

"Still think she missed out?" Archie snarked, and I stared up at the sky.

"Until she tries vag, I'm always going to think she's missing out," Rachel countered, and I did snort my champagne this time.

"Anyway," Ian intruded. "We're going to talk about the places and things you've seen and not the people you've done. If you girls want to catch up on that later, that's fair."

"Spoilsport," Rachel teased, then slanted a look at me. "He did ask about you.”

That surprised me, but I smiled. “I hope you told him I was well.”

“I told him you’d stopped denying your boyfriends and the five of you were living in a life of poly hedonism. He was very happy for you.”

I grinned.

“Poly hedonism,” Coop repeated. “I like that. And there, I didn’t think Frenchy was so bad.”

I just rolled my eyes, but Ian nudged him and muttered something about ‘move on,’ and I shot him a grateful look. Teasing was fine, but this was apparently going to be a sore point for some time.

Rachel, bless her, let it go, but I made a mental note to ask her for more later. If she needed to talk about it, she could absolutely tell me.

We spent a couple of hours at lunch and finished a bottle of champagne and then one of wine while we ate. It sounded like Rachel had an amazing adventure so far, but she promised that she had saved the Eiffel Tower for when I got there. She also didn’t mind retracing her steps with me.

I was lightheaded and relaxed by the time we went for a walk along the river. Yes, we needed to head to the hotel, but I wanted to see some things before we did. Ian and I made a beeline for the guitar player.

I was glad I wasn’t the only one who wanted to hear the music. We put some money into his case as he played. The others drifted over to join us, and Ian wrapped his arms around me from behind as we swayed to the music.

After, we wandered down to some of the shops. In the very first one, I found a selection of berets and bought several ’cause I had no idea what Chloe’s size was. I also found a couple of things for Patience and for Kelly, Hank’s wife. There was an apron that Coop popped around with that said something about Paris and the food and we got that for Jeremy.

Just ’cause.

There was also a stuffed black cat that reminded me so much of Tiddles that I couldn’t help cuddling it. I hadn’t been away from my cats this long in forever. A wave of melancholy hit, and while part of me knew it was the wine, I still wished I could hold one of them.

Archie plucked the cat from my arms and handed it to Ian along with our other purchases. I really didn't need it, but we all went a little crazy, leaving that shop and then the next few with more and more bags.

Rachel laughed at us, particularly after I picked out a rather obnoxious and colorful scarf and found one for her too.

Another thing I noticed, no one seemed at all askance when I kissed Coop or Ian or Archie or Jake one after the other. I'd walk into one store tucked against Ian and leave under Jake's arm.

"It's Paris," Rachel reminded me as we walked a little ahead of the guys. I was still tipsy, but a good tipsy and not quite so lightheaded. "They love love here, and you are surrounded by love. Of course they adore it."

"I've missed you, Rach."

"Of course you have," she said. "Because I'm me."

I laughed. We were in Paris. We were young, and she was right—I was in love.

"Come on," she told me, clasping my hand and hauling me forward abruptly. "We're going to get caricatures made of us…"

I didn't know how she'd spotted them ahead of us, but there were a bunch of artists.

We didn't get out of there without spending most of the euros we had in our pockets, but not only did I get caricatures of all of us, I found a stunning scene of the river itself painted from just that vantage point.

Some memories got selfies. Some got souvenirs.

This counted for both.

Chapter Twenty One
FRENCH KISSING AND OTHER THINGS

FRANKIE

We had a huge suite on one of the upper floors, so we had a long, and private, elevator ride. Our first twenty-four hours here had been a bit of a blur. After our wine and shop hop along the Seine, we retreated to our hotel where we unpacked, settled in, and the guys left me and Rachel in her room to catch up.

I had fallen asleep in there, but I woke up with Coop and Archie, Jake and Ian were heading out to explore while they also went for a run. I'd given it about five minutes of thought and went back to sleep after I gave them perfectly reasonable kisses. The next time I woke up, it was just me and Coop and it was dark outside.

Coop snored lightly next to me, but his hair was damp and his cheeks shaved. The rest of the room was empty, so I dragged myself out of bed, brushed my teeth, and showered. Okay, I hadn't expected jet lag to kick my ass quite so hard, but when I came back into the bedroom in a borrowed T-shirt, fresh panties, and damp hair, Archie waited for me.

"Come eat," he said, holding out his hand. "Then more sleep. You'll be great by tomorrow morning."

I glanced at Coop, but Archie just shook his head as he ushered me out into the sitting room. Jake and Ian were sprawled on the sofa, a movie up on the TV that they'd paused. Rachel had nail polish out and was working on her toes. She shot me a grin, and I managed a yawn.

Honestly, my brain was so stuffed with fuzz, it wasn't funny. It wasn't fair that everyone else looked normal. I was pretty sure they'd talked and teased, but I basically ate mechanically anything they put in front of me, drank a lot of water, and then kissed everyone goodnight, including Rachel, before I wandered back into the bed and crawled in with Coop.

Jake followed, chuckling as he tucked me in, and then kissed my head. That was the last memory I had until early the next morning when I woke up refreshed and in desperate need of coffee.

The plan was ten days in Paris. Then we were going to go across to London to see Torched for their very last concert. KC was excited. I'd talked to her on the phone for five hours the night before. Coop hung out with me on the balcony long after the guys had gone to sleep, though he had his ear buds on and seemed more intent on being there for company than anything else.

A year ago, if someone had told me that Kaitlin Crosse would not only have my number and I would have hers, but that she would blow up my phone and my email, I'd probably have laughed my ass off. She was a good kid though, a little lonely, despite her best friends who toured with her. Though she said they were more family than friends now, so they didn't count.

What she loved about me? I was ridiculously normal. The fact she enthused about my "normalcy" in the same conversation as demanding the details of our island escape and Disney World vacations prior to the private plane flight that brought us halfway around the world to the most romantic city?

Yeah, the irony was not lost on me, and it kept me cracking up all the way through.

When I finally got off the call, I leaned back against Coop, and he plucked one of his ear buds out and tucked it into one of my ears. The playful cadence of music washed over me, along with a French singer crooning.

"If you're taking requests, songbird, I'd love for you to sing to me in French. The sultrier the better."

"*Mon dieu, qu'est-ce que je vais faire de toi, mon amour?*"

His whole body shuddered behind me. "I know you said my god and my love, I'll take it."

Laughter swelled up through me, and when he tilted my head back for a kiss, I sighed against his lips. The French serenade just added to the sweetness, but I paid attention to the music selection. If Coop wanted me to sing to him in French, then I was going to sing to him in French.

Our third full day in Paris, Rachel and I left the boys to head to the Louvre. Jake loved the history of the city and the art as much as I did, but they were going out to scout some vineyards.

"Don't let Archie buy them all," I teased before they left, and Ian grinned at me.

"You mean you don't want a manor house here in France in the heart of a vineyard where you could play out every romance movie trope ever?" The playful dare in his voice made me snort.

"You really know how to paint a picture," I said as I tugged on the light jacket I'd picked out to wear. The weather called for rain on and off, so in addition to my umbrella, the jacket seemed prudent, along with the baseball cap and my hair pulled back into a braid.

"That's not a no," Ian pointed out, and I gave him a little shrug before leaning up to brush a kiss to his lips.

"No, it wasn't."

I winked before Rachel and I scooted out, and she laughed. "You're getting used to them spoiling you."

"More than a little," I admitted. "It's wonderful and frightening at the same time."

"But you're happy," Rachel said as we stepped out of the hotel. A car waited for us, our one concession to the guys not following us was that Archie's car service would pick us up and drop us off. "And I could get used to this traveling in style."

I laughed and pinched her as I followed her inside.

The Louvre was a magical place. I stared at the glass pyramid, fulfilling a years-long longing I hadn't even realized I'd possessed. Rachel said nothing while I gazed up at it. Some people called it a blight on the face of Paris, but I loved the design. I loved what it meant.

I just loved it, and more, I loved being *here*.

We took selfies together, then Rachel had me spread my arms, so she could snap a couple of me with the pyramid that she then fired off to the guys with the note that said, *Our girl looks good, right?*

Their immediate responses made me laugh. We snapped one more selfie blowing them kisses, and my phone buzzed with selfies of the four of them blowing me a kiss. I burst out laughing, and Rachel rolled her eyes playfully before linking arms with me and pulling me toward the main doors.

I didn't know which one of us started humming a song from French class, but we were both singing it together as we made our way inside. I was pretty sure the guys would have enjoyed the museum as much as we did, but it was fun to just hang with Rachel.

We talked about everything and nothing. She updated me on her family and asked about mine. I told her about Hank and Chloe. Rachel decided Chloe was her favorite. Staring at the *Mona Lisa* was an experience. Yes, it was smaller in person than I once imagined, but I'd also known it wasn't as big as it seemed in all the memes and graphics.

Still, I might have sniffed a little as I studied her. Thankfully, Rachel didn't tease me. Much.

We'd barely managed a third of the exhibits we wanted to see before it was time to find food. Café Grand Louvre beneath the pyramid was our dining choice, and I was in heaven.

"So, have you found a place in New York yet?" Rachel asked, and I grinned.

"I'm betting Archie has and is going to *surprise* me when we get there, what about you? I mean, the offer to stay with us still stands."

Rachel snorted. "I like to sleep at night, and I've heard you're loud."

I rolled my eyes.

"Besides, you guys are all sickeningly happy and in the honeymoon phase. I need my own space. Plus, you need a place to retreat to when they piss you off."

It was my turn to snort, but I didn't disagree. We'd been known to fight in the past, though I couldn't imagine anything would be so bad that I'd want to sleep away from them. To be honest, I'd gotten so used to them being there, I had trouble sleeping without one of them pressed up against me.

"That expression," Rachel said with an indulgent grin. "You have it so bad for them."

I did, and I lifted the wine we were having for lunch, and she clinked her glass to mine. The fact we could order alcohol without anyone blinking an eye at us just added to the atmosphere. We got the waiter to snap a pic of us, and I sent it to Madam, even with Rachel razzing me I didn't need to be teacher's pet anymore. Me flipping her off just sent her off into gales of laughter.

After lunch, I checked in with the guys. Coop had been sending me the best shots of the vineyards they were touring. He warned me Archie purchased a few cases of wine that he thought I'd like and was having them shipped home because…well, Archie.

God, I loved them.

Jake collected histories from the tour guides who spoke English and sent me notes. The part that was funnier was his commentary and subtle shots of Coop listening to their French. Apparently, it was only a turn-on when I spoke it. So I might have sent Coop a quick voice clip of me telling him about the museum in French.

The response was hilarious.

Phones away, we wandered back out to explore. There was no way to see everything, not in just one visit. And by the time we needed to leave to meet the guys for dinner, my feet were sore but my heart was happy. It was also raining outside, and I swore I swooned a little as we opened our umbrellas to make our way across to where the car would be waiting for us.

The fact Archie slid out to hold the door open for us and had his own umbrella just made me smile wider.

Whether we were romping at a water park in Florida, sunning ourselves in the South Pacific, or wandering in the rain of Paris, the happiness of just being with them was real.

One night, we did dinner on the Seine with a tour of the night sights. Another, Archie stole me away for a romantic dinner at an exclusive café, followed by a long walk through the rain-slicked streets. Jake and I nerded out on a tour of Versailles, then a day trip to Normandy, where I swore chills of the past kept shivering over me.

Architecture and the history of the ancient city held me in as much thrall as it did him. Ian and I escaped to more museums and an afternoon stroll across one of the old lock bridges. You couldn't put locks on it anymore, but they had painted it and we could do a picnic there. A part of me was sad, but then Ian found a lock necklace in one of the shops and he got it for me. Even better, we found a busker singing in English and joined him for a few familiar songs before leaving him a few euros.

Coop and I spent an afternoon just exploring and getting lost together while riding one of the hop on and off bus tours. I tortured him playfully for hours as I gave him his own tour, translating everything but also repeating all the French. We missed dinner that night, because Coop proved just how insatiable the French made him.

Ooh, la la.

Every evening, we did something different, including delightful cabaret shows, dancing, and romantic dinners. Rachel found a gourmet food walking tour, and the guys took bets on when I'd get full. I totally won though, because the food was to die for.

Finally, we went to see the Eiffel Tower, and standing on the observation platform as we gazed out over the city just seemed to fill my soul. We got all the touristy shots we could dream of and sent them back by the dozens to Hank, Alicia, Carly, Joe, Sara, and Jeremy. We kept the more salacious ones to ourselves.

All too soon, it was time to leave for London, and as excited as I was about seeing KC and the girls, I didn't want to leave Paris. We also had to say goodbye to Rachel. She said she would come over for the concert in three days, but she had some stuff she wanted to do before she left Paris.

We'd be back, but still…I didn't think I could love a city more.

London tasted different from Paris. The city was also ancient, featuring cobblestone walks side by side with modern improvements. The Tower Bridge swept me away to ideas of the distant past, when kings and queens took barges up and down the river to get away from the London heat. Scorch marks on some of the old buildings served as evidence of the Great Fire of London.

Our hotel wasn't far from the Tower of London, and our first morning there, we made our way to St Katherine's Wharf for breakfast and shopping. KC and the girls were waiting for us at the Starbucks. They sported baseball caps to hide their distinctive hair and sunglasses. Like us, they were dressed in comfortable T-shirts, jeans, and light jackets because it was chilly in the early London morning.

Granted, I was used to the suffocating heat of Texas, so the cool air even filled with the smell of exhaust from the cars and the fishier scents from the river was welcome. KC practically skipped toward us when we entered, and then I had an armful of girl in a tight hug.

Aubrey and Yvette followed her at a slower pace, and while their hugs might not have been as fierce, they were no less warm. I found myself wishing Rachel was already there. We took a huge table on the second floor and looked out over the wharf and the people hustling on their way to get to day jobs, open up shops, and tourists like us settling in to enjoy the view.

"You look fantastic," KC told me as she grabbed the chair nearest mine. I wished I could have said the same thing about her, but as soon as the sunglasses came off, all you could see were the black smudges beneath her eyes and some hollowness to her bone structure.

When was the last time she'd slept? Or even eaten?

Yvette and Aubrey were much the same, though it looked like Yvette had done her cosmetics with a careful hand as though to hide the signs of tiredness, but her eyes were red-rimmed.

"You all look like hell. How many more shows do you have?"

Aubrey actually snorted with laughter. "This is why KC loves you—you are not a suck up."

No, I wasn't. "I'm also starving. Can we go get food from downstairs, or do we want to go somewhere else?"

"I can't eat yet," KC said. "We have a photo shoot this afternoon, so this coffee is it until after. I don't need anyone yelling at me about rolls."

I blinked. KC was tiny, I'd say almost stick-like but that would be rude. If anything, she seemed like she'd lost weight since the last time I saw her. "How are you doing all those shows and not eating?"

"Eh," Aubrey said with a shrug. "You get used to it. Besides, under the lights and on the stage, it's hot as hell and you're in the moment. Too much food, and you're puking." She slanted a look at Yvette and then at KC. "We eat *after* the show."

"If we're hungry," Yvette agreed. "Sometimes, it's just some drinks, some water, a shower, then falling into a bed if we're lucky or a transport if we're not and on to the next show."

"But this is our last week," KC said. "We have three shows left. We're wrapping this bitch up where we started it."

Three more shows.

Still…

"Don't fuss," KC said. "This isn't about us. Trust me when I say we're used to it. I want to hear all about Paris. We were there a few weeks ago, but I don't think I even saw the city other than the route between the hotel and the venue."

"And please, for fuck's sake, tell her what song you want to do," Aubrey stated. "Then we can get our manager off our asses."

"Do you want to come to our soundcheck this afternoon?"

Was that a real question? Of course I wanted to go to the soundcheck. I also wanted to fuss more and to make sure she ate. As it was, we finished our coffee, and they had to go. Business meeting before the soundcheck, but KC handed us badges that would get us backstage and past security.

Ian and I had chosen "Reckless." It was one of their earliest hits and the third song of theirs on the album that made me fall in love with them. It was all about making choices and just because a choice seemed crazy, impulsive, or *reckless*, didn't mean it was a bad one. Besides the fun message, it had the crazy sexy beat that made it easy to dance to and a chorus that I adored.

KC's beaming grin at the choice made me feel even better about picking it. "I wrote that, you know," she told me as we walked them out of the shop and toward the side street where a car waited for them. The guys had been kind of quiet through the whole conversation, letting us dominate it.

But Ian promised we'd be there for the soundcheck and anything else they needed. We grabbed more hugs, and then the girls were gone. I stared after the car, and Ian wrapped an arm around me.

"They'll be fine, Angel," he murmured. "Three more shows and they're free."

I mean, I'd read between the lines of those emails, and it sounded like Ian had too. They were *exhausted*.

"You two are never going to tour until you are down to skin and bones," Jake said abruptly, and I glanced over to find him half glaring after the car that had picked them up. "I mean it. My little finger has more fat on it than any of them, and KC looks like she's one good stiff wind away from breaking."

"Yeah," Archie said slowly. "Not a fan. Not eating because of photo shoots? I get that the camera adds some weight, but not that much."

Coop, unlike the others, didn't say much, at least not on our walk back to the hotel. We had a few hours before soundcheck and I was starving, a fact I felt almost guilty about, especially when we found a little place that smelled sumptuously of bacon, sausages, eggs, and baked goods.

Even more, I felt guilty about the food we ordered. Coop studied me a beat and then said, "Exhaustion and stress do wild things to a person. You eating isn't going to make it better or worse for them. You're doing what you can by being her friend. By being all their friends."

"But she looks so damn tired."

"They've been touring nonstop, Baby Girl," Jake said, nudging my plate. "Eat. They know how bad it is, or I don't think they'd be taking a break from all of it."

"Agreed," Archie said. "And I agree with Jake, you and Bubba are never going to tour until you turn into a ghost of yourselves. I've seen you get worn away by stress. Hard pass."

It was Ian who summed it up when he said, "I'd never let them do this to her. Trust me on that."

I swore, one by one, the others relaxed, and Archie nodded firmly. "Good. Now, do we want to try and do some sightseeing before the soundcheck, or do you want to go back to the hotel and get laid?" The last he directed at me, and Coop burst out laughing.

"It's always good to have options."

We did go back to the hotel, and while I didn't get laid per se, the guys were very cuddly. Ian and I practiced our songs, and the guys heckled playfully. A huge lunch was waiting for me after my shower, and I stuffed my face happily, even if I was still worried about KC and the girls. Before long, we were at the venue and it was huge. From the outside, it looked large, from the inside, it was an arena. They could probably fit twenty-five thousand people in there.

More.

Terror bubbled in my stomach.

Maybe performing wasn't the best idea.

As if reading my thoughts, Ian threaded his fingers through mine and he leaned down to whisper, "You just look at me when it's time to go out there."

The simple note of command in his voice settled some of the nerves. KC let out a playful squeal when security guided us back to where she and the others were drinking hot tea. Apparently, it was good for their vocal cords.

There was food on one of the back tables, but none of the girls were eating. I considered scolding, then bit my tongue. KC shot me a grateful smile, and despite disliking not saying anything, it was the right choice. They were dressed up, cosmetics in place, jewelry gleaming, and KC's blue hair fell in a straight waterfall over one shoulder from where it had been tied up in a single ponytail on top of her head.

Grabbing my hand, she led us toward the stage. "Come on, it's freaky when you first get out there with or without people, so let's get that freaking out of the way."

My heart hammered triple speed the minute we walked out on that stage. It was empty, save for the backup band and others who were working and cleaning, and sound carried. The hollow arena didn't make it any less intimidating though. If anything, it was a thousand percent worse.

All the moisture in my mouth fled, and I stared around with wide eyes.

"It's scary," KC said from right next to me. "But when the lights come on and the music starts playing, it's the energy from the crowd that brings everything to life. For a few hours, on this stage, you become your pure self. No problems. No past. No future. No bullshit business contracts. No family drama. Just you and the music."

"Hey," Yvette said as she bumped KC on her way past.

"And your besties," she told me. "It's us against the world, but this right here—this is our world, and we own it. So, let the fear make you tingle and don't be afraid of the chill racing up your spine because when those lights turn on, ice becomes fire and fear becomes power."

I was still turning those words over in my head when they started their soundcheck. They wanted me and Ian out on the stage with them, and we both got wired up with mics that weren't on while the guys waited for us just off stage.

Coop and Jake both had their phones out, snapping photos of us and filming it. When one of the grips complained, Aubrey told him to get fucked and leave us alone.

I still wasn't ready when Ian and I had to do our soundcheck, and my voice cracked on the first lyric. Until Ian turned my chin up so I was staring up at him, and then KC was right about one thing—everything else fell away.

Despite the soundcheck, we weren't performing that night. KC tried to talk me into it, and I may or may not have ended up in the bathroom throwing up. They let me off the hook and guilt assailed me at the freakout. Still, she said, I was doing the last show if she had to drag me out there and just serenade me.

Rachel appeared at our hotel the next day, and we went out for a day of pampering, hair, nails, and the works. That night, Jake and Coop spent hours making sure I didn't think about anything but them.

The next morning, Ian and I were alone in our hotel suite while the guys went to do some shopping. I spent hours in ropes, teased and edged until I thought I would die, and when Ian finally let me come, he only did it after I'd managed to hum a few bars of the song. I was boneless all afternoon, and he soaked me in a hot bath before we got ready to head for the venue.

Even with the noise of the crowd seeming to make the floor vibrate and the energy surging backstage with everyone hurrying, I was loose and relaxed. Anytime my nerves started, all I had to do was look at Ian, and my body seemed to understand that relaxing was the only choice.

I still wasn't ready when they announced this was their final show and waxed nostalgic. I swore there were hints of tears in my eyes as I listened to them talk about what being Torched meant to them.

Those tears were still there when they introduced us onto the stage, and then we were out there, under the lights, and my heart fisted in my chest.

I could do this.

We could do this.

Over the crowd screaming, I still caught Rachel's "Yes, bitch!" from the wings, along with the whistles from Coop and Jake. Archie's gaze warmed my back almost as much as the lights in front of us. When the first chord was struck, I glanced from KC's grinning face to Ian's nod.

Yeah, we could do this.

Chapter Twenty Two
MAKE YOUR OWN KIND OF MUSIC

IAN

Frankie had been fighting nerves about the stage since the first day we came to hang out with the girls for the soundcheck. The fact she'd thrown up was our first clue. When it came to protecting others, our girl was fearless. But her own nerves? Those were harder to pin down.

All the sex in the world wouldn't chase them away, but the ropes and the knots? They melted the tension out of her frame. The denied orgasms refocused her. Then the orgasms loosened her muscles. Still, the tension was present when we stood off to the side of the stage.

They wanted to bring us out at the end of the show. Go out with a bang, KC said, and break all the concert rules. Because this was the last concert on their contracts. Personally, I agreed with Frankie—KC, Aubrey, and Yvette needed a few weeks of doing *nothing* as soon as this was done. I couldn't blame Frankie for being worried about how much weight she'd lost. The girl was practically skin and bones.

I had my guitar strap on, and I was ready for this. We'd let the girls offer suggestions on what to wear, but I'd settled for the muscle shirt with the Torched logo on the front in teal and jeans. Frankie had teased me that I looked a little like Bruce Springsteen.

No complaints here.

She'd gone with ripped jeans, a crop top, and a bright red baseball cap. The latter was from Archie. Red was her lucky color and his. The crop top bared her navel, which she'd informed us she wanted to pierce. I wasn't the only one who'd gotten interested in the idea.

But that was for later. When we were back in the States.

So much was for later—the new place in the city, college, recording music, writing more music, building our new lives. Warmth settled in my chest. So much of that included unknowns, but I was ready for it. We had found a way to balance all of this. My need to take care of her and Archie's desire to fix everything too. Jake's and Coop's needs to share her and protect her also added to the mix.

There were so many little things tying us together, but our competing desires also let us find common ground. Archie wanted to know more about the lifestyle, so did Jake. Coop was more than willing to learn alongside Frankie, but with her, and she wanted it all.

The girls began to talk about what Torched meant to them, from the beginning to this final tour before they took time off. They were closer than blood, and sometimes they wanted to draw each other's. There was laughter rippling across the crowd. But they wouldn't change any of their experiences, including meeting this duo and their family on one of their tour stops, and it was their pleasure to introduce us for the first time.

Frankie's eyes widened. Fear and apprehension flashed through her tears. But when her gaze locked on mine and I evened my breathing, she took in a deep breath and then let it out.

If I was grateful for no other part of how far we'd come and how much she trusted me, this would have sealed it. The fear abated, the apprehension relaxed, but the tears, they were apparently not going anywhere.

I could live with that. The guys began to whistle, and Rachel yelled as the floodlights sought us out, and I caught Frankie's hand in mine and walked her out.

Holy shit, the wall of sound from the crowd crashed into me, along with the heat from the lights and the smell of sweat. But beyond all of that was the energy buzzing over my skin. Frankie's smile grew wider as KC welcomed us out with hugs.

"Ladies and gentlemen, it's my rare pleasure to say I knew them when, and we get to pass the *torch* on to two of the most talented and genuine people I've ever gotten to know." The last bit she said as she cast a look at Frankie. "And to the girl who writes the best emails and is living her best life—you inspire me. Now," KC continued with a huge grin as she faced the crowd, "I hope they inspire you. Everyone, Bound Hearts is here to stay, and remember—you heard them with us *first.*"

Honestly, hearing the name we'd picked out called for the first time seemed to make it tangible. Beyond that, the smile that exploded across Frankie's face echoed my own. Hell yes, we were here to stay. If this was our only live performance ever, we were going to make it count.

The crowd surged with cheers, shouts, and applause, just as the band kicked off the first chord as I swung my guitar around. One of the grips ran over and attached something to the mouth of it to let me join them, even though I preferred my acoustic to the electric, and Frankie accepted KC's outstretched hand to dance with her as we played through the first several bars of "Reckless."

Thank fuck this was actually one of their songs I'd practiced and recorded for Frankie a few months earlier, so the notes were familiar. Even if my focus scattered some, divided between keeping track of Frankie and where the band was, I followed their lead guitarist with pleasure. The man could play.

So could the girls. Yvette had her own guitar out, and so did Aubrey. They were digging deep for every note, heads bobbing in time to the rhythm set by the drummer. Fuck my heart when we reached the first refrain and then returned to the top of the song, because Frankie opened it by belting out the first lyrics.

The strength her voice carried, but beyond that was the joy in her eyes when KC let out a scream over the first lines.

"Yes!" she shouted. "Let's do that again, we want to hear more from them, don't we?"

The surge of voices rising together seemed to rush over the stage, and we answered it by taking the song right back to the top. KC glanced over at me and jerked her head forward to join them, so I moved up.

When we kicked off the first verse this time, I fell in with all four of them.

I think I had a new favorite song.

I definitely had the best girl.

COOP

Honestly, even after listening to Frankie and Ian perform all those times and sing together, nothing could have prepared me for what it would be like to see them hit the stage, a real stage, in front of an audience of thousands. Frankie's terror morphed into something akin to joy, and I had both fingers at my lips to let loose with whistles for them.

Yeah, we weren't supposed to cheer from the sidelines. Fuck. That. Jake was right there with me, and Rachel about blew one of my eardrums out with her scream, but I didn't even mind giving her a hug when she clutched onto me abruptly as they segued from "Reckless" to "Pure Gold."

I glanced down and bit back a smile. There were tears sliding down Rachel's face, and I tightened my arm around her, keeping her tucked against my side. She was half hiding her face as she swiped at the tears.

I wouldn't comment. This was our girl out there, looking and sounding fucking amazing, with one of my best friends and a band that once seemed kind of just wild to admit we knew and now I kind of wanted to look after 'cause they were so exhausted.

Next to me, Jake had his phone up, and so did Archie. I kind of wished we could get footage from the front. Archie had even debated bringing in a drone, but they were filming this concert—all the ones in London apparently—as part of a farewell package to air in a few months.

We'd at least get to see it again, but I'd bet money Archie was already plotting how to get his hands on the footage. This was one of those moments we would never forget.

Instead of only a couple of songs, Frankie and Bubba—Bound Hearts, I liked it—stayed out with them for a full set of six songs leading up to their last. When they finally walked off, sweat slicked Frankie's face and her hair was damp. Bubba's shirt was damn near see-through, but they looked so fucking dazed and happy.

Jake scooped Frankie right into a hug, even when she complained about being all sweaty. Yeah, like that would keep our hands off her. The tears on Rachel's face were gone by the time Frankie turned to her, and I got out of the way for the girls to hug, even as Archie clapped a hand on Bubba's shoulder.

They were both panting, but the joy rolling off them was contagious. I passed a water bottle to Bubba as Archie pushed one into Frankie's hands. The crew had offered us some for them, but we'd brought our own. No offense to anyone, but Frankie wasn't taking a drink from anyone.

With Jake rubbing her back slowly, she gulped down half the bottle, then lowered it with a wild grin on her face. "Did you like it?"

"No," Rachel deadpanned. "It was horrible. Now half the world is in love with you, I'll never get my shot."

The perfect delivery shut all of us up, and then Archie dragged Rachel into a hug that had her squealing, even if it didn't carry over the music booming from the stage. He gave her a sloppy kiss on the cheek.

"Don't worry, they don't have a shot either," he informed her, and Frankie collapsed into Jake with a hand over her face as she laughed. Rachel slugged Archie in the arm as he smirked and then flipped him off.

Still, we shut up because out on the stage, the girls were winding it down with one last song. The stage darkened, the music slowed, and the crowd even seemed to hush. I tangled my fingers with Frankie's as she leaned into Jake, Bubba bracketed us, and Archie tucked Rachel between he and Jake too.

One by one in perfect acapella, KC, Yvette, and Aubrey sang their very first hit without any backup whatsoever. It took what had been a rock pop song that Frankie had danced around her bedroom to more times than I could count and turned it into a haunting, if brilliant goodbye.

The humming next to me pulled my gaze, and I glanced down as Frankie mouthed the words alongside them. Her eyes were glittering, even in the half-light cast by the three spotlights that drew together as the three members of Torched closed the distance between them, until it was just the three of them in a single spotlight.

And on the final note, the stage went dark and the girls were striding off toward us. We fell back as they grabbed water bottles, and beyond, the crowd began to scream and cheer.

There wasn't a dry eye among us, though Rachel seemed to hide hers better. Frankie hugged the girls and they grinned at her, but there were streaks of mascara from their own tears.

Handlers moved around them dabbing at their faces, and then the stage manager was there, his hand over the mic on his headset.

"Encores?"

"No," Yvette said. "That was our goodbye."

The last she offered up but still glanced at KC and Aubrey. "Definitely," Aubrey agreed, and KC let out a shaky breath.

"Hell yeah. Let's get drunk."

She grabbed Frankie's hand. "And all of you are invited." It was only the fact that KC was a tiny thing she didn't haul Frankie away from us, but no way we would say no. Not if they wanted to go, and I was pretty sure it was more about needing a friend than needing people to party with.

A fact made reality when KC and the girls didn't bother to change before they led us right out the back to a waiting car. We were whisked away to their hotel, which also happened to be ours.

That worked.

ARCHIE

At the hotel, we went in the back and used the manager's access to the private elevator leading to the penthouse suites. The Torched girls had gotten the one across the hall from ours. Since there was only two on the floor, it meant we didn't have to worry about anyone or anything interrupting.

"Everyone go shower," I told the girls and Bubba. "I'll get food and drinks up here. Any requests?"

"Everything," Yvette said. "I want everything on the menu. I'm starving."

"Ice cream," Aubrey said.

"Burgers," KC decided. "The biggest burger they have."

Frankie just grinned at me. Yes, I knew exactly what my babe needed. She kissed me as the Torched girls streamed across the hall to their room. The saltiness of her kiss made me smile.

"I loved watching you tonight," I murmured against her lips, and her eyes lit up. "Loved listening to you too. Did you have fun, babe?"

"I had an amazing time. It was… Archie, it was the most terrifying thing I've ever done."

"Nah," I told her. "You've done way scarier. Trust me." At her raised eyebrows, I motioned to the room. "You took on all of us."

Her snort just made my grin widen.

"Go shower."

"Yeah," Jake said, scooping her up. "Come shower. I'll wash your back."

"Hey!" Coop protested, but Jake laughed.

"You snooze, you lose."

"Ugh," Rachel grunted from the sofa where she'd fallen down and had her phone out. The sheer volume of disgust in her comment made me laugh. "You guys are disgusting."

"Don't hate," I said as I picked up the room phone to place the order. "I'm sure you want her to be happy."

"Mmm-hmm." She didn't glance up from her phone as she scrolled through images that from this angle looked like concert pics. "Yes!" She exclaimed, then held the phone up for me to see. It was a perfect shot of Frankie, Bubba, and KC at the microphone.

Hell yes.

"Grab that and send it to me?"

"Already done, Rich Boy. I want the higher res version when you're finished."

We shared a nod and then room service answered, and I turned away to get everything we wanted sent up here, including ice cream, burgers, beer, wine, and champagne.

Granted, I probably shouldn't endorse legal drinking for the rock stars, but they already had enough handlers. Pretty sure they didn't need me to add to it.

Bubba had gone off to shower, and Coop joined Rachel on the sofa as they continued to scan social media posts. The phone in my pocket kept vibrating like mad, and I'd just pulled it out to see who was blowing my phone up when Bubba walked out, hair damp and dressed in fresh clothes with his own phone in hand.

"Did you see these?"

I glanced over at him. "Was just looking?"

"Problem?" Coop asked, and I shook my head, because I wasn't sure yet.

The series of messages on my phone included a half-dozen missed calls from Wittaker, then a text that said to call him.

Bubba's phone had three missed calls from him and two from the entertainment attorney we'd hired.

"I have a suspicion that your debut got noticed," I commented. A low scream carried from the direction of the bedroom that elongated, then climbed. None of us said a word, but Rachel snickered, then Coop did, and I shook my head.

At least Jake had Frankie fully distracted.

"Call Wittaker, and I'll call…" Bubba began, and I nodded, the phone already at my ear as I headed toward the balcony.

Wittaker answered on the first ring. "Did Frankie and Ian sign any releases for their performance in London tonight? Also, a heads-up about public performances would have been appreciated, but I'm sure we can manage this."

"Good evening to you," I said drily as I stepped out and the sounds of the city wrapped around me. "It's always a pleasure to hear from you."

"I'm aware. Our conversations often bring me similar joy, however, I am concerned about what if anything they signed with regard to their performance tonight?"

"Nothing," I told him. "The girls didn't ask them to, and if paperwork had been involved, we'd have consulted you."

Wittaker exhaled a breath. "Good, then we'll be in a position to negotiate if they want to use that footage. It's already all over social media. The debut of Bound Hearts. Nice name by the way, very catchy. But my phone started ringing, including the last two producers who hadn't gotten back to us. The ripple effect was pretty instantaneous."

"Not surprising," I said. The ring of the doorbell had me glancing over my shoulder as Coop rose. The girls from Torched streamed in ahead of the first wave of waiters bringing up several rolling tables of food and drink. "They were pretty awesome tonight. But put a pin in any offers, run them by the entertainment attorney, and we'll commit to nothing until Frankie and Bubba both have a chance to review everything. Tonight was amazing for them, but Frankie did this as much for KC and the girls as for her and Bubba."

KC's very real excitement at seeing Frankie and having Frankie perform on stage with them had been echoed by the other girls. As exhausted as those three were, and washed free of makeup, hair up in braids and ponytails, while dressed in comfortable, if slouchy clothes, they looked like what they were— three teenagers. They'd gone out of their way for Frankie and Bubba because they *liked* Frankie.

I was pretty sure we were all accessories, and that was fine. I could handle being Frankie's arm candy. My ego took no beating at that thought.

"Glad to hear it, but those girls are multi-platinum and the videos are likely going to go viral. That will give Frankie and Ian both some serious traction when it comes to negotiation…"

I grinned slowly. "This all sounds very win-win to me."

"It's definitely the best negotiating position to be in."

"I'll take it."

KC had a plate full of French fries and was drowning them in ketchup. For someone who hadn't eaten anything the other day, she hadn't stopped since they wandered in. Frankie and Jake weren't out yet, but they would be in another fifteen or so. Frankie had been wound pretty tight.

Bubba had a pair of beers in hand as he made his way out to the balcony. Wittaker hung up, and I accepted the beer from Bubba when he joined me. The chatter from inside sounded like teenage girls too. Coop just relaxed back against the sofa, watching as Rachel joined the others in getting food.

"Apparently, I shouldn't sign anything at all until the lawyers get to look at it?" It wasn't a real question, but I nodded.

"So Wittaker said. But Frankie will want to give them any release they need."

Raising his beer, Bubba nodded before he took a long drink. "I'm inclined to let her. They didn't have to give us that opportunity."

"Nope," I said, agreeing with him. "They didn't. They were being friends to her and to you. At the same time…"

"Protect our own interests," Bubba said with a sigh, then shook his head. "We'll talk about it."

"Man, you killed it tonight. You guys looked fucking fantastic out there. If I didn't say it before, then hear it now—you have a real future in the business if that's where the two of you decide to go." And I meant it. I'd support them with everything I had too.

His slow grin was all pleasure, if a little embarrassed too. "That means a lot. Seriously."

"Good. Also, did you have a boner the whole time she was singing?"

"So bad," Bubba agreed. "It's the sexiest fucking thing."

I laughed. This was definitely one of those cases where I was glad that the guys totally got me.

Bubba clinked his bottle to mine, and we leaned there against the railing, drinking as the girls gathered around the living room with their plates of food— burgers, fries, ice cream, one of them with all three, and I wasn't saying a word about dipping fries in ice cream.

"You ever thankful you're an only child?" I asked Bubba.

"At the moment?" he laughed. "Yes. I don't know how Coop and Jake do it with the little sisters."

Agreed. I mean, I was grateful as fuck that Frankie wasn't my sister, but watching those girls in there, even as relaxed as they seemed, I worried. I'd kill anyone that let my family wear themselves down like that. I knew for sure Frankie would kick our asses if we let ourselves get that worn down.

We would be wrapping up soon and heading back to the States. But I had to admit, I was going to miss this freedom. June, I promised myself and them. Every June, come hell or high water, we were going to take off for a few weeks and just be us.

JAKE

Frankie's legs shook where they wrapped around my waist, and I tucked my face against her throat. My cock was still hard as a stone, but I'd been determined to wring a couple of orgasms out of her before I came and I still wanted more. I loved the way her fingers dug into my back and how open and hot her kisses were when I claimed her mouth.

As she spasmed around my cock, I had to fight the urge to bite down on the soft skin of her neck, and then she flexed those muscles and rotated her hips.

"Fuck," I swore.

"I want you to come," Frankie whispered against my hair, and then I lifted my head. There was redness around her mouth and her throat. The beard did that when I got too excited, though the burn wasn't as bad as when it was just stubble. She had a fistful of my damp hair, and I moved with her as she arched her back and rotated her hips.

Pulling back, I dug my fingers into her ass and lifted as I thrust upward. "You feel so fucking good, Baby Girl."

"So do you," she whispered, and when she tugged my face toward hers, I eagerly sucked her lower lip until her mouth opened. Tongues dueling, I ground upward, balls deep in her pussy, and I wanted more of her. The beaded tips of her nipples teased at my chest, and I wanted to suck on them, I wanted to finger her ass and fuck her ass. I wanted to be everywhere until all she could feel, taste, or experience was me.

That would never be enough. Not when she laughed as we kissed. Not when she fought to drag me deeper. Not when the low cries of her pleasure echoed off the tile around us, even as the water washed down. All these sensations were perfect, and I wanted to savor them.

"Please Jake," she moaned. "I want to feel you come."

Fuck, that had my balls dragging up tight, and I pressed her against the wall as I pounded into her. The friction had my eyes rolling back, but I needed her to come. I didn't care that she already had, I wanted to feel her shudder as I filled her. Working my hand between us, I found her clit, and it only took one brush and Frankie swore.

The clamp of her pussy on my cock dragged my own orgasm out, and I swallowed her screams, even as I answered them with my own moan. It was my turn to fight shaking legs as we clung to each other.

I hadn't totally meant to fuck her in the shower, but there was just something about a naked, wet Frankie I couldn't resist. A soft laugh escaped me, and I kissed her throat, then up to her jawline.

"What?" she asked, combing her fingers through my hair.

"I was just thinking that I can't resist you naked and wet." I grinned.

"And that's funny?"

"Pretty much." I kissed the tip of her nose. "'Cause I can't resist you dry and naked. Or wet and clothed. Or dry and clothed for that matter."

Her laughter eddied up to join mine, and she shook her head. "I adore you."

"Right back atcha." With care, I eased out of her, and we both let out a long sigh. We'd almost finished showering when helping her wash her breasts turned so interesting. "What do you say we kidnap the boys and drag them around the Tower tomorrow?"

"Oh," she said with a sigh. "I like that idea, but don't leave Archie alone with the crown jewels. I do not need him to get any ideas."

A snort escaped me. "Give that up. You know him—he's going to drown you in jewels if he thinks you'll let him."

Her soft 'hmm' made me smile. Over the years, Frankie had always been so resistant to letting us take care of her. Not anymore. Not that I was complaining, because she insisted on looking after us too.

"What about the British Museum?" She tilted her head up to look at me as she finished rinsing off. "They have the Rosetta Stone and the mummies and…"

I pressed a finger to her lips. "Sold, Baby Girl. We have a couple more days here, and we should have time to really dig into more sights."

"There's so much history here." That was my girl. She made a huge splash on a stage, singing her heart out and looking sexy as fuck, and now she wanted to go nerd out at history.

"I love you," I told her before giving her another long, lingering kiss that might have kept us in the shower longer, but her stomach protested.

One did not simply forget to feed the Frankie. With some reluctance, I shut off the shower, and then we were out and toweling off. I caught her watching me in the mirror as I ran the towel over my chest.

"Like what you see?"

"Oh yes," she said. "I love the way your muscles move when you're drying off. It's really sexy."

I flexed my glutes, and Frankie's grin grew.

"Yeah, I figured those were the muscles you were admiring." Not that I minded.

"Hey," she told me, all innocence. "I like your ass. A lot." Then she slapped my ass right before she scooted out the door and into the bedroom.

I laughed and managed to snap the towel to catch her on one butt cheek. "I like your ass too. And I'll happily spank it if that's what you're angling for."

"Maybe later," she teased, but glanced over at me. "I kind of do like being spanked."

"Oh, I know." But laughter from the other room carried as did the scent of food. We got dressed, Frankie went with sleep shorts and one of my sweatshirts, and I just dragged on loose drawstring pants and a T-shirt. We all slept naked so much these days, it didn't faze me, but at the moment, we had company.

And Rachel.

"Hey…" I said as she ran her fingers through her damp hair. "Don't fuss over Rachel too much. You moved her to tears tonight when you were singing, though she tried to hide it."

"Awww…"

"Yeah," I said. "You move me to tears often, but my masculinity can handle it."

Her delighted smile warmed me up. The sound of my cell ringing distracted me, and I glanced around for it. Took me a minute to locate it in my discarded jeans. My mother's name flashed up on the screen, and I nodded to Frankie.

"Go eat, I'll check in with Mom and the girls and be right out, okay?"

"Okay," she murmured, then blew me a kiss before opening the door.

"Hey, Mom," I greeted as I answered the phone. "I know, I should have called you guys but we've—"

"Jake," Mom interrupted. "There's been an accident."

Chapter Twenty Three
CATS IN THE CRADLE

FRANKIE

"You don't—"

I glared at Jake, and he closed his mouth.

"Thanks, Baby Girl," he murmured before pulling me tighter against him. We were waiting for the express train to take us to Paris from London. Then from there, we would take a second train to Germany and then to the base his father was stationed at. From the moment Jake walked out of the bedroom with that wounded look in his eyes, we'd become a whirlwind of activity.

Archie had booked our train tickets while Jake left a message for Klara. It had been late there, but all Alicia had known was there had been a training accident and Jake's dad was in surgery. Klara returned Jake's call, but his dad was still in surgery. They didn't know how serious it was yet.

No way could he not go, especially since we were in London, just hours away. Nor could I let him go alone. KC and the girls had offered some suggestions on the trains. We could do a flight, but with his father in surgery, trains would get us there in plenty of time and might prove a distraction.

The express from London to Paris was something we'd always wanted to do too. Still, not the way we wanted to do it.

Ian pulled Jake away for a moment to talk to him, and Archie pressed a card into my hand. I glanced down at the black card, then up at him.

"Don't argue," he ordered. "This time, I want you both to have everything you need when you need it. I'll send the plane for you in Germany when you're ready to come back." He frowned. "But let him take all the time he needs. We'll take care of New York and getting the place set up."

"You already got one." It wasn't a question, and I tucked his black credit card away in my wallet before stowing the wallet back in the inner pocket of the jacket I wore.

"Yeah," he admitted with a faint grimace. "It was a surprise, babe…" I pressed my fingers to his mouth before he could try to offer up any kind of apology.

"I love you," I whispered before rising on my tiptoes and replacing my fingers with my lips. His soft sigh as he wrapped me up pulled out one of my own. "I love that you plan fifty steps ahead, and I'll only scold you a little for not letting me help with the house hunting."

"You helped," he murmured before pressing a kiss to my forehead and tightening his hold around me. I sank into the hug, letting him hold me up and leaning on him. "You helped with telling me what you wanted in a place. You helped with opening your home to us in the first place, along with your heart. You helped because you give me purpose and reason to be better."

Tears flooded my eyes, and I rubbed my face carefully against his coat. Rachel had done something with my makeup this morning to hide the shadows from lack of sleep. I'd managed to get Jake to sleep for a couple of hours while everyone else hustled. We'd split our luggage up and packed me and Jake into one bag along with our laptops and Kindles.

Ian and Jake exchanged one of those quick man hugs. But Jake didn't escape Coop so easily. I watched them as I leaned into Archie. We'd said our goodbyes to KC and the girls back at the hotel. Rachel was going to hang out with them for the day, then head out to explore London. I was pretty sure Archie had extended Rachel's stay for as long as she wanted.

They were going to fly to New York after we got to Germany. They didn't want to be in the air until we were safe and sound. I got it, and I wanted them to get some rest before they dove into handling the move and settling in.

"You got him, babe?" Archie asked, and I nodded.

"I got him. I'll take care of him. You guys take care of yourselves?" I pulled back to look up at him, and Archie smiled before kissing me again.

"I hate like hell that you'll be that far away, but I can handle it. You call if you need anything, you understand? Absolutely anything."

"Even if I just need to hear your voice," I promised. One more kiss, and he let me go and turned to Jake. Ian was waiting right there, and he wrapped me up in a ferocious hug.

"Angel, you need anything…"

I smiled against his chest. "Right back atcha. You got Coop and Archie?"

"Yeah, I got them." No hesitation. "Jake's going to be defensive and hyper protective. He won't want to break down in front of you, and he's going to be arguing with himself."

"Because of how distant he and his dad have been." I got that.

"Yeah," Ian said slowly. "Coop will have more advice, but I only have this." He leaned back and lifted my chin. "Be you. That's who he needs. Just be yourself. Be every inch the stubborn brat I know you can be and the fierce woman you are."

I smiled. "I'll take care of him, and I'll jump him if he won't let me in."

A soft chuckle escaped him. "If all else fails…"

"Make him jealous."

Head back, Ian laughed, then shook his head at me. "Only you would play with fire as a method to handle one of us."

"You gotta go with what works…but I'll take care of him. I promise."

Cupping my face, Ian studied me, then gave me a sweet kiss. "Take care of you too. That's an order, Angel."

I smiled against his lips, then bit his lower one gently. "You too, Sir Ian. You take such good care of me, I need you to take equally good care of you."

"Done."

He backed off, and then Coop half picked me up into a hug, and he pressed his forehead to mine. "He's a stubborn ass, both him and his dad. They're both fighters too. All you gotta do is make sure you keep his head above the water and don't let him blame himself."

I smiled. "I can do that."

"I know you can. I'm gonna miss the hell out of you, but we're gonna step up our phone sex game."

A shiver chased up my spine. "Is now really the time to…"

He snorted. "Me and my hand spent years thinking about you, and the last few months, we've had you all to ourselves. Hell yes, now is the time to think about it, and trust me, Jake will appreciate the friendly competition."

"Let me guess," I teased. "You won't mind some pictographic assistance for our calls?"

"Video-chat works," he told me, eyes darkening. "Particularly when he needs a distraction, or you do."

I bit my lower lip because it seemed a really inappropriate time to be turned on. "I'm really growing fond of this possessive side of you."

"Good." Then his mouth claimed mine, and there was nothing sweet in his searing kiss. It was demanding, hot, and filled with decadent promise that had me panting when he let me go. "Don't forget about us."

"As if," Jake grunted, but he wrapped an arm around my middle and pulled me back against him. "I got our girl. We'll keep you guys in the loop."

"If you need us," Archie said as Coop and Ian both nodded.

"Thanks, guys."

We stood on the platform for one long moment, then Ian nodded to the train. "Y'all should go find your seats and get comfortable. Make some new memories."

"Is there a train club or something?" Coop asked, and rough laughter escaped Jake—the first real chuckle he'd made since getting the frantic call from his mom.

"Guess we'll find out, right, Baby Girl?" Jake's question washed over me, and I tilted my head back to smile at him.

"Maybe. You might have to earn it." Humor flashed through his pale blue eyes, along with heat, and he gave me a squeeze. All too soon, we were stepping aboard, and the guys stayed out there on the platform as we moved through the car to our seats. Jake had our backpacks, and he stored them before ushering me into the window seat and sliding into the seat next to me.

His humor dried up as he locked his hand around mine and lifted it to his lips for a kiss. The softness of his beard brushed my knuckles a split second before his mouth did. I squeezed his hand and then tucked my head against his shoulder. This wasn't the adventure we planned, and I was worried about him and his dad. I'd just met Hank, and it made me heartsick to think of something happening to him.

Jake and his dad had just started talking again. None of this was fair. Worse, we didn't know how bad the accident was, other than his dad needed surgery and there had been some kind of crash.

Klara hadn't been able to reveal details. Military protocol, I guessed. But I'd heard the worry in her voice, and so had Jake. His face had tightened and the look in his eyes—No.

Jake's dad had to be all right. But I couldn't bring myself to tell Jake he would be. I couldn't tell him what I didn't know. So I settled for whispering, "I'm here, every step of the way."

He kissed the top of my head and sighed. "I know, Baby Girl."

Then the train began to move and we were out of the station, picking up speed, leaving the rest of our family behind us.

The Eurostar had us back in Paris in a little over two hours. Jake hadn't said much on the ride, though he had fished out my Kindle and we pulled up a book to read. We'd finished the Hannaford Prep books a while back, and he'd read most of MK with me. So we loaded up the new rec from Rachel.

"Those guys are dicks," was his only comment about Dean and the other boys. But I was rather fond of Avalon, even if she was kind of a dick herself. But he read right along with me, and if nothing else, the book distracted him. He only checked his phone three times.

In Paris, Jake let me carry my own backpack while he handled the single suitcase and his backpack. We made our way to our next train, which didn't depart for an hour. "Hungry?"

"No," he said almost automatically, then glanced at me. "But you should eat."

There was a little café beyond the platforms where we picked up some pastries. He ate because I kept pulling my croissants apart and feeding him. The coffee was shit but we drank it, and then we were back to board the next train on time. Archie had booked us first class cars all the way.

Luggage stowed and in our new seats, I glanced at Jake. "More book, or would you rather watch a movie?"

He curled a lock of my hair around his finger. "Book is fine, Baby Girl, unless you want to watch a movie."

I rolled my eyes, and he tugged the hair gently. "I asked first."

"True, but right now, it's easier to not think because then I start wondering why we haven't heard anything more. Has he really been in surgery all night? Is Klara just exhausted? It's the middle of the night at home, but Mom is probably pacing, waiting to hear from me too."

She hadn't told Jake's sisters, yet. She wanted more information before she broke the news to them. On the one hand, I understood it. On the other, I didn't envy her that experience.

"Book then. We were just getting to the good part."

He laughed softly. "Thank you for coming with me, Baby Girl."

"Nowhere else I'd rather be." Not while he was hurting. Not when he needed me. It was one thing when everything was fine. But it wasn't fine. "And he's going to be all right. That's what we have to tell ourselves until we know different."

He nodded. "I keep telling myself that, but so far, I think I'm full of shit. You tell me, and I'll believe you."

I locked gazes with him. "He's going to be all right. From what your mom says and what I've seen, you and your dad are a lot alike. You're too stubborn by half."

A small grin tugged at the corners of his mouth. "Says the most stubborn girl I know."

"And you out stubborned me, so what does that say?"

He opened his mouth, then closed it again, a thoughtful look on his face "All right, you might have a point," he conceded.

Smiling, I settled the Kindle between us, and when he tucked his arm around me, I leaned my head against his shoulder. The gentle rub of his cheek against my hair hopefully gave him as much comfort as he offered me.

We were almost to our destination when Avalon kicked the crap out of Dean after he was a real dick.

"That's some real-life girl goals right there," I murmured, and Jake's whole body shook with laughter.

"Trust me, Baby Girl, anyone treats you like that and I'll beat them to a pulp for you, but I promise to keep up your fight training. I like you being a little badass."

Pleasure speared me. I loved that Jake loved me strong. More, I loved that he laughed.

"But don't get any ideas about that dick piercing. I don't care how many of these assholes you read about with them."

"I love your dick just the way it is," I promised him.

"And you've already got Coop half convinced," he retorted, and I gave a little shrug.

"I promised I'd pierce my navel whether he did it or not."

The heat in Jake's eyes sent another shiver through me. "Did you now?" He ran his finger along the hem of my shirt. "Just any piercing?"

"Something green to match my eyes and steel gray, so the gray-green matches his."

Jake nodded slowly. "I approve."

"Go with us when I do it?"

"You don't even have to ask, Baby Girl. I'm going to want you there for my dragon too."

"Hell yes." I tilted my head. "I can't wait to see you all inked up and colorful."

"Yeah?" He raised his brows. "All this clean, smooth flesh not doing it for you?"

I snorted. "You know you do it for me and then some."

"I do," he murmured. "Doesn't mean I don't mind hearing about it."

"Fair." Stroking my fingers along his cheek to his chin, I asked, "Have I mentioned how much I love your beard?"

"I think I heard a moan or two in that direction that last time I ate you out."

Biting my lower lip, I tried to swallow my laughter. If I didn't think we'd get booted off the train, I might climb on his lap right here. Still, we had a few too many in our audience, and my exhibitionist kink wasn't linked to a going to jail kink. "It feels so soft against my thighs."

"Particularly since you got that perfect pussy of yours all waxed and neatened?" He raised his brows and the stakes. "'Cause I love how silky you are on my tongue."

Heat speared through me, along with the warmth Jake's fingers elicited as he slid his hand between my thighs and gripped my leg. "So it's still perfect, even if it's not all wild curls?"

Were we really having this conversation?

"Baby Girl, everything about you is perfect. I'm just glad Rachel promised me she would make sure any waxing she talked you into would be handled by a woman. I didn't specify hetero, but I can handle a woman doing it but not a guy."

The corners of my lips twitched as I leaned in close to whisper against his ear. "I promise you, the only men who have ever seen my pussy are the four of you."

He rumbled with a bit of a growl before turning his head to catch my lips in a slow kiss. I just leaned into the contact, the heat gentle and giving as much as it was asking for comfort. I kept stroking his beard, savoring the soft brush of it against my cheeks. I hadn't been kidding about how much I enjoyed the tickle of it against my thighs and more delicate parts. It just added a whole other level of sensation.

One last thrust of his tongue had my toes curling in my boots before he let me have a breath of air. "You're dangerous and perfect."

No lie, I liked that compliment. I just grinned, then kissed the tip of his nose and glanced at the time before holding up the book we were still reading. "We have a few more minutes."

"Yeah, that's not reminding my dick to behave, but we can't fit all our luggage in the bathroom so you're safe…" He nipped my ear. "For now."

I could point out that I didn't want to be safe, but the distraction gave him a few precious minutes of peace. I would make it up to him later.

In Stuttgart, Jake's humor faded, and I took his hand as we made our way through the station. Fortunately, a good number of the people spoke English as well as German. French, I could do. Jake actually knew a few phrases, and he used them sparingly. I'd texted the guys that we'd arrived in the city and I'd be in touch as soon as we had news on Jake's father.

Their responses were swift. Their flight departed in a couple of hours, so we had time to get to the hospital at the base. I knew what they were waiting for. If the news at the hospital was bad, Archie would be directing that flight to Germany. They would be here for Jake just like I was.

Jake led us out of the station. I wasn't sure if we were going to get a taxi or hire a car. To be honest, I'd never been on a military base. Did we need to get permission to even go there? Or was there some other arrangement we could make? For now, I kept those questions to myself.

To my surprise, a familiar face waited for us as Jake and I crossed from the station entrance toward a parking lot. The dark-haired woman with the warm smile and a buttoned down, clean uniform strode toward us, and Jake released my hand and the suitcase to catch Klara in a hug.

She murmured something to him, and I held back to give them some space. Jake towered over the woman who had been as much a part of his childhood as his own mother. I remembered her, but I never equated her with family and a part of me felt bad about that. This wasn't about me, at all. So I refused to dwell on that. I was here for Jake and for Klara.

"How is he?" Jake asked.

"He's still in surgery," she answered. "I'm sorry I didn't get back to you with more details yet, I was hoping they'd finish by the time I'd done my report. Let's get the two of you into the car. I need to check you in with base security, then you can stay with us…"

Hesitation flickered over her face, but Jake reached for the suitcase and nodded. "We'd like that."

Relief flooded her eyes as she glanced at me. "Hello again, Frankie."

"Hello, ma'am."

"Klara," she told me. "I might be an officer, but you definitely don't report to me. Now, come on you two. You can catch me up in the car, and after we see your dad, Jake, we can call Alicia."

The tension in Jake's frame seemed to wax and wane, and he flexed his grip on my hand as we followed her.

"Can you tell me what happened? All Mom said was there was an accident."

"I'll tell you everything," she said as she unlocked the Audi. "I promise."

A training accident. Jake's dad had been with a number of other soldiers, airmen, and marines aboard a helicopter when it experienced mechanical difficulties. The challenge hadn't just been the crash though. They'd gone down somewhere in the Alps, and it had taken time for a crew to get to him.

My stomach cramped at the very idea. Jake sat up in the front next to Klara, while I road in the back.

"His leg is broken in three places," Klara said. "That's why the surgery is taking so long—they are having to put pins in and put the bones back together."

I shuddered, and I was not alone in that one.

"It could have been so much worse, but they were feeling confident."

Jake blew out a breath. "He goes down in a helicopter crash, and all he does is break a leg?" The dry humor couldn't disguise the sudden and keen relaxation Klara's news gave him.

"So far," Klara said with a wry smile. "They wanted to check everything else. He might have a mild concussion, but considering the way he was cussing when they were wheeling him in, I doubt that will keep him down for long."

I had to bite back a laugh, and Jake shot a glance at me over his shoulder. "That sounds like Dad." His eyes warmed though, and I mouthed a kiss to him. He winked. "How long is the surgery?"

"They said twelve hours when they took him back. But they had to do some other exams before they put him fully under. I had already called your mom, but I had to wait for him to be out before I could call anyone again."

Another reason she hadn't gotten back to us.

"He didn't want me to know?" Jake asked, his tone guarded. I didn't think twice about it, I reached forward and rested my hand on his shoulder.

"Jakey," Klara said, her voice soft but her tone firm. "Your father is a proud man, do not let this hurt your feelings. It would never occur to him that you would want to know to be here. He has always seen it as his place to protect you."

"Well, he can't really do that if he isn't around, can he?" The harshness in his voice underscored his worry.

"Jakey." That was it. Just the two syllables delivered in an affectionate if firm tone, and he sighed.

"Klara, I don't know how to talk to him anymore."

"Funnily enough, he says the same about you."

A part of me wanted to gawk at the sights. This was yet another country I'd never been to before, but the rest of me remained focused on Jake. I kept my hand on his shoulder, and he covered my fingers with his own.

"And I'm going to tell you what I tell him," Klara continued, and I felt more than saw her glance at me. "Love and respect him for who he is, but don't expect him to change. You are so alike, both of you. So fierce in your devotion and dedication. You also firmly believe you know what is right for your family. You saw him letting Alicia go as a betrayal."

Jake's fingers flexed on mine.

"He saw it as his duty, because she was unhappy and he couldn't make her stay where she didn't want to be. Neither of us could, nor would we. And she needed you kids. If he'd fought to keep you here, it would have forced her to stay too."

Jake shuddered under my hand.

"He won't tell you this and I will deny it if you claim I did," Klara continued, "but he has applied for two duty changes, he just didn't receive them because they need him here. When his twenty comes up, he may request early retirement."

"Fuck," Jake swore.

"Language," she corrected lightly, but then we were at the security gate to the base and she was showing her ID. We had to show our passports as well. Jake also had his dependent's ID. In no time at all, we were through the gate.

"It hasn't changed," Jake said as she drove.

"No," Klara said. "Not a bit. I think some of the kids that were here when you were are still around. Tamara still lives across the street."

"Trying to get me in trouble?" Jake asked, a hint of a smile in his voice.

"Not at all," Klara retorted. "First of all, I'd have to be blind to not see how you kids look at each other, and Tamara would be more interested in your girl than you."

I couldn't help it. I cracked up as Jake swore, but he glanced back at me with real laughter. "Keep it up and I will spank you," he threatened, but I just grinned.

"I didn't do anything."

"Yes you did. You're adorable."

"Ugh," Klara grunted. "Enough. You're going to give me cavities."

But that earned a real laugh from Jake, and I grinned. The more I got to know Klara, the more I liked her. Which was good, because clearly, she was family.

We went straight to the hospital on the base. My eyes were wide at all the activity on the base. There were people from all the different areas of the service too, based on the different uniforms. They were a purple base, or so Jake tried to explain, because there were so many different areas of the service all stationed here. They did a little bit of everything from this base, and it also played host to everything from training to rest and relaxation. Either way, it was a busy place.

I fired off a text to the guys that we were at the hospital and gave them a quick thumbnail on Jake's dad's condition. Archie let me know they were on their way to the airport and that Rachel was going to stay on in London. KC had sent her best as well, and she asked that I text her or call when I was free. Email would work too.

Inside, I walked with Jake as we followed Klara to the waiting area. She checked in with a nurse at the desk, and they spoke for several minutes.

Leaning against Jake's arm, I glanced up at him. "Feeling better?"

"Some. A broken leg sucks and that's gonna put him out of commission for a while, but he can recover from that."

And it wasn't likely to kill him. Or at least, it was not considered a fatal injury of any kind.

"What about what Klara said about him applying for reassignment to the States?"

Jake sighed. "I don't know what to do with that. Or what to do with the idea that he didn't fight for us because he didn't want to force Mom to stay here. Then at the same time, Klara's… She's amazing and she's family. It's not like he turned his back on us for some skank."

"Thank you," Klara said, and Jake stiffened.

"Sorry, Klara," he apologized stiffly, and she laughed.

"Relax, Jakey. I do possess a sense of humor, and you just called me family, baby boy. It's been a long time since you did that." She gave us both a warm smile, then motioned to the chairs. "Let's sit. Your father is in recovery, the surgery went well," she began as soon as we were seated. "They had to put a pair of rods in to reconnect the bones, and he's going to need physical therapy *after* he's healed. Probably at least six to ten weeks of very light duty, followed by conditioning duty, then a reassessment."

"He's gonna hate that," Jake muttered.

"Probably, but he'll do the work. Now, after the surgeon comes out to speak to us, we can go back to our place and get you two settled. He won't be awake for a few hours, and you've been running. You're also probably hungry."

My stomach growled, and Jake grinned.

"Hey," I said. "I can always eat."

"One of the things I love about you," he said with a wink. "But yeah, if you think it'll be a while before he wakes up… I want to talk to the surgeon, then call Mom."

"We can do all of that."

We did. The surgeon basically told us what Klara had, and he reassured Jake that it would be several hours before they lightened his sedation and let his dad wake up. The guys were on the plane when I texted them about the report, and Coop answered this time that they were going to head back and get to work on the new place and take care of the moving.

He promised to sneak me pictures. He also said I owed him at least one nice nude for being so helpful.

When I showed Jake the message, he sent Coop his middle finger and then said he'd think about it.

There was laughter in the group message after that, but even Jake seemed more relaxed. I sat with Klara and had coffee while Jake called Alicia.

"You're good for him," Klara told me, and I glanced at her.

"He's good for me."

"I'm sure," she said. "But he was so serious and so tense all the time after we first got to Germany. He was very determined to not like it here, and yet he wouldn't tell us why." She shot me a look. "I'm pretty sure I know why now."

I smiled. "He's happy now."

"Yes, he is."

And I planned to keep him that way. "Do you think he and his dad can work things out?"

"I do, even if we have to lock the stubborn bastards up and make them talk."

I laughed.

"You think I'm joking."

"Actually," I said slowly. "I don't think that at all. But I don't know that I'd help you lock him up."

"That's the right answer."

"Not that this was a test," I deadpanned, and it was Klara's turn to grin.

"Oh yes, I do like you."

That was cool, I liked her too.

Chapter Twenty Four
FROM WHERE YOU ARE

FRANKIE

"You look sleepy," Coop said from the screen on my computer. I was sprawled next to Jake in the bed, and I hadn't bothered with pulling the sheet up. Coop had video-chatted right in the middle of sex, and Jake answered then told him to wait. The fact Coop swore because Jake's ass was in the way competed with Coop's own suggestions had left me in stitches from laughter.

Worse, I'd been trying to smother it because Jake's dad was home from the hospital and they were only two rooms away. I did not need them hearing me, even if Jake had been all the more determined to make me scream. Turned out orgasms were even better when you had the giggles.

"I wore her out," Jake said with a wicked grin, running his thumb up and down my arm. The last week here had been a combination of playing tourist and history buff in and around time spent visiting with Jake's dad. When he came home from the hospital two days earlier, it had led to some tensions, and I had a feeling an explosion was imminent between the two men.

Jake's dad had taken to his convalescence probably as well as Jake would, especially since it also came with a wheelchair and orders to stay in it for at least another week, then they would fit him with a leg support and brace. Meanwhile, Jake had done the heavy lifting, and his dad had been a prick about it. Klara's words, not mine, and I was staying out of it.

For now.

Per Jake's request.

Mostly because he said if his dad snarled at me even once he was going to take his head off, and while I didn't think he would snarl at me, probably better to reduce the potential for violence. But seriously, his father was a grown-ass man, he needed to act like it.

"I don't know," I said as I tilted my head. My back was to Jake's chest, and I ran my foot up his bare leg. "I bet I could handle another round or three."

"Is that a challenge, Baby Girl?" I swore his voice dropped an octave, and I didn't miss Coop licking his lips.

"No," I murmured, biting back a smile as Coop's whole expression fell. "A challenge would suggest I didn't think you could handle it."

"Wow," Coop said as Jake started laughing. "I didn't know you had such a cruel streak in you."

"Yes you did," I retorted. "Now, stop trying to focus on sex. Tell me how the move is going. You guys have all been cagey when we've talked to you."

"You want me to talk about moving? Furniture? And real estate in a hot as hell city when the most perfect breasts in the world are staring at me?"

Jake cupped my breasts, covering them with his hands, and I swore my nipples peaked at both the contact and the way Coop's mouth dropped open.

"Problem solved," Jake offered as he began to massage them. "Tell Baby Girl what she wants to know."

Okay, there was something seriously hot about Jake tracing the rough calluses of his thumbs against my nipples as though taking turns torturing me and Coop. He caught my foot and trapped it between his legs so it spread mine, and the sheet drifted lower while he played.

"Um…it's a place, got rooms. Lots of new furniture… A little harder there, Jake, her nipples aren't quite red enough."

"It's a *place*?" That was what he came up with? Jake dipped his head down to nuzzle the shell of my ear, even as he slid his hand down and bared one of my breasts. Fortunately for me, his fingers dipped right between my legs. Unfortunately for Coop, he dragged the sheet up with his other hand to hide everything from view. "Oh, I like this."

"Traitor," Coop mumbled, but Jake just laughed at him as he began to play with his own cum and used it to tease around my clit. Considering how hard I'd come just a few minutes ago, I was still sensitive as fuck and it was hard not to shift against the bed. Particularly when the pressure was just enough to make me squirm but not quite enough to give me the friction I craved.

"Answer her questions," Jake said. "She's been a rock star for me and deserves everything."

Coop made a face. "She's a rock star for all of us. You're just the lucky asshole who has her to himself."

"Hey," Jake said slowly. "You know what? I do." He reached over and waved at the screen. "Night, Coop." Then shut it off as Coop complained.

I burst out laughing and twisted to roll over on him as Jake set the laptop aside and pulled me to him. "That was mean."

"Him and his blue balls are going to record you a video tour of the brownstone Archie purchased. It's a really nice place on the upper West Side, and we're not that far from Central and Riverside Parks."

I stared at Jake and then sat up abruptly, straddling his hips. But he pulled me back down before I could grab my phone. "Jake…"

"Nope, no freaking out, Baby Girl. Archie's surprise is excellent, and I am dying for you to see it. And until you walk inside that place, you do not get to freak out."

I gaped at him. "Do you have any idea how much real estate there has to cost?" I'd done some searching when we'd first looked at NYU to apply. Apartments there were a nightmare cost.

"Mmm-hmm, I have some ideas," he murmured, then rolled us so I was on bottom and he could pin me more easily. He rained kisses down along my jaw. "And I also know that we can afford a bigger place, a more secure one where you and Bubba can practice, and we have space to work, to study, and to even set up a workshop if we want."

I groaned as he nuzzled kisses against my lips. "He bought some mansion, didn't he?"

"You'll see," he teased, working his way to my throat, and the brush of his beard just added to the sea of sensations he seemed intent on drowning me in. His cock rubbed along my slit, and it grew stiffer with each slow grind. "Let Coop impress you. Archie's nervous enough about it."

"Archie likes to pretend he isn't nervous." That wasn't a betrayal if Jake had seen it too. He tugged at my earlobe, his teeth scraping gently.

"He does," he murmured. "But he also over plans when he's nervous, and he has a pair of backup spaces if you hate the one he found."

Another shudder went through me, and I dug my fingers into Jake's ass. The bite of my nails actually had him lifting his head. "Jake, how many places did he buy?"

"I didn't ask and he didn't offer," Jake told me firmly. "He said New York real estate was always a good investment and that some of those places were already in the family. My only request is we were nowhere near the place his mother is living."

I made a face. Yeah, I could live without seeing Muriel. I sighed and then met Jake's gaze. "Am I making too much out of this? I know Archie will say he can afford it and that I can too, now." Not that I would ever be quite as easy at spending as Archie was. At least not on myself. Spoiling the rest of them? I was down for that.

"No, Baby Girl." Jake's expression softened. "You have never loved Archie for his money. You have never noticed his money, not like so many others did. Honestly, half the time, I forget about it until he does something violently generous. We are never going to be those people where we take it for granted. That said…"

He raised his brows, and he didn't have to go on. I got it. "We are his people though, just like he's ours."

"Exactly." Mouth on mine, Jake didn't give me room to breathe much less respond, but I arched into the kiss, dragging my nails up his back as he mimed pumping with his hips. The slow push and pull dragged his semi-erect dick against my clit over and over. It was both lazy and sensual.

"You're going to think I'm crazy," I complained, but only a little, and Jake chuckled.

"Only if you keep thinking about Archie while I'm trying to distract you."

Okay, now I rolled my eyes. "I've had you come down my throat while his face was buried in my pussy making me come all over him. You've also fucked my ass while he's been in my pussy. I'm pretty sure I had his dick in my mouth when you were in my pussy too. Frankly, I think we ran out of combinations over my birthday. It's hard to separate any of you from sex now."

Mouth open, Jake studied me a beat, then shrugged. "Fair enough. Also, talk dirty to me some more."

They were all terrible. Absolutely terrible. And I loved them, but my next words went unspoken because there was a quiet knock on the door. Jake's eyes narrowed, and he made a face.

"Stay here," he ordered, then gave me a hard kiss before climbing out of the bed and grabbing a pair of boxers on his way to the door. I rolled onto my side to watch him. I really did love his body and the way the muscles moved when he did. I would never get tired of studying him.

The room we were using had been Jake's when the family lived here.

Apparently, they hadn't moved to smaller accommodations because the girls still came over to visit. He cracked open the door. As it was, they hadn't changed Jake's room though. Granted, it wasn't dressed up with posters from when he'd been younger, but there was a catcher's mitt on the dresser that was ridiculously small when compared to his hand now. The one concession to his age, however, had been to add a full bed to the room rather than the single he'd claimed had been in there.

"Yeah?" he asked as he cracked it open.

"Sorry," Klara said. "I did wait until the moans stopped, so I assumed you were done."

Oh. God.

I yanked a pillow over my head and hid.

Jake chuckled. "I like fucking my girl, Klara, but thanks for waiting. What's up?"

I sputtered at Jake's direct response, but my face was on so much fire, I couldn't bring myself to emerge and say anything.

"I bet. I need a hand with your dad. He's being difficult, and I want to shift him out of the bed and into the chair for a while."

"And he's being a dick and refusing?"

"Jake." One note of censure, and he sighed. I peeked, and he stood one hand braced against the open door but still blocking it so she couldn't see around him.

"Yeah, gimme a sec and I'll come help." Then he closed the door and glanced at me. "Sorry, Baby Girl."

I sat up, embarrassment forgotten. "He's your dad."

"He's being a dick." The scowl on his face worried me. "Would you do me a favor?"

"Anything."

"There's a place off base and in town that makes the best ice cream. Get dressed and ask Klara to take you? Tell her you have shark week and chocolate cravings? Just get her out of the place for a bit."

I slid out of the bed and reached for some tissues to clean up. Then glanced at him. "I can, but…"

"It'll be fine," he promised as he pulled a shirt out of our suitcase and tugged it on. "I promise. Dad being a dick to me is one thing, he's in pain and he hates being seen as helpless. I get that. But him being a dick to Klara is out of bounds."

My heart squeezed as I dressed. "You going to give him the lay of the land?"

"Damn straight. He raised me to treat women better. He and Mom both did, and I'll be damned if he gets to slide because he broke his leg." He hesitated a moment and then added, "And I need to talk to him, just him and me. Maybe set some things straight between us again. I don't know if it will help, but after what Klara said, I owe it to him to try."

I stuffed my feet into shoes and then rose up on my tiptoes to hug him. He picked me right up and held me tight.

"Fucks with my head that he could have died, and he might have died thinking I was still pissed at him," Jake said softly. "He could have set me straight a long time ago, but he didn't. He just let me think what I did and protect Mom."

"Because he was protecting her too," I answered him and stroked my hand through his hair. "I get it. Give me five to ask her for help and then take all the time you need."

He gave me another squeeze. "Thanks, Baby Girl."

"Jake," I said as he set me down. "Give yourself a break. The same one you're about to cut him. You didn't know what they didn't tell you, and you were doing the right thing. You were protecting your mom, and right now, you want to protect Klara too."

He nodded slowly. "It's hard not to be mad. And I don't have the best temper." He sounded so damn sheepish, it took everything I had to not laugh.

"You don't say," I murmured, and he gave me a wry grin. "You can only be you. And as far as I'm concerned, you are the best you on the planet. Now, go *talk* to your dad. Try that, and if that doesn't work…well, I guess yelling is the next best thing."

He laughed and then gave me another kiss. "Go get ice cream."

"You don't have to tell me twice." I gave him a little shove, and he chuckled. Fortunately, Klara seemed to be on the same page, because I'd barely asked and she grabbed her shoes and a hat. It was definitely colder at night here than in Texas, but I was pretty convinced most of Europe would seem colder to me and I was okay with that. It was never too cold for ice cream.

I didn't know what Jake said to his dad exactly, I didn't ask and he didn't offer, but the tension in the house dropped appreciably by the time Klara and I returned with all the supplies I could ever want for shark week. I wasn't due for another few days, but like I said, I never turned down ice cream.

The second week of our stay included card games that Jake's dad—he insisted that I call him Bill, and yes, that was weird for me—and Klara taught us, along with board games. Jake and I bought them a game console, and Jake spent an entire afternoon teaching his dad how to use it so they could actually play over the internet once Jake got home.

Klara's relief was a tangible thing, whether we were at their place or she was giving us directions to some sightseeing we might want to do. Bill and Jake also seemed more at ease with each other, even if their teasing still seemed a bit on the prickly side. We were happy to celebrate the Fourth of July with them, but I was missing the guys, even if I talked to them every day.

I was also missing the work they were doing, though it sounded like they had everything moved up to the new place. Then again, the tour Coop had given me over the phone had proven just how fantastic the new place was, and I had been floored by how gorgeous it was. The only room I hadn't been allowed to see was the master suite on the top floor.

Archie had interrupted the tour and announced I got to see that when I came home.

Fair enough.

The ache to see them just grew, and by the end of the third week in Germany, Jake's dad had been fitted for a leg brace and boot. It would give his leg support and help him walk while he continued to heal.

Essentially, he and Klara would be fine without us. While I was eager to get back to Archie, Ian, and Coop, I wasn't leaving Jake behind. So as long as he needed to be here, I was staying with him.

Also, phone sex had gotten very interesting, at least the way Coop and Archie played. Ian was killing me with new music. He'd been writing up a storm in the new place. I had picked up souvenirs for them, including a little beer girl outfit that Jake promised would drive them nuts if I wore it at home.

At home being the key phrase there.

I kidnapped Jake out of the house one day at Klara's request, and we went to see the Mercedes-Benz and Porsche museums. While I didn't care anywhere near as much about the cars or their engineering as he did, I soaked up his excitement and the notes he took. He also sent Archie about a hundred texts.

When we got back to the base, Klara and Bill had prepared an outdoor grill, and we barbecued like we were at home. It was a great night, and for the first time in my hearing, Bill asked Jake about his engineering degree and his plans.

Something inside me relaxed as the tension in Jake also eased. No more discussions about Jake entering the military and no more judgment either. If anything, Bill appeared genuinely interested. Klara raised her glass of wine toward me, and I clinked mine with hers and we settled in to enjoy it.

It was the last week of July when I called Archie and asked him to send the plane.

"Oh thank fuck," he said at the request. "I wasn't sure I could go much longer without seeing you, babe."

"You saw me day before yesterday on video chat, but I get it… I miss you too. I miss all of you."

"Yeah well, you're gonna have to suck up to Tiddles, I'm his new favorite." He sounded almost smug about it.

"Oh, I miss them too. Jake and I could book a flight…"

"Hush," Archie ordered. "I'll get the plane on the way. They're in London currently. I can have the plane there in a few hours or tomorrow, whenever you want it."

"Tomorrow is great. It's already late afternoon here, and we just spent the day walking all over the market. My feet are killing me, and Jake promised me a massage."

Archie grunted. "I hope he knows he gets the outside for at least a month when you get home."

I busted out laughing. "He does, and thank you for not making a big deal out of me wanting to be here for him."

"Babe, he needed you. We all get it. You needed to be there for him. And I know I'm going to hate myself for this, but your grandparents still want you to come out to the Hamptons when you're back. They asked Grandpa Ted about how much longer you thought you might be gone because they didn't want to bother you."

A snort escaped me, not because I didn't believe him, but because I'd talked to my grandparents at least once a week while here as well. "What did you tell them?"

"That I hoped by the first week of August." I could almost *see* him crossing his fingers.

"That works for me," I said with a grin. "That means I get a whole week with you guys and to really get a feel for our new place and the city before I go see them."

"Yes." His verbal fist pump just filled me with joy. "Labor Day at your dad's then?"

"Ugh, family is hard."

It was Archie's turn to laugh. "We'll do Bubba's birthday up right and he'll get you for whatever he wants, but I know you want to meet your siblings, and Labor Day is kind of contained. It's a long weekend, not too long but not too short for a visit, and we can drive up, which gives us the excuse to drive back early. I figure we can do the same thing with your grandparents, plus the drive to the Hamptons is really nice."

"And you get me to yourself for that."

"Oh yeah, I get you to myself for that."

No way I would say no to that. "Sounds like a plan."

"I'll take care of everything, you look after Jake and bring that beautiful body of yours home where we can spoil you."

"I can't wait."

"Oh, babe, you have no idea."

I had a few, except I really wanted to hear his. Jake and his dad were out in the living room playing and I was alone, so I slid out of my clothes and switched the call to video. Archie's expression made it all worth it.

"Why don't you tell me what you want to do?" I offered, and his grin grew. "In explicit detail."

"First, I want to kiss that lush mouth of yours while I fist your hair and feel those sumptuous breasts rub against my chest…"

Hell. I was rubbing my thighs together, and he'd just gotten started.

As promised, the jet was waiting for us at Stuttgart International. I let Jake say his goodbyes privately to Klara and to his father. I might have had to blink away a few tears when Jake gave his dad a hug. Then it was just the two of us making our way to the private terminal. We didn't have any real declarations to make, and the crew was waiting for us to get loaded. It wouldn't be long before we would take off.

It was strange as hell to board the private plane with it being just Jake and I. A low whistle greeted us, however, and I squealed when Coop grinned at me from one of the seats. I threw myself at him, and he laughed. "What the hell are you doing here?" Not that I wasn't happy to see him.

In fact, I didn't wait for him to answer as I kissed him. Jake chuckled as he dropped into the seat next to Coop's. "They've been taking turns being on the plane anytime it had to come over to Europe so one of them could fly back with us, but Coop was really hoping it would be him."

"That was sneaky," I said, almost breathless as I lifted my head and met Coop's gaze.

"Definitely," he said. "But I missed you like hell, and Jake and I still need our admission to the mile-high club."

I threw my head back as true joy exploded inside of me. Jake snorted. "Not like he couldn't wait or anything."

"Fuck off," Coop said cheerfully. "You've had this pussy all to yourself for weeks. Not to mention these breasts. And that smile… Fuck, have I missed that smile." He didn't give me a chance to respond before he was kissing me again. The only reason he let me go was because I had to be in my own seat for takeoff, and even then, he kept hold of my hand.

"It's good to see you," Jake told him.

"I know, you were broken without me."

They flipped each other off, and I just giggled. Yes. Coop was here, and I had zero problem with following him right back to the bedroom as soon as we hit a cruising altitude. I'd missed him and his big dick, but what I wasn't prepared for, however, was the dick he held in his hand and offered to me to examine.

Jake stared at it and then began to laugh. "You didn't…"

"She wants to know what a piercing would feel like, so I had a model of my dick made just for you with a piercing in it." He looked so fucking proud of himself, and I swore, I soaked right through my panties at the whole idea. "Now, we're going to experiment with that and the original model, and you tell me which feels better."

I was pretty sure the rest of me went up in flames then too.

Though, I wasn't going to lie, the fact I held a dildo of Coop's cock in my hand—suggested piercing and all—was probably one of the hottest things he'd ever done, and the man had been setting me on fire all year.

"Fuck me," I whispered.

"Oh don't worry, Baby Girl," Jake said as he pulled off his belt. "We intend to."

SUBJECT: BOUND HEARTS IS TRENDING

Okay, maybe you aren't *trending* per se, but you are making waves on our social media. Geoff—he's cool btw—grabbed the name on all the various social media sites about three seconds after I intro'd you. I should have thought about that. Anyway, we've got everything locked down for you and Ian. When you guys are ready, they're all yours.

Thanks for coming to London, thanks for coming out on that stage with us, and thanks for debuting your first performance alongside us. In a lot of ways, I think it reminded me of why I love singing in the first place. You guys made it fun.

Finally, I hope everything is okay with Jake's dad. Let us know when you're stateside, and if someone from our management team calls you, Aubrey said to tell them to fuck off. We'll sort everything out between us and keep the lawyers out of it. Stupid lawyers.

Love you, talk soon. I might sleep for a week.

KC

Chapter Twenty Five
WELCOME TO NEW YORK

ARCHIE

I wasn't the only one checking my watch the day Frankie and Jake flew back with Coop. Lucky bastard got to see her a few hours before we did, but Bubba and I took the car service to pick them up. We made a stop for a huge bundle of roses—Bubba's quick thinking because he spotted one of the flower shops on the way and we pulled over. I had him grab her three dozen and then had another three dozen sent back to the brownstone.

"Overkill?" Bubba teased without any real challenge, and I snorted.

"It's been over a month." And we'd done our best to stay busy. I'd taken a couple of meetings with my grandfather just to occupy myself. Coop had started volunteering at a local shelter to get out of the brownstone, and he'd voluntarily joined Bubba and I for runs.

Something we'd done every single day. Coop joined us four days after we arrived, and we all got it. I hated—hate—her being so far away. That wasn't going to change. Jake needed her, and we talked to her constantly, but it wasn't the same. Bubba had actually taken some calls with potential producers and the entertainment attorney. He'd also put them all on hold until Frankie and Jake were back.

As far as I was concerned, they could stay on fucking hold for a while. The ache of missing her last summer had been painful. The last few weeks though? These had been brutal and not because we were worried about when we were seeing her again, but more because it felt like I was actively missing a piece of myself.

The cats seemed to feel the same way, as had Jeremy. Though it amused the fuck out of me that Frankie's room, the bedroom on the top floor, was only cursorily set up because we wanted to make sure it was done her way.

We had added a sofa and chairs up there, so it was almost the perfect studio flat, save for the lack of kitchenette, and Coop had been the one to suggest adding a coffeemaker for when she went into hard study mode. Bubba countered though that we would need to make sure we set up regular meals then more than ever.

Jeremy had simply told us to continue with the rest of our work and he would handle dinner schedules and making sure we all ate adequately healthy meals on time. Since he'd also stocked the wine fridge with Frankie's favorites, I suggested leaving it in his capable hands.

We hadn't told her yet that Jeremy would also be managing the house here, but it was almost eight thousand square feet, four floors, and a full school schedule. Looking after the five of us would be a full-time job, and Jeremy's genuine thrill at being asked hadn't been lost on me. He was officially on *my* payroll now, even if he had been paid out of one of my trusts for the past two years.

While we'd been traveling, he'd finished the arrangements to move our personal items and selected pieces of furniture and electronics into the brownstone after verifying that it was ready for us. I'd debated hiring a service to handle the decorating, but Jeremy, along with the guys, all scolded me on that idea.

We would decorate it when Frankie was there and not a day before. The only rooms truly furnished and ready were the dining room and kitchen, as well as Jeremy's room and the formal salon that none of us were likely to ever use unless we had a party.

So probably never use, but it was also a room Jeremy could enjoy as well. The rest of us would live upstairs. The game room was set up, and the bed I'd ordered for Frankie's room, the one I'd been waiting to get since we'd all but moved into her apartment, had arrived the day before we'd come home and now it just waited for Frankie.

"Arch," Bubba said, and I cut him a look. "Your leg is bouncing like mad. Relax."

Fuck. I frowned and shifted in the seat. I usually played it a lot cooler than this. "You know what, I don't even care. I have fucking missed her, and it would be really nice if we could get out to Queens faster."

The driver glanced back at us. "Sorry, sir. There's an accident on the FDR. We'll be passing it soon, and I can make up time."

"It's fine," I told the man. The flight had another fifty minutes before it landed. We just wanted to be *right* there when they exited the private passenger terminal. It had taken some time to get used to being in the big city again, an entirely different pace of life, and I was so fucking eager to get Frankie here.

The night life, the theatres, the restaurants, and the access to so many different international offerings atop the museums and the fact this was a city that never slept? Oh yeah, I was ready for this.

Both of our phones buzzed when we were still ten minutes out. The flight had landed early. Our driver made good on his promise and made up the time. We were pulling up at the private terminal just as Frankie texted to say customs had cleared them and they were on their way outside. I handed Bubba one bundle of roses while I gathered up the other, and we were both standing outside the car when she strolled out into the sunshine.

The humidity faded along with the scents of exhaust and the roar of the planes overhead. Everything faded except the bright smile on her face, the roll of her hips as her stroll turned into a hop, a skip, and then a run. Bubba and I both stepped forward, and then Frankie was hugging us both, and I felt more than saw his shudder echoing my own as I buried my face against her neck.

She was home.

It was about fucking time.

IAN

We didn't linger at the airport, but for the first time in what felt like years, the gradual spin of my world on its axis shifted and then righted again as Frankie appeared from the interior of the airport. I'd managed expectations and missing her by channeling all of it into the music. I must have written a dozen songs since we'd said goodbye to her and Jake at the Eurostar in London.

It helped, but nothing helped like having her with us again or having all of us together again. Jake looked a hell of a lot better than the last time I'd seen him, and all the restlessness had faded from Coop. Archie's grin grew more playful and his manner more relaxed.

Yes, having everyone together again was the way to go. She loved the roses. Her delight seemed to sparkle in the air around her. Everything about her was brighter and happier. Or maybe the hot, sweltering summer day was just the perfect backdrop for my angel.

We took the long way back into Manhattan, per Archie's request. She and Jake filled us in on the trip and how Jake's dad was doing. We really weren't out of the loop to be honest, but having her tucked between Archie and me on the seat was doing wonders for all of us.

Jake looked a lot more at ease. We'd talked a few times, and Dad mentioned Jake had checked in with them about his father and later Dad said he'd talked to Jake's father too. Maybe the best part of the whole trip was the repair to the relationship between father and son.

Frankie hadn't been all that impressed by Jake's dad, but she was a huge fan of Klara's. The protective notes in her voice hadn't been lost on me, but those too had gradually eased over the past couple of weeks. I took all of the above as a positive sign, but if Angel needed to shut down and relax, then I'd make sure she got that time.

By the time we returned the brownstone, Frankie's eyes were the size of saucers. She'd smothered a couple of yawns in and around her smiles, but alertness returned to her expression as the driver pulled us up out front.

She stared up at the front of the place, and I spared Archie a glance. He'd gone still. Her liking the house was huge for him. I had zero doubt that Frankie would adore this place. It was fucking perfect for her. Everything about this brownstone screamed her name. At the same time, it was the kind of place that we could fill up with new memories.

Coop gave Archie a gentle shove, and Jake actually managed to cover his laugh. He had an equally curious look on his face, but this was Archie's show and we were just the backup players for this bit. Archie slid out when the driver opened the door, then held his hand out for Frankie.

Biting her lip, she slid her hand into his, and I grabbed the roses for her. She blew me a kiss just as Jeremy opened the door to welcome us back, and the look on Frankie's face, a combination of delight and surprise, made me wish I was a different kind of artist, just so I could paint a picture of that happiness.

Hand in hand, she and Archie jogged up the steps, and she startled the hell out of Jeremy by giving him a fierce hug and a kiss on the cheek. Or maybe it hadn't, because he wore the most indulgent smile as she let him go.

"Welcome home, Miss Frankie," he greeted her, and then Archie scooped her up as she squealed and carried her across the threshold.

"Asshole," Jake muttered.

"Brilliant," Coop countered.

"Both," I corrected them as I followed with the roses. Jake grabbed the backpacks from the driver and Coop claimed their suitcase and we followed after. Inside, Frankie hadn't made it past the downstairs salon where she'd dropped to sit in the middle of the floor with Tory. Tiddles stood on the staircase, and Tabby was likely upstairs in the game room that she'd claimed our first few days here.

I couldn't wait to show Frankie the studio Archie had added to the basement. The converted space was soundproofed and had its own piano and recording equipment. The piano bench was sturdy and well padded. I'd added a few extras, including some stainless steel eye bolts.

I might save christening the studio for my birthday. There was a bed down there too. Archie figured if we wanted a private space at home, the soundproofing would help there.

No arguments here. I appreciated his thoughtfulness.

That and the fact I could lock the door, which meant Jeremy would never go in there. Frankie deserved the privacy.

And there were still things I had no interest in sharing.

It took almost two hours to fully explore the place before Frankie finally climbed the last flight to her room, and I wasn't the only one eager to see her face. In fact, Coop and I took Jake up with us so we could be in there when Archie led her inside.

The moment she stepped inside, her whole expression melted, and Archie relaxed.

Like I'd said, this place was perfect for her, and the wide open space included two huge half dome windows on either side that allowed natural light to flood the room. There was a padded window seat with bookshelves inlaid into the wall. The bed was more than big enough for all five of us and took up nearly one-third of the space, and it had its own little platform so it offered a full view of the room. There were carefully inset eye hooks tucked and hidden away but placed for bedroom play.

The lighting overhead offered three phases, and she could turn it on and off from a switch by the bed. The en suite bathroom included a shower that took up one wall with three different nozzles and a tiled bench that would allow one to sit or lean or even lay down if it were to strike one. No more squashing to fit in the shower. Three or more of us could play in there easily.

The last fix to the place had been finished only the week before and it was the huge hot tub bathtub that she could lounge in or we could all use. The bathroom itself was ginormous compared to the others below, but this floor had originally had two full bedrooms and bathrooms that Archie converted into one sexy master suite.

Or mistress suite in this case.

"So?" Archie asked as though he couldn't read the answer on her face, and Frankie laughed as she tackled him onto the bed. I wasn't the first one to grab a pillow, but I had my shoes off and joined in on the pillow fight that sent the cats racing downstairs and away from the madness.

Later that night, breathless and spent, Frankie stared up at me with shining eyes. We'd welcomed her home with just Archie and I, since Coop and Jake got her on the plane, and the surprise and delight in her expression had made the concession more than worth it.

Besides, Archie wasn't so bad, as long as we discussed it ahead of time. He even had a few inventive ideas of his own.

"I swear," Frankie admitted, panting, "you two are determined to break my vagina."

Not true, but it was still funny.

"You know, babe," Archie mused from where he'd dropped next to us. "You make that sound like a challenge."

"She does," I agreed, and we both grinned at her groan. "Would you like us to take it as a challenge, Angel?"

Because we could do that again. It wouldn't take that long to recover, but only if she wasn't too sore.

We had all the time in the world to get it right.

JAKE

Even after seeing the pictures and the virtual tour and all the discussions with the guys, the brownstone was a hell of a lot more than I expected. Even better, we had all the space in the world. Yes, we had our own bedrooms, but the likelihood that we'd use them that often was slim. The space was more so we could retreat on our own if we needed it or with her if we wanted it.

Her room, even on date nights, had the biggest bed, and if everyone wanted to crash there, it was fine. Yes, we'd still have to rotate who got to sleep with her right next to them, but we'd figure it out.

The garden in the back wasn't that great, but there was a table and chairs and sunshine. Jeremy had already replanted the flower boxes, and while we had neighbors, we had privacy walls too. There was a place up on the roof if we wanted to go up there with more garden boxes, and Bubba and I decided we'd add a grill if there were no laws against it.

Honestly, the first week in New York, they barely let her out of bed and I didn't blame them. I didn't even complain that my rotation on date night got delayed by a week, because I had her to myself for a whole month. Beyond that, I joined the guys for their daily run and so did Frankie. She also spent a lot of time with her cats, and I couldn't blame her.

We mapped some routes to school and went to pick up textbooks. Even having read all about NYU, it was like when we got to Harvard. It was huge. And I wasn't gonna lie, there was some excitement over the idea of diving into my first engineering classes.

Dad even asked me about them the next time we sat down to play. The game console had been a good idea. *Call of Duty* let us bond and take our frustrations out on each other. Coop said it was healthy, I just said it was fun.

What cracked me up was when Bubba got his dad playing too and the four of us went after each other.

We made appointments to get Frankie's navel pierced, a job that required all four of us to be present, and I kept an eye on the guy who was going to do it. He tried to talk her into a hood piercing, and that conversation lasted all of five minutes before he shut the fuck up and laughed at me glaring at him.

Pretty sure his laughter died about the time the other guys joined me in glaring, and then it was Frankie who laughed at our possessive asses. While we were there, I settled on the dragon pattern with one of the artists and set up my first appointment to come back. It would take a few, and Frankie planned to come with me for all of them.

Classes started mid-August, so we didn't have that much time left before we had to dive into a new schedule. Frankie had promised to visit her grandparents in the Hamptons, so she and Archie left early on a Friday morning. They were going to be up there for the weekend, or at least until Sunday midday.

"Hey, Coop and I are going to check out a gym a couple of blocks over," Bubba said from the doorway. "You have time before you and your dad play?"

I checked my watch. A gym was a good idea. Even with running in the park, when the winter weather hit, we needed a place to train for more than just cardio. I also needed to find a place to work on Frankie's boxing. I'd promised her that I wouldn't let that slide.

"Yeah, I'm down. Are we supposed to be getting Rachel at the airport this weekend? Or is it next?"

She'd extended her trip an extra couple of weeks, then flew home to Texas before finishing her move to the Big Apple. She had space in a residence hall in Greenwich Village.

"Next week," Coop said. "Frankie verified it before she made plans to see her grandparents because she promised Rachel we would help her move in."

"No," Bubba corrected. "She promised her that she would help her move in."

"Same thing," I said at the same time as Coop and grabbed my wallet and keys before putting my shoes.

Bubba laughed. "Yeah, I know. Besides, the residences are furnished, I'm pretty sure."

"If they aren't," Coop muttered. "It will be when Frankie is finished." We all grinned and then headed out. It didn't take us long to get to the gym. The only problem I saw was getting there when it was winter. But then, we'd figure it out. Germany had been cold as fuck in winter, and I could handle the snow.

Even as we discussed it and then got to tour the place, we debated how often we'd use it. We didn't leave without a cost sheet and some free passes to come check out the facilities. They had locker rooms for the girls, the guys, and then a unisex one. If we used that one, it meant we'd always have her back if she was there.

"NYU is gonna have gym facilities too," Coop pointed out as we left.

"But that's an even longer trip on days we don't have classes. Then again, we could just make sure our workouts coincided with our schedules."

We debated the merits on the way back and diverted more than once to check out the local shops and bakeries. Some habits were hard to break. Like how close was the closest Starbucks and what bakeries had the best apple fritters. Since it was New York, we had to check out the pizza.

It was serious business, and we knew our girl.

The Natural History Museum was only four blocks away, but we hadn't taken Frankie there yet, so we carried slices of pizza into the park and settled down near the kiddie fields where pee-wee baseball was in full swing.

That pretty much set the tone for the whole weekend, though I had to field calls from all of my sisters, who each decided I was disowned because they hadn't gotten their souvenirs from me. I could handle it. I'd just keep them until Christmas if they wanted to be brats. Frankie texted after they got to her grandparents, but we didn't expect to hear much, though she and Archie responded if we asked them something directly.

At one point, she'd sent us pictures of the beach at Montauk. Next time, we were all going to go up there. It looked gorgeous.

Not as gorgeous as the island near Fiji. Speaking of that, I thumbed through the photos on my phone and grinned at the topless one of her striding down the sand in just her bikini bottoms.

Needed to get this one printed so I could keep it in my room. I loved the expression on her face, the freedom and the sensuality and just the openness in her smile.

"Jake!" Coop's voice carried from downstairs, and I shoved off my bed, leaving the engineering book I'd started reading behind.

"Yo?"

"Down here," Coop called and there was something in his voice, a tension that pulled taut. They were all in the kitchen. Bubba was already down there, and Coop looked tense as hell.

"What's up?" I asked, but Bubba held up a hand and nodded to Jeremy, who had the house phone to his ear. He hadn't said anything since I'd gotten down there.

"Are you certain?" Jeremy asked. "I see. Tell me what hospital."

What hospital?

Ice slithered down my spine.

I didn't have long to wait. As soon as he hung up, Jeremy looked at us. "Mr. Archie has been in an accident. Emergency services connected to the Ferrari called it in, and I was notified as his emergency contact."

Frankie was with him.

"Where?" Bubba asked. I wanted more details than that, but where would do.

"I'm calling for a car now," Jeremy informed us. "Get dressed."

He gave me a look, and I glanced down at my bare feet. Our own vehicles were stored in a garage a few blocks away. Coop was right behind me as I jogged back up the stairs.

She was fine.

He was fine.

Accidents happened all the time.

Except that was emergency services calling from the car and not Frankie or Archie.

"I texted already," Coop said.

"And?" I glanced at him.

"No answer."

Fuck.

Me.

Frankie and the boys will return in *Defiance and Dedication.* To keep up with Heather and all her series join her reader's group: https://www.facebook.com/groups/HeathersPack/

Afterword

Whew. Don't throw your phone or your kindle. If you did, um, go grab it. I'll wait.

Yeah, so—they did it! They graduated! Yay!

Right? That's the important part.

Okay, I can hear you now. You're still mad. Take a minute. Deep breaths. We have four more books. The next, *Defiance and Dedication* is right around the corner.

Still mad?

Right.

Can you breathe yet?

No?

How about a re-read? I'll be here when you're done. Promise.

xoxo

Heather

P.S. No, the ending won't change but you still get to have fun with them all over again.

About Heather Long

USA Today bestselling author, Heather Long, likes long walks in the park, science fiction, superheroes, Marines, and men who aren't douche bags. Her books are filled with heroes and heroines tangled in romance as hot as Texas summertime. From paranormal historical westerns to contemporary military romance, Heather might switch genres, but one thing is true in all of her stories—her characters drive the books. When she's not wrangling her menagerie of animals, she devotes her time to family and friends she considers family. She believes if you like your heroes so real you could lick the grit off their chest, and your heroines so likable, you're sure you've been friends with women just like them, you'll enjoy her worlds as much as she does.

Follow Heather & Sign up for her newsletter:
www.heatherlong.net

Also by Heather Long

UNTOUCHABLE

Rules and Roses

Changes and Chocolates

Keys and Kisses

Whispers and Wishes

Hangovers and Holidays

Brazen and Breathless

Trials and Tiaras

Graduation and Gifts

Defiance and Dedication

82ND STREET VANDALS

Savage Vandal

Vicious Rebel

Ruthless Traitor

Dirty Devil

ALWAYS A MARINE SERIES

Once Her Man, Always Her Man

Retreat Hell! She Just Got Here

Tell It to the Marine

Proud to Serve Her

Her Marine

No Regrets, No Surrender

The Marine Cowboy

The Two and the Proud

A Marine and a Gentleman

Combat Barbie

Whiskey Tango Foxtrot

What Part of Marine Don't You Understand?

A Marine Affair

Marine Ever After

Marine in the Wind

Marine with Benefits

A Marine of Plenty

A Candle for a Marine

Marine under the Mistletoe

Have Yourself a Marine Christmas

Lest Old Marines Be Forgot

Her Marine Bodyguard

Smoke & Marines

BRAVO TEAM WOLF

When Danger Bites

Bitten Under Fire

BOOMERS

The Judas Contact

Deadly Genesis

Unstoppable

Chance Monroe

Earth Witches Aren't Easy

Plan Witch from Out of Town

Bad Witch Rising

Her Elite Assets

Featuring:

Pure Copper

Target: Tungsten

Asset: Arsenic

Fevered Hearts

Marshal of Hel Dorado

Brave are the Lonely

Micah & Mrs. Miller

A Fistful of Dreams

Raising Kane

Wanted: Fevered or Alive

Wild and Fevered

The Quick & The Fevered

A Man Called Wyatt

Going Royal

Some Like It Royal

Some Like It Scandalous

Some Like It Deadly

Some Like it Secret

Some Like it Easy

Her Marine Prince

Blocked

HEART OF THE NEBULA
Queenmaker

Deal Breaker

Throne Taker

LONE STAR LEATHERNECKS
Semper Fi Cowboy

As You Were, Cowboy

MADISON, THE WITCH HUNTER
Every Witch Way But Floosey's

MAGIC & MAYHEM
The Witch Singer

Bridget's Witch's Diary

The Witched Away Bride

Mongrels

Mongrels, Mischief & Mayhem

SHACKLED SOULS
Succubus Chained

Succubus Unchained

Succubus Blessed

SPACE COWBOY
Space Cowboy Survival Guide

WOLVES OF WILLOW BEND
Wolf at Law

Wolf Bite

Caged Wolf

Wolf Claim

Wolf Next Door

Rogue Wolf

Bayou Wolf

Untamed Wolf

Wolf with Benefits

River Wolf

Single Wicked Wolf

Desert Wolf

Snow Wolf

Wolf on Board

Holly Jolly Wolf

Shadow Wolf

His Moonstruck Wolf

Thunder Wolf

Ghost Wolf

Outlaw Wolves

Wolf Unleashed